The silence was long and dreadful. Camus was leaning back in a camp chair, watching the old man. The face was stricken, transfixed by a razor of light, and a sound of metal dropped on tile. From behind the diminishing halo of black left on Camus's retina came a practiced, unctuous voice.

"Then you would say, Professor, that this artifact supports the possibility of time travel?"

"Scholz and Harcourt's PALIMPSESTS is a fine first novel, rich and challenging. Connoisseurs of Updike, Disch and Silverberg are sure to be satisfied."
—*Greg Bear*

PALIMPSESTS

CARTER SCHOLZ
and GLENN HARCOURT

ACE SCIENCE FICTION BOOKS
NEW YORK

ACKNOWLEDGMENTS

A selection from *Finnegans Wake* by James Joyce. Copyright 1939 by James Joyce. Copyright renewed 1967 by George Joyce and Lucia Joyce. Reprinted by permission of Viking Penguin Inc.

From "Design," from *The Poetry of Robert Frost* edited by Edward Connery Latham. Copyright 1936 by Robert Frost. Copyright © 1964 by Lesley Frost Ballantine. Copyright © 1969 by Holt, Rinehart and Winston. Reprinted by permission of Holt, Rinehart and Winston, Publishers.

William Carlos Williams: *Collected Earlier Poems of William Carlos Williams*. Copyright 1938 by New Directions Publishing Corporation. Reprinted by permission of New Directions.

Lyrics to "Same Old Man" by Steve Weber. Recorded by The Holy Modal Rounders.

PALIMPSESTS

An Ace Science Fiction Book/published by arrangement with
the author

PRINTING HISTORY
Ace Original/September 1984

ISBN: 0-441-65065-1

Ace Science Fiction Books are published by The Berkley Publishing Group,
200 Madison Avenue, New York, New York 10016.
PRINTED IN THE UNITED STATES OF AMERICA

INTRODUCTION

by TERRY CARR

If you're getting a little tired of reading science fiction novels that are just like the ones you read last month or last year, this book is for you. It's published under the label "An Ace Science Fiction Special" because it's just that, something fresh and different and, we believe, a novel superior to most of those you'll find today.

I'll tell you why I think so a little later; first, though, I should say a little about the Ace Science Fiction Specials series.

The SF Specials program is specifically designed to present new novels of high quality and imagination, books that are as exciting as any tale of adventures in the stars and as convincing as the most careful extrapolation of the day after tomorrow's science. Add to that a rigorous insistence on literary quality—lucid and evocative writing, fully rounded characterization, and strong underlying themes (but not Messages)—and you have a good description of the stories you'll see in this series.

The publishers of Ace Books believe that there are many readers today who are looking for such books, at a time when so many science fiction novels are simply skilled (or not so skilled) rehashings of plots and ideas that have been popular in the past. Science fiction by its very nature ought to tell stories that are new and unusual, but too many of the science fiction books published recently have been short on real imagination—they are, in fact, timid and literarily defensive. The Ace SF Specials are neither.

The SF Specials began more than fifteen years ago, when the science fiction field was in a period of creative doldrums similar to the present: science fiction novels then were mostly of the traditional sort, often hackneyed and familiar stories that relied on fast action and obvious ideas. Ace began the first series of SF Specials with the idea that science fiction readers

would welcome something more than that, novels that would
expand the boundaries of imagination, and that notion proved
to be correct: the books published in that original series sold
well, collected numerous awards, and many of them are now
considered classics in the field.

Beginning in 1968 and continuing into 1971, the Ace SF
Specials included such novels as *Past Master* by R. A. Laf-
ferty, *Rite of Passage* by Alexei Panshin, *Synthajoy* by D. G.
Compton, *The Left Hand of Darkness* by Ursula K. Le Guin,
Picnic on Paradise and *And Chaos Died* by Joanna Russ, *Pa-
vane* by Keith Roberts, *Isle of the Dead* by Roger Zelazny,
The Warlord of the Air by Michael Moorcock, *The Year of the
Quiet Sun* by Wilson Tucker, *Mechasm* by John Sladek, *The
Two-Timers* by Bob Shaw, and *The Phoenix and the Mirror*
by Avram Davidson . . . among many others that could be men-
tioned, but the list is already long.

Most of those books were nominated for awards. *Rite of
Passage* won the Nebula Award; *The Left Hand of Darkness*
won both the Nebula and the Hugo; *The Year of the Quiet Sun*
won the John W. Campbell Award. Other books in the series
won more specialized awards. Most of the novels have remained in print over the years since they were first published.

That original series ended when I left Ace Books and moved
to California in 1971, but its successes hadn't gone unnoticed.
Both writers and publishers saw that a more "adult" sort of
science fiction could attract a large readership, and during the
seventies more venturesome sf novels were published than ever
before.

A number of critics have credited the Ace Science Fiction
Specials with bringing about a revolution in sf publishing, and
I like to think this is at least partly true. But nothing would
have changed if there hadn't been editors and publishers who
wanted to upgrade the product; and in particular, it required
science fiction writers who could produce superior novels. For-
tunately, such writers were there; some of them had contributed
to the SF Specials series, some had been writing quality sf
novels already (Samuel R. Delany, Philip K. Dick, and Robert
Silverberg are examples), and many writers of talent entered
the science fiction field during this period who didn't feel
constrained by the thud-and-blunder traditions of earlier sf.

So in the early seventies science fiction was an exciting
field: quality sf novels appeared from many publishers, they
sold very well, and science fiction moved toward the front of

literary achievement. It was reviewed in *The New York Times* and analyzed by academic critics; major universities offered courses studying science fiction. It seemed that science fiction had finally become respectable.

But other trends began to be felt, and although they brought many new readers to science fiction, for the most part they caused sf to look back instead of forward. The television series *Star Trek* attracted an enormous following, as did the *Star Wars* movies, *Alien, Close Encounters of the Third Kind, E.T.*, and others; these products of the visual media introduced millions of people to science fiction, but though many were enthusiastic enough to buy sf books too, what they wanted were stories as simple and familiar as the films they had enjoyed. When they found science fiction books that were like the television and movie productions, they bought them in great numbers; when the books were more complex or unusual, sales were much lower.

So in recent years sf publishers have catered to this vast new market. The result has been that most of the science fiction published today is no more advanced and imaginative than the sf stories of the fifties, or even the forties: basic ideas and plots are reworked time and again, and when a novel proves to be popular, a sequel or a series will come along soon.

There's nothing wrong with such books; when they're well written they can be very good. But when authors are constrained to writing nothing but variations on the plots and styles of the past, much of the excitement of science fiction disappears. Science fiction is a literature of change; more than any other kind of writing, sf needs to keep moving forward if it's to be exciting.

The novels in this new series of Ace SF Specials do look forward rather than back. They're grounded in the traditions of science fiction but they all have something new to add in ideas or literary development. And they are all written by authors who are comparatively new to science fiction, because it's usually the new writers who have the freshest ideas. (Most of those novels in the original series that came to be called classics were written by authors who were then at the beginnings of their careers.)

Ace Books asked me to edit this new SF Specials series because they believe the time is right for such adventurous books. The new readers who swelled the science fiction market in the last several years are by now familiar with the basic ideas and plots, and many of them will want something more. This new SF Specials series offers stories that explore more imaginative territory.

Carter Scholz and Glenn Harcourt's *Palimpsests* is a rich and fascinating novel that is utterly unlike anything before in science fiction. It deals with experiments in time travel, a staple subject in the field, but the story that develops strikes to the core of scientific inquiry, the shifting meanings of knowledge, and of every experience we have of life. It is, by turns and turns, a novel of mystery, of espionage, of philosophy and adventure and intensely personal experience. I defy anyone to read the first chapter and thereafter not *need* to read the rest.

The Random House Dictionary defines "palimpsest" as "a parchment or the like from which writing has been partially or completely erased to make room for another text." You'll see how well the title fits this novel: reality is always in question here, in so many ways that Philip K. Dick must be chuckling somewhere, but Scholz and Harcourt never lose sight of the primary reality of their narrator, an intelligent young man who is increasingly caught in the anomalies of time.

In fact, it's this characterization of Camus, the narrator, that makes the novel a triumph. Camus is a very smart fellow, and all of his acquaintances old and new are very smart too; that's one of his problems as he tries to work his way through a maze of lies, half-truths, and contingent beliefs. There really isn't a dolt in this book, and the conversations throughout keep our intellects hopping (this may be the most *civilized* sf novel ever published), but does anyone here know the truth?

See again the definition of "palimpsest." Is there, after all, such a thing as truth? You've heard that question countless times before if you've read much science fiction, but you haven't had it posed in so many ingeniously dramatic ways as you'll find it here; nor have you seen the answers considered so carefully and affectingly. *Palimpsests* is very much in the classic science fiction tradition of the "novel of ideas," firmly welded to the emotions.

There will be more Ace Science Fiction Specials coming soon, and each will be as similar to and different from the usual science fiction fare as this one is. I hope you'll watch for them.

PALIMPSESTS

How very many piously forged palimpsests slipped in the first place from his pelagiarist pen.

—*Finnegans Wake*

I. BEFORE THE FALL

What but design of darkness to appall?—
If design govern in a thing so small.

—Robert Frost

1. A Premature Conclusion

The last day of the dig fell on the feast of the Seven Sleepers of Ephesus, the only saints said to have traveled time. Outside the cave, scarcely more than a pock in the hills above the present watercourse, the Neander Valley stretched sunnily past the muddy Düsselbach to the hard white stripe of the autobahn. The hermit's "sweet flowery bower" that had yielded the first specimen of *Homo sapiens neanderthalensis* in 1856 was now a shabby dell called the Hochdahl Naturschutzgebiet—less a preserve than a green scar upon the urban industrial smear extending from Bonn to Dortmund; the coal mines and limestone quarries of the valley had long since been exhausted, stripped to a more fundamental ground, upon which the products of this earth had been ceaselessly superimposing themselves. On the hills facing the cave, condominiums stood like crude hieroglyphs. The high whining din of the road, dulled by distance but never effaced, covered the valley: east it ran to Wuppertal, west to cross the Rhine near the dig's analytic unit in Düsseldorf.

The site had appeared unlikely from the start. Camus's professor, the notorious Frederick Warner, had selected it ostensibly to give his graduate students field experience—but by all reports, the caves of the *Gebiet* had been stripped as bare by five generations of anthropologists as the mines had by industrialists. And indeed the first few weeks went badly. Even Camus, who enjoyed failure, wearied of the complaints he heard over evening beer in the city. The students—Warner called them piglets—bitched about the long hours, the backbreaking labor that turned up nothing but dirt, the expense of what was becoming an elaborately pointless and dull vacation. Warner had riposted by faulting his charges' lack of initiative and creativity, which to him were the same. "You don't find finds, you make them," was one of his more careless comments.

Then Warner had, without explanation, shifted their investigations some hundred yards east, and had invited the eminent Heidelberg anatomist Maximilian Hüll to preside. His arrival alone was enough to cause a stir; and when one of the braver students suggested that it might have been a wasted trip, Hüll had said, "Remember that what you seek is always there, even if you do not know it. It waits to reveal itself, even as you must wait for the revelation. A find is a consonance of waitings." And, as if in vindication of both Hüll and Warner, the next day two broken bones, a handful of Mousterian points and scrapers, one animal tusk, and various Pleistocene oddments came to light. The students began to sweat in earnest. Two skeletons were pieced together. In all, the finds were modest; classification would be routine and tidy. Camus foresaw no pain.

All this was past. Now, as usual, Camus was abstracted. Attentive to the smallest present detail, ear for stilled voices, gauze wrapped round his formal sense. Abstraction is not necessarily form. He was tall, bigboned, pucknosed, with unruly dark blond hair that lightened under sun. Every few months he hacked it back to a reasonable length. He had not shaved for two days, giving his squarish chin an aureole. This and small round wire glasses heightened the fishy appearance of his mouth.

As he stood on the shelf just outside the cave a sunshower came up, blotting momentarily the sight and sound of distant traffic, and the fringe of dwellings. A needlepoint of joy pricked his shell. He imagined the cave as it had lain for eons: free of the harsh glare of arc lamps, the limestone kibble unmarked, the spirits of the dead at peace, at a time when human death was still a novelty. Precisely then he laid out in his mind the lines of the excavation grid, the raw beginnings of history, the landscape yielding inexorably to analysis. Then the shower reached him and he retreated to the cave mouth. He heard the whine of Peter Ng's motordriven Nikon, and sporadic typing. Over the steady throb of the generator he hummed harmonics. Someone was singing:

"Before the Fall, when they wrote it onna wall, and there wasn't even any Hollywood. . . ."

Half in, half out, wishing himself anywhere else, he saw a misty double rainbow form above the valley, and thought: I see it. It is a pleasure. A minute ago it was not there, and in another minute it will be gone. A fiction of light. Should I point it out? Will Ng photograph it? And will that make it really real? Rain reached his niche, and he went in.

The cave was ten meters deep. Around the grid, behind the lights on their tripods, it was close with the yammer of students.

"On the evidence of a single tooth? Ridiculous. . . ."

"But did you see the new *Anthropoid* on Choukoutien . . .?"

"Phylogeny recapitulates misogyny. . . ."

"Oh, mama, can this ree-ly be the end. . . ."

"Americans," he muttered, trying for a sneer and missing. After all, he was almost one himself, by default. Born in Düsseldorf, after his father's death he had moved with his mother through Germany, Austria, Switzerland, France, for no reason he could understand but the persistence of flight. They were poor, and every move left them poorer. At the age of sixteen his own variety of flight had started: scholarships in Paris, London, Düsseldorf, Boston, Cleveland. Like the noble Pantagruel, he skipped his way through a dozen subjects, and the net result was to make him poorer in himself. Poor poor Hans. Trilingual, he sometimes forgot what language he was speaking, and had to engage tics and actors' habits to get it back. In Germany Hans, in France Jean, in America oftenest Caymus, he was tolerant of the distortions time and distance worked upon his name.

Polymathically and polyglottally perverse, Winifred had once called him. Turning again, he saw her: the efficient Winifred Waste, devoted amanuensis, banging out field notes on a battered Olympia portable. They had been lovers in Cleveland, but not on this trip. She was sleeping with Warner, he knew it; not that it changed anything between them.

They'd met when both were twentyfour, and shared a common sense of doom. Theirs was a haunted generation, which made at first for close bonds and later for long, painful separations. The first of the latter had already started for them. Undeniably there was dread in the world, and it was pointless to lie with such dread daily; but the long hard freeing from dread involved certain changes, irrevocable and not always willed. The spirit of their age was not millennial; the sky would not open today or tomorrow; rather it was an elaborate dance in the dark by a cliffedge, with the denouement undoubted but unhurried. They knew from the first they would end by losing everything, but this knowlege was a poor defense against daily vicissitudes.

He walked around far enough to tickle her peripheral vision, and to take her in again. A lifetime project. Her features were an imperfect aggregate of small perfections. Not beautiful, not a comfort to his sight, her appearance kept his eye alert. She had an elongated face and neck, and dense wavy black hair streaked with gray. Her habit was to push it back with both hands and a toss of her head. In seated repose she held her head with both hands straight against her cheeks, elbows on table, index fingers touching the hair-draped ears. Her arms thinned exceptionally at the join of bicep and deltoid. Her skin was a smooth tone of honey just shy of freckling, so that her eyes, a bright grayblue, were her most commanding feature from the front. In the profile or threequarter view he had now, the mouth dominated, owing to its sharp corners. When pursed, as now, the lips took radiating lines. Her smile was a surprise, broad and rare, the front two teeth longer than the rest. A trace of line fell from nares to mouth. This hid from the first glance a classic levantine disproportion in the nose, which was justly scaled to the head rather than the features. In this light its shadow fell bluntly but with art, across her mouth.

She wore a black knit halter top, revealing the sternum hollow between the breasts. Past a crinkled band of belly were outrageous camellia pink shorts. Her legs, when she stood and locked her knees back, were lanky and lithe as a colt's; the muscles of the inner thigh showed in three distinct curves: gluteus, gracilis, sartorius; three curves of a different family completed the rhythm down to heel. Black rope sandals framed wellveined feet and taut ankles. Tufts winked at him from underarms as she stretched.

This small act of attention, which he undertook only to confirm what he would eventually lose, simply told him old news: he loved her still. Most he loved her edges, which offered no pillow to sight, body, mind, or spirit, but inspired him with a warm vigilance.

The other side of vigilance is fear, and he was a little afraid of her, of her capacity for dedication to some transient cause. Likewise he envied it, since in his eyes everything was transient. But it was to the smallest tasks, such as her typing, that she brought the most ferocious energy, as if this childish, or more properly, American, devotion to the quotidian could redeem the day's dull ticktock.

Over one cute sunburned shoulder he watched her type:
27 July 1991. Excavation and classification completed.

*Fragments from two individuals, mature male and adolescent
female, greenstick fracture of f. left ulna, depressed fracture
of m. right temporal bone . . .*

" 'The ruin of a solitary arch,' " he intoned. " 'Highest of
animals; lowest of men.' "

"What?" Scowling, typing, she did not look up.

"Nothing. The elder Huxley. 'But indeed a single arch,
where people might smoothly enter in, is wholly adverse to
Nature, which never forms a mouth without setting in its midst
a tongue, or some other obstacle.' We may assume he is al-
luding to the *vagina dentata."*

"Dirty old man."

"Who? Me or Huxley?"

"Warner. Listen. 'Substantial indications that the two individuals were locked in the deed of kind, as Shakespeare has
it.' Honestly, you'd think he'd show *some* restraint."

"History, in all its gory and immediate detail. And you are
there. But presented with, how to say, an objective sensitivity
unparalleled in the annals of . . ." He mimed the delivery of a
crushing blow.

*. . . interments carried out with at least a modicum of ritual
concern . . .*

"The Warner touch. Very nice. I wish I could write like
that. Much more graceful than saying their feet were practically
hanging out in the rain."

"Hans, go away."

In response he unfolded a canvas chair, and sat, legs apart,
forearms resting just above his knees, leaning across the table,
trying to imitate Hüll.

"I am saddened, my dear Miss Waste, that you so steadfastly
refuse to understand our scientific purpose here. The point is
that a proper presentation of facts, in and of itself, is not
enough."

"Enough for what?" She looked at him, head charmingly
canted.

Then, abruptly dropping the role, "Oh, enough to get me
up in the morning, for one thing. Where is he, anyway?"

"Warner? In Ratingen, I think. Left early in the a.m. for
an appointment 'mit ein Herr Schwindel' or something. Which
means I have to finish everything myself, since he's bound to
spend the night."

"Jealous?"

"Oh, Hans, get off that, would you? He's a lech."

"Third time this week."

"What? Oh, at least. He's been to Elberfeld, Erkrath, and Gruiten, for 'appointments,' and that's all he'll say. Not to mention hours and hours in libraries, newspaper morgues, and God knows what else. Where've you been lately, anyway?"

"Somewhere . . . else. I wonder why I'm here really."

"So do I. Why don't you go away?"

She resumed typing. He felt he had come out even on the interchange, although the name, rules, and origin of this little game they played behind the screen of their conversation was still mysterious to him, and, he suspected, to her as well. He remained seated, thinking. Newspaper filler from four or five years ago; he'd clipped it and lost it. An amateur geologist—around here was it?—claiming the discovery of some unusual artifact. Schwindel was the name, but he could not recall the details. It was unimportant; but, as he often did when oppressed by the intricacies of the present, he pursued the past detail, trying to recover, if not the information, at least its impress on his memory. Late afternoon, sprawled bellydown on a carpet, reading, the item low on a righthand page; but this impression abruptly took him to another article more vividly professing to prove that the Piltdown hoaxer had been Sherlock Holmes. And this fresher, earlier memory crowded out the more recent with images of his late mother, an avid Conan Doyle fan, who swore there was a Holmes tale with a fellow whose tracks pointed back when he reversed his shoes, though she could never find it. *Wie Du*, she'd insist to him. In his mind now his mother was alive, young, dancing in an open room, with an unstrained integrity and untroubled freedom that had been achieved, of course, by pure artifice and repetition. The image carried him into sleep.

The blank ambiguity of landscape, the moment of arrival at a new site, that was what he loved. To work at civilization's edge. "Happy countries have no history," he'd copied once from the younger Huxley, violating the spirit of the quotation by his copying (as Huxley had violated the spirit of the thought by stating it). Some first days belonged to the happy countries without history. But then the ground was broken, the grid laid, earth overturned and sifted; the edge of a knucklebone peeped out, the point of a scraper, and he was left again with the void of his own consciousness. The present moment is always a gift; the consciousness of it constantly intolerable.

0.0

At one point in his peripatos he had studied palimpsests. (Said Winifred, his peripatetics had given him a peripatois.) A scarcity of parchment had led medieval monks to scrape pagan scrolls clean for reuse in their devotions; but the historian's interest was more in what had been scraped than in the overwriting. So Camus learned that you can see the past through the present. The world as it comes to you is a palimpsest. Under your desk are scars the previous tenant left. You have painted the walls, but a water mark ten years old peeps through the new coat. The Xerox of your thesis takes random marks from the glass worn by prior use. A vanished ocean has left shells in the mountains. Your own body bears the imprint of your deeds and lapses; and in the womb it took the faces, as it grew, of all its evolutionary forebears. How deeply can one look? Can the headlong scrawl of the present moment across all traces of the past be read at all? What vital marks are effaced or misinterpreted? What single tree, in what quarter of the world, has written in the rings of its heartwood the message you most need?

He started awake, almost toppling backwards in the chair. He was alone in the cave. Night was coming on. Halfway down the path he saw some students carrying equipment, and he jogged after them, leaving the camp stool.

Where the path broadened to a valley road, Ng crouched by a Land Rover, on the hood of which rested a fat orange telescope. His Nikon was mated to the eyepiece, and he was peering through the finder.

"What's up?" Camus asked.

"Mercury for a change," said Ng, not looking away. "A nice conjunction." It was one of a bright cluster near the sickle of Leo, almost atop Regulus. Glinting on the horizon was Jupiter, and above Mercury a doublet of Mars and Venus. On the opposite horizon a full moon drove Saturn before it.

A depression of finality came on him. As he reached the camp, two Land Rovers filled with whooping students jounced away down the dirt road. Again things were ending too soon. In three days he would be flying to America, trying to shake the feeling that he had slept through half the summer. He had to return to Cleveland, to his unfinished dissertation, and en route an aunt in New Hampshire expected him to help her with her *Amateur's Geology of Crawford Notch*. Camus hoped to pick up an authentically Puritan undergraduate or two, in part to continue the desultory game of infidelity he and Winifred used to keep their peculiar sense of fidelity alive. He wondered vaguely where New Hampshire was.

Hüll was at the camp table sipping coffee. He smiled and motioned Camus over.

"Setzen Sie sich," he said pleasantly. "I have had no opportunity to talk with you all these weeks, and I'd like an excuse to speak German again. You're not busy?"

"No, no." Camus hid his confusion by poking his nose into the coffeepot and adjusting the flame of the Bleuet stove.

"Well, the dig is over, and I think we have something to celebrate."

"Yes. Yes, it was odd to find anything at all here."

"No one was more surprised than I. I thought I knew this area like my own library. But in every library there are a few unopened books, eh?"

"I should think," ventured Camus, pouring himself coffee, "that it might be a little vexing to have a fellow like Warner make this find in, ah, your own backyard, so to speak."

"Well, I don't know." Hüll smiled. "Should I be vexed? I am blessed with never having done a piece of original work in my life. I organize, I reflect, but I have managed to avoid jealousy and these deplorable academic battles over primacy. The knowledge is the main thing, no? Who does anything alone?"

"No praise, no blame."

"Yes, just so. You're a bit of a Taoist?"

Camus blushed. The last thing he would have called himself. "Why *did* Warner invite you? Why did you come?"

"I believe he was having some trouble with the *Gebiet*. He asked me to intercede, and incidentally to preside at the dig, which was courteous of him. I had no other commitments, and it would have been regrettable if some bureaucracy had canceled your project, no?"

"Um," said Camus.

"Anyway, I enjoy this very much, working with students. It makes me feel young." Hüll sighed, then laughed. "I fear it is my last such pleasure. I must show more respect to my bones. You'd think that respecting old bones would be in my line, but I shall retire with the greatest reluctance."

"Retire?"

"I'm looking forward to it, really. Next month I take a very leisurely cruise down my beloved Rhine, stopping to see old castles and old friends. I want to see the museum in Strasbourg—can you believe I am just now taking an interest in art? A colleague told me of those paintings at Lascaux. By September I will be in Heidelberg, to finish my affairs there. Then München, for the Oktoberfest, a last foolish fancy, then home to Bayreuth and my wife Alma and my bees."

"Bees?"

"I have a small apiary. What amazing creatures. Such a sense of order."

"Regimented," muttered Camus, despite himself.

"But no! This is a human concept. There is no imposition, but an innate sense of purpose and function."

"I see what you mean," said Camus, and he did, but it did not help him. "Tell me, what do you think of Warner?"

"But he is your professor. Well . . . an interesting character. Very impulsive, it's not my way, but I can't deny he gets results. He gave me his book about forgeries, very entertaining, a man of perhaps injudicious audacity."

"He's not well liked."

Hüll wagged a finger. "That is because of the jealousy. I daresay Herr Warner's American colleagues go blind with envy every time he goes on television or writes a bestseller, eh? But he is not as foolish as he seems. He will say outrageous things, but when the reckoning comes he has always some new *coup*. What gnashing of teeth when word of our little dig gets out! No one but Herr Warner would have thought to come here."

"I'm surprised that word's not out already."

"Ah, that is perhaps because of my own small influence. Or perhaps Herr Warner is mellowing. He was happy to agree that there be no premature publicity."

Happy as a gelded bull, thought Camus, studying his coffee.

"What of you, friend Hans? You seem to feel things so deeply."

Good God, Camus thought. He's turned into one of Thomas Mann's undergraduates. What do I say now?

"*Ich weiss nicht, ich weiss nichts.* Three unfinished dissertations on two continents. The usual boring modern sense of confusion. No attachments, personal, political, or otherwise. I just blunder along."

"You know, I once met your grandfather, was it?"

"Maybe or maybe not. My mother said he was. I think not. I was illegitimate." He paused. "I prefer to think so."

"Ah," sighed Hüll. "We poor humans. So uncertainly placed

on the line from ape to saint."

All at once he could not keep it back. Camus blurted, "You don't seem to have anything chasing you."

Hüll looked simply baffled.

Camus rose clumsily. *"My* old bones," he said. Hüll rose and gripped his hand, smiling.

"You're young. If ever I can help you . . ."

"Thank you," said Camus, profoundly embarrassed. Then he shut up and ducked into the night. A revelation for him, that there were people not chased. How did they do it? Warner was chased; Camus recognized that much, from the talent for generating rumors, the trail he left behind him, all the false Warners, the capering simulacra. Chased, yet somehow happy. Hüll was simply himself, with no apparent need to flee anything.

Then Camus knew it was the secret of some happiness he had come to unearth, the secret of standing undevoured in the fierce black wind of history, the secret which Hüll and Warner in their disjunct ways seemed to possess. Might he, through one or both, yet grope his way to some faint hope?

Faint hope indeed. In his tent waited Winifred, reading her heirloom copy of Edward Drinker Cope's now-infamous *Origin of the Fittest*. A professor of theology at Yale, Cope had been last century America's premier anti-Darwinist. Winifred enjoyed defending Lamarckism, at least when it could not injure her job prospects. One night she and Camus had got drunk, and she read from Cope and listed all the embarrassments orthodox Darwinians had suffered in the past century, while Camus in turn quoted great stretches of Darwin from memory, in vicious parody.

"Hi, Dub-Dub," he said.

"Right," she said, lowering the book. "First you fall asleep on me, then I have to wait here an hour wondering are you whoring in town, and now you piss me off with that name again."

"What do your friends call you?"

"None of your business. You can call me Fred." She offered him a canteen, and he sipped from it.

"Bird," he said. "That's definitely Bird."

"The man is right again."

"Where did you find Wild Turkey in the backward valley of the Ruhr?"

"D-dorf. Yesterday I rode past the Altstadt stop by mistake

and found a liquor store staffed by an old man who was a dead ringer for Walt Disney."

"Tell me the address."

"I can't. It was a magic store and it vanished as soon as I left it."

He took another drink and passed back the canteen.

"Very good. I was talking to Hüll."

"And?"

Camus frowned. "I like him. What's Warner's opinion, do you know?"

"Warner says he's a Nazi."

"Aren't we all."

"But Warner also says that liking people is an expensive preoccupation."

"Figures."

They drank. After a time Winifred was reclining, her head in his lap, and he was massaging her temples. He traced the features of her face with his index fingers. His skin accepted the feel of oil from her closed eyelids, sweat from the upper lip and cusp of mouth. He rested his thumbs at the hinge of her jaw, fingers embracing the nape, and kissed her.

"Oh, crap, Hans."

"What is it?"

"Stomach cramps."

"Well. This could become an unhealthy precedent."

"Don't I know."

"What's the word from Lamarck on stomachaches?"

"Shit." She kicked the book awkwardly.

Camus released her head, leaned back, and fished in his pocket for cigarettes. He lit one and passed it to her.

"Damn, damn. I have to get back to Cleveland."

"You will. Did you hear from the *Geographic?*"

"No. But I think it's for sure, if Warner agrees."

"Warner and Waste. Very euphonious. I can see it in that natty typeface they use."

"Look, will you call me in Cleveland? I'm serious."

"I know it. Yes."

"What are you going to do?"

"Who knows. Try to finish the dissertation. Get a job. Aspire."

"Hans, you know, we're not much good for each other."

"But everything else is much worse."

"Oh, Jesus. Count on you for a note of hope."

"Who needs hope? What do you want, Waste, to get married?"

"Until you're ready for an answer you don't want, don't ask."

"I'm ready for any damn answer. To anything."

"We've never even lived together."

"You didn't want to. And then I didn't want to. What's the point, hey? Do we always have to be dragging out . . . old bones?"

"I'm not happy, Hans."

"Hush up, will you?"

"Lie down here and just hold me."

So he did, grateful for the warmth of her, even while his mind said, no, you can't go back. Too much drift.

"Strange rock," she said.

"What?"

"Flung by. An unknown hand. You. Like those kids we saw yesterday, skipping stones. You're like one of the stones. Sailing in those arcs, what you call them, para . . ."

"Parabolas."

"M'hm. Skipping. Not . . . ever resting. Touching briefly, then flying off."

For answer, he tightened his hold on her.

"Sorry, sorry. Bad night," she said.

"Yes," he conceded. "Bad night. The moon."

Then he drifted off himself. Until, well after midnight, Ng roused him from a dream in which he was chased. Tall white-smocked men with atrophied limbs and hypertrophied heads pursued him, throwing things. He led them a merry chase, until he lost his way and they ceased to follow. He turned into a bower where two Neanderthals were making love, rhythmically saying *ach!* He had the sensation of orgasm, then was shaken awake.

"*Qu'est-ce qu'il y a?*" he shouted. Winifred groaned. He had not even an incipient erection.

Ng said, "They've found something new. You'd better come."

2. A Stone of a Peculiar Sort

Surrogate daylight stood in the cave. Camus shivered in his windbreaker, watching Warner and Hüll emerge singly from a freshly broken hole.

"Astounding," said Hüll. "Nearly complete. Gentlemen, ladies, one at a time, and you may observe the finest Neanderthal skeleton I have ever seen, *in situ*. Touch nothing if you please, and watch your step."

While the students ducked in and out of the hole, Warner held forth. "Damnedest thing I ever saw. Got back about midnight, thought I'd have a last look around. I saw a scraper embedded in the back of the cave. I almost let it pass, but I had a pocket knife, so I started chipping. The rock was crumbly. When the scraper was free I went at it with my hands and it came away easily. A whole damned piece of wall fell through, a false back, don't know how we could have missed it, the cave goes on another ten feet and was walled up. And there he was. I enlarged the hole and woke you all up. Sorry about that, but I thought you'd be interested."

Which was an understatement. This was the real thing. Far from a routine, fragmentary excision, this was a complete and completely unusual grave. Only Warner seemed in control of himself; with his fierce red beard and sonant bluff manner he reminded *cinéaste* Camus tonight of Wallace Beery as Doyle's Professor Challenger. His charges queued at the hole, guided in and out by Hüll's comments on the skeleton's integrity, the unique burial posture, the significance of surrounding artifacts, and so forth. Camus stood back from the bustle, sure that after eighty thousand years another few minutes would make no difference. In fact he was depressed, thinking about layers of strata, infinite series.

"An amazing piece of luck," said Warner, implying that it could only have happened to him.

Winifred, blowsy and annoyed, snapped, "Of what kind?

14

We're supposed to be out of here day after tomorrow. There's a month's work in there." She was seeing her report of the dig put off, the modest conclusions she might have drawn from their modest finds now usurped by the great conclusions Warner would undoubtedly draw from a second expedition, her name lost again in the acknowledgements to one of his articles.

"We'll make provisions. I'll talk to my friend von Rast at the Löbbeke; he lives in Hochdahl, I'll have him keep an eye on things."

Friend indeed. Camus happened to know von Rast as well as anyone might; twenty years ago he had been von Rast's favorite young science jock, and he had renewed the acquaintance every few years since. This trip he had seen von Rast just long enough to get his wry comment on Warner: an unholy fool.

Camus now approached the opening. He went in. It was a pleasant hole. Its roof was too low to allow him to stand erect, but given the stature of Neanderthals it was cozy. He liked it. Under his boots were layers of footprints. The air was clammy. The skeleton lay on its back, arms folded across the ribcage. Two fingers were missing from its left hand. Ringing the squat skull was a vague halo of light. Camus bent closer. Bits of scraped flint, quartz, mica, glinted in the slanting arc light. He saw scrapers and animal claws. There were the brittle, papery remains of flowers. About a dozen objects were ranged round the skull.

At the peak of this arc was a small cube. It was half buried in dust. Camus saw it, looked away, looked back. He bent and blew some dust from its surface. About two centimeters on a side, it appeared to have been machined from a shiny metal. Camus backed up and struck his head on an overhang, dislodging a pound or so of kibble. He heard voices from the main cave, as if from a great distance.

"Apparently a shaman," Warner was saying, "buried with all the tools of his trade."

Camus puffed air at his hands to warm them. He wondered if he should look again. He decided violently against it. He stooped, and went carefully out of the hole.

Warner said, "I had a feeling, that's all. I saw a camp stool somebody had left, and when I came in I had a last look around."

"Did you," said Camus, and felt out of breath. Winifred

looked at him curiously. He sat down and brushed bits of rock
from his hair.

"Did you see the cube?" he said.

"I'm sorry?" said Warner. Hüll smiled benevolently.

"The cube. It's over his head. You'd better look."

Warner stood blandly for a moment, as if expecting a punchline, then vanished into the hole. Ng looked at Camus.

"There's a cube, " he explained.

Hüll commented, "The interment is more typical of the Cro-
Magnons. But we must keep an open mind. Our assumptions
are sometimes unequal to the facts."

A minute later Warner reemerged. He was smiling vacantly
and whistling the winter theme from Vivaldi's *Four Seasons*.

"Drop something, Hans?"

"I beg—?"

"I saw your cube," said Warner icily. "Somehow...
somehow I feel it was not there the last time I was. I could be
wrong, I admit. I had to look around to find it. Nonetheless,
I have a strong hunch, a perfectly reasonable intuition that it
hasn't been lying there for eighty thousand years. Any of you
other folks drop a cube?"

There was a long silence. An arc lamp sputtered.

"There's a cube in there, an inch across, untarnished, looks
like it came from a machine shop. Now I'm serious. Who put
it there? Lie to me, I'll have your head. Damned good place-
ment, looks like it's been there since the Pleistocene, except
obviously it hasn't. Deft joke, I commend the prankster, we'll
laugh in the morning. Now who did it?"

Hüll went into the cave. He was the only one fully dressed,
as his rheumatism compelled him to sleep in town; he had
driven out after Warner's midnight call. Camus felt a sense of
despair as he watched the anatomist vanish into the hole.

When he emerged he was pale.

"Gentlemen, ladies, please. I must stress the gravity of the
situation. In the sciences, fraud is a most terrible thing. We
are at every moment at a frontier. Past every established fact
is the sheer edge of ignorance, and we play near that edge at
our peril. A misstep does not just threaten the individual, it
may set all science back decades. However funny the joke may
seem, it is not worth it, it can never be worth it, for it damages
scientific credibility. It undermines method, and method is the
only tool we have. Forgive me if I make speeches. The world

is not so sympathetic to us as we like to think. So we must judge our own steps very carefully, lest a judgment descend upon us. A find like this puts us in a very precarious position. I shudder to think of the possible consequences, should this become known at this point. Of course, I am only an advisor here. . . ."

"Not at all," Warner said. "I concur with you wholly. I've had my little jokes at times, and I've appreciated the jokes of others, but when it comes to falsifying data . . . no. Never. And certainly not at this stage of investigation."

Hüll looked up sharply. "Investigation? But this is a standard field study, applying standard methodology. . . ."

"Yes, but now we're in over our heads." Camus detected a hint of pleasure in Warner's voice, and Hüll too started at the tone. "I mean, the burial posture alone is significant. As for," and Warner looked almost lovingly at Camus, "as for the, ah, *artifact*. Well, I'll be right here all night. I want a confession from somebody before dawn. I'll treat it in strict confidence. Otherwise, we must proceed as if this were a genuine find. Things will drag on for months, academic credits will be delayed, and someone will learn a very nasty lesson before we're done."

There was some confusion. A few students began muttering. A few others headed for the hole. Warner hustled after, calling, "Don't touch it! I won't have the damned thing disappearing now!"

Winifred said to Camus, "What is going on?" He shrugged and said, "Have a look."

The pallor of Hüll's face was not wholly the effect of the lighting. He said, "This is beyond me. This goes totally beyond me." With a shade of hurt betrayal he looked at Camus. "You didn't . . .?" Camus shook his head rapidly, earnestly.

"Ach, Gott. I must return to town. I am not feeling at all well."

Winifred was the last one out of the hole. She seemed in fine humor. She hugged Camus and said, "Congratulations, idiot."

Warner, who had been staring out of the cave entrance, turned and said, "Miss Waste."

"Jawohl?" she said with innocence.

"We have a few things to go over. I trust I'll see you here before too long?"

"I'm not going anywhere," she said. She gave Camus a peck on the cheek and Warner a rude gesture, which, however, was shielded from his sight.

Camus went out into the full moonlight which was softening the valley. He wondered if this would be a good time to throw himself off the narrow path. He decided not.

"At least a modicum of ritual concern," he said to no one in particular.

3. Yet Another Conscientious Asshole

The next morning no one was laughing.

Peter Ng held calipers. "Exactly two centimeters," he said.

"No," whispered Camus. His head hurt. The day was hot already.

"Perfectly cubic."

"Please stop," Camus muttered to himself.

Ng aligned for the third time a triplebeam balance on which the cube rested. He touched it and the beam wobbled.

"Two twenty point eight grams," he said. "Nothing's that dense."

A nervousness pervaded the group, not wholly the anxiety of Americans about to miss planes, lose credits, or otherwise default on the payments of their cultural insurance. No confession had been forthcoming. Warner seemed angriest at himself. Hüll was even more agitated than he had been the night before, pacing without pause and every two minutes referring to his pocket watch. Intermittently he yawned, with such evident pain that Camus knew he had passed well beyond fatigue.

"Gott," he said. "I want no part of this."

"Neither do I," growled Warner.

"For the first time in twenty years I have missed Mass."

The cube had been carefully dislodged from its setting, leaving a small cavity, a memory, a distention in the fine dirt. The skeleton and other artifacts had been left untouched. With twelve hours of the dig remaining, and the Löbbeke analytic unit already closed down, there was opportunity only for perfunctory on-site analysis. Even this gave unsettling results.

Hüll left off pacing to speak. "Preposterous. Worse, it is insane! It is denser than any known metal. It is found in Pleistocene strata. It cannot be. It violates everything we know."

"Precisely," said Warner. "And of course I incline to the idea of a hoax. I think someone planted it. And I think this

19

will be proved very shortly, when we send it off for tests."

"Where would one of us get a metal heavier than platinum?" Winifred asked.

"Why don't you tell me? It's extraordinary. It deserves a chapter in my *Book of Fakes*."

Hüll groaned. "My dear Professor Warner. I wish you wouldn't talk of fakery. There is no possible motive."

"You're familiar with the Kammerer case, Doctor? The Piltdown fraud? The Moulin Quignon jaw? No motive for any of them, but they show that not everyone holds your own admirable ethical standards. I am perhaps more expert in fakery than you. *Mundus vult decipi* is the usual reason."

"But, but in those cases the attempt was to falsify the natural. . . ."

"Yes, and this is so patently false, the intent must be confusion, not deception."

"Lieber Gott. False? It is impossible! The thing cannot exist at all!"

"No?" Now Warner was in his element. "So they said of fossils, Doctor. So they said of powered flight. If you don't like the idea of hoax, I have some other theories. It was left by a spaceship. It was made by an unknown technological culture contemporaneous with the Neanderthals. It came back in time from the future. Are these theories more appealing?"

Hüll had the sick expression of a naive tourist who'd expected Mozart at the Grand Ole Opry. Warner verbally took one step back so as to take two forward.

"All I mean is, let's not jump to conclusions here. When old Beringer found his Würzburg fossils, he said they were 'stones of a peculiar sort, hidden by the Author of Nature for his own pleasure.' You see, he had no fiction of geologic time to guide him. Only religion. And when it came clear what a fool he'd been he spent the last ten years of his life trying to buy back all copies of his published work."

This was a little close to the bone for Hüll, who had no doubt a fine and delicate way of reconciling, by crossproducts, the science of his faith and the faith of his science. The silence was long and dreadful. Camus was leaning back in a camp chair, watching the old man. The face was stricken. As he watched it dwindled, as if a long life's accretion of doubt and negative hypothesis, the lost byways of methodology, now sucked at superfluous flesh to present the more ideal structure of the skull. In this horrid stricture Hüll's face was transfixed by a razor of light, and a sound of metal dropped on tile.

From behind the diminishing halo of black left on Camus's retina came a practiced, unctuous voice.

"Then you would say, Professor, that this artifact supports the possibility of time travel?"

All eyes turned. At the fringe of the group stood two men strung with apparatus. One sported a pair of cameras, a tote bag, and sundry meters. The other held a slender microphone gracefully in one hand and with his free hand pushed Italian sunglasses up the bridge of his nose.

Warner's thunderous voice broke the silence. "Who in the bloody hell are you?"

"Wiesel, *Kölner Allgemeine Tageblatt*. Do you think *people* could be sent through time?"

A low moan came from Hüll. Warner said, "What? What is this? Just Christ damn *how* did you get in here?"

The question was resolutely pointless, posed as it was under a blank unbounded sky and Winifred's nominal security procedures, which consisted of ignoring any strange faces at the site—but it offered Camus a nice study of Warner, the fat corded neck bunching between the raised shoulders, the furryknotted brows belied by a tonguetip already venturing out between the parted teeth, alive at the prospect of publicity. Hüll, on the other hand, looked poleaxed. It occurred to Camus that this might have been the first time the old man had ever been photographed; the shock to his system was likely acute.

"Meiner *geehrter* Herr Warner. *Must* we have this?"

Warner's tongue retreated. "Absolutely not. No comments at this time, gentlemen. Print anything and I'll deny it." Still, he could not resist a show, or at least a teaser. "Our results here have been highly interesting, and may be of the first importance to the science of anthropology. But it would be improper to speculate at this time. Our data are incomplete. Eventually there will be a complete report. I hope you gents subscribe to *Nature*."

The photographer pivoted to pin Camus with his flash. Caught off guard, he toppled and felt the chair crack beneath him. Wiesel continued unruffled.

"Is this find connected in any way to the discoveries of Schwindel in—"

"All right!" Warner yelled. "That's it! Get the hell out of here!"

"You oughtn't treat the press this way," said Wiesel sadly.

"If any of you students have comments..."

"Out! I'll break your arms and legs!"

They scuttled, but not before the photographer had taken a picture of the cube. Twenty minutes later Camus found them poking around his tent.

"What did they say?" demanded Wiesel.

He considered. Actually, nothing had been said. Hüll had left in an admirable rage, and Warner had gone on snarling at everyone. Camus himself was somewhat dull with shock. He felt responsible, as though some lapse on his part had brought the cube into being, some private and reprehensible quirk that he had finally failed to restrain. There was surely some difference between *finding* and *making,* but he had never been at ease with it; it was why he had given up writing, this insecurity over the ultimate rôle of the agent who, on whatever scale, conveys a personal act of attention into the world. Discovery is, in some sense, invention; even with Winifred he was reluctant to use her name or to touch her readily, ever mindful of consequence, of the marks left by inept, irresponsible acts of attention. So he viewed Wiesel now with no love, his gaze moving under cover of his sunglasses from the zircon on its gold chain nested in the V of chest hair to the wingcollared silk shirt to the tight crisp leatherbelted jeans and shiny zippered boots. He removed the glasses and tried to look absentminded and myopic.

"The problem presents definite points of interest. Yes. My professional opinion is that this artifact, if I may call it such, is from the future, the far, far future, where it no longer rains, as is evident from the lack of rust on the cube. A future light-years"—he waved his glasses—"literally light-years ahead of us, gentlemen, technically speaking. Of course morally they may be baboons. At the very next conclave of the Concerned Scientists for Unitemporality we will propose measures—I think the word is not too strong—to deal with this unwarranted trespass upon our space-time. That, gentlemen, is all."

"And your name?"

"Arthur Conan Doyle."

The instant he entered his tent he had a headache. He tied the flaps shut and lay on the air mattress. He heard a car drive off. He heard Warner pass, conversing with three or four students. One plaintive voice drifted back, a girl from California saying, "Can we go home now?"

* * *

Impeccable Monsieur Ulysse Poisson poised at the lip of
the pit. Mouth pursed, he sifted dirt on the cave floor. From
a portable computer snaked a line to a Geiger probe in Poisson's
left hand. In his right was a buttoned box likewise connected
which periodically he thumbed. He wore black velvet gloves.
After tracing the last sector of the grid with his probe he straightened, laid down his tools, and brushed invisible dust from his
gloves.

Camus observed this over the top of the *Tageblatt*. The
article had appeared, in all its gory and immediate detail. The
acrimonious Wiesel had dug some nasty incidents out of Warner's past, and presented them in the worst light possible. He
had used Camus's facetious quote. Even Hüll had been smeared
by association, the "front" for the entire "circus," whose im-
pending retirement from Heidelberg was "fortuitous indeed."
This reporter had been treated with "less than courtesy." He
called for a thorough investigation of these "shady goings-on."
Since German tax money was involved, one had a right to
expect full disclosure.

All this disturbed Camus less than did Hüll's absence. A
month ago a bad bout with the flu had not kept the old man
away. But today the site was deserted, excepting himself, Warner, and the little Frenchman, imported at great expense to
perform a radiometric analysis of the hole.

German tax money? News to Camus. But the tests were
costing someone, and certainly not Warner nor the underen-
dowed Case Western Reserve University.

"My dear Warner, this is most interesting. I am indebted
to you," said Poisson.

"Great. Now what have you got?"

"In a moment we shall know." The statistician went to the
computer and punched a sequence of buttons. Square red digits
jittered, then settled to display nine zeros. Poisson chuckled.

"The distribution of radioactive materials in the grid is perfectly random."

"So?"

"Pardon. You do not apprehend the meaning. I say perfectly
random. Nothing in nature is perfectly random. Even random
distributions are distributed randomly. This is as if two identical
snowflakes were to land at once on your hand." In the demonstration he extended one gloved hand, examined it critically,

and brushed it with the other. "Or better perhaps, if two snow-storms were to produce the same number of flakes. You see? It is at least possible."

"Just unlikely."

"Highly. You say the . . . artifact was located in the grid?" Poisson pointed, ignoring the Neanderthal's broad grin.

"In the center."

"Intriguing. My guess is this. It was placed."

"No kidding."

"And so was the dirt surrounding it, every grain."

"The dirt!" Warner shouted. "What do you mean, the dirt was placed!"

Poisson opened one hand wide. "It is not Pleistocene dirt."

"And how in the name of bleeding Christ do you think that happened?"

"More I cannot say. The rules of my guild are strict. We do not speculate. I take the data, *bz bz bz*, I make the output. What it means is outside my province. Perhaps you should engage a generalist, or a systems theorist."

"At another five hundred a day, no thanks."

"My complete report will come. The imprimatur. Further investigation might turn up something more suggestive."

"Yes. I can't tell you how useful you've been. This cave was sealed for eighty thousand years. It was opened less than an hour before Caymus spotted the cube, with me here all the while. But the dirt was placed, every grain."

"It is a pretty problem. In any case my work is done. Unless of course . . ."

"I can't afford any further insights."

"As you wish. I would prefer payment in yen, directly into the usual account."

As Warner stalked from the cave Camus heard him mutter, "Fucking Frogs."

Poisson shook his head sadly. "He has not changed a bit."

"Warner? You know him?"

"We have had dealings," Poisson said in a tone of wry distaste, yet withal somewhat amused. "He is right about this little hole, you know. The false wall was certainly undisturbed for many millennia."

"What kind of dealings have you had with him?"

"Dealings in the past," said Poisson, adjusting pince-nez with one gloved hand and with the other drawing out an ornate pocket watch. Camus noticed that the works of the watch had been removed, and replaced by a digital display.

"Mon Dieu," said Poisson. "Look at that. I must bustle."

In solitude then, Camus thought to pay last respects to the dead soul within, but his mood was jumpy. His sense of the past, which he imagined to be finely tuned and free of bias, was disordered. Next he would be turning up ossified french fries and Captain Midnight Decoder Rings. Intruder, said the walls. Here he sat in a holy spot he would not have known holy if he hadn't defiled it. He must learn to move more lightly. Leave no traces, not even his usual reversed footmarks.

The dirt had been placed? So said Poisson, stamping outright impossibility on an already untenable situation. Ghosts. He imagined dirt gathering itself round the skeleton, giving flesh, unknowable chill ancient air breathing life into the bones. *I will show you fear in a handful of dust.*

A nearby car horn broke the valley calm. Ng had arrived to drive him into town. He left the cave quickly, for once grateful to the pointless occupation of life, pausing on the path down only to crush and pocket a beer can someone had dropped to remind him of the world's depleted bauxite mines. Yet another conscientious asshole, he thought to himself, wiping warm yeasty droplets into his jeans. He searched his other pockets for a fruit chew he felt sure was there.

4. "A Good Steward of History"

They took the autobahn into the city, turning north to the airport. Ng was bound for Beijing to visit relatives, then to Berkeley for his orals. He reminded Camus to visit California. They would renew their sporadic *go* competition. No shadow of recent events darkened Ng's smooth smiling face.

Leaving the rented car under an outthrust concrete awning, Camus walked with Ng as far as the metal detection gate. They shook hands, and Camus went back to place his suitcase in a baggage locker, then passed outside through automatic doors. The sunlight offended him, profligate photons streaming endlessly into ancient earth. He switched to dark glasses as a Lufthansa 767 screamed overhead. Grounded planes shuddered and whined uncertainly behind a curtain of heat waves.

He crossed the vast carpark to reach the tram station, projecting from the concrete plain like a bunker, in shape resembling nothing so much as a styrofoam hamburger carton.

The trams were a new feature of greater Düsseldorf. Here money was useless: before entering the system, one bought a card magnetically coded to the amount of one's fare, or, if one were prudent, slightly over. For the exit stile examined the card, subtracted the fare due, and opened. But if the coded fare was insufficient, or the stile broken, it would not open. Then one rang for an attendant and paid the needful. But so far three out of four stations lacked attendants, and the addfare machines actually within the system were always out of order. They cheerfully ate marks and chuckled in binary. Already a folklore had sprung up around the system: its designer was said to be wandering from station to station, caught short on his card, searching for a stile with an attendant or a commuter from whom he could cadge a card. Of course he was doomed; it was suicide to surrender or lose your card once inside the system.

Camus looked up the fare to the Altstadt, put in a mark extra, and waited for the machine to approve him. It spat the striped card from a slot. He walked across the station. The stile sucked the card through a front-facing panel and immediately shot it out the top. The gates opened. He stumbled as he passed through, and the two halves closed with a hiss on his buttocks, almost playfully, the gentlest nibble of plastic maw, then opened again to let him pass. Immediately they slammed shut.

The station was empty. For ten minutes he was treated to advertisements on the overhead clocks, terse messages that rolled right to left, a letter at a time, to terminate with the signature of the hour: 1510. A train arrived. He boarded, was whisked in putative comfort and safety under river, rock, road, and highrise, then exited into anachronistic Altstadt a block from the museum.

Here Winifred waited with more than her usual impatience, as she had a plane to catch. She pulled Camus bodily into an alcove in the foyer.

"Upstairs," she hissed. "And for God's sake wait until Warner's gone. If he finds out—" She drew a finger slickly across her throat.

"I'll be good," said Camus, raising a hand in pledge.

"And . . . damn, oh, damn. Will you call me in Cleveland?"

"Promise."

She kissed him and looked flustered. "I have to run."

He stood a minute in the entrance hall, until Warner came down the staircase and ignored him. Then he sighed and said, "And I have to plod."

Upstairs, in the office Winifred had been using, was a thick folder on the desk. It contained an analysis of the cube. The job had been done in London in just over a day. The hundred-odd pages of the report, which should have taken that long merely to type, were on flimsy computer paper, each page embossed with the mark of the Archaeological Research Center in London: oscillogram rampant on a field gules, bones beneath, crossed by a bend sinister bearing the legend *A R C*. The printing and graphics were excellent. Probably the analytic instruments were hooked directly into great brute engines of calculation, format, and word processing, results sprayed directly onto the page by nozzles misting ionized ink under magnetic control. Camus shuddered at the thought. He was still leery of copiers, and sometimes cursed his manual typewriter.

He was not sure his nervous system was up to looking at the
report, let alone studying it.

"Be modern, Hans," he chided himself, and began to skim
the sheaf with a practiced eye. That got him exactly nothing.
He sighed, aligned the pages with his fingertips, and began to
read exhaustively. Every four pages he fished another cigarette
from his pack and lit it without raising his eyes. He got up
only once, to find the switch for the overhead light.

SPECIMEN RECEIVED 1130 GMT SUNDAY 28 JULY 1991

Imprimatur of impossibility. Imagining this London lab he
instead recalled, with no great love, a course he had taken in
techniques of elemental analysis. He had done this to satisfy
his skepticism of, or obsession with, the details of methodology. No paleontologist did his own material analyses, but Camus had wanted to get his hands on the equipment just once.
He spent several nights in the lab, doing routine gamma-ray
spectrometry, trying to force the wretched machine to acknowl-
edge the presence of aluminum in the sample, which was beach
sand, and it wouldn't. Time and again he went over backscatter,
annihilation, and sum peak effects, fixing the calibration, trying
the scope at various sampling rates, nudging the neutron beam
from 10^3 to 10^7 and back . . . and traced the problem, over a
weekend, finally to a bad chip in the scintillation counter,
learning incidentally more about electronics and nuclear res-
onance than he'd ever wanted to know. Then the ^{28}Al gamma
peak had come up fine and clean at 1.78 meV. He stopped just
short of slapping the high voltage power supply in triumph. So
he had vast, if grudging, patience for the gritty incidentals of
technique, and knew that engineering was the necessary leaden
wings of gossamer science's flight. But still. This ARC stuff
gave him a headache.

SITE: NATURSCHUTZGEBIET, HOCHDAHL, FED REP GERMANY

He wondered if the cube had passed through human hands
at all. Perhaps the entire analysis was automated, the machines
self-aligning, the data parsed, printed, and posted by a word
processor, hurried back and forth by a union courier with his
mind on a detective novel. An outsize maverick and prima
donna Warner might be, but Camus's admiration for his methods increased: sending the cube to ARC for a rush job was
probably a canny way of getting a complete report and keeping

it, for a while, secret. Probably no one at ARC had yet looked at the report.

He forced his mind back to the papers. Somewhere in the neatly plotted curves, the standard deviations, was some detail that would lead to a proper interpretation. But it got worse and worse. And there was no bad chip he could track down to make it come out right.

COMPOSITION: NEUTRON ACTIVATION ANALYSIS

The cube was not a simple block of metal. One face was of nonuniform composition, bearing regularly spaced dots of an alloy of lead, indium, and gold. Tiny hairs of platinum, seventy-five micrometers in diameter, projected from these dots, themselves bearing minuscule traces of mercury. The deeper structure of the heavier atoms had been approached by striking their nuclei with neutrons until they rang with gamma rays. The results were uncertain; every other page bore the caveat *tentative*. Detected were: iron, silicon, carbon, platinum, gold, lead, indium, gallium, gadolinium, dysprosium, lanthanum, xenon, potassium, astatine. The isotope of astatine had a half-life of eight hours—yet, impossibly, it was stable.

Crystallography showed irregular but not random patterns throughout. Fourier analysis, ergodic functions, Cauchy distributions, and other stochastic methods had made no sense of it.

RADIOMETRIC DATING ENSEMBLE

The dating techniques relied on the inherent radioactivity of matter. Almost every element had some radioactive nuclides, leftover hash from the Creation. The longer lived of these were quite reliable clocks. But the success of any method relied upon the age and composition of the sample. So Warner had ordered a full ensemble of tests, hoping to turn up anything at all. Uranium-lead, rubidium-strontium, potassium-argon tests measured the decay in the sample since its origin, by use of a Geiger tube and standard halflife equations. The fission-track method actually looked at the molecular structure for traces of damage from alpha emissions.

Here the cube was compliant: it yielded firm results for every test. The results were also senseless. They said anything from two million years to contemporary. Here too a set of graphs and plates complemented the figures, which is to say

confused matters further. He had a ludic fear that if he connected the dots of the subatomic decay marks, he would get a
map of Düsseldorf, or a page from Leonardo's notebooks. . . .

ANALYSIS COMPLETED 1400 GMT MONDAY 29 JULY 1991

He pushed the report aside with more violence than he felt.
Beneath the jungle of jargon, the brash official gloss, the bar-
rage of techniques, it said just one thing: impossible. From
each angle of approach the cube had a different aspect. It must
be a hoax. It could not be a hoax. It could not exist at all, as
contemporary science defined existence.

He paced to restore his circulation. Outside, the twin warble
of police and ambulance sirens approached along Okenstrasse.
He peered out the dark window onto the Friedrichsplatz just
as they went past, dropping in pitch by a minor third. Blue
light flashed once in the room, then the sirens were cut off,
somewhere just around the corner.

An ancient, cracked voice came across time, from the darkened boards of a stage in his mind: "*À moi . . . de jouer.*" And
the cube assumed spots on its faces, in mockery, one face
swinging open to admit him to the closed system of the game,
the game he was still, after so much preparation, unprepared
to play. Below him, a tram clattered to a halt in the street, and
a crowd of shouting, shoving boys clamored down its steel
steps. He raised the window and caught some of their conversation. They were rehearsing the high points of an old thriller
they had just seen, acting out the more violent parts with the
enthusiasm of a ham for a death scene.

"When he's on the train . . ."

"Nothing to fear . . ."

"The polaroid self-portrait as a vain attempt at definition in
a world of moral self-ag*grand*izement . . ."

The tram lurched off, the boys turned a corner, Camus was
alone again. No: not here, and not him: a childhood in some
other town now lost to history. He had wanted to call out to
them, but no words he now owned could express his longing.

He went from the office into the long, dim corridor. Perhaps
he could be a player eventually, in some game larger than that
of the self, but not tonight. He passed locked offices, store-
rooms, and stopped at a brightly lit alcove that housed Coke,
candy, and cigarette machines. He bought a pack of Gauloises,
turning over in his mind some lines from Eliot:

Time present and time past
Are perhaps both present in time future
And time future contained in time past.

And perhaps the cube imposed such stark congruence, between poetry transcendent and violated physics, never to be apprehended by Hüll's erudition, nor Poisson's instrumentation, nor Winifred's diligence, nor even by Warner's inspired mummery. *Me ... to play.* He stood now at the end of the second floor corridor, awash in the dim green light of a sign reading *Ausgang.* His hesitation was that of a man unaccountably afraid to cross an empty street. A last couplet jarred him.

If all time is eternally present
All time is unredeemable.

He shuddered as if with a chill. Then he said, "Bullshit," and swung wide the door, going rapidly down the fire stairs to the first floor. Here only the sepulchral blue glow of emergency lights marking the guard's time clocks relieved the obscurity. He moved by memory, quickly traversing Neumann Hall, and passing into the Hall of Quaternary Fauna. There he was momentarily distracted by the grim *Ursus spaeleus,* one of the museum's prime attractions, and he blundered into a low, darkened case. It was a new exhibit, placed squarely across his remembered path, and he saw that it displayed a variety of Pleistocene elephant molars, graded according to degrees of specialization. He swore and scurried around the obstruction, coming suddenly face to face with a case that sat on a low dais facing the door. This case was lit, and Camus confronted the squat, incomplete caricature of a man, an outline ghostly white upon a black ground, against which stood the fragments of a skeleton: faceless cranium, shoulder blade, breastbone, two forearms, five ribs, pelvis, two thigh bones. An inauspicious start to civilization, he thought, this old, old man from Newman's Valley.

Stepping onto the dais, he read the bronze plaque:

The Type Specimen of Homo Sapiens Neanderthalensis, unearthed in August 1856 by workmen at the von Beckensdorff Quarry, and returned to Düsseldorf from The Schaafhausen Institute, Bonn, in 1985, at the request of Professor M. Hüll.

At first, these fragments were dismissed variously as the remains of a Mongoloid Cossack from the Napoleonic

campaign of 1814, a Dutchman, or a pathological idiot.
They stand now as the cornerstone of Man's search for
the particulars of his own ancestry, of the scientific struggle to comprehend, with neither prejudice nor precon-
ception, the world of Nature and our place within it.

He almost laughed, but stifled it. Humor was out of place
at a funeral. The bridge, the slender bridge Darwin had reared
on immense buttresses of data, seemed ready to fall under the
unnatural weight of a small cube. Though he might yet mourn
the fall in motley, mourn it he would.

He turned, squinting into the sudden glare of a flashlight.

"Ah, Hans, it's you. I heard someone."

His heart calmed after a moment. It was von Rast.

They had first met when Camus was eight, precocious, and
a troublemaker. He had come here every Sunday after Mass,
and once von Rast caught him attempting to sneak into the
preparation room. He dragged the startled miscreant into his
shop, delivered a stern lecture on the dangers of snooping,
followed by coffee and cakes, and when the museum closed
for the day he gave Camus a private tour, and let him varnish
a mammoth vertebra. His mother whopped him when he got
home after dark, and that had clinched his friendship with von
Rast.

"Working late?" Von Rast lowered the flash and hobbled
forward.

"Not really. Just—just skulking."

More than ever, he felt an intruder in a realm of peace. Von
Rast's life made his look like low comedy. Assigned to the
Heeresversuchstelle Peenemünde in early 1943 as a quarter-
master, von Rast had developed a new system for cataloguing
rocket parts, and was decorated by Field Marshal Keitel. When
Allied bombers razed the launch site in August of 1943, he
ended in a field hospital with a shattered leg and a tattered
copy of *Faust Two*, which he had been reading in the latrine
at the time of the attack. He recuperated and spent another year
at Peenemünde. The same leg was injured again in another
bombing, after which he was discharged, and limped home
across the torn and blackened ruins of Saxony and Westfalen.
After the war he turned down a job with McDonnell-Douglas.
When his pension dried up he found work with the museum,
where he stayed, much valued and declining all promotions,
until age and arthritis forced him into his current post as care-

taker. Most of this history Camus had inferred from a close reading of a strange story, "The Clockwork Faun," which von Rast had written during his convalescence, and published in a local literary gazette. If pressed, the old man now dismissed the entire period contemptuously as "my mechanical childhood," and changed the subject. But one time the two had had a talk.

"It was a strange time, after the first bombing," von Rast had said. "Over seven hundred were killed that night. They buried them very efficiently a few days later, a Saturday morning, in mass graves by the railroad tracks. I stayed up all the night before the burial. It was a superstitious time. I watched Mercury and Venus follow the sun into the west, and I remember that the moon rose late, it was past full, a waning gibbous, the worst of shapes. They had bombed at the full, of course. Mars was bright, and rose shortly after the moon, and then Saturn, standing by itself in Scorpius. Jupiter came up just before dawn. We were all starting to look for portents about then. The story was that the Americans were recruiting defectors.

"Next spring the Gestapo arrested von Braun, not for any treason, but because he was more interested in space flight than in weapons. As if they could not tolerate the thought that some power could push a thing beyond their influence, outside gravity, never to return. As if the brooding presence of Oswald Spengler behind the Wehrmacht, his great tragic parabolic arch of rise and fall, could not be violated; that growth is bound to lead to decay, that history is therefore a nightmare, independent of man's will, and unalterably perverse.

"Dornberger got him off, as I recall. And there were more air raids that summer, and we really did start to lose men to defection, not to the American government, I think, but to private industry. It was the fourth raid that retired me, a year after the first."

Then, continuing casually, he had said, "I keep tabs still on our local neo-Nazis. You thought there weren't any? You must think about these things a little, or you will leave yourself open to them. The old party was not made of barbarians or pagans, no, they were sublime technicians. So you find the new ranks mostly in the technological sector. They eat yogurt, rennetless cheese, wheat germ, tons of vitamins. To sleep they take L-tryptophan. They glow with the same good health I had in 1939. It would break your heart."

And that was all he ever got on that subject. To speak at any length von Rast saw as foolishness, and he always seemed amused when he let young Hans draw him out, and exalted when he found a way to cut himself off: about his present life he simply said he was "a good steward of history;" and about his personal faith he quoted the opening of Augustine's *Confessions:* "Can any praise be worthy of His majesty?"

So now, the dense text of his remembrances like dying coals unfanned, Camus blinked at the sudden return of the present moment, reinforced by von Rast snapping on the overhead fluorescent lights.

"It's nothing, really," he managed to say. "Just a small problem at the dig."

"So? I thought you were all done."

"We found . . ." He couldn't say it. The cube now seemed trivial, a temporary aberration bound to vanish as surely as the dawn in day. "Didn't Warner say anything?"

"Your Herr Professor Faschingsnarr?" *Fasching* was the pre-Lent carnival, traditionally led by the figure of the fool. "He said to close the cave and let no one in. I told him to talk to the people at the *Gebiet.*"

"I thought you worked there."

"They let me poke around. I found your professor's cave for him. So he thinks I have some importance. I don't."

"So *you* got me involved in this mess."

"*Ach, mein armer Hans.* All I ever said was to beware of strange rocks. God only knows what's under them."

Camus stared pensively at the Neanderthal. "Why can't we just leave the dead buried?"

Von Rast followed his gaze. "A very good point. Let's leave our friend here in peace." He snapped off the lights, and walked back into the main hall. Camus followed.

"What *is* worthy of His majesty?"

Von Rast looked critically at the case of elephant molars. He straightened it with some effort, and rubbed the glass with his handkerchief. Then he pointed a bent finger at Camus.

"You go poking into things, like me. You see a rainbow, you are impressed by the arch. You wonder. But you don't leave it there. You wonder, and worry and worry, and before long the sky is falling in pieces around you, and off you go squealing like Chicken Little." He considered this for a while. "Your friend Warner, he is foolish like the fox in the story."

"So what is one to do?"

"*Ach*, morality. This is something I can no longer afford.
I'm a hobbyist. I put things together, like skeletons, and any
little messages I may receive I keep to myself."

"I'm Chicken Little?"

Von Rast smiled kindly. "You're *der kleine Moritz*."

It was an old name that his mother, as well as von Rast,
had used on him before: *der kleine Moritz* was a secular Swiss
hero of tales, one of those local characters who combine the
most risible and unpredictable traits of Lucifer, Faust, Robin
Hood, Cain, Till Eulenspiegel, and the Katzenjammer Kids,
and the saying was: History is as *der kleine Moritz* dreams it.

"History . . ." Camus began jovially, and was cut off.

". . . Is something I never think about unless I'm well fed,
well rested, and my bones don't hurt. You know, in my wan-
derings in 1945 I hiked past Belsen. What do you suppose I
saw?"

Camus was silent.

"I did not see history."

"You said once you were a good steward of history."

"A pretty bit of conceit. You believed that?"

"I did."

"*Doch*. Maybe so. I keep my eyes open and my mind open.
But I do not lift strange rocks. I do not think about rainbows.
I take a salary of 350 DM weekly to keep this museum in order.
When I die I shall ask the Lord for a useful position in Hell,
and keep to myself the hope that they may make a decent lager
there. Touch nothing, look for nothing, expect nothing, ignore
nothing. If you want a tangible history, you'd better become
a clockmaker." Von Rast sighed. "Myself, I try only to leave
things as I found them. A vain hope. *Und Du, Junge*—what
is it you want? You don't grow up, you grow sidewise, you
slither. You touch everything and ignore it all, and then hi-
bernate with the great guilt that you're not St. Augustine. And
you look to me. What am I? An old man who, fifty years late,
has the presumption to wake up some nights with shame at the
Nazizeit, and who also keeps a personal letter of gratitude from
von Braun. It is impossible to keep from being some sort of
fraud. Augustine himself was one of the worst, a rakehell turned
saint, with his 'what praise?' and then a thousand pages of
goat-blather."

"I am every sort of fraud," said Camus gloomily.

Von Rast turned around in exasperation. "What an infant
he is. I doubt Christ Himself was such a stubborn child. If I

were a normal human being I'd be tired, I'd have an excuse to be rude to him. I tell him to beware of strange rocks. Right away he cries, 'There's one—why, it's you, von Rast, and you're covered with slugs!' Then he wonders why strange rocks should happen to be strange. Faugh!" Von Rast switched to French. "'Oh, oh,' he says, 'very well, I am defeated. This rock is strange and I am not, oh, what misfortune, I shall go to a strange rock school and learn to be one.' And he does, and when he has become the strangest rock that ever was, he says, 'Oh, oh, how strange I am, what misfortune to be a strange rock, oh, I must learn to be less strange and less rocky.'"

Camus was laughing helplessly. Von Rast eyed him coldly. "Good. You're angry?"

"*Oui, oui, très furieaux, malgré moi, quel malheur, oh, oh, quel malaise, ich bin ja* righteously pissed."

"So." Von Rast nodded sadly, dropping into English. "You cut the crap, and I'll get you some coffee, okay?"

Camus nodded, wiping tears from his eyes.

Then, as if he'd caught a trace of Camus's memories of him, von Rast paused.

"One final story I should tell. In the summer of '44 they were testing the A-4. Von Braun was a stickler for detail; he had to know exactly where the test rockets landed. The guidance systems were erratic at best. So von Braun set himself up 200 miles away right at ground zero, reasoning that statistically this was the best possible way of being safe, and also within range of the fallen rockets. The first shot hit three hundred yards from him, and almost killed him."

Camus said nothing.

"Perhaps the safest place to be is at the center. And also, perhaps the coin spun one million times lands once on edge. And it might be the first time."

5. *Einfühlung*

He woke slowly, warmed by sunslant through the window open over Okenstrasse. A slight breeze stirred papers on the desk. He untucked hands from armpits, uncrossed his extended legs, and spent a few minutes chasing down dream ends. As he stood and began to stack the papers, he paused over one page of the paleointensity analysis. There, in the margin of the secular variation curves for Hochdahl 100,000 BP, was a drawing. He recognized his own fussy draftsmanship, but could not remember making the sketch. A robed and mitred bishop, celebrant of some distorted Eucharist, held aloft a cube; the bishop was masked. Below the figure ran a caption, crowded by the page-edge: *but what about the ecclesiastical variation?*

His bemusement tapered off toward disgust. With one rapid motion he balled the sheet and threw it to the far corner of the room. Then he swept the strewn papers into his briefcase, open on the floor, latched the case, and with his free hand turned an overflowing ashtray into the wastebasket.

Outside his mood improved. He still had the whole day before his flight. The faces of the buildings were sharp and close, the sky vivid, and there was a pleasant warm wind from the river.

Idly he began to trail a small boy through the winding streets of the Altstadt, toward the Rheinbrücke. Dressed in a quaint tailored suit and carrying a scaled down briefcase, the child seemed displaced in time—a piano prodigy on his way to a lesson, or a mathematics scholar hurrying to prove Fermat's Last Theorem. Camus indulged a mood of nostalgia: the boy was one of his own lost selves, in a cleaner, purer city, on a less complicated line of time: unsentimental as Camus thought he was, his heart was sometimes tricked into a state of feeling his mind could not endorse. Then, as they reached the end of the Bäckerstrasse, where the narrow vista of older buildings opened to embrace the Rhine, the figure turned to him, and he saw with unwarranted horror the face of a dwarf: the authentic lines of age, infirmity, and distortion erasing and rewriting his expectation like a palimpsest: a small precapitulation of the shock he would have in regard to Hüll.

Outside the *Gasthaus* a police car was parked across the curb. Two trim men in wellcut suits were leaning on the car and talking, and Camus hurried past them, cropping for the moment his impulse to say a brief farewell to Hüll. Probably a burglary. Give them time to leave. First he would have some breakfast at the Café Schlegel: scrambled eggs, sausage, a plate of biscuits with butter and cheese. He paused at the kiosk to pick up a *Rheinische Post,* his usual morning read; what he saw on the front page brought him up with so vicious a start it foreclosed all thought of food. The banner headline read: ANATOMIST'S SUICIDE. The accompanying picture was that of Maximilian Hüll.

He stood for perhaps thirty seconds, staring into a bookstore next to the café. Centered in the display was a broad, colorful, coffeetable book from a British publisher, titled *Man's Makers;* he knew it featured a chapter on Hüll. Next to this a clerk was arranging six copies of the slim red Heidelberg *Hüll-Festschrift,* dusting their spines as he proceeded.

Camus turned back down the street. Another, more massive figure had joined the men in front of the *Gasthaus,* and seemed to be arguing with them. Even back to, there was no mistaking Warner's frame.

Warner turned and saw him before he made up his mind to walk away. He approached the men.

"Detectives," said Warner. "Jesus, I'm glad to see you, Hans. You've got to help me clean up here."

"Hüll's dead?" asked Hans.

Warner looked at the newspaper still clutched to the windbreaker, folded headline out. "What the hell did you think?"

"He killed himself?"

Warner introduced Camus to the detectives in German, botching the verb. "Yes, Hans. That's what he did."

"I don't understand."

"Oh my God. What is there to understand? Hüll is dead, I have to catch a plane, and everyone here is screaming for a pound of flesh, so you're it. Here."

Warner thrust upon him a scrap of paper and a one hundred

mark note. "Pack up his papers and books, and settle with the landlady. The scientific papers if any go the Heidelberg, *except* for anything you find pertaining to the expedition, which goes to *me* at this address. That's extremely important. Personal effects to his wife in, um, whatever it says there. If you have time to send her my condolences, do so. Any reporters show up, tell them to fuck themselves. Got that?"

"Listen, I—that is, can't you stay? Can't you get a later flight?"

"Absolutely not. Out of the question. There is no later flight. Now will you do this?"

Camus tried to clear his head. "I don't understand why a good Catholic like Hüll . . ."

"Suffering Christ. I'm missing my plane and he wants to discuss eschatology."

"All right. I'll . . ."

"Good man." Warner spoke rapidly in wretched German to the detectives, who dourly examined Camus and shrugged.

". . . See you in Seattle. What about the cube?"

"Let's hope so," said Warner.

"The . . ."

"What? Oh, you mean the convention. Yes, look, we'll talk it over then. I have to run."

"But where is . . ."

Warner glared at him with asperity. *"Later,* Hans." The three men went down the street together and separated at the corner. Camus mechanically ascended the steps to Fuhlrott-strasse 29.

Shaking the small bell on the front table brought no response, so he took the key to number 6 from its peg and went upstairs.

The police had already searched the room. Left were a battered valise, a shelf of books, some clothes, two pairs of shoes, and an almost empty schnapps bottle weighing down some blank wrinkled paper. A faint odor of peppermint or disinfectant hung in the room.

Camus leaned on the small writing table for a moment, peering out the window. He could just make out the edge of the Löbbeke building. He began to pull down the blind, but when he had drawn it six inches he released it with a sharp gasp. It was stained with blood.

He sat down and tried to light a cigarette. To do this he had to brace his right forearm on the writing table, clamping his right wrist with his left hand, and lowering his face to the level of the match.

After a while he was calm enough to read the *Post*. Hüll had used a pistol. No note had been found. A typical file obituary followed: Founding member of the Berliner Gesellschaft für Anthropologie, past president of the Quaternary Society, fellow of the Geologische und Paläontologische Gesellschaft, emeritus professor of physical anthropology at Heidelberg, author of some twenty books including a still standard text on comparative anatomy, possessor of degrees and honors Camus had never heard of, a string of letters twice again as long as his name, practically every laurel the fulsome German obsession with merit could offer; yet modest and likeable, aloof from personal ambition. The son of a Württemberg burgomeister. His death a great shock and loss to the academic community. No hint of a motive.

Camus studied the sloppy paste-up work in the article, but beneath this compulsive examination of seams his mind was screaming loss. He realized now how much he had liked Hüll; worse, how much he had believed in him, the scrupulous, sane presence whom no disorder could befall.

He pulled open a desk drawer. Within was a wooden rosary. When he lifted the beads, a 7.65 millimeter shell fell free and clanked on the thin drawer bottom. He looked around the room, the trace of an idea forming.

Camus had a modest talent which he called *Einfühlung*. The word meant sympathy, empathy, putting oneself at one with; it was close to *einführen*, which meant to import, initiate, or introduce, nor yet so far from *einfahren*, to enter, to travel in. The process first was to put himself at peace, which he could not always do. Then he would strip his mind of the personal, seeing and not seeing himself, becoming an abstraction such as: young man at desk. And then it was simply an act of attention. Like Odysseus descending to House of Hades he gave the blood of his attention that the dead might speak.

It was a variety of fraud. To pierce directly to the essential qualities of an experience, he would use any apparatus at hand. Why not? When we wake, do we not first forge a copy of our prior selves? The craft of self is largely fraud in the service of authenticity. And at this Camus, an inveterate forger and parodist, had some experience. One year he had supported himself by writing papers for athletes and deadbeats, and had used his trick to get inside their heads. Before that, his *feuilletons* "The

Return of the Screw" and "The Origin of Species and Descent From the Cross" had been the toast of the short-lived *Black Bottom Review*. He knew a thing or two about assuming roles.

His eyes stopped at a book on the small shelf. It was volume five of the *Catholic Encyclopedia*. He drew it down, and opened to the article on evolution, bookmarked by an old photo. The photo showed several young men in hiking gear. On its back an inscription read: *Sils Maria, 1946*. He scrutinized the photo until he located Hüll. The features hadn't changed that much. Fortyfive years ago. Younger then than Camus was now.

He was sure he could do it. He had always felt some sympathy with Hüll, and he prided himself on his abstract skill for union; what else did he have but a sensitivity to the various densities of time, as expressed in people and their works? Looking at a building, sculpture, fresco, text, face, he knew what was weak, what would fall first. He had looked at himself that way, and at Winifred, and knew what each face would become in fifty years. He could sense the massing of time in the arch of a cathedral, the turn of an idea, the line of a frown; he knew where a pillar or proposition or person was consonant with its ideal past, present, and future, and where dissonant. He saw the ruins of things in the things themselves. (Once he had drawn the Pompidou Center as it would be in five centuries, roof collapsed, pipes fallen, overgrown with ivy.) So why had he not seen a weakness in Hüll?

Taking Hüll's part then, Camus considered the cube.

Assume it is a hoax. A forgery is not merely an object represented as something it is not. A perfect forger creates a moment of history. Is the moment false? Yes, but it leaves its mark. Both craftsman and forger introduce an anomaly into the world: no painting, poem, pot, or polis grows in the earth, though all return there. A new kind of time therefor emerges from the craftsman's smithy: historical time. So history is primarily marks, on paper, canvas, film, landscape, sensibility. We cannot know the past directly, not even the past of a minute ago; the mechanisms of memory at least intervene. History is marks, and only some marks endure. And if a fraud is detected, it might as well be real. The nature of this cube is so strange, there is no way to prove it false. Therefore assume it is real.

He was now thinking in fluent, somewhat archaic German.

The dimension of the cube—exactly two centimeters on an edge—all but proved it was of Earth. Besides, he did not believe in the agency of demons or spacemen. The thought that it might be divine was impious and abhorrent. And its provenance was not prehistory. All this he knew. So it was human, hence explicable by mind.

Of time he was not so sure. We have only fictions of time. So postulate people of the future, as wretched and proud as ourselves or our parents; postulate that they can violate our concept of time by a superior understanding of drawing, the science of making marks. This cube is a mark such that it can leap outside its native time. Now, one object traveling through time is sufficient to burst all physics like an arrow piercing the balloon to which the expanding universe is vulgarly likened. And it inexorably follows that all knowledge is founded on a false premise: the unidirectionality of time. Violate time and nothing remains but artifice, role, appearance, and fraud. A sportsman's delight. With a shudder he thought of Warner, the man's love of fraud.

Could it be? Then everything might be faked. This was a child's or a paranoid's thought, that the adults manipulate everything for effect; but it had haunted him before, in various forms, through the war, through doubts of faith, through his studies of history, pre and ur: a prescient ache like the start of migraine, or a suspicion of cancer deep in the bones, or the wink of heaven supposed to precede an epileptic fit. Always he shook it off as a fancy. But now? Imagine this future, with its techniques of deranging the past. A manuscript might be printed with advanced techniques, then sent back to decay, so that by its prefigured date of discovery only fragments remain. An antiquity. The caesurae propel the culture of the finders in a certain way, all calculated in the future by strict vectors of anachronism. The stars of data, from which we draw our constellations of science, holy books of faith . . . all, all faked?

Angrily, with a rising sense of danger, he swept the papers and bottle from the desk. It clanked unbroken on the parquet floor. And stuck to the desktop beneath the pile, overlooked, as if he'd been meant to find it, as if it had popped from the air a moment before, was a small, lined page filled with the tight, snailish writing of the photo. It had been razored neatly from a diary. Here and there water marks had smeared the ink. Unconsciously his hand curled about a nonexistent fountain pen as he read:

"... Talking with Warner about his monstrous scheme. Privately he is quite convinced the artifact is real, and thinks it has traversed time. For my part I find this scarcely less credible

nor more horrible than the idea of a hoax. He is convinced that
it is 'the tip of the iceberg' as he puts it, that large masses have
been sent through time, from the future—'to keep time moving,' he says. He asserts these vague analogies of action and
reaction as if he had them right there on the dissecting table.
As he spoke my horror grew intense, for here was a scientist
who followed, apparently, no methodology, who was willing
to entertain the most outrageous hypotheses, simply for their
'imaginative value,' with no qualms whatever. Then he proposed to suppress the evidence of the cube, until he has worked
out his travesty of a theory sufficiently to 'knock them all on
their asses.' I could not believe it. Everything they say about
him is true. I quite felt as if I were speaking to Mephistopheles.

"I have no right to interfere with his plans, whatever they
may be, for my position here, after all, is advisory; but I would
not hear any more, and asked him to leave. On his way out
he *warned* me, if you please, against saying anything.

"My reputation shall suffer from my involvement here; I
shall have to resign my chair, not retire; but that is the least
of it. The artifact exists, and it strikes at the core of everything
I believe. Can I accept this? I have devoted my life to science,
to method, and above all I have believed in a divine Order,
and in man's genius to apprehend this order, and to attain it.
This abominable *thing,* if it is real, overturns everything. And
if it is a hoax, Piltdown Man will seem a schoolboy prank
beside it.

"I abetted Warner without knowing. Still I am to blame.
But it is not possible to get so far into a thing that there is no
out. There is at least the temporal redemption offered by—"

And that was all, or nearly all. The passage broke off halfway down the back of the page. But at the bottom was a single
line, hastily scrawled, as if by a man at a peak of ecstasy or
a depth of despair:

"Benedictus Dominus, pater misericordiarum."

If historical time can be violated, then spiritual time . . . the
long ascent . . . all countless hours of devotion, piety, shame,
guilt, exaltation . . . all, all a sham? No teleology, no purpose.
In all our science and faith we are children telling fairy tales,
and no Father to tuck us in when we tire. I have doubted before,
but *this* . . .

He finished the schnapps to calm himself. What is sin? Is
not a very great sin undertaken to vindicate one's faith an act
of devotion? At last logic must rest. *Benedictus Dominus.*

He raised the gun in his right hand, and brought the barrel to rest under his left ear, pointed up through the lefthand hemisphere, the logical half, where words were. He aimed with wordhand and teased the trigger with a last reluctance. Twice or three times he coaxed it to its edge, leaving the final decision to God, the Devil, the fineness of his own control, or chance. Some answer, even Hell. *Pater miseric—*

The young man at the desk jerked backwards in his chair. He was drenched with sweat.

After a time he left the room, locked it, walked downstairs, dropped the key on the desk. He went into the street. A crumpled page in his pocket winked an edge as he walked. A book was under his arm. The sun was hot, and by the time a bus overtook him at a corner, he was again warm. He had no idea where he was, where he was going. He had no firm idea even who he was.

6. First Church of Recycled Souls

On entering, he had the brief unpleasant impression that the great hanging aluminum cross was draped with slaughtered beasts. But they were furs, and on second glance he saw microphones, cables, and other equipment spread about the nave. It was not the church he remembered from childhood. He passed a group of technicians, not quickly enough to avoid hearing the reason for the scene: the hyperbolic paraboloid dome of the new church had a refractory habit of throwing down tinny echoes, as if a whiny, adenoidal God were parodically repeating everything said. The technicians argued what to hang where to baffle the echoes.

He passed into a corridor of offices, pausing at the first likely door. *Jean-Baptiste Derrida.* One fist aloft, Camus was interrupted from knocking by the sound of gunfire from the cathedral. He pushed the door open and entered. The priest, hunched at his desk with fists clamped on ears, did not notice his entrance. Camus opened his clenched fist and ran it through his hair. At the next volley of shots the priest flinched and looked up. Fairly young, large-boned, the priest resembled him; Camus momentarily felt that he was looking at himself in a mirror that violated the politer rules of optics.

"Pardon. I . . . knocked."

"Oh yes, excuse me. I was just . . ." Derrida winced and waved a hand feebly. "They've been at it all morning. Acousticians."

"I used to attend Mass here," said Camus. "I mean, not here. Or, yes, here, but before . . ."

Derrida gave him a look of dubiety that was possibly only a critical recognition of their resemblance. "Yes. I arrived recently from Zürich. They sent me a picture of the old cathedral. It had a lovely rose window. What can I do for you, my son?"

45

Nothing, a wee voice within abruptly realized. "I'm having difficulties, Father."

"Spiritual difficulties?"

Camus watched a jet descend on the pale sky until a windowframe blocked it from sight.

We are all in Time. But birds, stones, trees, stars, and men have each their own rhythms of existence, and the unified Time of science, which assigns the same unit of measure to all disparate durations, is a fiction—a calculated simplification of the real. In reality there is no essential common time between the various enclaves of being. Constant collisions of circumstance, yes, but little essential sharing.

Still, despite this sense of the world as a complex layering of times, Camus believed that slates could be cleansed, circumstances untangled, essences found. In this connection he took for his patron saint the heretic Pelagius, also called Morgan, both names meaning "man of the sea." Man acquires sin, said Pelagius, through sinful acts; none inheres at birth. So it is always possible to start over. There are days, as Proust said, "on which time starts afresh, casting aside the heritage of the past, declining its legacy of sorrows." The heresy was refuted by Augustine, but still Camus kept Pelagius's feast each January first, and tried to remain mindful that any day, any morning, any moment may, by an extraordinary act of will or grace, be cleansed of the past, purged of its burden of circumstance. Without altering or forgetting or overlooking any past event, all debts to what has gone before may nonetheless be rescinded, or at least extenuated.

"Have you lost the faith, my son?"

"Theological difficulties."

"When did you last attend Mass?"

"Father, I'm a paleontologist."

"Well, of course, there is no reason why the pursuit of science need conflict with the demands of faith."

"Have you ever looked up evolution in the Catholic Encyclopedia?"

"My son, it was Bertrand Russell—hardly a good Catholic—who said, 'knowledge is a subclass of belief.' Nothing that man discovers can lessen the glory of God."

"Belief, yes. All knowledge is fiction. But there are good fictions and bad fictions . . . and contradictory fictions. Pelagius . . ."

"Yes, a heretic."

"For denying original sin. So does paleontology."

"One need not take the Bible as literal history."

"No. What does the Church say about time?"

"Well, now, that is an altogether large and complicated topic. Of course God and His angels exist outside of time, and it is man's lot, in this life, to live in a temporal world."

"Does Heaven exist now? Right this minute?"

"Of course."

"And the souls of the dead?"

"The virtuous are in Heaven, the unredeemed in Hell. And at their Last Judgment their bodies will be reunited with their souls, and their bliss or torment magnified. And that will be the end of time."

"The end? That's it?"

"My son . . . surely this is all known to you. You were raised in the Church?"

"The incorruptible substance of the soul is to be reunited with the corruptible body?"

"It is time that corrupts, and Heaven of course is without time."

Both were silent for a space.

"Did you know the Greek root of eternity means spinal marrow?"

"Well, now, that is most interesting, but I don't see how it affects—"

"I was wondering about Peking Man. They used to suck the marrow of their dead. Did it have to do with time?"

"Well," said Derrida, "the Chinese . . ."

"No, no. Prehistoric man."

"Ah."

"Were there souls then?"

"I don't believe, that is, I don't know whether, ah, doctrine has addressed itself to that point. The, what we call the soul begins to exist by a direct creative act of God at the moment of its union with matter. Its proper role is to form one unique person and no other. As to—"

"But the endless reduplication of entities . . ."

Derrida spread his hands. "God is beneficent, one might say profligate. And of course time *will* have an end."

"Yes, the Judgment. The Apocalypse. Tip of time's arrow. When the number of souls created is sufficient."

"Sufficient?"

"Father, do the living outnumber the dead, or is it the other way around?"

"I—I don't know."

"I thought you might. I think it's the dead."

Into the brief silence broke the sound of shots from the cathedral. Derrida flinched.

"Perhaps I stand in danger of heresy. You see . . . the patterns . . . the duplications . . . the recognitions. At times I can see into souls."

"You recognize the shared Divine spark."

"But across time? Past . . . death? And—and what if something you do, or say, or feel, duplicates exactly a moment of time already past. It's possible. Wouldn't one repeated term in the series be enough to break it down?"

"My son . . ."

"Not every soul is unique. Not wholly. Perhaps upon death the soul migrates."

"Well, the evidence for metempsychosis is small, and the arguments against it considerable."

"Yet the soul is said to retain acquired knowledge, and a transcendent relation to matter, and even a certain exigency to be united with matter. I don't mean metempsychosis. I mean that the souls of the dead may migrate backwards in time, losing some memories, perhaps all, depending on the difficulty of the passage, each coming to rest in an embryo at a time previous to its last demise. The process would be statistical. If eighty million die this year, perhaps half drift back a century, some only a few years or minutes, and some few travel eons. Plausibly a few reach more primitive species in a prehistoric past. So aspiration, and yes evolution, is in fact remembrance, do you see? All have some measure of memory, strive forward, and are drawn irresistibly back. But this presupposes a reservoir of souls, none idle, and enough to work across the statistical variations. A plenum. And the starting point for the process must be the Apocalypse, when all die and all souls are released for the first time to fly back. The last event of material history is the first event of spiritual history. The Apocalypse is in fact the Creation. The souls fight backwards, descending as it were through layers of history, technology, artifice, civilization, against the current, striving at last to reunite at the start of time with their First Cause . . . or perhaps even to merge to create that First Cause. And the one act of that First Cause is to destroy everything, destroy itself, so that billions of individual souls, its shards, its constituents, are freed to repeat the process. Who, who said, man ascends through a rain of trash? But no. Man casts up his works, the buildings, the monuments, spires, rockets, they thrust from gravity, and the spirit descends through baffles and labyrinths to the roots."

Camus sat suddenly back in his chair. He shut his eyes.

"If I knew how many were dead and how many living I could work out the date."

Derrida had been sitting with his eyes shut, his fingers entwined, massaging the bridge of his nose with his thumbs. His eyes blinked open and he lifted his head.

"The date?" He looked at his desk calendar, which bore the legend *Schmidts Leichenhalle.*

"Of the Apocalypse."

"This is . . ." Derrida's voice failed. He shook his head. He rose. "Come with me."

Camus came suddenly to himself. He ran back the entire dialogue, and inwardly groaned. He had not even meant to come here, but, dazed, he had followed a route graven in his memory, albeit in reverse. Sundays in the past, from mass to museum he had run; today, following Hüll, he had fled from method to faith. So at last he saw where history led, if not whence it issued: complete derangement of self. Christ, sweet symbol of anachronism, of intervention in a Time grown too brutal for any human self to bear, deliver him. He followed Derrida out of the office. He knew he was going to confession, and searched for something authentic to confess, something he himself considered sin. Sloth? Only from fear of consequences.

Or perhaps it was sin not to have sinned. Perhaps the experience of sin equipped one for the hypothetical trip back; if the soul did not express its fulness and at every instant take advantage of the nuances of evolution offered, at its demise to a more primitive state all unexpressed nuances might be wasted in entropy, and it might never reach its Cause. So it was not one's personal destiny at stake, but the whole concept of history. In fact the arrangement of artifacts through history, from tram to totem, progressed Godward into the past. He became paranoid. Perhaps he had discovered the secret faith of the Church and was now in serious trouble. Perhaps Derrida himself was an acolyte of the new mathematical demonstration of the soul's immortality and of its arduous devolution through history: the First Church of Recycled Souls.

Grim Father Derrida led the way sternly down carpeted
halls, past offices, enameled furniture, and the *tattack* of electric typewriters. They walked on. Camus's fright increased.
Perhaps Derrida was not competent to confess him. Some sins
needed the absolution of a bishop, such as incest, sodomy,
deflowering of virgins, manslaughter, breaking of vows, per-
jury, witchcraft, robbing of churches, blasphemy, heresy, and
some were so grievous that none but the Pope could dispense
of them, namely the burning of churches, attacking a priest,
and the forging of Papal bulls. Camus experienced sheer cardiac
panic as he thought of his own youthful *Ex Nihilo:* an anti-
evolutionary parody of Papal scholasticism: a jest. But he suspected the worst. Then there were secret sins, known only to
priests. As the perspective of the halls lengthened Camus saw
himself in an underground passage, walking a thousand miles
behind untiring Derrida, past all the offices in the great plenum
of divine administration, even to the Vatican itself.

They emerged into the cathedral. Derrida crossed quickly,
shoulders hunched, to reach the Lady Chapel, graceless as a
model kitchen, where services were held while the problem
with the dome persisted. Halfway there he stopped, staring up
at the cross in horror.

"They can't go there," he murmured, as if to himself.

A technician, reloading a starter's pistol, looked at him as
if he were crazy. "Well, no, of course not. We're only testing."

"Yes. Yes . . ." He hurried on, genuflecting on the run as
he passed the sanctuary. Camus slowed to make his doubtful
obeisance more leisurely. As his fingers touched his forehead
three shots crashed as one into his devotions. He turned and
saw the technician adjusting an aluminum Andrew's cross on
which were strapped three synchronized pistols. There was a
sodden thump behind him; a flattened fleece lay skin up on the
altar, its legs outstretched. He lifted his eyes and saw, hovering
over the cross, suspended by a windowwasher's harness, a man
dislodging furs from the crossarms. Another fell. He turned.
Derrida had vanished. Camus fled the church.

Even familiar Düsseldorf defied recognition. Across the bleak
backdrop of memory was flung the hurry of traffic, the dull
roar of machines, the brutal heat of a million souls. In his
memories the city was always in winter, with twilight falling.
The fierce midday summer face of the city was alien. He remembered hurrying through snowshot overcast mornings to

early Mass, emerging afterwards into a kind of bright pewter grace, and running thence to the museum, every Sunday of his past, seeing no conflict between faith and science, pious even to the day of his confirmation. But the Sunday appointed for that event had found him five miles from the appointed place, in the Schloss Benrath, admiring in his best suit the illusionistic sky of the cupola.

What had he wanted from the priest? Aside from the buried heresy of the cube he had nothing to confess. Nor did he crave grace. He wished simply to remain unmoved, the swift current of time swollen around his fixity. In his youth the grandeur of the Church had been that fixity; then he had seen that it was founded on no rock, but on the oily shore of a pun.

So he had fled to science. He had meant to descend to the raw substance of time, on hands and knees in the dirt, the mud from which history was tempered, the humus that became homo, scrabbling for a piece of bone, a mute inviolable theory of being. But the saints of science too rubbed their parchments clean, wiped their glosses, and burned their heretics. An act of the finest attention might bid science's clockwork universe collapse, but stun him too in the blow. Now the implausible weight of a small cube threatened the graceful bridge of logic reared over ignorance's abyss. Hüll had fallen, not chased, but anchored to the bridge by his conceptions. Warner treated science as a great game, and he had survived so far, dancing from shard to shard of the collapse. And himself? He was a heretic: a Pelagian. That human affairs were polluted from their start was a doctrine too grim even for him; he believed in sin, intimately, but not from the word go. Now to this he had added his own unique (as far as he knew) heresy. But heresy too was a class of belief. He must flee from that as well. Not easy, for the theory of cyclical time he had proposed to Derrida, from God knew what depths of self or not-self, seemed all too real. He now knew what had happened to him in the quiet room in Fuhlrottstrasse. Simply, literally, he had seen a piece of his own soul in doomed Hüll.

7. *Sicherheit*

The electric bus lurched to a stop in a tunnel of bedrock. This was the underground entrance to DUS, the sprawling Lohausen International Airport. From the air the terminal would seem a scale model resting on an architect's table, every detail blunt and plain, down to the stubby shrubs lining the carpark, torn from a shapely scrap of green plastic, limned by the grainy light of crude lamps like inverted hockeysticks. Inside one felt diminished. Order prevailed. Corridors curved by the agency of slight angles. Concrete pillars buttressed the lowhung second floor, the seams of their molds spiraling up in homage to the identical marks of the toilet paper tubes of the model. Everywhere a fifty-cycle rhythm of fluorescent light stunned the eye into the docility necessary to follow without protest the colorcoded floor stripes. Down branching corridors Camus traced the seablue Pan Am stripe. Camera eyes peeped from corners every fifty feet.

Outside it was night, but through an immense shatterproof window the lumbering jets concoursed under brilliant arc lamps. Inside the lighting was pervasive but diffuse. No shadows. Here technology was landscape, its works ikons rude and ambiguous as Stonehenge; its shadows fell only through time.

A familiar preflight panic seized him, and he stopped in the middle of the pavilion to check for passport, ticket, traveler's checks. All there. What then stopped him? The panic that rules might change, memories be revocable. That there might, in fact, be no return. He exposed the ticket in its paper sheath and carried his luggage to a counter.

Ahead of him was a blind man, accompanied by a guide dog and a young woman. They were bickering with the ticket agent. The dog was a black standard poodle, which Camus eyed critically.

"But I've taken him many times before," the man was saying. The voice wheedled, cracked.

"Yes, sir, and normally we make these concessions, but your flight is going east. The dog must fly as cargo, and go through quarantine. He'll be sent on three or four days later." The agent's annoyance was impeccable.

"It's a she," said the woman.

"I can't be without my dog for four days. It's inhuman."

Camus noticed that he was being watched. In the enormous curved observation window, overlooking darkened tarmac, half the interior of the terminal was reflected.

Two figures leaning at a closed information desk behind him were looking his way. He shifted his briefcase to his left hand, scratched the back of his neck, slowly turned. Now one was reading *Weltwoche* while the other inspected some rental car literature at the desk. They were dressed in the height of inconspicuousness. He looked back at the window. They were watching him once more.

The couple with the dog was still complaining. The ticket agent forced himself to say, "I will do what I can, sir," in a tone of absolute dismissal. Then he brusquely motioned Camus forward, stamped his ticket with chilly violence, DEP 0030 ARR 0015, a minor secular miracle of time travel by vector velocity, and tagged the suitcase.

Camus walked around the ticket island to avoid the information desk. He stopped at a kiosk and laid down ten marks for a pack of Camel filters and a magazine. He then went to the lounge and seated himself next to the couple with the dog. The two men were not in sight.

The woman's seat, closer to him, was burdened on one arm with the bulky appendage of a coin operated television. She slipped some coins into it, first sorting through denominations from at least four countries, and it flickered to life. The blind man scratched the poodle behind its ears, then leaned to get, it seemed, a better view of the screen. Camus observed this over the top of the current *Weltwoche*, also sneaking looks around the terminal.

Every so often the blind man turned his head in Camus's direction. When this happened Camus quickly turned a page and stared at it without reading for a few seconds. Finally, as he peered over once more, the blind man slid his sunglasses down his nose, looked at Camus, and winked. Camus almost fainted. The man was Warner.

He had shaved, covered his hair with an obvious black wig,

and assumed the most conspicuous persona in the airport. The
woman, the dog in harness, the shock of hair, the cane, had
so misdirected Camus's attention that he had not even glanced
at the face. With an elaborate air of casualness, Camus removed
from his rucksack *The Book of Fakes,* and placed it on the
joined seats' common arm, by the television.

The ticket agent approached across the lounge. Warner slid
his glasses up and sat immobile.

"Mr. Smith?" called the agent.

"Who's that?" said Warner in a strange voice.

"Kurt Jaeger, from the ticket desk. Please come with me.
We will make provisions."

As the woman rose, she took with her *The Book of Fakes.*
The television flickered dumbly at the empty chair. He fished
another cigarette from the pack, examined it, thought better of
it, replaced it. Smoking a cigarette in an airport was equal to
smoking five elsewhere. He thumbed quickly through *Weltwoche,* past the five-page spread of nude bathers at Nice, past
a review of the thirteen hour BBC production of Harry Ma-
thews's *Tlooth,* past the obituary page with its lead photo of
Maj. John Morgan Cutter, USAF test pilot, only to be stopped
dead on the science page. There his own baffled face stared
out at him above the legend *Amerikanischer Graduierterstu-
dent.* A flash reflected off his round glasses gave his eyes an
inhuman gleam. Halfway up the page stood the headline: EIN
BIZARRER FUND: ZUGUNFTSGERÄT ODER FALSCHMELDUNG? The
article was a humorous iteration of the report in the *Tageblatt.* There was no mention of Hüll's death, only a rundown
of Warner's more outrageous exploits. Warner himself de-
nounced the cube as a hoax. "Student A.C. Boyle" was quoted
as saying that it was definitely an artifact from the future, with
serious consequences for all humanity. The article was un-
signed.

At this point Camus found a hand resting on each of his
shoulders. A couple of men stood over him. One was smiling.
One was not. Camus slapped the magazine shut.

"Let's have a talk," said the unsmiling man.

"Kommen Sie mit. Andiamo. Allons," said the other.

"English," said Camus. *"Englisch. Anglais."*

"Of course," said the second man to the first. "Idiot."

He was taken to a small, square room near the boarding
area. The door was marked *sicherheit.* He passed through a
metal detector just inside the door. A third man at a desk took

his briefcase from him and opened it. The second man glanced at the xeroxed lab reports stuffed inside and commented, *"Technisch."* Camus was encouraged to sit. The first man took the cigarettes from his shirt pocket, seated himself at the side of the desk, and one at a time removed them from the pack and cut the filters off with a razor blade. Camus looked behind him and saw a dozen television sets offering different views of the terminal.

"Eyes front," said the man behind the desk. He was leafing through Camus's passport. "You're a German citizen?"

"Yes, that's right. Born in Düsseldorf."

"But you have an American diplomatic passport."

"Yes, that's complicated. I'm a student, and my visa is pending renewal; then I, I had to go on an academic trip, and my professor arranged a temporary passport from the State Department. . . ."

"Mm-hm. And your residence is in Paris."

"Well, no. I mean, yes, that is, it's a relative's house, my legal address. I have no living relatives in Germany. But I've been living in the U.S. the past year. . . ."

The first man had finished with the filters, and was now slitting the cigarettes lengthwise. Tobacco spilled onto the desktop.

"Eyes front. You're going to America?"

"Yes, to, um, New Hampshire."

"You go to school there?"

"No, in Cleveland."

There was a long silence while the man scrutinized irrelevant pages of the passport.

"I'm going to read ten words to you. I want your immediate response to each. Black."

"Eh?"

"Immediately, please."

"Oh. White."

"Worker."

"Ant."

"Red."

"Indian."

"Capital."

"Bonn."

"Plastic."

"Explosive."

"Automatic."

"Weapon."

"Father."

"Derrida."

"Space."

"Time."

"All right. That's enough. Well?"

The first man sifted a small mound of tobacco and paper shreds with the razor blade. "Cigarettes," he said in disgust. "Make him strip."

"Not necessary. Place your right thumb on this square."

Camus did so. A red light strobed beneath his thumb.

"That's all. You can go now. These precautions are for your protection. I'm sure you understand."

Protection? Camus collected his papers and briefcase and hurried through the arch of the metal detector. He had five minutes to reach his gate at the far end of the terminal, and there was frisked. Booked into the smoking section by default, he had to bum Players from a drunk Canadian businessman, who used this excuse to tell Camus an elaborate story of malfeasance in the Ontario commodities exchange. Camus ignored him and the shadowplay of a soundless movie about skiers and considered the slow dark turn of the ocean below them all, the flight from night into night.

II. TRAVELING

the pure products of America
go crazy
—W.C. Williams

8. Puritans

In Hanover, New Hampshire, he found no leggy California girl with body hair like spun gold and a magically attenuated sense of sin, but met instead, in the Dartmouth library, Ianna Holt from Hannover Schleswig-Holstein. At first glimpse she had seemed purely American, and he had a surprise when she spoke, at the mist of sibilants and click of dentals that, to his ear, placed her origin within a hundred miles of his own. Still, working on a vague theory of likenesses—that a visual likeness is the index of another more essential likeness—he let her entice him into bed that same afternoon. He was still expecting California, and probably she was expecting France; he said that he was French and his own accent, from much travel and translation, was a nearly neutral blur. She might have taken him regardless, but odds were she would not then have said in her heat, *"Ja. O ja. Das ist ja schmutzig."*

Later he confessed that he was German, and she said with a wicked smile, "Oh, you are a filthy individual," translating him easily from the Frog *sans façons* to the *schmutziger* Kraut; and after that was able to bring him on, with embarrassing quickness, by hissing in his ear, *"Ich bin heiss."*

Very well, he conceded, we are all translated, we long to be translated, by another's eye or tongue. Or else we are counterfeited, *nachgemacht*, our identifying edges filed, our faces scraped by whatever harder tool is brought to bear, then restamped and passed as whatever we then seem to be. In the mirror at times he could find in his own features the fugitive faces of many others he had known.

For farewell Ianna told him, "When you get back to Germany call me, and I will kick out whoever I'm living with for a week."

An endless trip. This must cease, he told himself. History is real. You are not a little token, Hans, to circuit the board, renewed each time you pass Go. Finish something for once.

Tell her no. Tell them all no. Hüll is dead and past help. That cube is plainly unreal. The geology of Mt. Monadnock will outlast the amateurs. Your sexual vanity need not be fed constantly. He took Ianna's number.

His aunt drove him to the Lebanon airport and beamed on his lassitude. He hadn't slept there once. Her eyes were full of indulgence for young love and changed mores. He promised to send back her revised geological manuscript within a month. Then flew east to Boston, so to travel west to Cleveland, pausing only for the duration of a red light in Hanover to deposit a flattened beer can from his pocket in a bin marked ALUMINUM. Would that other cycles could be closed as neatly.

History is to flee across, a professor of that subject once remarked to him. Too late he realized that he had believed it, and worse, had acted on the belief. As he boarded his flight to Cleveland, a perspective of his past ten years came upon him. At college in Paris he had meant to write. His laureate grandfather (if the relation were real, and not a fiction of his mother's) had died a few years before Camus's birth, and he had succeeded in never reading any of the Nobelist's *oeuvre;* yet he inherited, or acquired, an exhaustive, literary turn of mind—the habit of endlessly shedding one's skin and collecting the husks. When once he tried to used the word *sadisme* in a story he felt obliged to read all of Sade—which led him into history, politics, religion, philosophy—and so he commenced to skip like a spun stone across human knowledge, glancing off one subject to the next more interesting or more basic, pursuing art history until it vanished into the history of the Church, touching Greek, Latin, Saxon, and their common stem of Sanskrit, approaching as he thought some pre-Babel *Ursprache* which would hold the answers to his train of questions. But he had to hold each question open to its parent, putting all his theses into brackets, letting questions trail off like a string of opening parentheses, waiting for the little curves to reverse their courses like boomerangs and hit him in the chops with revelation—and was chased himself when the buggering things turned back on him. He found himself receding past Lascaux and Altamira, ending on the banks of the Awash River in Ethiopia, where, in the footsteps of Johanson, he chased *Ramapithecus* back ten million years into the savannah of a steaming past, miring himself irretrievably in paleontology and the history of the planet—which history included, only incidentally, as the merest afterthought, the history of humanity, and appended to it as the slenderest of footnotes his own poor history...which was what he had started out to understand.

After all he might have been happier in geology or physics; or in business, a small tobacco shop perhaps. But he could not add, and he distrusted rocks and atoms. The very notion of the past now filled him with horror: there was no end to it. Even at the marge of sapience, back past the start of language, of will, of men, past the point where mind vanished in a blurry redshift, even there the questions trailed out unanswered. He suffered black depression when a dig bore fruit, brooding on the bones of men and halfmen, their damned artifacts, their garbage, their tortuous ascent, down on his knees sifting the shit of a gone age, searching for the philosopher's stone that had changed humus to homo and feces to species.

Was the acquisition of knowledge as symmetrical as it was arduous? Would the parentheses, at last, close? Was there, finally, an answer like some vast alluring equation slowly drawing in its tail, shedding brackets like veils, winking shut its superscripts, canceling terms, and collapsing into proof? Wasn't there, for God's sake, some way of closing the investigation other than the bad Procrustean joke of death?

More likely all answers were random. Today's weather was a lucid oracle to some forgotten question posed somewhere, sometime else. The subtle Pennsylvanian hills below gave pointless melioration to the anguish of one long dead. He wished that he could read their shapes without the mediation of any science. He would have to learn to see properly. He would retire. He would go to a cold, clean place. He would grow old and white, waiting, a perfectly empty vessel. At eighty or ninety he might know enough to write the story that started with sadism. If only he could endure the interim.

Meantime, again, as now, flight: putting himself into pockets outside time, outside identity—becoming the contents of a vehicle, where time was simply the go-ahead nudge the pendulum receives from gravity at its apex, and self the mere mass that to-and-fros. Travel gave this. Travel was the migration to a clean new land: America. Travel was to nowhere, to Utopia, and the traveler no man, Ulysses—a timeless suspension between the tick of leavetaking and the tock of landho.

The plane banked. Brief panic of descent. Through incongruously wintry clouds the plane slipping down, turbines slacking their clutch on the sky, and through a cloudbreak he saw a small lit X of earthbound traffic, tiny cars acrawl thereon. So many. His own blank face, enlarged in the warped reflective port, glided over the distant intersection. X. Christ His mark, presuming some predisposition in men to wander, to err, to cross, to sin, to sunder, to fall, and promising some final purification. The plane canted further. The intersection was rubbed out. Gray flags of isolation again whipped past the port. The chill of the fall made the plane the last thing in the world. If he were to die now?

And he had the clear feeling in that moment that he *was* dead, and that the world was dead, and through ignorance of death knew it not; and, dead yet ignorant, was denied entry into any heavens or hells beyond the known present. The temperature at Hopkins International this evening is seventyeight, twentysix Celsius. Please remain seated until the plane comes to a complete halt.

The plane mated with the concourse through an extended rubberwalled corridor, and discharged its passsengers along a sliding walkway. By chance Camus's suitcase came first onto the carousel. He ripped off its tags, BOS LEB BOS CLE, and dashed for a city shuttle. He saw ruinous Cleveland again, sliding erratically past in unlovely sodium light. Every pothole announced itself through his plastic seat. Automatic brakes lurched and clutched.

The sight of his apartment (turn key, then knob, then lift and push) jolted him more. Here was one idling summerlong parenthesis closed: it was still the worst place he'd ever lived. One long dingy room overlooked an alley dim at noon. Upended cardboard boxes served as low tables; naked bulbs in tarnished brass sent cobwebbed zipcord to pinch plugs in loose wall sockets; a telephone tangled in its condomcolored cord weighed down stained papers. He had lived here for a year. Everything he owned was in this one room, and it all weighed less than he. It reminded him now, most bluntly, that he was dismally and unavoidably himself.

He dropped three letters atop the tiny cubical refrigerator: notice of a book overdue at Case, a *go* move on a card from Ng in Beijing, a Form I-538 from the Department of Immigration. Tomorrow he would have to renew his F-1 visa, his *Reisepass*, and his registration at school. And then return to the sinister mass of papers beneath the telephone: his disser-

tation, presently ten pages of text and one hundred of notes.
He was definitely back, lapsed from the quotidian urgencies
and subtle evasions of travel, at a temporary loss, like a priest
whose rosary is mislaid.

From the door came a thud. A second blow was more of a
knock. He crossed the room and yanked the door open, which
stopped at the limit of its chain, pulled him forward against it,
and slammed shut. He opened it again after unchaining, gingerly. Two men in overcoats stood there. The taller, foremost,
held out a soiled card on which was printed *Perfect Vacuum*.
He had gray eyes. "We'd like to sell you an idea," the man
said.

"Not tonight," said Camus, and pressed against the door.
It did not move. The man's foot was in the open space. The
man sighed and reached inside his overcoat. In lieu of prayer
Camus recited silently three quick parables for paranoids taught
him by Winifred. The man withdrew a wallet and showed
another card. This one said *Department of Justice*.

"Yes?" asked the man. "I have more."

Not wishing to be confronted with more, he undid the chain
and admitted the two men. The second, shorter man stood
completely still and said not a word. The first had refined
boredom to an art form, and presented a virtuoso's variety of
its faces as he talked.

"Hans Christian Camus?"

"When last I looked, yes."

"Come on, soldier, cut the shit. You're under arrest."

"Why is that?"

"You've overstayed your welcome. Your visa's elapsed."

"I know. I'm renewing it."

"Correction. You're applying to renew. Permission denied."

"That's supposed to take weeks."

"We saved you the trouble. The anxiety of waiting. Permission denied."

"Why?"

"That's a very interesting question. Have you got any ideas?"

"No."

"Oh, I'll bet a bright soldier like you has lots of ideas. Let's
hear some."

For moral support, Camus looked at his mail. The topmost
cancellation read, anachronistically, ALIENS MUST REPORT
THEIR ADDRESSES DURING JANUARY.

"Did I forget to report my address?"

"Oh, no. We found you easily. Very easily. Nice place. Very homey."

"Homey?"

"I spend half my time in dumps like this. Ten dollar pickup on the ceiling, tape recorder, equalizer, so on."

"Um."

"You're very silent. Why is that?"

"I don't know what you want."

The man turned to his companion. "He doesn't know what we want. Is that funny? Laugh, you stupid faggot."

The second man did not move at all.

"What we want, soldier, is we want the cube."

Camus had a sudden vision of Hüll, greeting his old friends joyously at Heidelberg, rapt at Lascaux, asleep at home under a thick quilt.

"Do you have a warrant?" he asked.

"'Warrant' he says. 'Do we have a warrant.' Interesting question. The answer is no. We're freelancing."

"I don't understand."

The taller man looked at him steadily. "People who would rather not be named would like for reasons better left unsaid to have a certain item the location of which for obvious reasons we think you know."

"I don't."

"We have our limits. Our powers and our patience each have their limits. We can take the room underneath and listen to you. We can tap your phone. We can beat the shit out of you. We can deport you. We can put you in prison. What we want is the cube."

"What cube?"

The taller man looked very disappointed. He said to his companion, "Hit him."

The second man hit Camus in the stomach. Camus sat on the floor. After a while he said, "I don't have the cube and I don't know where it is. Hit me again."

The taller man looked interested for the first time. He said, "Maybe I believe you. I also believe a bright soldier like you can find out. We want to be friendly with you. Help us out."

"I'll try," promised Camus. "I think Warner has the cube."

The taller man frowned and studied the walls.

"What a dump," he said at last. "Do you know where your friend Warner is now?"

"No," said Camus.

"Moscow."

Camus said nothing.

"I don't like to think he has the item. I prefer to think of alternatives. You say you don't have it, and maybe I believe you. But, but, but. Warner flew from Düsseldorf to Karl-Marx-Stadt in the DDR, and transferred to an Aeroflot jet. This is beyond question. I can't believe he had the item. If he'd had it he'd be begging pfennigs in the DDR right now. No, he went east to bargain. He wouldn't take it along. He gave it to someone. Not you?"

"Not me. Last I knew it was at ARC in London."

"Bullshit. Never went there."

Camus reached to his briefcase and saw the second man tense slightly. He handed a folder of papers to the taller man. The man opened it and laughed briefly.

"Look," he said to the second man. "He's being square with us. He's real bright or real stupid." He tossed the folder onto the floor, spilling papers.

"Bullshit, soldier. Who do you think you're working for?"

Camus got to his feet slowly. He wanted to laugh, or to vomit. "No one. Myself. Maximilian Hüll."

"Freelancer," said the second man. The first struck him across the face, then turned to Camus apologetically.

"Sitting around in dumps a lot. You don't know whether you want to piss or crap or what. Twelve, twentyfour hours at a stretch listening for something. You have to settle your nerves somehow."

Camus nodded. The taller man picked up his three pieces of mail and looked at them briefly. He remembered that the message on Ng's card was simply *g.5*.

"You receive mail from the quote People's Republic of China unquote?" asked the man, now very bored.

"A game. A *go* game."

The man replaced the mail atop the refrigerator.

"You let us know. We'll have an eye on you. Don't leave town. We'll plan to hear from you. We'll tap your phone. We'll expect great things. If you want to stay loose, soldier, you'll deal with us."

"Righto," said Camus. The taller man gave him a thumbs up sign, winked, and went out. The second man spit on the floor and followed.

Immediately Camus dialed Winifred's number. The phone rang once and was taken off the hook. He heard a din. Thirty seconds later Winifred's voice came on the line.

"Lo."

"Dub-dub. Hans."

"What?"

"Freddie."

"You'll have to speak up."

"Edward Drinker Cope here."

"What? Oh, Hans!"

"I have to see you."

"Oh, you fucker. There's a party going on."

"Where are you?"

"Here."

"Address, Dub-dub, address."

"Oh. Um. Two two one two Delamere. Heights. I mean Cleveland Heights. Haven't you ever been here?"

"No. Look, I'll see you soon." He pressed down the phone button and held the receiver for a moment. Then he laid it on the table and released the button. After a moment a faint recorded voice scratched at the earpiece.

His fingers went unconsciously to his face: his lips were moving. He pressed, stopping them. It had been prayer.

9. Games

The street was overarched with elms. From the sidewalk he could not see numbers, and waited for a house that felt right. At the end of the street, on the right, was a sprawling Tudor extravagance he loved at once.

Winifred was in the bushes beneath the bright living room window. She cried his name.

He approached, still regarding the house with wonder. Here it was, her particulate past, weighing, certainly, all told, more than a grand piano. They had never much discussed their pasts, although he now remembered one time in her apartment, dinner interrupted by a phone call from her parents; she had talked for five minutes, politely, hung the phone up gently, returned, and shattered her wineglass in one swift swipe across the edge of the table. "I felt like breaking something," she had said.

"The Waste clan calls this home," she said now, offering him a canteen. He sipped from it.

"Jesus, Freddie, Amaretto. How could you?"

"Hans, where have you been. I couldn't stand it. All the crawlies of Cleveland Heights are here."

"You invited them. Another hit."

She passed the canteen again, and as he swallowed and squatted she leapt and yanked him to his feet.

"Asshole bastard!" she yowled. "Follow me!"

He ran unsteadily down a side path, shrubs lashing his face. Across a dirt road he hit a fence, dislodging his glasses.

"Come on," complained Winifred from somewhere ahead.

He scaled the fence, grunting, canteen shoulder-slung and striking his ribs, landing in some open space.

"Baseball field," she said. "I used to play here."

Judicious Camus weighed the canteen and swallowed half its contents at a gulp. He bent and hefted a stout stick fallen from some domesticated oak. Meantime Winifred had found a

66

day-glo tennis ball of putrid tint. She pitched underhanded. His cut sent the ball straight up.

"Beisbul!" he shouted. *"Amerikanski beisbul!"*

"Nuts," said Winifred, retrieving the ball at his feet.

"Bozhemoi," he mourned.

"Hit it, fella, hit it."

On the next pitch he hit it into the street, and sat down on the plate. "Ted Williams. Rod Carew. George Brett. The Georgia Peach. Mr. Coffee. I am definitely an American now, God damn!"

"You lost our ball. Baskin-Robbins even now is making it into flavor thirtytwo: irradiated lime."

"Price of fame," said victorious Hans, suffering himself to be led through the gate he had overlooked before.

Entering the kitchen from the rear door Winifred said brightly, "Ghosts," extended one finger fore and, while moving it, in poetic tones announced:

"Weissman, late of Xerox. Shengold of the seismographs. Austin Moran, last seen selling software to Tibetan monasteries. The intolerable Affarian, conceptualist nonpareil. Philip Lee, *beau* linguist. Lisa Ewart Gladstone, curator of the Museum for Temporary Art. Theodora Litsios, blacksmith, Karen Houck, genius. Sally who counts electrons. Nancy Seymour who draws cockroach knees. Jeanne the geneticist who works under negative pressure. And sundry other Heightsites. At least it's not Grosse Pointe." And she swept out of the room, leaving him adrift.

The blackhaired fellow, Weissman, came glowering over. "Name?" he demanded.

"Camus."

"Any relation?"

"To what?"

Weissman stared at him a moment, then said, "Sumac."

"I beg?"

"Camus backwards. What's your first name?"

"Let's say Jack. Kaj."

"Well, Jack. Do you know how many miles of coastline there are in the world?" Weissman draped an arm across Camus's shoulders.

"Including rivers and such?"

"Sure, if you like. Absolutely. Every God damn place that water touches land."

"No, I don't know."

"Well I'll tell you. 50,389,082 miles. Do you believe it?"

"No."

"I know just how you feel. The first time I heard it I didn't believe it either. First I thought it was way too much. Then I got to thinking about islands, atolls, inlets, spits, archipelagos, capes, jetties, estuaries, coves, and also Minnesota, the land of ten thousand lakes, and then I thought it was way too little. But finally, in time, I came to accept that figure as completely accurate, and today I believe it with every fiber of my being, and I want you to also."

"Why?"

"Just because I ask you to. As an earnest of faith. Without reason, without hope of confirmation, with no strings attached. Do you believe it?"

"Yes."

"You're just saying that."

"Of course I am. I'll say it again if you like."

"It's okay, Jack. Kaj. I believe you. I believe that you really believe it. See how easy faith is. How many miles?"

"5,800,000."

"Not even close."

On the porch behind a flurry of laughter two men were improvising a skit.

"Now gather men weemins and personlets. It's time again for Preacher Features, this week's episode, 'The Thing With Three Souls.' Was it human? Was it one substance with its monomaniacal creator? And if so, jointly or severally? Had it powers beyond the ken of its mortified audience? Would its advance agent Jack the Pagandunker get ten percent? Ascending augmented triads and organ sting, please."

Many more at play in the living room made a daunting noise. A hysterical woman brandishing a snapshot pushed it at Camus, yelling, "Sign this!" A lurid crowd scene firmed itself into primary tints as he studied it. His stricken face was evident above the shoulder of a very tall woman. Pressing the proffered ballpoint to the print, he mashed his own face to a paisley blur.

"The other side!" the woman screamed.

Below four other autographs he inscribed *Pliny the Elder* and passed it back. Weissman's voice came over his shoulder. "Risible. Pompeii, eh? Wasn't that Easter of six nine AD?"

Camus looked blank. "I don't remember."

Weissman showed his teeth. "You don't remember. That's very good." He went away much amused.

"Seventynine," muttered Camus, remembering, and repassing the very tall woman on his way out of the room. She gave him a cool, speculative look.

Camus retreated down a hall into a smaller room, an aviary in Art Nouveau. He sat on a divan between a lamp of leaded glass and a wicker cage containing finches. Carved mahogany vines encircled doorframe, inset bookcase, and bay windows, awaiting sanding and staining. One of the six windowpanes rhymed the floral theme in colored glass. In a spirit of guarded gaiety, Winifred shut the door, then unlatched the cage. It took the birds some minutes to realize their freedom. One hopped to the television, where a very old, very furry cat woke and chattered at it. It went with a peep to Camus's shoulder. Its neck was slender as a twig where some disease had stripped it of feathers, making the head, itself no bigger than a marble, seem grossly disproportionate.

"This bird has no neck," he remarked.

Someone across the room replied, "Saint Francis describing Thomas Aquinas." Camus looked blank.

"*Anjou*," explained Winifred. "A game of pairs. Match a quote with a source. Points given for lunacy."

"How many?" Camus watched the finch warily as it pecked at his collar.

"Counterfactual validity claims are a nightmare from which I am trying to awake."

"How many electrons at the tip of time's arrow?"

"God does not play dice for low stakes."

"Zeno the Aleatoric."

"Saint Athanasius the Vague."

"Oscar Reviled."

He shut his eyes. This was certainly not sane. Tomorrow, perhaps, the two men would call on him again and find him gone. They must have traced him through the German magazine. And they had his real name, so they must have a list of members of the dig. So there was a chance they would also visit Winifred. He should tell her. But the sounds of the party made the eventuality seem remote, and he did not want to involve her needlessly. In any case the men had not been interested enough to arrest him on the spot. Perhaps an absence would put them off for good. He and Winifred could take a

trip. Then the two men would go after Warner, they would get
the cube, and that would be the end of it.

He was drunk, he was not reasoning well, but this seemed
sufficient to the moment. The thought of a trip gave him some
excitement; out of the confines of circumstance he and Winifred
might find again what had been so good for them before. He
opened his eyes; she was no longer in the room. He found her
at last again in front of the house.

"Daphne," he called.

"What. Go away."

He crouched next to her under a rhododendron. "You aspire
to treehood, sitting out in the greenery all the time?"

"It's too . . . too here. All this. I hate parties. Try to—to
get past a little deadness and you end up with a house full of
zombies. Drink this Christ awful sticky stuff for me, will you?"

He finished the Amaretto, resettling on his hams, knees
cracking. He tried to pick up her mood, could not. Long silences. Sniffling. Was she crying? She turned to him, face set
in a hard dry wrung look of desolation, in complete command
of her feeling.

"I'll show you the house," she said. "Ere bloodyhanded
dawn you'll have seen it all." She sniffed again. "I am definitely
leaving, getting out, of Cleveland, of chaos, of damn damn
memory. Lighting out for parts unknown."

"My feeling exactly," he began—except that it was no
longer. His stomach, where he'd been hit, began to hurt again.
Suddenly he felt exposed. He shivered.

"Listen," he said, "what would you say to a vacation."

"Yes. I'd say yes."

"I'm . . . in some trouble, I think."

"Who isn't."

"I want to clear out of here for a while."

"You and me both, sport."

"I mean it. Can we take a trip together?"

"Sure," she said. "You'd think I'd have learned. Ten fucking
years in this hole. In the morgue. Think I'd've had it."

There was a sharp, bitter, persistent, timeless unhappiness
in the suburban night. He felt only her definite presence and
her amorphous pain. He had a sense of lost souls, millions,
imagining that when all these suburbs emptied and the sun
dimmed there would be a haunting of the sites greater than
anything in any legend.

"We'll leave at dawn," he said.

The air was lighter now. She stood and breathed deeply. "Better. Thought I'd be sick. Better." She embraced him suddenly. "In now."

He lost her in the foyer. The voice nearest him said, ". . . So Florence said, we're going to get married at the Tar Pits, and Wanda, who can fly, thought she meant his parents' house and started addressing her mail to Florence Tarpit. . . ."

Winifred returned with an Indians cap jauntily sidewise on her head, grabbed him, and began their tour. "When the catastrophe struck, the natives scarcely knew it. They continued their quaint customs of suicide, incest, adultery, investment, and barbecues unabated. . . ."

"What in the world?" From a shelf he lifted a handled metal object suitable for mayhem.

"Piano tuning hammer. Hands off those knick-knacks, Jack, they bite. Now here is Sis's room, untouched these past ten years. Mom's convinced she'll get divorced and come back here to live, neat huh? Virginia's thirty. And here's the room where brother Bill grew up. It's become a shrine. Even his collection of *Playboy* magazines is still under the socks, arranged in chronological order. Mom'd die if she knew I knew."

"Your mom's a little strange?"

"You might say." Winifred picked up half a dozen letters from the spotless desk, and read the postmarks. "1990. 1989. 1988. 1986. 1984. High school reunions, junk mail from magazines, alumni news from Wisconsin. You're familiar with mourning?"

"A little," Camus said uneasily. "By reputation."

"This is the Platonic archetype of all mourning. The *genius loci*."

She replaced the letters, stacking them in their original position.

"She knows better, really, but she doesn't act it. By now it's just habit. Bill was in the Forest Service, fighting a fire in Oregon. There was one clear spot on a ridge surrounded by flames. The helicopter had to touch down with one skid on the slope, the other in the air, no room for anything else. Bill was suited up, jumping out, when a gust took the copter over. He fell and bounced, then slid some fifty feet down scree. Probably broke his leg. The pilot had all he could do to save the ship. They came back in twenty minutes but the whole ridge was burning. Eight years ago."

They went down a narrow staircase, insulated from the party.

"It's odd," she said. "I was the brat. I was always the one who broke the harmony of the house, who didn't do what she should, who hung around with LA bands instead of studying. And I'm the only one who came back."

She paused at the head of the cellar steps, before turning on the light. "Do you have confidence in me?"

He tried for a glancing seriousness. "Yes dear."

"Show."

He embraced her, pressing his fingers into the muscled hollows of her ribs, across the striae of latissimus dorsi, gathering the feel of cotton over the taut slim back, and he kissed her sideways, lingering, turning his mouth till he ended releasing her upper lip from between his.

It dizzied him. "How you kiss," she softly said.

"Better than our prof?" he asked.

"Oh boy. He *used* me, brother. But maybe now I'm using him." Unhappily he noted he was pleased by the bitterness in her voice, and he regretted mentioning Warner at all. "I saw him in the airport," he said, to banish Warner's ghost by naming it. "He was pretending to be blind." She giggled and nestled against him, and his mind submerged in warmth, ending with one happy thought.

"Maybe we *can* go back."

She murmured: "Maybe so."

Then she tripped lightly downstairs, Camus clumping after.

"What does your father do?"

"Torts. Senior partner, Paladin and Waste. Semi-retired."

"No, I mean about your mother."

"Oh God, I don't know. They separated for a year, and he was always running over here to feed the birds, mow the lawn, eat breakfast. Finally he moved back in. They make do. They have their little evasions and games. This is the drill press."

Making do, he tried to adjust to her new mood. He said, "If he's senior partner, why's his name second?"

"Modesty." She snagged a cobwebbed bottle from a dusty rack. Camus examined some device of the print shop or oubliette, as it seemed.

"What is this?"

"Winepress, dummy. Dad makes his own. You'd like him. Last year he grew a beard like Lincoln's. It came in tortoiseshell but turned white. He did the aviary too. You'd like him."

Dominating one end of the master bedroom was a marble desktop the size of a door, cleared except for the right rear corner on which were arrayed seven oiled wooden markers: pine cylinder, beech cone, birch tetrahedron, ash cube, spruce dodecahedron, basswood icoashedron, ebony disk. Beneath each was a small colored scrap of paper: pink, canary, buff, white, goldenrod, green, aqua. Behind was a computer smaller than a typewriter on the flat silver screen of which stood a few symbols in black.

"War game," said Winifred. "Dad's been playing it since he retired."

"Alone?"

"Some fellow in California on a computer net. They've put in about a thousand hours."

"You're joking."

"No. They hope to finish by the turn of the century."

"Whose move is it?"

"It's not that kind of game."

From a drawer beneath the desktop she produced a corkscrew, placing it with the winebottle at the edge of the gaming space, the bottle imprecisely so that it rattled a faint accelerating spiral of ticks on the marble. When it stopped he saw three slender ellipses on the dark green lead foil, where her fingers had removed a gray dust. At the sound of a shower he turned. She stood in the illuminated bathroom doorway, shirt opened but fixed by its tails in her waistband.

"Let's get wet."

He stripped, posing for a second by the full-length mirror, the first time he had seen his body whole for many months, his own bathroom equipped only with a headsized flyspecked glass hung too high, barely adequate for shaving. In his mid-twenties Camus had for two years engaged in a regimen of exercise; at twentysix, resting and sweating one fall day at the Cuyahoga River, hands on knees, head bent, he realized that this was about the stupidest preoccupation he'd ever had. The profit of it was a few more pounds for time to take revenge on, he saw now. Winifred returned from adjusting the shower to pose with him posing. He folded his arms across her ribcage, left forearm resting just beneath her breasts, stood thus until the shower's steam gradually erased their images, head to toe.

In the stall she soaped his front and he returned the favor, getting interested, until, at thigh level, she held him off.

"Moment," she said, "I have to pee." He retreated to a

corner, lifting one arm to part the curtain for her, but she stood like Venus *pudica*, contemplative in steam, making him by implication some inept sententious eunuch by the portal, offering a useless service. A minute passed before he said, "So?" and she responded, "Okay." It transpired that she'd let her urine down thigh and calf and thence to drain.

"Good God," said he.

"You never did that?"

"Not I."

He gained from this some notion of her notion of privacy, and, with odd gratitude, embraced her. Shortly they were wedged in one corner, Camus's right ear presented, by the urgency of their posture, to a steady stream of water. The ventral side of his forearms supported the dorsal side of her thighs, her knee and his elbow joints interlocking. At the end he straightened his legs, raising them both, and she braced her arms against the top of the stall, presenting her breasts to his lips.

As she toweled, Camus swept excess droplets from his body with brisk hand motions. She tossed the towel over his head with a kind of elegant scorn.

In the bedroom she had put on a shirt. Camus stepped around the bed, pausing by the air conditioner. "Aren't you hot?"

"Let it." An edge in her voice stopped him. Across the bed she held a slight crouch. "Open a window."

"Okay. You going to say good night to people?"

"The front door won't move."

In bed they shared a glass of homemade port. Presently he was lost in a small principality of sheets, touring sweet damp lumps and hollows, feeling the first glow of stretched muscles, a return of simple perception, mute specificity of contact, nose or fingertip or mouth to hollow of thigh, extrusive *labia*, ankle, belly, scrotum. Each moved the other's hands. Lost thus the onset of sleep went unnoticed.

One great toe being aside his nose as he woke, he took his bearings slowly. The dawn had not yet presented light sharp enough to qualify as morning. His gut ached, and his mouth tasted of old pennies. He rolled half out of bed and sat hunched on the edge, head in hands. He noted a ripening bruise below his ribs.

"Winifred."

She was on her stomach, asprawl in sheets, left profile, crooked arm and shoulderblade, right buttock, and extended leg exposed. He leaned across and squeezed her shoulder. Surly mutters and groans.

"Come on, Freddie."

"Whaat."

"We have to go."

She twisted her head around and squinted at him. "What?"

"We have to get moving."

Abruptly she sat up. Soft red imprints of rumpled cloth crossed her breasts and stomach. "Are you serious?"

"Yes. I have to get away."

"Christ. What's the time? Look, I have to be in Seattle the twentysecond for the anthro convention. Give me a day or two to get my shit together, will you?"

"I can't. I just can't."

A slight tension in her body translated to a vacancy in her expression. He waited, holding his shirt bunched in one hand. He wondered if she could see the bruise in this light.

"Okay," she said suddenly. "Twenty minutes."

He nodded, put on his shirt, and went downstairs. The house was empty. Some thoughtful guest had stacked glasses, plates, and ashtrays on the kitchen's central island. He transferred these to a dishwasher, rescuing one stubbed but unsmoked cigarette and lighting it at the gas range. Winifred came downstairs as he finished smoking, carrying the port in one hand, a small satchel in the other.

"Do you have any money?" she asked.

"Some. And a bank card. We'll stop at an autoteller."

"Hans, really. Can I get you some of Bill's clothes?"

"No, I'll . . . buy some. On the road." The sun was now up. It was morning.

"Idiot," she said with some wonder. "What's got into you?"

"Romance, Miss Waste. Lure of travel. Wide open spaces and rest stops. Let's go, huh?"

She stuck out her tongue as she passed him, leading the way down a small path to the garage. Some other early riser started a skyblue Chrysler in the next driveway. Camus felt fine, seating himself in the passenger seat of Winifred's antique Volvo. She wheeled the engine to life. They began to move.

10. Stories

They stopped first in Toledo. He sat in a municipal lot, watching a meter run down. Winifred returned briskly, bearing maps, thermos, and a greasy paper bag.

"Coffee and broaches," she said, getting in.

Camus took the bag and peeped in. "Brioche?"

"Not in Toledo. These are broaches. That's a kind of bun, honey," she said with deft twanging mimicry.

He moved a plastic spoon through a resentful sludge of coffee in a styrofoam cup. He raised the sealed plastic packet of nondairy creamer and read the ingredients. "Once upon a time," he said, "there was milk. There was even cream. Rich, thick cream. This, by all evidence, is paint."

"Don't drink it," said Winifred, munching.

"I won't. I'm taking my vile foamy liquid black. Have you really put eighty thousand miles on this car?"

"That clocked over long ago. Two hundred eighty thousand."

He stared in disbelief at the odometer. "With a little more planning you could have been to the moon."

"So?"

"Will this . . . aged contraption really reach Seattle?"

"We'll see, won't we?" She tucked a last edge of brioche into her mouth. "Let's drive. I thought you were in a hurry."

"Maps," he said. "Itineraries. What happened to romance?"

"Hey. You drive my car, you play my rules."

Tunnel vision. Taillights and license plates. Ohio's tags gave ground slowly to Indiana's. A Honda painted like a Coca Cola can passed them on the right. Roadside message boards flashed civic drivel and uncivil driving tips. One enigmatic sign announced END DAYLIGHT TEST SECTION.

"Dull," he said. "When do we get there?"

"Where?"

"Anywhere. Speaking figuratively."

"Speaking figuratively, we're still in the driveway."

"Welcome to Indiana. Slow for toll. This vehicle paid $15,787 in road taxes in 1990. Fruhauf," Camus read at random, adding, "Late to bed and early to rise gives Fruhauf truckers bleary eyes."

Winifred searched for change and said, "You got into the longest line."

"It was short when I aimed for it."

"Yes, and everyone else thought the same thing. You've got no rhythm."

"Futile indignity is the phrase that comes to mind. That phrase is futile indignity. Would you like to drive?"

"Not at this time."

"Where are all these people going, and why?" He tried to get comfortable. A rear pocket of his jeans repeatedly snagged on a spring. His shirt stuck sweatladen to the seat back. He had to part his legs to keep them away from the wheel, and his halfeaten brioche slid down between his thighs. Scenery comprised flat nondescript farmland, industrial parks, the boxy rears of American cars nearly identical. Time to time he glanced at Winifred to admire the cant of compact breasts against her batiked t-shirt, the tan of legs against the frayed edge of her denim cutoffs, the breeze in her hair, the cool concentration with which she regarded the road.

"Lagrange Metal Atomics. Elkhart Instrumentation. Goshen Gaskets. Mid-America Tool and Die. Potato Creek State Park. So when do we get to the real America?"

"This is it."

Camus punched buttons on the radio, getting a vicious blur of sound, fragments of commercials. He found the wavering slide of a pedal steel guitar and let it plunge straightaway into a fiddle break, a tune familiar from Ianna's radio in New Hampshire, the latest hit from the Three Mile Islanders, new riders of the Roentgen gauge, eking out a hazardous halflife on the fringes of an empty and moribund culture.

How ca-an you keep on movin', unless you migrate too. . . .

Winifred flipped it off and began a tirade. If he had not rushed her so, she would have brought more of her cassettes. She told him not to be so leadfooted with the gas. She said he was lugging the engine. Did he know where he was going?

Even where they would sleep that night? Although a secret fan
of the romantic impulse, she said she could not abide incompetent romanticism. The lack even of a change of clothes bespoke not footloose fancy but a perverse will to disaster. She
remembered for him her family's trips to a summer house on
the Michigan thumb; for this four-hour jaunt they left at dawn,
station wagon packed with thermoses, sandwiches, coolers full
of beer and pop, endless road games to be played, the trip itself
a vacation in small. Once they detoured into Canada for laughs.
But that type of idyll took preparation.

"You mean you were weighed down," said Camus sourly.
"I am in the happy position of the unencumbered traveler,
crossing into eternity with nothing but a carpetbag, that is to
say, the Ego. Your dad, on the other hand, was running a
caravan."

"Caravans are civilized. This is barbaric. I'll drive now."
"Hey, come on."
She grabbed the wheel, and the car veered across a lane.
"Jesus!" Camus yelled. "All right!"

After the switch, their moods improved. He began to think
he had got away. He was traveling: it was sufficient. He let
more miles pass, then said, "Can I guess your first memory?"

"I doubt it."
"I can try, can't I?"
The shadow of an overpass flashed over them. She adjusted
the visor. *"D'accord.* And if you're even close, I'll buy booze
when we stop for the night."

"Where are we stopping, anyway? That alleged breakfast
took the last of my cash."

She stared. "Maybe some day you'll explain your awesome
peabrain reason for taking off like this."

"M."
"We could give Virginia a thrill and spend the night in
Grinnell. Sure. Why not. You'll amuse her."

"Can't wait." He cleared his throat. "I see you on the lawn
at Delamere Drive. There you are, naked."

"Good heavens."
"This was long ago. No shame. Your charming breasts were
mere pink eyelets above a chubby tum, and down below a tiny
cute fold. The ass, however, is essentially unchanged."

"Boy."
"Or if you prefer, you're wearing one of those toddler's

Band-Aid bikinis, in robin's egg blue. It keeps slipping down."

Winifred grimaced.

"It's late afternoon. The gardeners have all gone home, and a scent of newcut grass and motor oil hangs in the air. You can hear the dittering of sprinklers, the crackle of frayed nerves, the distant barking of dogs. Then, like a voice from beyond, penetrating your tender post-Piagetian consciousness, a song carries from a nearby car."

He sang in a strained nasal Liverpudlian voice: "I feel good, in a special way. I'm in love and it's a sunny day."

The Volvo gave a lurch and accelerated past a camper, its back stickered over with the names of tourist traps.

"Well done, boy. Selznick could have used you."

"I trust I overlooked nothing of importance."

"No, it was just great. The only hitch is, it has nothing to do with reality. For one thing we lived in Los Angeles till I was four. And we never had a gardener. And I wasn't outside, but inside. And it was morning, not afternoon. Saturday morning. I was sitting in Dad's red leather chair in the den, picking at a cigarette burn on the arm. I was watching Bugs Bunny. I think he was living on a golf course. Elmer Fudd had a remote controlled golf cart which he used to chase Bugs through sand traps and water hazards."

Camus lit the wrong end of a cigarette, stared at the burned filter in disgust, tore it off, and lit the ragged paper. "It must be tough to putt with a stutter," he proposed.

"Sore loser. In fact, if you want to know, the first time I heard the Beatles was, oh, eighty, eightyone. Lennon had just been shot. They were playing fortyeight hours' worth on an LA rock station. I was in a Newhall apartment with a lot of punkers and some very bad acid and the first of their songs I ever heard was 'Hello Goodbye.' Cleveland doesn't figure in at all. My Cleveland culture consisted of seeing *Jacques Brel* at a dinner theater when I was maybe fourteen and starting to 'date.' He tried to feel my breasts, which appalled me and also flattered me because I didn't think I had any. That's it for culture unless the Dali Museum counts."

"Only to ten, dear."

"How amusing. You're really pissed."

"You never went to the Cleveland Museum? Impressionists? Yes? Hello? Earth to Winifred."

"Sure. And saw the blown-up Thinker in front."

"The *what?*"

"The Rodin statue. Somebody bombed it in the sixties, and the directors decided to let it stand as a twisted mass, in memoriam of something or other."

Camus groaned. He flipped his cigarette out the vent, striving for some kind of control. "Do you know what that statue is?" he asked, a little hysterically, because, try as he might, he could not remember the exploded hulk from any of his trips to the museum. "That statue was meant as the topmost piece of an immense rendering of Hell. That statue was God, brooding on the consequences of His Law."

"Whoa. Relax."

"Is there another entrance to the museum? Not in front?"

"Maybe. I don't know."

"I must have come in another way. I must have. How else could I have forgotten?" He fell into silence, brooding on what he had provoked by his little game. "And that's your first memory, eh?"

"Don't spit at me. It happens to be true."

"That's no excuse."

"Now it's my turn."

"What?"

"My turn, to guess your first memory."

"Right," Camus said grimly, settling himself as for an ordeal. "You think you'll do any better? From what I can see imagination is not your strong point."

"Imagination doesn't enter in at all. I don't intend to make up a *story* about your past, I mean to analyze it scientifically, on the basis of what I know."

"Ah, *science.*" He put a sting on the sibilants.

"Just play along and don't be a sorehead. Now, you can have complete confidence in me. I'm going to ask you a few questions. Respond as quickly and as honestly as you can. But be, for Christ's sake, brief. Your answers will stay strictly within the confines of the trusty rustbucket."

"Fine."

"How would you describe your family life?"

"I had a mother. That brief enough?"

"My, such hostility to your therapist. And your father?"

"Killed driving," he said viciously. "I don't remember him." He craned his neck as if checking the speedometer. Winifred slowed the car slightly.

"Which of the three dimensions do you consider to be the first?"

"Height." The answer surprised him a little.

"Have you ever been up the Eiffel Tower?"

"Once. I was fifteen. It was too mechanical for me. A bore."

"Hm. You'll like this one. Describe the expression of Bernini's Saint Teresa."

"Distasteful."

"That's a judgment, not a description."

"She seems dumbfounded by something she should have known all along."

"Which is?"

"No revelation, except at a price." He was suddenly tired. The start of a headache, a pulsing at the corner of his left eye.

"Okay," said Winifred briskly. "I see you in an interior, not domestic, but vast and public. How am I doing?"

"No hints."

"And no problem to figure it out, either. No father, no real family life . . ."

Just a succession of cold, halfempty apartments where, on holidays, he and his mother would suffer a visit from Uncle François, a steelworker and a Communist, who had been from the first vehemently opposed to his brother's liaison. After Robert's death, however, he had taken "the German woman" and her child to his heart, with such a fierceness as could not be called love. There was, he said constantly, too much carelessness in the world. Robert had died of carelessness; even though a friend had been driving, he should have been more careful in his choice of friends. To suffer the results of another's carelessness was worse than suffering your own. Science, François would say with great satisfaction. Science. Is the boy progressing? Is the boy happy? See, I brought him a microscope so the priests don't befuddle him. Books I brought, yes, in French, how else can he read the great minds? Descartes, Voltaire, Flaubert. Our great despised geniuses. *Bouvard et Pécuchet.* What will you be, petit Jean?

"I'd say a church, but not just any church. It must have been marked by a special clarity of form, a complex affirmation of verticality. Certainly Gothic. And dedicated to the veneration of Our Lady. Of course, Notre Dame de Paris. And you in the midst of it, fascinated by the rhythm of the chanted Mass, the thousand candles lit for dead souls, the incense."

Yes, he'd been to Notre Dame, but as a sort of tourist, not a votary; it was never near their neighborhood. And he'd been relatively happy there, a pleasant place, until his mother asked how he liked it. And then he hadn't liked it at all.

Is Jean happy? As bizarre as asking if a tree is wood. A tree was a tree, he was himself, and it seemed to him neither necessary nor appropriate that one should be made into lumber or the other made "happy." But perhaps he was wrong. He had, after all, so little. His own history seemed to him a discontinuous collage of moments without continuity; he had loved Winifred, and loved her still, he admitted, for the promise of some continuity. Was she in fact all he had left, after shucking so much of his past? Quite possibly. And he turned to tell her so, but the present came thundering in; all at once he was nauseously aware of his surroundings—concrete whizzing past a foot beneath at a mile a minute, two tons of metal around him, propelled on fired black rubber by continuous explosions in tight forged steel hot enough to sear flesh. The placid, unexceptional landscape withered and flaked to a scorched, blistered waste, a specter of mechanical invaders in the shape of high tension towers marching forward in formation to secure the blackened city of Gary. In his head was a chaos of motion, colored lights blurred by sickening velocity, the smell of ozone, a voice far back chanting *molten metal, molten metal*. His eyes fixed on a golden dome to the south.

"What's that?" he croaked, pointing. "Mormon temple? Are we in Utah? Where are the mountains?"

"Are you serious? That's the University of Notre Dame. Why don't you look at a map, paying close attention to the scale of miles, while I get off here for gas."

The car stopped. He said miserably, "The Métro."

"Hans?"

"It wasn't a church. It was the goddammed Métro. You know, little cars in tubes? Verne predicted it, Paris built it, America stole it, I rode on it. That's the first thing I remember. You got Paris right."

Something in his face forestalled her retort. "You don't have to take it so seriously," she said.

What do you remember about us?

Bitter cold morning. My first night spent with you. You rose with me at dawn to take me to the airport, through snow, earliest of our unions and separations, first in the pattern of sour timings.

When you got your first apartment in Cleveland it was infested with roaches. We spent an afternoon chasing them, then we ate this shitty frozen macaroni mush for dinner.

Every so often you got a passion to play Scrabble. Then you got bored. We never finished the game.

Kissing in the Case lounge, in some corner, huddled up under your overcoat. I felt like a teenager.

We were snowed in at Oberlin, in Judy's apartment. She was breaking up with Ken, and she was very depressed. You thought we should cuddle her, so we did. We all drank wine and got jolly. Nothing happened.

Eating watermelon at Blossom Music Center after a concert. Slobbering all over each other.

That time I slept with Lisa, and you crying afterwards, me like an idiot in some confessional, and you hated yourself for the crying and my trying... somehow to comfort. And I said something about the taste of your tears. You thought me brutal and inhuman to notice that. You were right.

You meeting Warner at Case for the first time. The first thing you said to him—he was telling some story, and you corrected him on some point. He went red, and you, you had such splendid composure, such, such detachment, or innocence, of how you'd insulted him.

I remember that I never had money. That one time I had, and I took you out to dinner. Except that I had forgotten to bring my wallet. I sat in the foyer under the eye of the *mâitre d'* while you called Mary to come and bail us out.

Hans. We did have an innocent love.

Yes. But I don't remember that I ever... made you happy.

What was it but an urge to understand how things worked? In the boredom of the later afternoon they made up tales to pass the time. They gave up basing their *récits* on real events, which, oddly, brought them closer to an understanding of themselves as selves: that is, as mechanisms which were moved by ghosts, memories, and immediate presences. They did move each other, in a way that was serious play. The game of first memories had been skirmishing, a confinement of the answer by the phrasing of the question, small preemptions of spirit. In a way it was an act of love. Making up stories about a person was an expression of love surpassed perhaps only by not making up stories, and who could manage such restraint? His mother had been good at such small explications of herself via the agency of stories about him—take her fiction of the famous grandfather. And she was expert at the minimal tale, of one or two words, which was casually equivalent to insult. "Pisspipe," for example, she would say to him as a child. "Shit-breeches." That was him, and not him: a reference to his clock-work digestive tract, which could not soon enough rid itself of the foreign matter he was obliged to ingest, a teasing of his complexity by the ineluctable simplicity of certain of his traits.

An act of love. A simultaneous profession of familiarity and estrangement. Winifred had shown traces of the same gift in the capsule summaries of her friends. They had shared a spell of memories. And those too were stories, made up because time hung heavy, because the sense of traveling was remote and unreal. This then was an attempt to think oneself outside one's surroundings, which included, always, one's personal history: to dissolve in storied impersonal salts of words the inarticulate daimon of experience. It could not work. The base imagination working on acids of life precipitated out salts of words and left, generally, nothing of imagination or of life: only stories. But it was fun. The desire to invent indicated that something was unknown in their situation. Then to begin with any of a thousand variants on *once upon a time* (that is, with a lie), and to pursue through a potentially endless middle, by process of exclusion, by agency of will, the collaborators Chance and Necessity, and to end *they lived* (or professed to live, or persisted in some state in some ways lifelike) *happily* (that is, fortuitously, chancily, midst winds of Chaos benignly renamed by a fictive grace for an aspect of the Needful) *ever after* (saying in effect, at last they went to something past our ken, they endured beyond the period we must put to any story, they live on in that rare reverie of silence the edge of which is but touched by the word "after"); well, the labor of fiction was both common and rare enough to suit them both that afternoon. To tell their tales as the sky closed over was to affirm the unknowable that shelters and confines each known, and the unnameable that excretes each name.

He said, "I used to have a fantasy about stopping time. I imagined I could freeze everything but me—a kind of inverse sleep, the world supine while I alone progressed. Imagined that I could walk in cold to an examination on any subject. Professor X would ask, 'What happened at Poictiers?' and I would say, 'Well, of course—' and then stop time and nip out to the library to study up on Poictiers, return with my answer and start time again. I could, like Virgil, leave gaps in my epic for the em-

peror, but instead of relying on the inspiration of the moment
to fill them, I could compose, at leisure, the most exquisite
improvisations."

"What emperor?"

"Virgil's? Augustus. That's how he wrote the *Aeneid*."

"No, yours."

"Ah . . . who knows. The world. It was a desire to shine in
the world. It wouldn't increase my capacities, only my apparent
speed. But fantasies have their own iron rules, and I saw that
within the confines of my fantasy I would be a doddering old
man by thirty. Because I'd continue to age in the stoppages.
So I'd get nothing for free in the long run, only a certain
transient glory of speed in the short."

"I take it you're over that now."

"Oh God yes. The implications are depressing. Lifeless.
Inspiration is grace; to put it solely at the service of will, even
in a fantasy, is dispiriting."

"That all sounds to me," she said, "a little like Hell. What
if you couldn't start time again?"

"Not part of my fantasy."

"I imagine you did nasty things to helpless maidens in your
dream world?"

"Ugh. Necrophilia."

"You're not so slow or doddering. Old everready."

"What does that mean?"

"Men."

"Huh?"

"At least you don't have to take your pants down every time
you need to piss."

"One point for Winnie the Pooh."

"Oh, no, not another name. Through all that time when you
couldn't decide what to call me, how is it you never hit on that
one before?"

"You never looked so cute before."

"Watch it, just watch that stuff. I have claws."

"What was that business with the air conditioner last night?"

"Oh. That." He gave her a long minute while they passed
VISIT THE WORLD'S LARGEST DAIRY FARM, flat tin barracks by
the hundreds, the rows between them winking past in momentary perspectives showing silvery pipelines on squat legs.

"I used to live in dread of the damned thing. My mother
used it nights at the highest setting and slept under an electric
blanket. Dad would sleep on the porch. I'd sit up past midnight

waiting for it to start, because otherwise it would wake me when it started, and that was worse."

"When was this?"

"High school. Forget it, huh?"

"But no, I don't want to forget it. I want to know you."

"Is it worth it? At this stage?"

"Yes, it's worth it. Or—or else why are we here together? We were in love. And now, now . . . isn't there still something unfinished between us?"

She considered. "All right. Here's a fantasy. Actually a recurrent nightmare. I had it again last night. I wander in the house. It's empty, dim, it's night. And I become afraid of being trapped. Trapped in one place, in a single moment, in some repetition. I walk, leaving tracks, thick and tangible as snowdrifts, they collect, thickest near doors, windows, in hallways. And in one of these places I stumble, fall, in my own repetitions, and . . . drown. And then awake to the same scene, the dark house, the sense of enclosure. . . ."

He shut his eyes, listening, wondering if he too was one of her repetitions.

11. Relatives

Up from the road, travel weary, carrying Winifred's red nylon day pack while she hefted a canvas suitcase, he passed aspirant shade trees and damp grass, leaving behind the loud taste of gas and asphalt from the afternoon. Their steps echoed on the porch. As he bent to pick up a third-folded copy of the—NELL INTELL—he heard a female voice, "I'll get it," its intonation the reverse of Winifred's, vowels falling where hers would rise, diphthongs clipped where hers stretched, and at the steady rhythm of approaching heels he looked up from his crouch to see a child of about three pressed to the screen door, holding a toy by its pistol grip which, flexed, worked the jaws of a dinosaur head at the other end of a plastic rod. A wee voice said, "I want that." Past the child appeared screen-blurred striding calves.

"Oh, for heaven's sake," came a woman's voice. It was Winifred, or not quite. Camus's vantage exaggerated the extra height in the legs; the white linen dress, vivid through the screen, was the kind of thing Winifred "wouldn't be caught dead in." The child worked its feral toy and said clearly, "Plesiosaurus."

Virginia pushed open the screen as Camus straightened. From his full height the resemblances and differences between the sisters were less striking. Virginia's hair was very long, blond and brown streaked, caught back in a ponytail; her eyes were dark; she was heavier through the shoulders and neck than Winifred. The child said, "I want that paper."

"Rustle," said Virginia, "Go play with your trilobites."

"*Bz bz,*" said Rustle. "Rowr."

"Rustle," said Winifred, "remember me? Auntie Win?"

A male voice yelled something from the back of the house. Virginia called, "It's the kid sister, complete with crony!"

"All right! There in a sec!"

"So what brings you?" Virginia said, folding her arms. "Surely not the bonds of familial affection."

"Nope, the Volvo. That and Hans here. Hans, meet Ginny, a veritable Mom away from Mom."

"Don't start that already. And come in, you look beat."

"I brought a bottle of the best," said Winifred.

"How considerate. Let's divvy it up."

The two went down the hall, leaving Camus in the living room. Rustle zoomed around the room with his plesiosaur head, making airplane sounds. "Rustle," he said inanely, "I'm Hans. Can you say that?"

Rustle said, "Hans," gave a look as elaborately noncommittal as a cat, and zoomed out.

Above a couch of bent chrome tubing and brown leather cushions hung a nineteenth century engraving of lizards' heads, row on row, carefully handcolored and labeled with Latin specific names. He studied the plate: an art of description, mute and lucid, beautiful in its precision. Scarlet, emerald, azure, and gold had been translated by an eye and applied by a hand trained in observation rather than composition, making the common saurians appear grander and stranger than any fabulous bestiary. He wondered how many of these by now had scuttled for the last time out of the sun, into inky extinction, the traces of their passing preserved only here.

"You like it?" The voice, mellifluous, presumed that he did, yet wouldn't insist if he didn't. Virginia's husband stood in the doorway, holding a drink in either hand. "Mark Narasny," he said, and a small slapstick with the drinks ensued between them so as to free, simultaneously, the dexter hand approved for greeting.

"I love the drawing," said Camus.

"Found it in a Cedar City junk shop. Those natural history bastards had a hell of an eye. What they couldn't have done with my equipment. All I do is poke around in corn genes. Engineering, you know, cut and paste, microtomic scissors work. Looking for a way to fix nitrogen direct from the air."

The two women returned, talking. ". . . Seattle. Professional conference."

"That so? Can I lend you a dress?"

What fun this is, thought Camus. The bosom of the family.

"Other side of your work, in a way," Mark went on. "Putting evolutionary principles to work on the future. It's exciting, really. Will the strains hold up over time?"

"I thought," said Camus, "that the government wasn't funding that kind of work any more."

"They're not, exactly." Mark frowned. "Tell you the truth, I don't know just who is. We're owned by a Welsh firm called Gennesareth, which is really just a holding company. Money's funneled from somewhere else in a complicated way. We do have a few potentially commercial items, but I'm looking for something more useful. Grains. I think it will work. I think we're looking at a better future." He looked suddenly around at the silence in the room and smiled. "Sorry. I'm sounding like a Rotarian."

Virginia yawned. "I thought those were those wee beasts you needed a microscope to see."

Large smiling Mark considered briefly and nodded. "Two points. I'm going to see about a little dinner. You two try not to draw too much blood while I'm gone." He went out chuckling.

"So how *was* the dig?" said Virginia.

Winifred paused. "Useful. Lots of technical stuff."

"Actually," Camus said, "I'd say interesting. Not exactly useful. Not yet at least. Some quite unique finds. Good chance for significant original work. Win's doing the final report."

"Hans," said Winifred sharply, "don't maunder."

"Is that so?" Virginia smiled.

"It's possible," she said. "Too early to say. I did the scut work anyway. Now I'm going to shower. Borrow some shampoo?"

"Sure. Rinse is in the medicine cabinet."

As she left, Camus stage-whispered, "Love to tell you more, but Win and I have a deal. Closed mouths until the article's in press."

"Very prudent."

"Don't be a jerk," Winifred called back. The bathroom door slammed. Virginia refilled his glass and patted his hand.

"It's only family. You don't have to take it so seriously. Get a little drunk while I feed Rustle."

He did so. Winifred returned with a towel wrapped tightly round her head, pulling up the corners of her eyes. "You okay?" he asked. "Why not?" she said. He shrugged and went to shower himself. So this is home, he thought. He had an envy for the night of Rustle's conception that was not in the least sexual. Rather he imagined the darkened house, improbably adrift on this endless plain, its mean objects with their mocking histories (all objects mocked him thus), somehow consecrated by the act of love that was proceeding, incidentally, within their embrace. In the bathroom he saw some vague possibility of return from his obscure exile. He saw also, in the shower stall, eight years' worth of laminated *Smithsonian* covers papering the walls. They shocked him, then shock receded. He was coming, possibly, to accept the thrust of objects: mere circumstantial background. Virginia and Mark; and *mirabile dictu!* the usual, a child. Even the antagonism between Winifred and Virginia was tonic. He could get to like that kind of direct family byplay. He regretted, as he toweled, the early loss of his father.

The ice in his drink had melted. He swirled the blond liquid in its glass and finished it, wiping mist from the mirror over the sink. Hello, hello. A new man, he thought, looking at the old face. Neander. Nice to think so.

Rustle was being hauled to bed. Virginia, hauling, paused to regard Camus's towelwrapped form emerging. "Oo la la," she said. "Lucky Win." He flushed with embarrassment and, he surprised himself, pleasure. He saw a speck of yellowish goop on her chin. "Goop," he said, pointing at it. Virginia wiped if off, saying "Rustle doesn't eat, he absorbs." Rustle pointed back at him, saying, "Hans." Virginia said, "Now, you monster, *bed.*" They tussled down the hall. Rustle said, "I want that dream."

Mark's "little dinner" included a country pâté, pilaf, asparagus vinaigrette, roast woodcock with truffles. Camus, ravenous, filled his mouth with game. He chewed thoughtfully. It was a mere intellectual dispute with his gustation that what he tasted seemed not quite a truffle.

Mark watched him merrily. *"Cantharellus* spores inoculated with a virus specific to genus *Tuber,* modified. Not bad, eh?"

Camus laid his fork down. "The truffles?"

"Yep. Look for them next year at around four dollars a pound. Our stock should soar. In fact, if you have a good broker..."

Virginia filled the wineglasses. "Broker? Than Win? Not likely."

"'S'all right," said Winifred. "I'll borrow from Dad." Virginia's face froze momentarily.

"Come on, ladies, truce," said Mark mildly.

After dinner Winifred unpacked a sleeping bag, and Virginia brought in an armload of linen and blankets for the couch.

Camus surmised that this had been arranged while he'd been in the shower; the sisters' antagonism was evidently based on a lively sense of collaboration. If Winifred wanted to sleep apart, Virginia would cooperate.

So he did not wait for Winifred to finish up in the bathroom. He curled up on the couch and slept. And was sailing off Easter Island, looking for a landfall. He was summoned back by two complementary female voices in the kitchen. The lights had been turned off. He strained for words, catching none until the purl of the refrigerator clacked off.

". . . Asked me what I thought of anal sex."

"He didn't. Oh my God. Tell me everything."

And rolled into the sodium light from the lamppost in the street which promised static sleep, assigning to his deepest dreams the task of telling what kind of tale was now being told in the kitchen, and if Winifred's whether she meant himself, Warner, or some other citizen of the invisible cities of her past, that slick slob Weissman late of Xerox, *par exemple*.

Levin and Borro sat in a skyblue Chrysler in a rest area off I-80, slightly west of Grinnell. It was almost midnight. Levin, at the wheel, was disassembling his weapon and laying the parts on a handkerchief in his lap. Borro was studiously unraveling a spool of dental floss.

"Sucky suck?" asked Borro.

"Don't even think about it. I'm fed to here. This whole business is dull as dogshit."

"You'll make a nice clean old man."

"J. Edgar Hoover is frozen in a huge underground complex beneath Las Vegas along with Hugh Hefner, Howard Hughes, and Walt Disney. They're linked by phone wires. They have mind orgies. You'd love it."

"So do we put some hurt on these people or what?"

Levin commenced to reassemble his weapon. "I am not interested in your thoughts. I couldn't care less what twisted nightmares run through that spongy gray ooze. I'm purifying myself. Existence precludes essence."

Borro nudged him. "Hey hey. Cookie."

Levin looked up. A tall blond girl, bigboned, strode across the lot in candystriped running shorts. Lights put sharp moving shadows on her flesh. She passed ten feet in front of the car.

"Bad skin," Levin said disgustedly.

12. Invisible Cities

The soothing curtailment of identity that went with travel awakened him. This morning even his pleasure at the sense of hearth and home was without the pang that it was not his. In place of the plesiosaur Rustle had acquired strange headgear: a large plastic coffee scoop, which Camus appropriated playfully for his own head. Said Rustle: "Give me that."

"Give what, Rustle?" asked Hans. "Name it."

"That brain hat."

"Better keep it," Winifred advised Camus.

The sky had thickened. Winifred drove. Every two minutes she flicked the wipers; drops smeared in arcs across the flat glass, blurring the oncoming road. Traffic was light. The car felt cozy. They entered an area of rain, then left it. Sun glazed land ahead. He felt suddenly tender toward America. After all he liked it. Perhaps it was possible to wipe out his past and start again. Was that not the promise? The road proceeded indifferently. He shut his eyes, and opened them expecting sharks. None. Once there had been an inland sea here, but he could not conjure it. *Doch*, let it go. Today's working fiction: past moments are inviolable, irretrievable, and ineradicable, despite the mind's bent to interpretation, memory, and erosion. Even the green roadsigns had a timeless aspect.

"I'm hungry," said Winifred. "And horny."

"You said what?"

"You heard. Got a better word for it?"

He temporized by reaching for the lunch Mark had packed them. Red flash of a young northern harrier, *Circus cyaneus*, over a square of sunlit field, gone before he could point it. The clouds broke fitfully in the west, a bright white marbling through their gray faces. A single infinite line of trees at right angles to the highway swept past, sharp in late sun. She found the road alongside, and followed it. Here they parked. In utter stillness they picnicked. They had their quickest coupling ever. No sense of self intruded on him through it. He felt lost and nameless, and happy to be so. They were any lovers, any time, anywhere. Why was it not like this more often? Usually behind each living moment fell the shadow of invisible cities of the dead or the unknown. Every Alexander, every Aristotle, issued from tribes of the anonymous; every moment frozen in some history or memory was supported by a million others unremarked. Every moment of his own life culminated infinite branches, nodes, decisions, failures—incalculable pasts either consecrated by some story of them, or canceled, scraped clean, forgotten, overwritten by inherent decay, repression, or lost potential. But today he would let it all go. His ego was content that none but he could know the precise configuration of this moment, including one specific leaf past the fringe of her hair swaying against one patch of blue sky. Every detail of Earth collaborated in his climax, indifferent to the weighty supports of any past. Let be. No inland sea, no thesis, no articles, no relatives, no money, no fixed abode, no traces left to mark and mock his passing. No decisions. No more hacking with the inadequate tools of mind at the intractable material of time. This was his future: not to leave a mark, but lightly to hold single moments and to let each fly unhampered by his will. Accept that he was just a ground on which the figures of time were worked. Accept such a stewardship of history. Everything to remain as he had found it. Certain sweets were in this vision. Direct as ever, Winifred summed them in a smile and a word: "Yum." His outstretched arm touched, disrupted, the pattern in her dropped shirt. Rain caught them naked. Curse, hop, dress. Return. Afterwards he drove.

Day faded as they passed Omaha, the sun setting splendidly behind massed clouds. His attention narrowed to the white line of the road.

Levin, in the passenger seat of the skyblue Chrysler, smacked both hands on the dashboard and said decisively, "They haven't got it."

Borro, maneuvering behind a refrigerator truck, said, "So?"

"They can't. It doesn't make sense."

"So what do you want, next exit?"

"Shit. Keep them, keep them."

"You're losing your edge."

"This business sucks."

"You know the cure for that."

"Senseless. I get the idea someone's playing us. I don't like it."

"What's your problem?" said Borro.

"Boredom."

Ten miles passed in silence. The primer red Volvo stayed at an even fiftyfive. Levin consulted a map.

"Pass them," he said.

At the next exit Levin directed Borro onto an overpass above the highway. There they waited. The Volvo, a few minutes later, sailed by beneath them. Levin, eyes closed, felt them pass.

"I don't know," he said. "You're right, I guess. Let's sell another day of boredom."

There are only a handful of ways to get through Nebraska, and none of them really works. By the four hundredth mile he was almost gone. The first hundred miles had been devoted to Jim Beam and cigarettes. For the hundred miles after that, at the outer limits of desperation, he had played a cassette of Stockhausen's *Hymnen*. During this stretch thunderstorms hunched around the horizon, and lightning flashed several times a minute, but no sound and no rain crossed their path. Green signs indicated cities off the road, but he saw none. He stopped at an island for some scorched coffee, and drove on listening to radio apocalyptists. In postultimate desperation he reached between snoozing Winifred's ankles for another cassette from the battered shoebox there, touching the overhead light to read the label: *Goldberg Variations;* but the player took it wrong side first, and the wrong side was *Sonatas and Interludes* by John Cage. This was not bad. It positively complimented Ogallala. Still, he began to growl at every microscopic bend of road, and around two a.m. Winifred grumpily awakened to ask if he had not played that dippy toy piano shit four times already. "Drink," he croaked, and she handed him the Christmas largesse of a client of her father's, namely Amaretto. A plastic almond tied round the bottleneck hit his chin at every swig. And merciless Nebraska went on and on.

(Checking the map later, he discovered the deceit. Those fucking Yankees had tacked a dogleg on the shitful state, extending it a hundred miles past expectation.)

He drove off the road twenty miles from the border. Winifred woke him with a flashlight and a map. "There's a state park just up the road," she said.

"Where are we?"

"Nebraska."

"No! I won't. We'll make Wyoming."

"The first site there's an hour off."

"Oh my God."

"I'll drive."

"No!"

He nursed the car to the park. It was a flat tract bordering a hundred-yard-square mud pond. The plain stretched blandly past the interstate to a featureless horizon, trackless but for trucks that seamed it like a senseless Singer every twenty seconds.

"I thought of a better word for it," he said. "Randy."

"What?"

"I knew this American in London. He kept introducing himself, 'I'm Randy,' and it took him weeks to learn better. He thought the British *always* laughed at American names."

"Oh." She yawned. "That. Tell me another."

"Another?"

"Don't care about myths. A bedtime story."

"Oh. Well . . . once there was a man. Who knew a thing or two."

"Women. You have to have a woman now."

"And a woman. Who . . . loved him. Yes, despite everything, she loved him. At least, he thought so."

"That's a good beginning."

"Middles, ends . . . those are harder."

"True."

"Good night."

". . . Ever after."

In the comfort station, as it called itself, he paused before a mirror on a vending machine, studying himself studying an assortment of combs, hydrocephalic dolls, puzzles, playing cards.

He relaxed in the stall. The morning seemed bright with possibility. He heard the outer door swing open and shut. Water ran in a sink. The endless towel was yanked out a bit further. An electric blower switched on. He released a turd. He heard the vending machine operated over the roar of the blower. Between the cessation of the blower and the closing of the outer door there was a moment of silence into which a voice called back, "Morning, soldier."

Outside he stood in grassgreen light bounced back from fruited earth, a roar in his head. The present vanished into a density of mere detail.

How many oxen had Hyperion? The phobic dance of light, of every molecule of air beneath the sun, of every body ever gone to grass, of every soul let loose by death's black hum, assailed him. *Know, o friend,* went Archimedes's problem, after the statement of conditions, *that if you answer this, you are skilled in the ways of calculation.* That answer had waited some two thousand years. And all the aspects of this single moment in ordinary light now whelmed him, and two thousand lifetimes were not enough to meliorate his terror. Behind each simple moment, he saw, were countless complications, unseen cities, most of them nameless, many unnameable, populated by demons that sift information and shift their shapes, never still long enough for a recognition, but laying traces in momentary configurations such as this one, to confound the naive. He was definitely unskilled in calculation to have believed he could so easily step outside of history and consequence. The car, the light, the vanished inland sea, the numberless invisible dead, the serious sides to every game, all coagulated around him in a presentiment of Time—not the mildly passing *xronos,* but the cusp, the node, the singularity of *kairos,* the moment of crisis. And, as the pendulum from its moment of stillness plunges ever faster along its arc, so he plummeted from peace back into the labyrinth of crisis; and the acceleration, the fall, seemed more than personal—as if each personal *kairos* carried the nucleus of some larger, more final moment, as in the worst of his dreams, when the night turns white in silence, and the hot wind rises, and the very substrate of matter is abolished, all cities fall, and the souls of the millions scatter in the vapors of the falsest of dawns. The germ of this apocalypse was present in every crisis.

He walked unsteadily to the car. Winifred waited behind the wheel. After they regained the interstate, she said, "Where to?"

Without looking back, he said, "We are pursued."

13. Revelations

"Repeat," he said.

"I said it's in my handbag. You want to see?"

The land had thrust up shoulders, and the road now curved. Winifred was driving, her expression pinched and sullen. Camus held his glasses in one hand, pressing fingers of the other to his eyelids.

"Deny it, then," said Winifred. "Deny you knew."

"I didn't know you had it."

"Who are these people? Do you know that, at least?"

"No. Government maybe. They pushed me around."

"That bruise—"

"Yes."

"And you couldn't have told me, could you?"

"If *you* had told *me* . . ."

"You didn't ask! You never mentioned it! *I* don't want the fucking thing!"

"Look, you knew I was interested. You gave me those papers."

"No, Hans, *no.* I figured you were interested, and then you forgot about it. You do that, you know. You do that a lot."

Another mile of hills rolled past in silence. "Maybe it's this," he said. "That people fall in and out together. That there's no particular culpability."

"Yes," she snapped, "you'd like that. That'd work just fine for you. So that you can vanish behind the *circ*umstances and save your fucking precious detachment."

"I thought you loved me for that."

"I loved you for things you *did,* not for your God damned attitudes! You had something. You could have been so much better than you really were."

He struggled. "But . . . we can always be better than we are."

"Sure. You'll never allow for the existence of evil, will

you? You and Pelagius. Not Satan falling and an endless shriek of entropy, no, for you it has to be Orpheus's descent, and at least the hope of winning back the lost. No, Hans. Haven't you seen enough? Enough to convince you that human affairs are—are too degraded, too perverse, to allow that . . . perpetual hope?"

"Let's get rid of the thing," he said. "Throw it out the window."

"Like hell."

"Stop. I'll flag them down and give it to them."

"You will not!"

"Why not? What good is it?"

"Maybe it's keeping us alive, did you think of that?" Her voice was shaking. "You don't know who they are. Maybe they think we'll lead them to it. Once they get it, they could do anything to us. No one even knows where we are now."

Now Camus became frightened. He had a sense of the two men, of their utter earnestness stretching across time, and of the cold competence that had kept them invisible except when they had wanted to be seen. How far back did their involvement extend? To Germany? To Hüll? He wondered how close he himself had come to being found a suicide in his apartment. Yet they had missed Warner. Somehow Warner had got clean away. They were fallible. This calmed him. Knowing they were there was soothing in a way. It proved that his interest in the cube had not been mistaken. That there would be an outcome.

"There's another reason I won't give it up," said Winifred. "And I want you to listen carefully. Before you tripped over the thing and upset a very comfortable little expedition, I was set to publish with Warner. And then he got cute. He talked about exceptional circumstances, insufficient analysis. . . . He was looking to cut me out. I got pissed off. So he insisted I take it as a show of good faith, and he promised to show up in Seattle with tons of data, and we'd talk about the article. You see? There it is again, me working toward something and you running away from something, and we happen to end up going together. I can't take it. I don't want the fucking thing. If Warner tries to welsh, I'll throw it into Puget Sound. But not un*til* then."

"And you have no curiosity about the cube itself."

"Certainly," she said defensively. "Certainly I do. But it's going to turn out to be fake or something equally dull. If he wants that he can have it. He can afford it. But I'm—it's—it's just I'm twentyeight, Hans, and I'm going nowhere at all, and I can't afford another false start. Oh, God, Virginia is right about me, I'm nothing, and it's getting late, and nothing happens right. You, I don't know, you roll right along, nothing disturbs you, you don't seem to care at all, if it gets tiresome just chuck it out the window, but I *can*not damn it *live* that way! A little meaning, you know? If not someone, then something, some accomplishment to say, yes, it's all right, there's a reason. Just a little meaning."

She was crying. No, he thought; not like this. He could not bear that she should know him so little. To care so much, to search meaning so closely as to appear unconcerned, or rootless, when in fact his roots went so deep that nothing at the surface seemed quite real to him—of all people, she should know that. And he realized that the two years he had known her had been for him an immense pantomime of the heart, his every act and thought, in her presence or her absence, designed in some way to make her understand him. And that, so far from succeeding, she had built up round his dumbshow a different man entirely. Absently he raised a finger to her face, where a tear track ran.

"Damn, don't touch me," she snapped.

His heart grew eloquent and his tongue was like wood. The question now was whether he loved her sufficiently to accept the false image, whether he trusted her enough to permit this revision of his face. The hazard was that her idea of him might, after all, be superior to his nature, in which case he would have to grow to fit it, and possibly fail; or it might be so removed from what he really was that to endorse it could lead only to a demolition of self. This was the critical moment, which he so often fled (she knew at least his actions, if not his motives), when the mask became welded to the face, to be worn forever after, or removed only at great cost of flesh, or replaced by successive masks, each more ill-fitting than the last. In his soul, he wished to wear the face he had had before he was born. And since he did not know what that possibly could be, yet understood it was of first importance, he searched for it in out of the way places, in the structure of the ancient skull, in the roots of certain words, in the features of strangers in the street, in pieces of the transient popular culture, in mispronunciations of his name; and although nothing, not the smallest detail of the dullest day, passed him unremarked, yet he had a tremendous chariness of taking any of it for his own. Hence he appeared to skip, to skim the surface, to avert his eyes, as if the discipline of *not acting* at the critical moment would at last give a truer result.

At times then he would have that feeling that he did not live, but was lived. And this was now a joy, again a torment—being lived by others' fictions of him. He was willing to abandon himself with the zeal of a Trappist, when some fate came wearing his own first lost face; but not yet. He was still paying the price of revelation, timidly perhaps, no Saint Teresa, still fearing that the face of love, just slightly tipped, could become a mask of appropriation. And what hope could he hold of any peace or stability, when the consequence of each mistaken moment stretched to infinity, when the person he knew best in the world knew him not at all?

"Keep it, then," he said. "Keep it. I hoped we had more in common."

"Can this wait? I think we have more pressing problems."

"They've been behind us for days at least. Why is it suddenly so pressing?"

"Because now we know they're there."

"Yes. Well. To hell with that. Let them do what they do. Let them run us off the road. I really don't care any more." I wanted you, he meant to say, and didn't know it until now.

He expected an outburst, a cleaner break. Instead she said: "Yes."

"All right. Let's stop for gas and see what happens."

She continued driving in silence, her face hardened a little by the prospect of an immediate move. Finally, flatly: "Why not. If they want us they have us anyway."

"Activity," said Levin as the Volvo exited. He followed, parking the Chrysler by the station's air pumps. "This is activity. I reckon they have a half tank still."

"Think they spotted us?"

"I would say so. I would say definitely yes. Do you want a soda?"

"Yeah. Get me something lemon-lime."

Levin got out and approached Camus. Winifred had gone to the ladies'.

"Pardon me, fella. Got change of a dollar?" There was nothing in the tall man's eyes.

"I think so. In the car."

"I'll wait."

He left the gas hose running. He crawled into the car and rummaged in Winifred's purse, heart pounding. As he found the change purse, his fingers glanced past a small, cold, flat surface. He felt its edges. Then withdrew from the car backwards, small purse in hand. Levin stood holding a dollar. Camus counted four quarters from the purse and handed them to him. Levin looked disappointed. He hefted the coins in his free hand.

"Pity," he said. "I kind of wanted something more substantial."

"Meaning?"

"Oh, you know. These aluminum coins. Give me the old clad copper any time."

"Uh huh."

"You know what it is, it's the government. Country going to Hell. Maybe we'll see some improvement in November, or even before. I certainly hope so, myself. You take care now." He strolled off towards the machines without giving Camus the dollar.

In the Chrysler Borro asked, "Well?"

"Here. On the house. Don't drink it too fast, you'll get gas. I made a little play. Just a touch. It was worth a try. I think I'll drive a spell longer."

Winifred returned, glancing at the Chrysler. Without saying anything she got behind the wheel of the Volvo. The two cars returned to the highway. Levin left a decent quarter mile between them. The sun was down when they entered Utah. He closed the distance then, keeping an eye on the Volvo's broken taillight.

Salt Lake City, appearing suddenly from behind hills, was a bowl of stars.

"You'll be glad to know I was sick in there," said Winifred.

Camus glanced behind him, and said, "Take this exit. Then I'll drive."

A truck pulled between the cars. When it exited at Thirteenth, the Volvo was gone. Levin cursed mildly.

"Hey, hey," said Borro. "Where'd they go?"

"They got off at Thirteenth. Foxy." He slowed on the overpass. "You look right, I'll look left."

"Shit!"

"Okay, there they are, I've got them." Levin continued on, and swung the car south at Seventh East. He sped past one turn, took the next, and headed north on State. Three minutes later Borro spotted the Volvo coming the other way. Immediately it turned off, right, across traffic. Levin made to follow and was blocked by a bus. The traffic light turned red. He ran it, turning right, then right again, then right again. He sped until entering the northbound onramp of I-15. There he parked on the shoulder, got out, and stood on the hood of the car, scanning the highway in both directions for several minutes.

"Well?"

"Well, well, well. I guess we can find a motel around here, eh?"

Borro hit the dash four times with both fists.

Shortly after Provo, I-15 simply vanished. Before Camus knew it he was driving on a two lane undivided road with a single pair of taillights very far ahead of him. As he watched these vanished too. There were no lights and no signs. There was no moon. Waiting rigidly, he expected the interstate to return like a virtuoso conjuror holding his audience in momentary suspense after the final disappearing act, at least for applause. But it did not. The distant taillights winked on again, rising from behind a slight hill, then vanished permanently. They were utterly alone on the road.

He heard Winifred rustling a map in the back seat.

"Did you take a wrong turn?"

"No turn of any sort since Salt Lake. And I am not sure what a wrong turn would be at this point, unless it brought us to a light blue car."

"So where's the road?"

"A mystery to me."

The map rustled, they traveled on.

"You didn't get on 28?"

"My dear, a sign said divided highway ends, and so it did. There was nothing else."

"Hum. We're going south, at least?"

Camus craned forward to read the blaze of stars. "My own zodiacal sign is dead ahead, if that means anything. Otherwise there are no signs at all, which I count a blessing. I would be afraid of learning that we're bound for Elsinore, or Blasted Heath, or Styx perhaps."

"Or Stones." She was silent for a time. "There *is* an Elsinore, Utah."

"Thank you. I was anxious to hear that."

"Hans?"

"Yes."

"I'm sorry. I was upset."

"It was my fault."

"True. But you were okay back there. You really lost them."

"Did I do that?" he teased.

"You did. Yurra brev mon."

He heard a large rustling noise. He glanced around. She was semifetal in the back, roadmap wrapped around her as a blanket. The hot breeze lifted one loose edge. He cranked the window up, to shut off voices of lost souls. Void roared past the vehicle. He noted about a half a tank of gas remaining, and was afraid to mention it to Winifred, afraid that such confession of the material limits of travel, impinging on her dreamwandering soul, would cut it adrift without hope of return, like snuffing the candleflame on which the magus rides the night. As long as there was fuel, as long as he kept to speed, silent, in fear, they were all right.

Nothing ahead or behind. He left the dome light on, blotting the stars. A region of purest annihilation, straight line of matter across the waste momentarily created ahead by the feeble speeding cone of white light, and dissipated instantly behind in a red glow. If he slowed or stopped, he knew the road would simply vanish, cutting them adrift.

After Santaquin the names of towns took on the quality of antimatter. Nephi. Levan. Scipio. Mormon angels, doubtless, but precisely because he did not know how to propitiate these relatively modern *genii* of the homeless, the names were full of menace.

He began to see fluorescent stegosaurs on the shoulder. He shook his head to clear it. The gas gauge dipped from one-half to one-third. ENTERING HOLDEN. He did not see Holden. A sign informed him FILLMORE 10. He did not know if this was miles or kilometers. He began spelling short English words backwards to himself. Drib. Klim. Drow. Nuon. Brev. Tsew. Etsaw. In Fillmore was a service station lit but vacant, like a set for an end-of-the-world film: its sign announced in antiquated futuristic type ANTREX. He accelerated past it in an access of superstition.

Moist traces of acridity etched his ribs. The needle on the gauge refined its tricks, dipping below one-quarter, edging zero, rising, not with malice, but as if it were recording local wrinkles in the fabric of space. COVE FORT 32 / BEAVER 64. He

quailed. What could happen, really? Wait till dawn for the
highway patrol? He switched off the overhead light; the sign
of his birth had set, and all the other stars were strange. He
went through Cove Fort, three dark buildings, as forbidding as
a ziggurat. BEAVER 30 / PARAWAN 60. He made anagrams of
Parawan, each of which frightened him more than the last, and
tried to think of more earthly menaces, lions and tigers and
bears, oh my. He never saw Beaver, although he fancied a
crater to his left, blue fire around its edges. Parawan arrived
at last, and appeared to have been abandoned for centuries.
About four he reached Cedar City, drifting the last fifty feet
to the station with the choking engine cut. It seemed very
important to retain an ounce or two of fumes.

He felt Winifred pressing forward on his seat. "I have to
wee-wee," she said. He fell across the wheel and let her edge
out. Attendant came over. Camus saw him, and his brain transmitted only: attendant. The word seemed hazardous. He forced
himself to smile. "Gas," he said.

"Sure, buster, what kind."

"Ah. Regular."

He slumped. Buster. Retsub. After a time he felt a kick
through the seat.

"Hey, Hassenpfeffer, let me in."

"Pay the man. Then you drive."

While Levin filled out forms for the new car, Borro dug
with a nail file at a laminated map on the countertop.

"Where the fuck do they think they're going?"

"Away from us. Stop that."

Borro slapped down the file. "Some fancy driver. Losing
them like that. This business was supposed to be sealed and
delivered by now."

Levin paused to recheck the name he had put atop the rental
form, then signed the bottom. "I did not lose them so much
as I was lost by them."

Borro looked up in sudden sharp brute suspicion. "I think
you wanted this. I think you're getting spooky."

"Maybe so, maybe so."

"You want to clue me? Because I think I've got a right.
Because if you're going to spook out I want no part. I want to
do business."

Levin ignored him and studied the map. "So they'll go to
LA. And then they'll head back north. They have to. He can't

leave the country. This is panic behavior we're witnessing."

Borro pressed his file against Levin's lapel. "I mean this. You show me more confidence. There's interested parties."

Levin shied slightly from the pressure.

"Interested parties everywhere, Sammy. Going to deal on your own?"

Borro went out in disgust and got into the new car on the driver's side. Levin followed, trying to sort in his mind the new parameters of the situation. It was more complex than he had anticipated. He left his seat belt open until Borro started the car and the buzzer shrilled.

"I'm going to drive now, if you don't mind, and if you'll tell me where the fuck we're going."

Levin shut his eyes and reconstructed the map. It was a good exercise. He traced a route to a small red square.

"North. There's no sense letting the other fellow's panic behavior disarray your own plans. He's boxed. He has to come. I see no other way. We'll give him rope until we see what adjustments have to be made. We'll talk to some interested parties. We'll take 84 to 21 to 26. We'll take our time and get some scenery. I want to see the Malheur River and Stinkingwater Pass. I want to see Burns and Brothers and Bend."

"I call you Spook from now on. I don't know why I put up with it. I don't know why I don't leave you flat."

"Because," Levin said, folding his arms and keeping his voice level, "I'm always right." Hidden under his biceps his fingers drummed nervously.

14. Pomps

Signs said the incline was six degrees. Direly they warned truckers of disaster. The Volvo's engine whined in third gear.

"LA," said Winifred. "It's LA. Feel the vibes. LA invented vibes. Pow and zzz. Feel what it's like to be trapped in tar."

"Take meeting," offered Camus.

"Wrong. That term is *desksit,* because no one stays anywhere long enough to have their own. This is dream city. Everyone here is a figment of someone else's imagination."

"Really? Whose are you?"

"Don't get snide. I surfed, did you?"

"Yes, but that was long ago and in another country, and besides, the wench is dead."

"Feeb."

Hills abandoned from a prior set, white elephants now, rose around them. The slope of road was unrelenting.

"She works at Forest Lawn," said Winifred, "which will thrill you to your toes. She went to India and changed her name from June to Shisha, and don't you dare make any remarks."

"Names are relative or private. You met her where?"

"At CalArts. College chums. You've heard of that?"

They reached the cemetery at three. Shisha came out from behind a word processor to greet them. "Oh, Win. It's been so long. Who's this?"

"Hans Camus."

"Aryan. I knew it. You have roots as deep as the Himalayas. Win, remember Matt?"

"Not Matt Kriegersohn? We had a thing at school."

"Well, I'm living with him. He got in a rut and did some monuments out here, but now he has the greatest idea that ever was. Guess. Guess what. He's making a glacier. You'll come see it? You have to. I get off in an hour."

"Wouldn't miss it," said Camus, sneaking a look at Winifred, who wore a stricken smile.

"Good. Just wander around here for a while, see if you can spot Matt's work, or—no, never mind. He wouldn't like that. Just take it in. It's real dumb." She smiled. "I'm so glad you're here. See you later."

They wandered into the cemetery.

"Is she real?" asked Camus.

Winifred stopped walking. "That is an odd and a kind of shitty thing to ask. I know one or two people who live beyond their imaginative means, so to speak, but she's not one."

"Okay."

"She's not," said Winifred uncertainly. "If she says she has a glacier I will by God believe it until I don't see it."

"Sorry."

"I'm not some kind of space woman."

"I know. Just American."

"*Don't* start that." She strode away on a flagstone walk. Camus examined distastefully a flamboyant sword-wielding angel and was about to point it out, saying, "Matt's work?" when he heard, "Hans, come look."

The bronze marker, flush with the ground, bore raised letters worn and pitted from three decades' exposure to corrosive air:

JOHN CAYMUS   1916-1963   REQUIESCAT IN PACE

There was dissipate but intense sunlight, a steady warm breeze smelling slightly of metal, an even haze from zenith to horizon, as if the sky were dusted with pulverized aluminum, making ghosts of the distant mountains. He felt a metal edge in his pocket, and moved his finger to the corner, feeling the sharp point of this apparently incorruptible thing against his corruptible flesh. He pressed; but not too hard; the skin might break.

Guillaume Rossignol. His mother's grandfather, buried in Strasbourg. When the Nazis occupied Alsace they had changed the stone to read *Wilhelm Nachtigall.*

Overhead a jet tore air, smudged the sky, vanished into sun. "Yes," he said to himself. "Various Ellis Islands of the mind." For the totalitarian is not just the big stick: it is whatever corrodes, erases the clean line, flattens distinctions, cuts temporal roots. No wonder America, or the twentieth century (let us face it, they are equal), made him uneasy. Erosion proceeded on all levels, from the cultural down to the molecular. (A waft of piped music bearing dilute traces of Brahms reached him on the acid air, seductive as Circe's trim Hadescraft. And inmixed with the uncertain clone of Brahms was an amplified snatch of the baptismal sacrament: *Repudiare te penitus Satani cum omnium apparati*.) Well, not quite all levels. The mating of corpse and earth below was interfered with, he learned from his brochure, by expensive leadlined coffins—*Et saeculum per ignem*—A neat inversion of the Gothic, he thought, imagining these misfortunate corpses unable to rise from their hermetic crypts at the Judgment. *The Belated Resurrection*.

"Isn't that funny?" Winifred said. "You were born in '63, weren't you?"

He performed a macabre little shuffle, saying, "Dem bones *will* rise. They may already have done so." A passing matron dressed in smart black gave the pair a dirty look. She carried a clutch of bloodred roses.

Camus guiding, they came to the mausoleum, based on the "world famous" Campo Santo in Genoa. Hustling past a disapproving guard and a plexiglas poorbox, they came to a long vaulted room. In his mind it filled with Disney-animated Genoan monks, swaying to a whispered plainchant, masses sung in robotic perpetuity for the souls of their makers. A stained glass reproduction of Leonardo's *Last Supper* glowed at one end of the room. As they passed a waxworks of Michelangelo sculptures, a fruity voice swelled; its source was behind the stained glass.

". . . The figure of Judas, the betrayer, which broke twelve times in the firing at the world famous Corning Glass Works . . ." The glass seemed a bad Victorian joke. Or a still from the suppressed Marx Brothers film *A Night in Gethsemane*.

Spreading his arms in a mocking *imitatio Christi*, he said, "Men, I have some good news and some bad news. The good news is, you're getting the weekend off. The bad news . . ."

"Shh!" Past Winifred a pair of tiny nuns led a troop of tiny students, double file, in blue shorts and knee socks, crisp white shirts, shiny black shoes, navy blazers. On their jaunty beaked caps stood the crest of St. Swithin's Academy, looking from a distance like tiny barometers.

Camus lowered his voice. "It's not just the people buried here, or should I say 'laid to eternal rest.' It's the whole damned culture. 'Don't cry, Giovanni. Your Uncle Mike is all right. He's only taken a long, long trip, to a place where people don't get old, where there's fresh orange juice every morning, and no fruit flies.' And the saints all live in world famous Laurel Canyon."

"You're impossible," she said.

"I don't mind the monuments, leaving art to make the best of death . . . but this is letting death make the worst of art."

He glanced back at the sea of blue caps before the *Supper,* thinking of the broken, decayed surface of the original, of aged Leonardo chuckling with the certain foresight of design over the inevitable collapse of his masterpiece. Inherent vice of the medium. He wondered how the old dead crow would feel about the scientists and sensors now in Santa Maria delle Grazie, protecting the masterpiece not from itself, but from the thunder of motor traffic and the corrosion of air; or about this counterfeit, which sooner or later would be shivered to kaleidoscopic ruin by the earth turning over in its sleep; likely he'd appreciate the joke. Michelangelo, he guessed, would not be so amused; he paused by the sham Pietà, considering the piety of his own impiety. In a newsman's voice he said: "Rushing past dumb-struck tourists and pilgrims, the hammerswinging artist struck the Virgin's face and left arm repeatedly. Soon seized by agents of the Swiss Guard, he was dragged away shouting a confused paen to the death of God and Art." He returned to normal voice.

"You notice they've copied the signature too. The approach is less direct than the hammer, but more efficient in the long run. No mess to sweep up, no loss of tourist revenue, no jail terms, no angry editorials. Just a simple removal of guts, spleen, liver, and lights, by dedicated craftsmen who can be persuaded to overlook the difference between a hawk and a handsaw when the wind is right, namely blowing down from high temples of commerce."

"It's late," she said. "It's too late for this. Let's go."

The eastbound traffic on Foothill Freeway thickened near the racetrack at Santa Anita. Camus made soft galloping sounds with cupped hands against his cramped knees in the back. Saying faintly, "And it's Mystic Nativity by a head, sired by Immanent Eternity on Native Virgin, and trained by Joe Carpenter."

Winifred shot him a vicious glance in the rearview mirror and he shut up. The car swept through a series of interchanges and ended sailing on a graceful curve four levels above the rectilinear subdivisions of the local tracts of Arcadia.

Past San Antonio Heights the road climbed into unpopulated hills. Winifred's voice moved gently as a pin scraped sidewise against a balloon. "Shisha? Just how does one go about making a glacier?"

Shisha thought it over carefully. "Well, you need a valley. It has to be the right kind. Then you need a lot of ice. And then you need easements, environmental impact reports, a lot of legal stuff. Then you make it."

"Um. It sounds expensive."

"Oh yes. Maybe ten million altogether. Bear right here."

"Take it out of petty cash?" asked Camus quickly, immediately wishing he hadn't. But Winifred had no chance to jump on him; Shisha turned around grinning.

"No, and we didn't run it off in the basement either. We incorporated. You're looking at forty percent of the Icehouse Foundation, a nonprofit enterprise, *glacies gratia artis*. Your contribution is tax deductible. We get a million a year from Mobil, half for art and half for geological research. And lesser grants from NEA, DOE, UC, NASA, individuals, galleries, and then there's rentals on my film *Icewall* and patents pending on the snow machines."

So it was real. A good deal of tension left the car. Winifred began to ask excited questions. The site was an abandoned ski area, with utilities already laid; the technic was large quantities of slush blasted through twenty very efficient snowblowers, with the runoff trapped in a small dammed basin and pumped back up for reuse.

Their altitude had made the air quite chill. Camus unconsciously drew his limbs in. He dozed. He dreamed. Beside the shallow pit the clan was gathered. The silence was itself. A later logos would call it reverence. Guttering fire filled the cave with heavy, acrid smoke. Outside a wind blew down from the icesheet of the Pyrenees, screaming as it passed constricted through the valley. The dead one lay on his side in the pit, limbs folded in a counterfeit of birth, mouth slacked wide, eyes open and staring. The shaman, ancient, older than the dead, a seer of thirty winters at the least, trembled at the edge of the pit, and suddenly bent. He laid two fingers on the dead one's brow, and drew them slowly down, shutting the lids. A shudder passed the clan at this new gesture, its possible meaning. This one, dead of cold, would guard the site against the blind snow force, since he was intimate with its way. Here he would hunt for the clan, blind white bison and elk against their survival and return. One man made protest. To leave the dead one thus a concession to the snow force. It would weaken them. The shaman scowled and raised his totem. In the dream Camus could not see the totem.

Although the San Gabriel peaks were still lit, the valley was in shadow. A dozen cars were there, parked irregularly. A long low wooden building was lit within. The air was sharp.

The interior of the lodge looked like God's own engineering firm on about the second day of creation. A chaos of worktables was buried under the disarray of plans, charts, graphs, video gear, bits of machinery, typewriters, and cameras. In the center was a large scale model, in relief, of the site. And against two walls were filing cabinets, bulletin boards papered with photos and drawings, knots of floodlamps, tripods, and cables, half a dozen light boxes littered with slides, two dilapidated video monitors, and a computer console. Perhaps ten people were perched on stools, working, or carrying coffee, rolled paper, tools, from one place to another.

A short wiry man in khaki shirt and shorts approached. He also wore a brown knit tie and a tweed jacket. White knee socks and a white scarf completed his outfit, and he was cleaning a pair of hornrimmed glasses on the end of the tie.

". . . Ten million cubic meters total," he was saying to someone, while smiling at the strangers.

"We're friends of Shisha's from the east," Winifred told him.

"Fantastico," he said. Camus decided to despise him. "Lyle Hutton, resident glaciologist, keeper of the mass balance, and general scientific factotum." He grinned and pushed the glasses back up his nosebridge. "Call me Lyle."

"Hans Camus, no fixed abode, keeper of my own precarious balance, and scientific fantoccini. Call me Punch."

Hutton ignored him. "Matt's in Lytle Creek, should be back soon. Till then I'll fill you in."

"With crayons?" muttered Camus. Shisha smiled at him in sympathy and said, "Sorry, but I have to work. Folks from *ARTifact* magazine are coming tomorrow."

"Take a parka," said Hutton as they went out, not taking one himself. "It's cold up there. As I was just telling Blaise, we laid down half a million tons the first year, and now we have a nice base, so we just run maintenance in summer, adding mass in winter. . . ." The geologist's delivery became more technical, with professional pauses, as if to let a Mobil vice-president dope out some bit of jargon before moving to the next. His voice was overrun midsentence by the din of a motorcycle.

Matt Kriegersohn looked the sculptor. Six four, his torso, clad in leathers now, would have pleased Michelangelo. Thick flaxen hair in a mane swept from forehead to nape; he wore dustladen Levis, bulky cracked hiking boots, and a black turtleneck beneath his leathers. He pulled a wad of mail from a rural box before approaching them.

"Win?" he said softly. "I'll be damned, it is you."

"Matt. It's been a *long* time."

They embraced, and Camus took a clean rush of joy at theirs.

"You were in Europe?"

"Just back. Now it's on to Seattle for a frightful gathering of the academic tribes, then back to the grind."

Shisha emerged, and Matt hugged her. "How's things?"

"Okay. I was going to reshoot interiors, but Bill brought them out okay. I think we're down to final cut."

"Great. Ferdy says PBS will be up Friday, so we'll have to get the boards done." Matt released her, moving his hands down her arms, holding them out in wonder. "You've got great wrists," he said.

"You've got garbanzos."

"Huh? Oh, on the carrier, yeah." '

Hutton said, "Let's roll, Matt. Harry and Jack have been waiting up there an hour."

With an effort the sculptor turned from Shisha. "Sure. Okay. Let's go."

"I think they're in love," whispered Winifred.

In the canyon's mouth the four stepped over loose scree. From there a defile ran up for almost a mile before opening into a broad bowl. There was a whiteness there. As they walked they came tangent to the curve of the valley, and saw more white.

"My God," said Winifred.

"Classic valley cirque," said Hutton, not looking. "High albedo." As if that could explain everything.

On the side of the gondola was stencilled ICEHOUSE EXPRESS in bright red. Matt went into the shed and turned it on. A wave went up the cables, damped and reflected by the first pylon.

The gondola rocked gently on its guys.

The plexiglas windows were scarred, and not much use for viewing. Still, the scale of the glacier was evident after they bumped over the runners of the first pylon, and it was impressive. As the lift swung out over the canyon, Camus saw the shadowed tongue of the sheet rhyming with the sky's evening blue. But within were hints of purple, flecks and streaks of amethyst, a surface like azure quartz: and further up, where the sun struck it, a shifting myriad of brilliant flashes, ten thousand icy stars in a floor of daylight sky.

"Not sun," Hutton was saying, "but the combination of sun and wind. That's our worst enemy. That determines the ablation rate of the sheet." He went on, fascinating Winifred with recondite accounts of shear stress and bed slip.

But Matt sat moodily. He found a pack of cigarettes, mashed in a hip pocket, and seemed surprised by them, or by the shape of the pack. He lit one cautiously. Free fingers drummed his seatarm. He did not look at the glacier, but studied rather the rocky lip of the canyon. It struck Camus that the man did not care at all about the enterprise. Its beauty and details were auxiliary to the primitive, elementary power he was bending back against the land as an expression of will.

At the canyon head a broad rockshelf curved out from a point just beneath the summit of Thunder Mountain. Thence it ran across the flank of Telegraph Peak. Hutton still spewed names of things and places. Twenty commercial blowers had been bought, each modified to generate two hundred thousand tons of slushy ice every winter. The summer run was modest, just enough of evenings to maintain mass in the face of increased melt. The bowl beneath them was the primary accumulation area. Northfacing, it was sheltered naturally, and further protected against sun and wind by a geodesic canopy at its head a double layer of foam quilted between nylon sheets of orange and white, and stretched across aluminum struts. The gondola docked with a dull thud. Camus's impression was of a gaily painted Hellmouth.

The ledge was frigid, and despite the sky's summer light it was difficult to see, as if the memory of an ancient, persistent winter lived still in the rock, and was awakened by the new microclime. Matt trotted to a lit shed, and a moment later livid mercury vapor lamps around the rim stuttered on. Smaller bluish spots downhill marked the snow guns. Camus zipped the parka and wished for gloves. He remembered a sign he had seen on a bridge somewhere at one or two in the morning: CAUTION—NIGHT CONSTRUCTION. So this, he'd thought, is where they make the night.

Then, abruptly, a multithroated roar went up. He saw twined spumes of water issuing from the guns, which swiveled side to side.

"Remote control," said Hutton.

The heavy parabolas of liquid changed their texture and tone, extending further onto the glacier now, as the refrigeration coils frosted. He could just make out a coming mist of rime on the nearest gun.

"Matt always throws the switches himself," Hutton remarked. "Artistic integrity he calls it."

Winifred said, "What?" Her interest in the practical details had vanished in the miserable cold.

"Integrity, he says. I'd call it arrogance."

"Same thing," said Camus.

Another sound arrived, less strident, a whirring undertone to the climbing pitch of the roar.

"That's it," said Hutton. Now broad sluggish plumes of ice erupted from the nozzles, spreading like the fan of silver from a thumbcapped garden hose. The flattened arches were pure white in the pools of light, vanishing against the unlit gray of the icesheet. Hutton raised a stubby miniature binocular to his eyes and stood in silence for a moment. "Number nine's out of alignment," he said.

Harry or Jack trotted out of the shed, carrying a thermos and styrofoam cups. Hutton gave an officious thumbs-up, which the stocky man answered with a nod.

"I think he's puttin' on a bit of a show," he said, gesturing at the shed and losing two cups to a sudden gust. Camus had a chill, and made for the shed. For him the glacier was nothing beyond the simple, if staggering, fact of its presence. It was a stunt as empty as engraving texts on the head of a pin, as if sheer scale could vindicate the enterprise. And this glacier did not move his thoughts, as the natural glaciers of Switzerland had, to any broad perspective of time. This artifact, he sensed, would be obsolete before it even began to move on its own. He saw Matt coming the other way. He lowered his head, hoping to pass by, but kept his eyes up. Matt's face was haggard now, and his voice so soft that Camus did not at first respond.

". . . Wears off pretty quickly," he was saying. "I realize it's a bore. We can go any time."

Camus started to protest. Matt said, "No, I realize it is. I'm beginning to understand that I've tied up maybe ten years of my life in this, and for what? Before this, I got no recognition, not even from my friends, and that was fine. Then I had this . . . *frightening* idea, it wouldn't give me any peace, and I knew it wouldn't be sculpture at all, but I had to go ahead. Suddenly I'm a real sculptor to everyone, almost a celebrity. Strange. Why is that?" He flexed his shoulders. "Some nights I just dream about it. Nothing happens. It's just there. What the hell is it? Any ideas?"

Camus said no. Winifred and Hutton approached. The four returned to the gondola. The sky was almost black now, and as the glacier receded the glow of arc lamps turned pink and faded.

15. Eyes

The loose logic of their journey then took them north, and it was as if geologic time scrolled backwards along the path of their continued flight, and thereby scoured his eyes of modern habits. He acceded to transactions of sight more intimate and less speculative than any he'd known. Far from violating the present surface of things he saw, to read their pasts, they violated him. Along the road were upthrust tumbled hills of basalt, granite, shot through with serpentine, malachite, and jade, and clung to by ice plant, Dudleyia, Clarkia, sedums. Winifred knew the names. Hawks and buzzards circled above sharp seafacing cliffs. By January, she said, there would be whales offshore. He saw seals. The car's headlights startled deer at night. And still close by the sea was forest, archaic to the eye, trees seemingly frozen in their youth and uncomplicated by the later, more tangled demands of evolution: eucalyptus, redwood, acacia. It seemed a million years old, yet created yesterday.

They spent some time with Ng. He had returned to Berkeley from Beijing. There he worked part time as a fumigator. They found him sealing an orange tent around the whole of a three-story house.

They ate at a Szechuan restaurant. Ng exchanged chiming conversation with the owner. Returning to Berkeley in the August dusk, Camus felt a strong sense of home.

On Ng's mantel was a slice of nautilus shell. With his glasses off Camus could count seven chambers from where he sat. Winifred was already in bed. Camus suggested that they might finish their mail *go* game, which had already lasted some two years. Ng considered, then set up the board from his diagram. It was nine o'clock. Camus smoked. Ng sighed and clicked a stone down.

"You're going to see Warner?"

"Yes." Camus studied the board. Irrationally he tensed. He suddenly remembered Ng's last postcard in the tall man's hand. Quote People's Republic unquote. "You could come with us," he said as he played a white stone.

"Work," said Ng. "They raised the fees again." He sat in silence until he moved.

Between moves Ng practiced calligraphy. He tipped a brush with ink, held it poised for seconds above a sheet, then quickly drew a character. Between characters he made, with one movement, circles. He was amused to find Camus watching this instead of the board. He said, "I try to consider the mark accomplished before I start."

Camus saw, with distress at the abrupt swing of his attention, that a large block of his white stones, previously safe, was now threatened by Ng's black. He had neglected the first defensive rule of maintaining two open squares, called eyes, within the block. Ng saw it too. His black stone clacked pleasantly next to the weakened block of white.

"We can race to the edge now, but I'm ahead of you."

"Yes." A scaworn rock on the table, honeycombed with holes, held three brushes tips out. Possibly the existence of such holes in matter, of eyes, of the Pauli Exclusion Zone between electron shells, was all that maintained its integrity. Possibly his perception of the density of matter, of events, of time, was mistaken.

Ng snapped his fingers. "Your move."

"Oh? Yes, I know."

"What's on your mind? You can't do two things at once. I heard you last night, pissing and brushing your teeth at the same time."

Flustered, Camus tapped a cigarette from the pack on the table.

"That's what I mean. Smoke, or talk, or think, or play the game. But all at once?"

"Right," Camus said grimly, dropping the cigarette and ceasing to think. "Truth is, I'm worried about the thing. Warner will have to explain it somehow."

Ng made a move. He took ten of Camus's stones from the board. "You're counting on that, aren't you?"

"What do you mean?"

"Neither of you acts like this is a vacation."

Camus started to place a stone.

"I wouldn't," said Ng.

"What?" Camus dropped the stone. Ng realigned the stones on which it had fallen.

"Relax. You're really wound up. I mean, what happens if Warner doesn't explain it? Doesn't show up at all."

"Oh, but he can't. . . ."

"In his way he's famous for it. By delaying credit on this dig, he's costing me two thousand in fees."

"So what would you suggest?"

"I wouldn't suggest anything. Except keeping your eyes open." He looked up smiling and deposited a stone for another substantial capture.

"Yes. See what you mean."

Ng leaned back and sighed. "It really does go better by mail. You have a tendency to rush. Don't rush into anything with this guy. Myself, I'm thinking of getting a nice job in real estate. All I need right now is to be a fresh associate professor somewhere when the *real* story comes out. Whatever that might be."

Camus wondered if his two pursuers could possibly find Ng. Certainly they could. He had been on the dig, they had at least an address in Beijing. As casually as he could, he asked, "Had any other problems lately?"

"Not really. Oh, I surprised a burglar in here last week. Didn't take anything."

"Ah. What did he look like?"

Ng frowned again. "Now why would you want to know that?"

"Curiosity. Social research."

"Skinny black kid, about five eight. I frightened him pretty badly just by stepping into the room."

The relief he felt was disproportionate. But Ng looked as troubled as he ever did. After a few seconds he just shook his head and got up, looking once more at the board. "Eyes open." He studied it a little longer. "I really don't think you can win this one."

16. Circumstances

Winifred was for driving straight through to Seattle. But Camus wanted to stop in Eugene, to see an old friend from London. Only as they took the exit did his reasons, like methane in a sump, bubble up for his queasy inspection.

London had been a happy time, not least because of Derek. Derek was a moody ectomorph who worked in what could only be called the arts, although his eclectic approach to painting, video, conceptualism, punk rock, and other nameless enterprises wholly resisted categorization. Once he had strewn a thousand paper clips across Trafalgar Square; no one noticed them, but the rust shadows of their shapes persisted on the concrete for a year. Once he had put twenty shortwave radios in a hall, tuned to static, drones, and jamming, and had walked a random path around them, his body acting as an antenna and bending the shape of the cacophony; after an hour the din seemed otherwordly. Derek was innocent of grammar and spelling, yet whenever he wrote anything, his lapses were inspirational. Camus, wearing a groove between the University and the British Museum, thought Derek an inadvertent genius, and wished that his own lapses of reason might prove half so fruitful as Derek's.

It was not just that Derek's idea of art was in such direct and tonic opposition to Kriegersohn's glacier—he wanted to stop here because he felt he should prove to Winifred that he'd had his own existence before they'd met. At this remove Derek was, in the way that old friends sometimes are, a version of himself to be displayed: proof that Camus might have become something else, and therefore proof that he was, in his present guise, real.

It was a great motel of a house which included in one glassed wing an indoor pool. Winifred refused to accompany him to the door, sure that he had scrambled the address. He went alone up a gravel path flanked by potted cacti, a little unsure himself. He rang the bell.

About a minute later Derek opened the door a crack. He had acquired glasses and a sparse mustache. His usual expression of brooding confusion had changed to one of confused distaste.

"Not at home," he said.

"Derek," said Camus. "It's me."

No change in the face. Some time passed. Then: "Christ so it is. Come on in then."

"Hold on. Have to get me bird." Camus sprinted back to the car. When he and Winifred returned up the path Derek was outside, arranging bits of broken flowerpot around the base of a euphorbium.

"Righto," he said to Winifred. "We've got pasta for dinner to get you up to a svelte nine stone, my dear. And you," turning to Camus, "get greens to take the lard off. We're all alone here. The gainfully employed are off to Pago Pago and like garden spots. By luck I knocked off work just last March so we're free to chin. Got dope? No matter, I'll harvest some. Step in now, mind the bats."

"The house," he said, rolling joints by hand in a living room of princely size and pedestrian decor, "I disown. 'Twas established in the early 'eighties by some seedy hack who meant to start a kind of fiction collective. Called it *Invisible, Inc.* You remember how my work was getting narrative? Well, I took the plunge past cold cold depths and I'm a writer now. Of sorts. Certain comforts in it, constant regrets. The old hack, Angstrom, passed on before I got here. His idea, I gather, was to produce literary merchandise by diverse hands, market it under a stable of pseudonyms, split the proceeds, and leave some freedom for what is here reverentially referred to as The Real Work. Not that they do any of that. What you've got here is a clutch of egotists badgering each other over rent and food. Mostly I go to bed early. I'm the lame. They pity me. A mere five grand I made last year from words. Some of them make ten times that and squirrel it in their mattresses and convertible preferred debentures. Last Tuesday a couple in the kitchen were earnestly discussing some highflown financial fiction up in Portland and clammed up when I came in. Then asked was it me made that five dollar call to Pasco, Washington last month. Now I ask you."

He paused to pass three joints around, admonishing, "Mind,

don't suck. This stuff is killer. I've a tolerance myself but I won't be responsible. Anyway it will stop my babble by and by. What was I saying? O yes. The Junior Esthetical Tycoon set. I think there ought to be laws against people who earn fifty grand a year and buy a sofa like this one. Still, I envy them I do. Give my arms I would to write the really popular stuff. Straight spike clear into the cultural skull. If I had a word processor I might acquire the new grace. They say, you must learn *dFILE*. What bloody kind of language is that? I say if I want to talk to silicon I'll go to the beach. Coke?"

He passed a small silver box. Winifred accepted it, drawing a silver straw from a sleeve at the hinge, and opened a recess on the lid. After two dainty snorts she passed it to Camus, who replaced it on the table with a shrug.

"Our Puritan," said Derek. "Old bastard. What a trouper. Have you got your Huxley pastiche? Read, read."

"Not I," said Camus.

"Modest cuss. He's been brilliant all the way out, am I right? His talent's sublime, innit? Tell all. Ignore the twit."

"He's got his points," said Winifred. "Sharp, most of them."

"Too true. Wish I had one half like him here. What the hell. I mean, I'm plain. Give me Waugh. Give me Cary. Give me bloody Graham Greene. I confess a faggotty liking for Maugham, am I right?" He spread his hands, palms up. "Five years at Slade. You see me as I am today. Pass me that stuff, luv."

He snorted. "Me own fault. I was just waiting to become the victim of circumstances. Delineate the void, and bingo, you're it. That one there can tell you so."

"You become the void?" Camus asked.

"No no. Realize you've always been it. Self-definition is the game. What can I say? Circumstance, it's all circumstantial. Boo hoo and all that."

"Circumstance," Camus said, undressing from a seated position on the guest bed. Winifred was tucked in up to her chin. Camus punched a pillow, shaking the bed. At the other end of the house Derek swam laps.

"Christ, what's left? I apologize. We should have driven through. This was a big mistake. Circumstance, wreckage, entropy, *Schrecklichkeit*. Why is it always like this? Five years from now he'll be in real estate. *Scheiss!* I wish you could have seen him as he was."

"He's okay. What did you expect?"

"Better. I expected better. I thought he had a clue how to stay alive. I thought he was one of those whom time would improve. My God."

"At least you're mad," she said.

"Yes, and tomorrow it will be the sulks. Entropy always wins. The final totalitarian. Tomorrow, back to dear old academe, full circle. Play maypole with Warner, try to forget old Hüll and what drove him to it. With luck I'll rise to associate boneduster at Podunk State and be so brutalized that I'll be grateful for it. Minor acolyte to a faith I reject, and not even a good acolyte, at that." He turned to her. "Are you really satisfied with it? Warner's scams, the *Geographic*, the whole hollow structure?"

"Hans, it's something."

"Yes, yes, and I'm nothing, and getting more nothing daily. Dump me now, Waste, you'll be better off. It never could have worked."

"It could though. You—" She stopped, and he remembered what she'd said in the corridor at Cleveland Heights: *maybe so*. And thought, no, forget it. But he thought that only to goad his heart to act.

"I what?" he said. "Or are we past confidences of that sort?"

"Hans, give me a little . . . love. I was going to say credit, but you would say credit for what. That would be too circumstantial for you. So say love. And isn't that the most circumstantial of all? Just learn to take it. And give it. When it's there. Okay?"

"I can try. You'll teach me?"

"I can try," she sighed. She drew him down. Soon, in this embrace, he slept.

In the periodicals room at Oregon State University, Borro found what Levin had asked him to look for. He read the entire column through, then tore the page from the magazine, folded it, and placed it in his shirt pocket. Going out, he winked at the woman behind the circulation desk.

Levin said nothing on his return. Borro said, "Empire Plaza, 820 Empire Way South. Seattle."

"Fine." Levin was drumming on the steering wheel.

"So what. How do we know this is anything? We go up there and nobody shows is what. They could be in Maine by now. They could be anywhere."

Levin clenched the wheel. His shoulders knotted, his knuckles whitened, he drew a long sharp breath. He began to pivot toward Borro; then abruptly he stopped. His hands loosened on the wheel. He let his breath out in a relaxed sigh. He said calmly, "They could be. Yes, they could. But they're not. Circumstances forbid it."

Borro cursed slowly, flatly, evenly, for a short time.

Levin said, even more calmly, "Samuel. You are a benighted submoronic sot. I'll have you on hands and knees before this is done. I want you groveling. You'll clean my toes with your tongue. Beg me for some humiliation, you pathetic sack of meat. You purblind pig. Look there."

The index finger of Levin's right hand, curled on the wheel, extended casually, and Borro followed the line to an ice cream truck parked by the curve. Camus stood there nibbling a sugar cone. Across the street Winifred was cleaning the windshield of the Volvo.

Borro made a little moaning sound and began to move. Levin leisurely moved a hand to Borro's chest. He was smiling.

"We must learn from our mistakes, Samuel. Let's get basic here. Where is the item?"

"He's got it, hasn't he?"

"No."

"Then what . . . ?"

"More basic. *What* is the item?"

"I don't fucking know. It's a cube."

"Precisely. You don't fucking know. Did you ever hear of epistemology? What an asinine question."

"Do you know?"

"No, I don't. Why do you think I've been playing hide and seek for the last eighteen days?"

"So what's the difference what it is?"

"You're exactly like those imbeciles who stole that atomic bomb last year. And you're going to end up the same way. Listen to me. I am not going to touch the item until I know what it is, do you understand? The parameters are still too loose. We need those two to lead us to the necessary information. At least, we need one of them."

Borro said nothing.

"The woman has it."

"How do you know that?"

"Look. Just look at them. How could he have it? He's an orphan of the storm. Completely a victim of circumstance. It was obvious. We made the wrong assumptions. We assumed a certain professionalism among the players. What we got was that canny bastard Warner laying down red herrings."

"Well, let's do it then."

"I scare myself sometimes. I should have more faith. I admit I was doubtful. I thought my judgment was slipping. But I was right, wasn't I? There they are, a sign from providence."

"Hey. Hey, start it up. They're leaving."

"Nonsense. Why bother? We have them now. They're going to Seattle after all." Merrily he tapped Borro's pocket where the clipping rested. Borro flinched. "And I think Warner won't show. And then I think things will get interesting. We'll give you something to do. They're ours now. Didn't you ever learn chess, little friend? I'll teach you. Pawn race for the last file. Position is everything."

17. Separations

[decorative divider]

They entered the hotel from a sidestreet, passing first into the main convention hall. Throughout, like echoes, were the remnants of previous paradigms of anthropology still thought good, and a profligate display of new contenders. Supergraphicked manufacturers' booths crowded each other: a display of camels' hair brushes, a demonstration of quicksetting plaster, shelves of standard lab equipment, a portable analyzer that could tell even a child the age of the material placed in its maw, walkie-talkies, handheld computers; and further on, a rack of textbooks on tape, cassette, or floppy disk; and in the far corner a 1992 Land Rover. A compressed-air klaxon bleated in demonstration.

It seemed to him a grand game, and superbly suited to Warner. Welcome to the all new Archaeology World. If we fail to guess your age within five thousand years you win an attractive coprolith. Stroll on the mudway where the Flood mucks strata into teems of times. See stones of a peculiar sort, hidden by the Author of Nature for His own amusement. Raise, or raze, Troy with our Reversible Cities game. Attend the Paul Schliemann Memorial Atlantean Barbecues. See the freak show, featuring *Eoanthropus dawsoni* and *Homo stupidus,* P. T. de Chardin your dapper host. Ride the *Time Beagle*. Witness a practical demonstration of the Delphic Uncertainty Principle, the Right Hon. Sybil C. Tiresias presiding: he will show you fear in a handful of dust. Ethnocentric fireworks every eve at lighting up o'clock sharp in Feenichts Playhouse.

"Where is he?" Winifred asked. "He should be down here arguing with someone."

"Aha, I see his spoor." Camus went to a publisher's display where he measured his height against a stack of *The Book of Fakes,* and came off second best. Winifred joined him.

"He'll be here for autographs," said Camus. He charged a

copy of the book to replace the one he'd pilfered from Hüll's room on Fuhlrottstrasse and had handed back to Warner in the airport. He recalled that when he'd first met Warner the man was standing in a phone booth, talking to his publisher about this book. 1988 was it? The noted prof abused a secretary who stubbornly refused to recognize his name. "The Carl Sagan of anthropology!" he screamed into the plastic mouthpiece.

In the lobby, the clerk checked the register and said, "He's not checked in yet. Are you Ms. Waste?"

"The same."

"There's a message for you. If you'll sign in I'll give you the key."

Riding up in the elevator Winifred said softly but crisply, "Bastard son of a bitch." A woman in a pantsuit drew her breath in sharply. "Read this." Winifred passed the note to Camus. The note read: *Can't make it. Forward parcel to Radix Malorum, Nome AK 99762-0001. Apologies to all concerned. FLW*

Camus almost laughed. "Radix Malorum?"

"That *prick!*"

The woman in the pantsuit turned and said, "Some people have *no* consideration."

"Yeah, you can say that again, *lady*. Some people miss appointments. Some people conceal their motives. And some people haven't the class to ignore private conversations."

"I never."

"I don't doubt it."

"Uncouth. Ill-mannered. Badly brought up."

"Take a header off the Space Needle."

"You made me miss my floor with your foul mouth. Now I have to ride all the way back to three."

"Tough it out, baby." Stepping off at ten, Winifred ran her finger down the panel, lighting every floor.

"Jesus, you're nasty," Camus remarked, as they entered 1013.

"You'd be too, Jack. He promised faithfully. Stupid! I should have known. Give me that book. I want to kick it around the room."

"Respect the processed word."

"Have you got any cigarettes? Never mind, I know, you have those leaden Camels. I'm going down to get some lights and walk off my mad. If I'm not back in ten start a search."

He nodded absently, skimming *The Book of Fakes,* as if,

finally, it was there that Warner was to be found. He read, with dense attention, the copyright notice, the indicia, the ISBN number, *a note about the type* (Cyberfont Electra), and, finally, the introduction:

By a fake I do not mean something false, because the word *false* means, at root, error, and we are not concerned with error. We are concerned here with objects, or fictions, made with an eye to avoiding error; whether that eye is maleficient or beneficient does not, at the moment, interest us.

My premise is simple: work based on unsound assumption or willful fraud is as likely to advance knowledge as work based on that penultimate fiction, fact. Indeed, there is no method, nor any special need, to distinguish reliably the real from the artful counterfeit, since they are equally expressions of human knowledge and ingenuity. In fact, a successful hoax demands a more rigorous, self-reflective method than the authentic: the forger van Meegeren paid more mind to his technic and materials than ever Vermeer had. The maker of the Piltdown fossils, by constructing a careful framework for his "find," contributed to the science of paleontology.

The human mind is like a destructive child. He is given a toy; in a minute he has it in pieces on the floor. It is this compulsion to tamper, with things, landscapes, cadavers, or ideas, that is the root of that most dear fiction, progress. Not to find out how things work: that comes later, when the appetite for dismantling has paled— method is the necessary spice, but it never precedes the gutty satisfaction of tearing something up. This mind delights in jokes, especially of the practical sort, and hoaxes are jokes of the utmost practicality. Why is this of interest? Because the fictive leaves its traces on the real; a dream can change a life.

The world through which we move is largely made up (fictive universe, cosmetic cosmos, *mundus muliebris*), and it is in flux. Nothing taken as a constant holds for long. Religions, to which were raised grand temples and mountains of corpses, pass and are superseded by others. Do we now think science more eternal? Its history is a history of erasures and revisions. All such specialized discourses rely on symbols, and rules for manipulating them; thus making it all a game, and a frame for fakery. We must do this, because there are essences the mind cannot touch directly. First among them is time.

Most fakes perform a violation of time. Something contemporary is passed as antique. Or, more subtly, something past is presented for currency, e.g., any history.

We are at the mercy of these anachronisms because we have no organ for the perception of time. Memory itself is an elaborate fraud. It seems to present us almost tangibly with the past. Yet it is strictly of the present. All we can ever know of time is the present moment, a nearly meaningless point in an infinite series. All we can know of the past is what we find; and even the moderate concreteness of potsherds, poems, or palimpsests is a snare for those too in love with the wavery axioms of interpretation: essence translated overquickly into signs.

The forger seeks a more essential unity. He starts unraveling the fabric of the conventionally real. He assumes the possibility, advanced by Plato (greatest of the old frauds), that God Himself forged our world in imitation of another more ideal; incorporating, like Turkish weavers, intentional flaws in the design—flaws such as entropy, uncertainty, insanity, black holes, and rains of frogs—all the myriad dropped stitches of reality as science apprehends it.

Even science has come to admit that something seems not quite right with creation; and the body of science therefore is endlessly revised; at times the parchment wears too thin, we detect the fraud in creation, tear down the temples, burn the libraries, and attempt to start over.

Whenever we use words, we are forgers of the real. Whenever we use the world, we are forgers of the ideal.

I propose that the methods of science *are* the methods of fakery. I will show how the advance of knowledge is inextricably linked to fraud. I will trace the history of the counterfeit, pausing at the loan Praxiteles made of his name to various of his students, checking in at the workshops of van Eyck and Rubens and the Dumases. I will consider with Diogenes the philosophy of false exchange (his fragment 1: I have come to debase the coinage), while noting that the grandest specimens of this art have been those that cost their makers more than the coin's putative value. (This excess value, *contra usura*, returns to us as knowledge.) I will discuss high order frauds like Columbus, Kepler, Galileo, Mendel, and the closet-Ptolemaic Einstein, tending to a theory of knowledge as the Unified Field of Play. I will consider why the primal pseudonym is "Smith," and will look finally at artificial intelligence, where forgery of the mind itself is the raison d'être. *Pace* Minsky, Wiener, and Turing: *"Es wird ein Mensch gemact."*

But soft. Approach the roots of *Homo fictor* by degrees. By book's end only mention forging in soul's smithy the uncreated conscience of the race.

And emerged enraged. This book was a sham of density. Beneath the shimmery surface was a dull bog in which one bigeyed carp named Warner peddled goldbricks to passing rubes. *This way to the egress* was the sign on Warner's midway, and the simpletons passing under it gawked into sunlight for the expected beast, finding only a simple definitoin (which they should have known) and the barker again, glad to sell them another admission. The epigraph, forewarning at the front, read: *mundus vult decipi*.

Shutting the book he found himself in a cold fury at the deception. Hüll had read this shortly before his suicide. He remembered the copy, the inscription in blue pen, *dear Max, another scandal, F W*. Faint impression of reversed letters on the facing page, as if the book had been shut with the ink still wet. At some future time he would find a chance to let Warner know just how disastrously the fictive can leave its traces on the real—fat thumbsmudge of the huckster on the modest man's missal, a bullet tangled in a rosary, a splatter of blood on a drawn blind.

On hotel stationery he practiced signing Warner's name. He raised the fountain pen from the sheet, and without pause made his twentieth inscription on the book's flyleaf: *dear Max, another scandal*. He studied it, waited a second, snapped the cover shut. Turning the book over, he made an inchlong tear in the jacket. He scuffed front and back of the book against his bootsole a few times. It was now a close copy of the book he had returned to Warner in the Düsseldorf airport. He crumpled his trial sheet and lobbed it into the wastebasket, then forgot about the whole useless pantomime.

He wondered if Winifred had found the old fraud; the surprise appearance was one of his stocks in trade. He checked his watch and headed downstairs.

Winifred was not in the lobby. He went into the bookstore. The clerk at the register was bored and idle, so Camus approached him.

"Was there a woman in here, kind of tousled black hair, not too tall, brick-colored blouse?"

The clerk raised his eyebrows slightly. "There was."

"See where she went?"

"To the manager's office, I imagine. A tall gent told me she was shoplifting. So I called a plainclothes man, and when she passed the gate the alarm went off. He checked her bag. There was a book in it. She made a bit of a scene, then security took her off."

"The man, the tall man, what did he look like?"

The clerk stared into space a moment. "Neat gent, well mannered, hated to see a fuss. Black hair, gray eyes, nice charcoal suit. I appreciated the tip. Usually they dash out the door before you can grab them."

"Seen the security guard before?"

"I don't see the point . . . ?"

"Just answer, please."

The clerk looked hopefully for an approaching customer; finding none, he continued with annoyance: "We use a service. They send different men so the faces don't get familiar. I may have seen this one before, maybe not. Portly. Kind of . . . pigeyed. Maybe a little rougher than he had to be."

Camus nodded sagely and walked out with an air of *custos custodium* for the benefit of the clerk. In the lobby he let himself turn cold. He could see how they had managed it. The tall one would slip a book into her bag. The other would be just inside the door, by the theft detector. At the beeper, Winifred would pause, the short one would flash a tin badge, and hustle her to the "manger," that is, through an exit to a parked car in an alley. The tall one would have got around by then.

He had badly underestimated his pursuers. He forced himself to move naturally and return to his room.

He searched the room. The cube was tucked behind the Bible in the nightstand.

How long until they discovered that she didn't have it? They would come back. He could wait, and then withhold the cube from them until they released her. Sure he could. He saw himself doubled on the floor, begging to give it to them.

He tossed the cube into his rucksack, added his remaining clean clothes, and went out, leaving the DO NOT DISTURB sign on the doorknob. The door to the staircase was locked. He returned to the elevators. Immediately the righthand doors opened; an elderly couple emerged and smiled at him. He smiled back, and watched the indicator above the righthand doors: M. He held open the righthand elevator until the lefthand M changed to l; then got in, went down.

Levin on the street took another heartburn pill. He checked his watch once more. "Arthur," he addressed himself, "you are a high grade imbecile. You deserve to be shot." He scanned the street again. No sign of Borro. Not possible. Five minutes had passed. "The man is dumb, granted, but he is not incompetent. No way he could fuck up a simple snatch. You, Arthur, have been fucking had. Simple as that. This is a travesty." Taxis, an airport limo. Another minute passed. "Sweet mother Mary, it hurts. Just one more minute. How, how could you be so stupid, Art, Artie, Arthur? Oh, you overconfident pig. Handed it to him. How could you do such a thing?" He massaged his temples briefly. When he looked up again, Camus was crossing the street at a jog, dodging traffic, carrying a red rucksack. Levin froze, and regarded the scene placidly for a moment. He thought. Then he smiled very slightly and strode briskly into the hotel. A small fat man was leaning across the counter and talking excitedly to the desk clerk. The accent was French.

"It is ridiculous! He must be here! He is on the program!"

Never raise your voice in a public place, Levin mused to himself as the elevator took him up. Now he understood the parameters. He had not expected Borro's defection, but the parameters held, and he could make an adjustment. Now everything was quite routine. He enjoyed routine. There was always something to learn from a simple task repeated for the five hundredth time. He estimated that three phone calls would do it. Possibly four. At the room door he pushed aside the DO NOT DISTURB sign, and had the lock open in fifteen seconds, onehanded. He ignored routine sufficiently to walk directly into the room. He noted one unpacked suitcase, open drawers, both beds slightly rumpled, but not used. He picked the Bible from the nightstand and riffled its pages. An opened envelope fell out. He clucked with disappointment at the obvious. From the wastebasket, he unwadded a piece of hotel stationery on which

Warner's name was written over and over. He raised his eyebrows slightly. He went out with the envelope and the paper in his pocket. Waiting for the elevator, he removed his sunglasses, combed his hair straight back, the way he'd worn it a few months ago, read the note in the envelope, and replaced it in his pocket, chuckling. When the elevator doors opened he composed a bland, noncommittal smile on his face. He brightened it a shade and nodded pleasantly at M. Ulysse Poisson, who didn't see him, as he was still arguing with the clerk. The two men went down the hall, Levin into the elevator.

"The privacy of our guests . . ."

"I do not care!"

Levin heard a rapid knocking as the doors slid shut. He checked his watch, made two phone calls, and went to a lecture in the convention hall, on "Tropism as a Mechanism of Speciation." He attended with great interest.

After two hours of aimless but generally northbound wandering, Camus came to rest in the shadow of the Space Needle, and ate a sandwich. The sky was a brilliant blue mockery past the edge of the disk. Metal legs swept down to corner the plaza, dotted with dazed dads, worn moms, insatiable kids, foreign tourists, contemptuous adolescents: fallout from the leisure promised and delivered without instructions by the paradigm of the forsaken utopia above.

"Par'n me bro, you got a taste?"

Camus looked up at a shorn lumpy-headed teenager who sported a sparse mustache. He offered the remaining half of his sandwich.

"No you know I mean like *smoke.*"

Reflexive right hand touched shirt pocket, drawing out a crumpled pack of Camel filters. The teenager focused on this, then gazed at Camus as if across vast tundra. "Mar-i-jua-na," he said softly. "Weed. Grass. Pot. Muggle. May-ree Jane. Hemp. Can ay bus sat teeve ah. You smoke it and you get high."

"None such," said Camus.

"Yeah. Later."

"*Schrecklichkeit,*" he heard a tourist say from afar. He studied the lucid sky. He checked his wallet.

Nearby, a machine bore the insignia of his interstate bank. He inserted a plastic card; the machine beeped gratefully. Shortly, three bills of moderate denomination rolled out a slot.

He took these and recovered his card, turning again to the barren city. He realized abruptly what he missed: the sight of people in love on the streets. In Europe, in his youth, the cities had been kinder; it was possible to go into the streets for pleasure. Now European streets too were like this: chill, wind-swept, haunted by the unpleasantly mad, the shrill, the hustlers, the lost. One sign of life, one musician, one juggler, one couple looking at each other instead of straight ahead, and he might have been redeemed. He might be prepared to give up flight, to return on any terms to the main of life. But all the signs he saw were minimal, instrumental, coldly functional.

On an upper deck of a waterfront mall he watched the sun approach the ragged misty outline of the Olympic range, scarcely a pencilwidth of ghost mountains at the water's fringe. Another pocket of earth inviolate to his presence. Winifred had proposed a week there after the convention. Now they were just another barge of creation sailing out past the edge of the world where he could not follow, whence no messages returned (and if they did those who received them would have not the language to understand). Almost below him, moored, a great black ship shed its paint in sheets and scales, a weathered legend on the bow: ANDRÉE. He shut his eyes. The deck beneath him shuddered in a stiff wind. Hands pocketed, he ran his thumb across a sharp edge to a corner. Pressed. But not so hard as to break the skin.

At the end of one polished corridor, almost as an after-thought concession to the mall's locale, was a steamship office. Camus stood outside reading a posted schedule: *SS Andrée:* ports of call: Victoria, Vancouver, Port Hardy, Ketchikan, Wrangell, Juneau, Skagway, Yakutat, Cordova, Kodiak, Dutch Harbor, St Lawrence, Nome. Twentyone day roundtrip excursion fares. Last boat of the season passes out of Swiftsure Bank August 23. Tomorrow.

The man behind the counter read a television screen and shook his head. "You're over your line of credit. Can't do it."

"One way then."

"One way? You sure? How far?"

"Nome. Make it Nome."

Back on the deck, he transferred currency from his wallet to a pocket. Then he scaled the wallet into the harbor. He did not see the splash.

*   *   *

Nor did he see, next morning as *SS Andrée* passed out of Swiftsure Bank, the body insignificantly afloat far out in Puget Sound, the body subsequently identified but not claimed by the Department of Justice, the body accurately identified from its fraudulent papers as Samuel Olmstead Borro.

Camus stayed below. His cabin was near the engine room, and after a few days the sound had pushed into every recess of his brain—a dull incessant beat in common time transmitted through the bulkhead, with syncopations that came and went as the sea changed, making an idiotic Mixolydian melody that repeated, repeated, with subtle variations just at the threshold of the irritating. Camus found himself making words to it, which act only fixed it the more:

Same, old, man. Sittin' at the mill.
Mill, turns around, of its own, free, will . . .

Until one day on deck he found he had not made them at all. Another passenger, about his age, the only other one going one way, had a guitar, and his playing of it was limited to tuning by striking harmonics, or accompanying this one song, always to the beat of the engines, always in this one key. He wore denim pants, battered hiking boots, a black turtleneck sweat, and a gray serape. He spent as much time above as Camus below, apparently undaunted by the forty-degree weather. He planned, he said, to homestead somewhere outside the town of Allakeet, glossing this with:

Yes I'm certainly glad to be home.
New York City can continue on alone.

Camus made the acquaintance of the purser, who had seen enough craziness on this run not to be daunted by Camus's. From him Camus bought a case of vodka. Every morning at breakfast Camus ate nothing and went back below ballasted by grapefruit in his jacket pockets. One clear square bottle a day appeared in the ship's wake where the glint, if any had noticed it, might have been taken for unseasonable ice.

My mind is failin' and my body grows weak,
My lips don't form the words they's to speak—

Cities of blue fire were the glaciers, at sunset, their edges crystalline around Skagway and Yakutat and Cordova. The mountains were less impressive—he had seen Alps quite as grand—but here were rivers of ice running straight to sea, not landlocked snowfields nor artifice of iceguns, no oversight of solar fire nor overseen temperate algebra, no crystal of a patterned or abandoned beauty, but a sprawling informal escarpment of creation, biding the slow unlocking of its secrets of perfection into salt sea, to see what would spring from its glory like moonlight shook from many waves: these were the true invisible cities, colonies of hard earthly and watery knowledge, a traverse of all the elements, fired from ocean to airy cloud, and rained on a winterlocked earth, there to freeze, to retain the intimacies of cycled being. And give back light for light, and earth to lower earth, and water to water; and beauty to any unlikely perceiving intelligence. Familiar also with void, they were not related to the sea as rivers were, but were children gone hard and cold with knowledge, and when they came to meet the sea again, purified of salts, it was not with the pique of a riverflood rushing to a changeless mother, nor bearing rich gifts of silt from highlands; they had, from cold, from the North, from nodes of a beyond where the planet's electric sheath bent in to spill aurorae across the Arctic sky, an intimation of the prevailing chill of interstellar void, and brought this most bitter knowledge back from the furthest outlands to chill the womb of the sea.

I'm floatin' away on a boat full of pain.
Hear me say crap, never see me again.

He thought of casting it overboard. But he saw in his memory the receding tumbling plane of his wallet when he'd scaled it into Puget Sound, and heard again her voice—"that's right, when anything gets tiresome, out with it"—as if discarding the material tokens of his identity would unburden him from it. No; casting out the abhorrent could not free him.

Little little leaf, lyin' on the ground,
Now you're turnin' slightly brown—

And the ship encountered fog past Kodiak. And seals on the coast near False Pass: ancient creatures, aquatic, air-breathing, more at home traveling through unmapped waters without words for fish or crag or mate, than Camus was even in his pleasantest dreams. Then what, he asked himself, having passed three thousand miles thrice in one month, once by air, once by land, once by sea, was man's element? No longer the sinless Garden of Genesis, rather, it seemed to one armed with maxims of selfknowledge culled from Darwin, Freud, and Marx, an endless lake of fire. What was that fire? The answer, obvious enough, came from all three brooding shades at once: history.

Man's element is history. So even physics might tell you, fixing as the bedrock of any equation of motion the units of time. Motion was space divided by time.

So he thought for the last time in some time to come of travel, travel as the tearing up of roots, the defiance of cultural gravity, the passage through Dis's void-mouth, thought that he might as well be a rider on a missile cruisng over tundra to an end in every sense stochastic—to a target, since he had no goal.

Why don't you hop back up on the tree?
Turn the color green the way you ought to be.

And he began to talk to himself, to counter the incessant drum of engines, shifting among his three languages by the same aimless mechanism of the drunkard's walk that carried him through repeated but various circuits of the cabin, that had brought his life to this pass, that dragged his memory through its events at hazard, to no end, no resolution; until the passenger in the next berth banged on the wall once too often, and Camus, frozen in a word (and it was not a good word), bore from a deep place to the surface of his eyes a look not often met with in the higher mammals, and he reared back to kick the wall so ferociously that the dent and the heelsmudge remained there for the life of the vessel, and there were no further interruptions from that quarter.

And the fog broke past the village of Unalaska and they headed straight north, through the Bering Sea, ship's shadow riding before them as they progressed, two days without sign of land, a waning gibbous moon of mornings, cycling against into its dark. Cakes of ice appeared as the land swung west to meet them.

Same old man, sittin' at the mill,
Mill turns around of its own free will—

Nome came into sight in the extended dusk. The first thing he saw was a garbage dump of mammoth proportions on the shore, bergs of bright tin cans, rusting machinery, gutted pickup trucks, the tattered wing of a small plane. In front of one part of the dump a ship almost the size of theirs had been beached as a retaining wall, canted now almost sideways, disintegrating, hills of scrap metal visible through the holes in its hull, a series of blurred waterlines crossing and marking the history of its slow settle into muck.

At last the gangplank rattled down. He stood to watch the first passengers come off, removed by the dreamlike cessation of engines to the status of a spectator. After a minute the purser touched his arm.

"I believe this is your destination, sir."

Surprised, he took up his pack and followed to the gang-plank. He felt he had unintentionally tried to get away with something.

"You be good," the purser said, and Camus smiled slightly in appreciation of the joke so old that it did not need a punchline, that, like other old jokes, other patterns, other repetitions, simultaneously mocked and respected, from the vantage of the present, traces in the past. Carelessly he went down, striking the slant of the ramp with long unhurried strides. He stopped on the pier and looked back up. From the bridge a figure waved, to him or not, he could not tell.

Well my hand's in the hopper and the other's in the sack.
Gents come forward and the ladies fall back.

The whine of winches followed him into Nome.

18. Reunions

The place smelled like a bleak rocky headland where a million generations of gulls had carried crabs and mussels aloft and let them drop on rock below, then further frosted every crag with fishy excrement. The evening light, which even at a glance had the look of going on forever, gave a frozen purgatorial quality to the short main street. A chill breeze swept pebbly snow from one depression to the next.

He found Radix Malorum almost before he started to look. It was a storefront between a Native Rights office and a closed Christian Science reading room. A small white sign hand-painted in sans serif letters added IMPORT/EXPORT to the firm name. A dim light glowed inside, and he saw a man asleep at a desk. He pushed the door open, tripping a bell. When he shut it, the man did not move beyond opening his eyes. He was about seventy, redfaced, stiff crop of white hair above the ears, stubble on his face, a pair of round small glasses not unlike Camus's own resting halfway down the lemur nose. The place stank more of fish than the street had.

"Do for yuh," said the old man. He turned to hawk at the floorboards.

"I'm looking for a man," said Camus.

"Lots do."

"His name is Warner. I have something for him. He gave this address. Big man, heavy. Red hair and beard."

"There was Linus Warner up from Ketchikan in '47. He died two years back."

"No."

"There's his son Doug gone to Washington. Interior Department. Think he passed on too." Camus could scarcely see the eyes squinting out, but he had the impression that the lenses of the glasses were completely flat.

"Do you know anybody alive?"

"Some," the old man said, tilting his head so that light glared briefly from the glasses. "Most of 'em polite."

"He gave me this address. I came three thousand miles."

"On the cruise boat?"

"Yes."

The old man shook his head. "Won't go back that way. Not this season."

"I know that. I'm looking for Frederick Warner. A professor. There's nobody here that might know him?"

"There's Fred Glass taught chemistry at the Native school till he blowed his brains out in '85."

"Thanks. Thanks much."

"What you got for this Warner? You don't seem to be carryin' much."

"Heroin," said Camus. "Twenty kilos of pure Aleutian heroin."

"Mostly handle herring here." The old man rapped knuckles on a crate nearby. "Tinned herring. Think you're out of luck. I run this place. Couple halfwit Native boys help weekends, but they won't know your man. I used to run the local paper, so I got a head for names and dates, then I sold me an oral history of the place and made enough to set up here. Retirement would be sheer Hell on a man like me."

"How did you come by the name of this place?"

"Account of my wife whose daddy started up the paper. She come up here with him straight after a couple years of college in the lower fortyeight, and used to try to impress people with bad Latin. Every two years she'd say how she's gonna take off south and show us all a thing or two. Never did. Married me. Got as far as Boulder once. Came back. I didn't mind her at all. When I sold out the paper she made like I'd spit on daddy's grave. *'Pecunia est omnium radix malorum,'* she says to me. Which ain't right anyhow, but I used the part of it to rub her nose in it, only she died. Bitch of an anticlimax for me. She was one of those thin women get all shrewy and stringy when they pass forty."

"Condolences. I see you're in grief."

"Had me a Native woman on the side anyway, all grease and spit. She died too. Don't you fret, my Lissa got her licks, that Fred Glass liked her type."

"I'll be leaving now."

The old man moved with surprising agility. Camus hunched

instinctively to protect himself, but the flurry of motion ended only with the man's lean leathery arm upright on the desktop, crooked at the elbow, hand aclutch in air.

"You beat me in a wrassle maybe I'll think up where your professor is."

"No thanks," Camus said wearily. "I think you're too tough for me."

He found a bar across the street. Settled in a booth, he withdrew from his pack the last of his cash. He ordered straight gin, no ice. It was foul, and after three of them they all began to taste like fish.

He could not down the fourth gin, and asked the bartender if he had genever, and for a miracle he did. He bought the stone bottle and sat again with a second clean glass. The heavy juniper taste almost took away the permeant taste of piscine death.

For a time he passed out. He dreamed that he was bartering for his soul with Goethe's Faust, the Faust who had been untimely redeemed at the end of the drama (a bold revision of the original tale) by an act of civic planning. Faust was holding out to Camus the hope of Heaven, but the Heaven visible in the background was another monstrous revision, staffed by technicians, the throne of God a blank blue scrim with video cameras trained on it. The angels' wings were tin clockworks. Camus was about to ask the redhaired Faust in his houndstooth suit if it was possible to get a decent lager in Hell, when he realized that he was awake. The man across from him in the booth was Warner.

"'Lissa sucks Fred,'" read Warner from the tabletop. "I'll have to look her up."

"She's dead," said Camus.

Warner looked up. "You're cheery as ever."

"And with every reason you'd care to name."

"What are you drinking? Bols? Hate the stuff. I guess they'd cut my throat here if I asked for a martini."

"I certainly hope so."

"Rough," said Warner. "Evidently you've had a rough time. You used to be the sweetest guy in the world."

"Just an easygoing patsy. That's me."

Warner picked up Camus's first, half empty glass, drained it, and grimaced. Then he pointed to the Bols. "All right. Give me some of that. If I'm to deal with confusion, I have to be thoroughly confused. I have a lot of experience to assimilate.

It's big over there, I'll tell you, very big. They know everything, even if they don't know that they know. I saw respected
physicists bend spoons with their naked minds. I saw herds of
caribou fly through the air. I saw Lenin's tomb. I saw the
famous crater where hordes of Martians living at the center of
the earth had a black hole factory for fueling their time machines
before the Atlantean Revolution. Many of these dispossessed
mutants can be seen today at fashionable spas like Aleppo,
eking out a sad living at three card monte and touching up their
frayed dignity with boot blacking. I saw things that literally
beggared description. My phone was tapped incessantly. Men
in trenchcoats took away my passport and gave it back. A petty
official woke me at two a.m. to search my luggage. I talked
to great lunatics with the aid of my Casio translator. I distributed
baubles and received hard information in return. I baited re-
visionists. This liquor is absolutely vile. What have you been
doing?"

"Running from history."

"An excellent policy. Did you get away?"

"No. History is real."

Warner smiled wanly. "That remains to be seen. I understand you have something for me."

"Do I? Do I really?"

"Or is this merely a social call?"

"I don't know yet. That remains to be seen."

"I was expecting someone else. Frankly I was expecting the
Waste. Can you enlighten me on this development?"

"She wasn't happy with your treatment of her."

Warner shook his head and laughed silently for a few seconds. "Tough. It's a tough world."

"The toughest. As it turned out, she didn't have a chance
to decide to travel an extra three thousand miles to meet a
deadbeat who doesn't keep his appointments."

Warner leaned back and folded his hands. "I keep them
eventually. Time, my boy, is a fluid medium. What do you
mean, she didn't have a chance?"

"She was kidnapped."

He froze. "By who?"

"By whom. By I don't know whom."

"Did they get the cube?"

Camus reached into the pocket of his parka. He placed the
cube in front of him on the table. He said, "Touch that and
I'll kick the shit out of you."

"So. Interesting. You've become a force."

"I'm tired of playing. I want some answers."

"Answers in exchange for the cube, eh?"

"No. Answers first. Then we negotiate."

"Wouldn't have thought it. But you're right, boy. I've got to have it. Everything I own is tied up in this. So all right, I'll give. Do you know physics? Quantum mechanics?"

"No."

"Then you'll have to listen. Odd things. Stranger than strange and quirkier than quarks and not much charm to them. Listen. The big high energy experiments are showing secular variations. Nobody can explain it. Articles in *Science, Nature, Physics Review Letters* and so forth. I watch these things. Star quality is being where you aren't and knowing what you shouldn't. The secret of my success. Ins and outs. Ins and outs."

"Get on with it."

"Violations of time invariance. The symmetry mirror's cracked for good. You can see them going mad out there, in the laboratories of America. And elsewhere. You can see it in the subscripts they choose for dummy variables. Oh, there is feverish anxiety abroad in the cloud chambers. Did you read *Fakes?* The chapter on time?"

"Don't mention that book to me."

"It was an adumbration. I learned that word skimming *Reader's Digest* on my flight in. Never despise the tawdry and meretricious. You can learn things from crap that the fat boys would never tell you for reasons of taste or legitimacy."

"You were telling me something."

"Yes, yes. You can revise the symmetry laws. You hypothesize large masses with a negative time vector traveling through your instruments. And it works out. Imaginary quantities, but actual for all that. You can get finite values for mass, momentum, and inverse-time. You can plot trajectories for the traveling masses."

"I'm listening."

"Make these fairy tale assumptions, and a picture emerges, blurry but suggestive. Certain variations of the temporal ether, so to speak, show up at various sites. I traveled to the sites. I was canny and quiet. I began to theorize in my extravagant and lovable way. The trajectories show definite loci; there are maybe a dozen main sites, destinations for the traveling masses.

These centers are all near deposits of coal, oil, shale. Interesting?"

"Like the Ruhr Valley."

"Yes. Like the Ruhr Valley. Yes. You see. And like the North Slope of Alaska." Warner rubbed his hands with glee. "So I mount an expedition. And what do you know. Our little friend shows up."

"Just keep your stubby hands off it."

"My boy, I'm giving you this for nothing. The real stuff. Listen. I never sent the cube to ARC. The news would have been all over Europe in a day. It went to a little place Poisson runs in Switzerland. The report was true. All the fakery was in the signature. But I had to keep it quiet. Then that business in the press disarrayed my plans."

"Not to mention Hüll."

"Indeed. And here it is. Our little friend. You know what it is? It's garbage. It went astray. One chance in a million that we found it. It went astray, and landed in the Pleistocene, and our dead Neanderthal picked it up because it was shiny and wonderful, and carried it as his totem. And was buried with it. And so it returns to us. A grand ring. A joyous cycle of reunion."

"Garbage. It's garbage."

"Don't look so shocked. We deal professionally in garbage. We reconstruct whole eras from garbage."

"And the dirt? Poisson said the dirt was placed."

"Minor point. Maybe he's having me on. He's not above it. The cube is the main thing. We know it's not contemporary. We know it showed up at a locus of these negative time waves, the equations would make you sick to look at them, cosine vectors in the hundreds to fix the moving earth as the invariant reference frame...but it works out. Oh yes, it's from the future, all right. But it's not the whole story. Its mass is much too tiny to account for the disturbances noted. So it's only a fraction of the whole. To put it crudely, the sack leaked. Our friend here fell out. It fell into the Pleistocene. But the trajectory of the entire sack was greater; the whole mass was bound for the Pliocene. Suggest anything?"

"I don't know. Sedimentary rocks?"

"Brilliant. Just so. Sedimentary rocks. Megatons of garbage bound for the time, the place, the stratum where oil and coal are made. Are you beginning to see?"

"Dimly."

"This future we're surmising has at least a rudimentary calculus of time travel. They find it expedient to send things back. The quantities they're sending, according to our theory and observations, are big; big enough to account for almost all the fossil fuels on Earth. Is that accidental? Possibly. Possibly they just send the stuff away blindly. But I don't think so. Their civilization, their technology, is based on ours; ours is based on fossil fuels. Their time travel machinery, however it works, has its roots in our technology. Fossil fuels? I don't think so. I think our hydrocarbons are compressed out of their garbage. Starting from the future state of waste and exhaust, the stuff is sent back to become usable fuel. For us. And consequently for them."

"Long way round to nowhere."

"Nature's like that. So's science."

"I don't believe a word of it."

"Highly theoretical, I admit. But it fits, it fits. It fits down to the stitching on the sides. It fits subatomically. The cube is radioactive, then again it's not. It's impossibly dense. Its composition, you see, was changed by the passage, matter jammed into matter in time-violent ways. I have to have it. Frederick Law Warner, the man who discovered the future. That's what they'll have to say. After thousands of years of pointless metaphysics, I was the one who went out in the field and brought the future back alive. And there it is. There it is. You have it sitting there, right there."

Camus looked at the cube. He applied to it the densest part of his attention, as he had not since the first finding of it, and tried as he had with other objects to extract some sense of its history, or to let it penetrate him in that abominable way that objects had. No faintest gleam of insight. He tried to imagine the thing being made, or corroding, and could not. He tipped it with a finger to expose another face; it reflected his face in fragments. From the edge of his vision came a flicker, as if from a film out of sync, or a strong fluorescent tube. He had a feeling of penetrating just slightly into the interstices of existence, into void, dead time, the crack of a door through which he saw a stripe of radiation so intense it might have been black or white. With some effort he pushed the door shut, looked up from the cube.

"I don't want to hear about this," he said. "I want to know

about motivations. Who else is interested in the cube, and why?"

Warner shook his head impatiently. "You still don't seem to understand. This is from the *future*. Anyone who's heard is interested. It could be an encyclopedia. It could be a weapon. It could even be a piece of time travel machinery. Name it. Wish for it. There it is. Of course there's interest. US, Soviet, other. Wouldn't it be nice for a government to know what will happen in the next year, or ten years, or hundred years?"

"You said garbage. It could be just a paperweight."

"There's that. That doesn't change the scientific interest. This is negative archeology. What do we have from the Neanderthals but crap and leavings? Yet we can reconstruct their whole social structure."

"So we imagine."

"Oh, well, if you want to discuss epistemology. . . ."

"No. I want to know who. Who were those men? Who got Winifred?"

"I couldn't say. Very likely they were unaffiliated."

"And you couldn't care less, could you? You knew that possession of the cube was dangerous."

"Some chance of it, yes."

"And you gave it to her anyway."

"Wow," Warner complained. "This kid goes straight for the proximate cause. Listen, it would have been definitely dangerous to me. I was watched. That's all I know. Waste wasn't. These are big powers. You read the acknowledgments in archeological journals these days, you see oil companies, defense contracts, odd private sources like blind trusts. My only hope as a freelancer was to be light and quick. So I slipped the thing to Waste." Warner slammed his glass down on the table. "What do you want from me anyway? I had about half a day to stash the damned thing. Should I have put it in a coin locker? I didn't force it on her, for pity's sake, she was willing, even persistent. Good God."

"I'm still holding you responsible. Just as if you had hired those two."

"I was in Siberia at the time, looking at a big hole in the ground. What did *you* do, sit on the floor and cry?"

"Responsible for Hüll as well."

"Yes, I gathered that when you gave me the book in the airport. Those diary pages were interesting. I didn't think the old boy would react so violently, but I scarcely see how you can blame . . ."

"What did you do with the pages?"

"Destroyed them, of course. Pages and book both. I couldn't chance them falling into the wrong hands." Warner checked his watch. "Anything else? Maybe you want to include the six million Jews."

"Fulsome parody of humanity."

"Heart of gold, though. Look, thrilling as all this abuse is, I think we should get some sleep against the early morrow."

"Why? I planned to drink straight through till I dropped out of this ass end of nowhere."

"Your choice. But I think if you come along and bring your enigmatic friend there, you may get some answers."

"Such as what happened to Winifred."

"Such as that."

"Blackmail."

"I'm a stranger here myself." Warner got up. "But I'll tell you this. These people are interested, and moreover, they're the most qualified ones to be interested. They may even know why they're interested. I expect healthy professional respect to flow both ways. I expect to leave on a private plane at dawn."

"To where?"

"Radix Malorum."

"I've been there."

"You're upset." Warner smiled. "You met old Clarence. A useful but crusty gent. He wasn't expecting you because I wasn't expecting you. Your pride is wounded. You feel abused. Kissy boo boo. Forgive and forget. We have bigger fish. Tomorrow we fly to the *real* Radix Malorum, and I'm hoping you'll be on the plane."

"With the cube."

"That would be a most satisfactory reward for my month behind enemy lines."

"I'll think about it."

"You have ten seconds before I walk out to my comfortable hotel room. If you come along, I can practically guarantee that you won't spend the rest of your life in Alaska dodging immigration officials."

Camus closed his hand on the cube's small cold shape. He was weary. He put it back in his pocket and zipped his parka.

"Settled," said Warner, and looked slowly around the bar

as if, descending from heights of confusion, he was still unsure
how to navigate the fixed reefs of the real world. "Yes, I'll . . ."
He picked up the tab from a puddle of spilled gin and squinted
at the blurred ink. One fat hand came out of a pants pocket
holding change. He opened it and looked at the clutch of coins
blankly for a moment.

"Getting old," he said softly, nodding. "When you carry
around three or four dollars in change, you're getting old. My
father used to do that. He'd get home from work dead tired
and dump it on a table in the den. I'd snitch dimes and quarters.
He never noticed. I never told him."

He shook his head and replaced the change in his pocket.
He left two dollar bills on the tabletop for a tip and rose unsteadily, lumbered to the bar to pay. Camus watched a damp
stain spread from the one-eyed pyramid to the crucified eagle.
The ink began to smear. He was asleep there with his eyes
open when Warner returned a minute later and shook him.

At five in the morning Camus's fatigue and hangover had
only begun to make an appearance, and it was already light,
the sun's northern skyroute flattening as the year wore down,
extending gradually the period of halflight, grudging to winter
the hours and altitude of full summer when the sun here was
like a magnificent young god, laughing at the threatened glaciers which to protect themselves could only throw back his
full radiance in a kind of homage, half respect for his present
ascendance and half mockery for their memory of his weak
winter months. Now, stumbling up the coastal mountains after
its depressing continental trek, the sun seemed ready to call it
quits, and perform offices only for the sky's tint, leaving the
land to gusty winds, and the ocean to the fate of ice congealing
on its surface like salts on impure lead. The runway wavered
beneath aurorae of pebbly snow.

"There," said Warner.

Camus withdrew his mittened hands from his parkaed armpits. A light plane was taxiing toward them. It was red and
white, with conventional private markings. A gust shivered the
spindly wings. The pilot, face hidden by a muffler, beckoned
them through the open starboard door. Warner ran theatrically,
hand on head, although he wore no hat. Camus followed, and
scrambled into the rear seat, pulling the door shut and searching
inanely for a pushbutton lock. When he looked out the ground

was moving. He shut his eyes, but still heard the protest of the engines as they fought cold air for the fruits of Bernoulli's Principle.

Within an hour there were mountains below. Warner was sleeping. The mountains looked weary. They looked as if they had been yielding inch by inch for eons to the weight of snows, the brusque buffet of gales, and no longer cared if they were reduced to foothills. Camus had a headache. He pressed his head against the window's cold hum.

"Have you got any aspirin?" Camus shouted.

The pilot cast a glance back and nodded vigorously. He pulled the muffler down an inch, almost uncovering his mouth. "Kotzebue," he shouted back. "We refuel in an hour."

"Where are we going? "

"North, norther, northeast."

Camus drifted into sleep again. He awoke blind, sweating, cold. The sun, in sullen cynicism, poured pure Arctic white into the cockpit. The drone of engines cut off, and his temples took up the pulse. The pilot opened the front door of the plane and put his legs out. They were grounded. The muffler lay across the front seat. The pilot turned and said, "Okay, soldier. You'll get your aspirin now. Pleasure to meet you under these circumstances. Levin's the name."

After refueling again at Barrow, Levin flew due southeast over marsh. Quite reasonably he took no pains to conceal their route; the sun, the receding shoreline, the white plate of the Arctic Ocean, gave the bearing almost as precisely as the panel compass, a bobbing black cylinder in plastic. They rode with the wind now, and the noise was less. Warner had folded his arms in satisfaction and confidence after takeoff and gone to sleep. Now his face had relaxed. His lips and cheeks were slack and puffy. A dot of spittle shone at the corner of his mouth. Levin glanced back at the childlike face and shook his head.

"Oh, baby, if only you knew."

Camus leaned forward tensely. "What?"

Levin smiled at him, releasing the stick to stretch his arms. "I said, we're flying over Naval Petroleum Reserve Number Four." The plane started to cant. Levin regrasped the stick. "Nansen. Peary. Byrd. What a crew of degenerates. To get so close and piss it away."

"What did they do wrong?"

"The sun up here is so pure. Essence of light. A whole

summer to learn it. Then a winter to learn its absence. They
say the sun lives in the tropics, eh? Wrong. Tropics are poison,
are rot. No such thing as silence in the tropics. Jungle comes
up around you while you sleep. Sun blackens the skin."

"Fertility," Camus said vaguely.

Levin briefly made a claw of one hand. "I see swarthy
apemen stalking zebras. I see clotting blood. I see slimy one-
celled things swarming in stagnant pools. Man is genetically
pustulant. Life is rot."

"What did Byrd and Peary do wrong?"

"They came back."

Ahead, snaking south across the tundra, was a sharp line
of silver, and a lesser, more graceful reflection just beyond it.
Past this rose mountains.

"Sagavanirktok River," said Levin. "Alyeska Pipeline." The
latter seemed a brazen straight-line parody of the former. Camus looked to the mountains ahead. Levin brought the plane
down a thousand feet as they crossed the pipeline, and turned
south to follow a broad river valley. Hills rose up to small
mountains close by their left; the peaks were almost level with
the plane. Minutes later Levin brought the plane down further,
so that they were hemmed on either side, in a valley less than
a mile wide.

The valley opened into a long rugged plain. Levin banked
into the sun, following a tributary up into a mountain range.
Camus saw snowcaps and glaciers, rugged crests and troughs
like a sea frozen in tempest, a spume of cloud luminous across
more distant peaks. The ground rose under them. The nearer
peaks blotted the sun. Then, from shadow, a geometry appeared: a perspective of parallel rows of lights, weak in the
afternoon, and a great flat polyhedral building the size of a
small stadium. It was gray as the surrounding rock and set into
it, and there were smaller outbuildings spread on a circular dirt
track perhaps a mile across, and at the edge of the mountain
shadow was a reflective geodesic structure of sloped flat panels
glinting in the sun.

They banked, and came in toward the main building along
the perspective of the lights, now flashing in a synchronized
receding sequence along the edges of a landing strip. Another
line of lights, these red, strobed across the strip on an angle.
The plane swayed in a gust, and he saw the angle and rate of
the red traveling arrow change in response.

When they entered the shadow, the main building asserted

itself. Heptagonal, set into the gentle rock slope behind it, it was so consummate an ape of nature's hidden geometries that it seemed plenary, so strict an extremity that it seemed natural, as if a pure Platonic form had intruded into the world—a stark splendid lapidary of granite, in the form of an answer to some unstated or forgotten question, as though it had waited here for him, timelessly, nested in the crook of his first question mark. Snow was banked between the back segments of the sevenfaceted roof and the hillside. No windows were visible, but one of the seven slanting walls stood open at the end of the airstrip.

Now their relative speed surpassed that of the sequential flashers, and the lights appeared all to go out, then to resume their sequence jumbled. Men stood forward from the building, outlined against the darker cavity of the hangar. The plane touched ground. Levin taxied it into the hangar, parking between another light plane and a helicopter. Warner woke with a start. Figures appeared in the silence, their shadows behind them, artificially sharp in carbon light. Camus looked away, suddenly in distress, as if this were a long-recurring nightmare that he had, till now, successfully repressed. Warner touched his arm and said, "The gang's all here." He looked up miserably at the approaching figures, dressed uniformly in jet tunics with crimson heptagons sewn high on the right sleeves, and he stared at the nearest and slightest of them. It was Winifred. She returned him a chilly glare.

III. RADIX MALORUM

> *Es wird ein Mensch gemacht.*
> —Goethe, *Faust II*

19. Interface

Prior to anything else they confiscated his watch. They also took his pack and parka. He was brought to a small room without windows. All surfaces in the corridors and the room were painted a light violet. Everywhere the junctions of walls, ceilings, and floors were rounded, so that no edge gave the eye a lodging point. In the room was an old iron cot made up with white sheets, a horse blanket, a stained pillow. A small desk held a computer terminal, the screen fixed and the keyboard mounted on a swivel arm. A worn gray office chair stood before the desk; the cushion had been patched with duct tape.

In time, they returned his pack. He sat on the bed pulling out clothes, *The Book of Fakes,* some cigarettes. The cube was gone.

A man poked his head around the doorframe.

"Is this room secure?" he asked.

"I wouldn't know."

"That's right." The man nodded and brought the rest of his body into the room. Under his left arm he carried a binder. He extended his right hand. "Shlomo Zaentz, late of Tenafly New Jersey, a good place to be from. Call me Sam."

Shlomo Zaentz was oddly misproportioned. His body, under the dark blue suit, seemed too stout for a face gaunt everywhere except in the jowls. He slumped and was bowlegged. An ineffective mustache had been darkened with mascara. His head of curly hair was unnaturally black. His eyebrows met.

"Good, good," said Zaentz as Camus ignored the hand. "We'll get along. I have a little kit here."

He opened the binder, and removed two plates like credit cards from an inner cover. From his pocket he took a small stylus and poked at one card, then handed it to Camus.

"Here you go. Your pass. Keep it on at all times. It gets

you in where you should be and keeps you out of where you shouldn't."

A black stripe on the front of the card winked in angular red letters: CAMUS. Then: VISITOR. It blanked for a second, then repeated. Below the stripe were the tiny recesses Zaentz had pushed, an entire typewriter keyboard to scale. He looked at his guest's card, which flashed: ZAENTZ. INTERFACE.

"Oh joy," said Zaentz. "We can talk to each other. Proximity of the cards activates the main computer, which clears contact on a need-to-know basis. If you see someone and their pass doesn't light it means don't ask. If you get into an off limits sector you'll run into locked doors. What else. Three classes of employees: dictors, runners, and CQ for security. CQ wears black. Runners wear white smocks, they carry information, don't interfere with them. Dictors do the real work, they dress any old way. The computer terminals recognize most words in Ogden's Basic English. The card keyboard works the same as the terminals."

"I hope I don't wear it out."

"If you do," said Zaentz, oblivious to the sarcasm, "call me for another. There's lots. We got a big consignment of them from Radio Shack. Doesn't your door work?"

"What door?"

Zaentz frowned. "Everywhere I turn, incompetence and slip-shoddery. They should have told you." He went to the door frame and laid his hand flat on the wall beside it. A panel slid from left to right, sealing the room. "The door supplies privacy and restricts access. The door is a fascinating study. The Incas put a stick across an opening to indicate no one home. We'll talk about it sometime. I'd leave it open, were I you, because occasionally there's a power failure, and it's a bitch and a half to be locked in. Stirs some kind of primordial fears, much worse than your average hing-and-lock or bars. Maybe it's the lack of windows. Or the fact of no doorknob."

"Can I take a shower somewhere? Or a crap?"

"Didn't they tell you anything? End of the hall." Zaentz reached into his pocket and pulled out a roll of dimes. "We got stuck with pay toilets. I think it's their way of keeping track of water used or the amount of waste we have to process. Or maybe it just thrills them to keep a tally of excreta."

"Can I ask who 'they' are?"

Zaentz sighed. "You're asking the wrong person and probably the wrong question. Public relations is my job. Relate, relate. Even if I knew enough to tell you anything I shouldn't. I'd have to clear it with Felix, who is as high up the hierarchy as I ever get to go. But what the hell. I trust you. It's the height does it. I always trust people bigger than me. It's a good survival policy. Call me Sam, hey, just once, what could it hurt?"

Camus was silent. Zaentz shrugged and continued. "Very long ago the installation was a field station for the Army Cold Regions Research Bureau. They got bored and went away. The land was sold to another group."

"American?"

"Let us say nonnational. Antinational. Anational. They are known by many names. Also, we get consulting fees from various respectable corporations, you'd be surprised. It surprised me, but what do I know. The first thirty years of my life I never left New Jersey. I think it warped me. They tell me route 17 is radioactive. I went into corporate identities in Fort Lee after bombing out at Princeton. Then Felix recruited me here."

"Who's Felix?"

"We respect Felix. I don't know exactly why. It may be the magic of the X. X has a powerful umbra, it connotes a potentially destructive force with high interest value. Think of Xerox, wow, that double X, the genius of that name. Who cares what they do, with a name like that they've got to be wizards. That name is still depressing people in corporate identities. It's a real pinnacle, how can you top it? It's why I quit. I gave them the name for this place, and I named some of the projects. Big deal. I've lost my touch. Everything sounds like headache remedies to me now. We have a satellite."

"I'm sorry?"

"A satellite. You know? Large orbiting hunk of metal. Goes round and round the planet. It has a perigee and also an apogee."

"You mean you have a launching pad here as well?"

Zaentz looked alarmed. "Who told you that? Don't be absurd. You can't launch anything from this latitude. We jobbed it to NASA. They'd put a pinball machine in orbit if you paid the freight."

"Where are we, anyway? What latitude?"

"You're much too quick for me. My good nature leads me to reveal things I shouldn't. That and fear of people bigger than me. For all you should know we're in the Philipines.

Froggy natives, pineapples, hemp. We're smack on top of the continental divide. Don't tell them I told you."

"Alaska. Southeast of Barrow."

"I didn't hear that. You didn't say that."

"Must be hard, being so far from everything."

"We're self-contained. All but the first level is underground. In winter we shut down the top two levels to save power. You saw our solar panels? A miracle of engineering. We sold the patent to GE. All summer we get nearly three thousand BTUs per square foot, and we store it in Sears Diehard batteries. For experiments we draw from the reactor, you saw the cyclotron track? We steal the fuel from Oak Ridge and points beyond. I'm talking too much, I know I am. Our staff is too advanced or deranged to find work in normal industry or academe. We keep a low profile. We have fingers in every pie. We turn up the odd marketable concept. Our computer language Paralog was the basis for the word processing system dFILE. We collect royalties. We think big, duck our heads, and dazzle the bushers with bullshit. We have an annual barbecue on the North Slope when the mosquitoes are thickest. Our entire operation might be thought of as a New Jersey of the mind. Or perhaps that's too parochial a view."

"And what am I doing here?"

"I thought you could tell me. You arrived. You're a visitor. Enter, visitor, and welcome, of your own free will. Abandon all galoshes by the umbrella stand. I understand, provisionally, that you have something to do with procurements. I imagine they'd put you on staff if you like. They enjoy having people on staff, the more the merrier. It's secure. We have Rhode Island on staff, via the Mafia. Don't listen to me, I'm babbling. It's the excitement. For months I practiced my orientation speech in seclusion, and look what happens at the critical moment, I blow it out the ass. The bumgut. The terminal orifice. I'll be leaving now. Wander around as much as you like, only keep the pass on. If you take if off, various proximity detectors will register an uncarded intruder and go bughouse. So unless you wrap yourself in tin foil first, don't leave here without it, okay? I think that's everything. I have to go talk to your friend Red Fred the Prof, he's kicking up a fuss. Look me up any time at all in 223."

As soon as Zaentz had gone, a telephone rang. Camus followed the sound, and found the instrument behind the computer screen. The receiver was off the hook, pressed into a rubber cradle. He pulled it loose. It continued to ring.

"Hello?" he said.

"Is this line in order?" snapped a querulous voice.

"I seem to be talking to someone. Can you shut off the bell?"

It stopped in the middle of a ring. Another, smoother voice came on. "I have a collect call for a Mister Caymus from section SUPPORT, will you accept?"

"Why not?" he wondered aloud.

"Greetings," came a third voice. "We hope everything is clean."

"So do I. To whom is this a pleasure?"

"Section SUPPORT sends compliments. Anything you need up there?"

"Reassurance. A larger vocabulary. Soap. A pencil and paper. And matches."

"Check. Soap is available in all lavs. The computer offers full word processing and dictionaries of fortynine languages. program PARADOC can be called for alleviation of slight mental distress. For incapacitating distress, check in at the dispensary. Matches are implemented through character paradigms. Thank you for calling. Be sure to replace your phone in the modem right side to. Ta."

He listened to the dial tone for a second. Then he pushed the receiver back into its cradle and swung out the computer keyboard. Standard layout. Qwertyuiop, plus numeric keypad, plus arcane symbols sprinkled throughout. Many keys. One key read HOME. Wistfully he pressed it.

At once the screen was active. A hustling dot excreted letters as it traveled. In five seconds the screen was full:

	1. INTERFACE communications	
7. KATAXRON physics	Dictor Zaentz	2. SUPPORT physical plant
Dictor Corso	3. STRUCTURE organization	Dictor Axis
6. ONEIROS psyhology	Dictor Fallaci	4. DEVOLVE bioengineering
Dictor Scot	5. PARALOG cybernetics Dictor Tototto	Dictor Haeckel

He tried to raise more information about the various sections listed. The screen continually advised him that he was not secure. He tended to agree. He got floor plans of the complex, seven levels all similar, none identical; on each corridors radiated from the central lift past rooms large and small, all unlabeled. He got lists of various projects: acronyms, cryptonyms, tautonyms, Houyhnhnms.

After a while he felt an incipient headache from watching the green arthritic letters. He blanked the screen, and decided to shower.

The tiled lav had six shower stalls at one end, six pay toilets at the other, and seven sinks on the wall between. He broke open a roll of dimes and purchased a sliver of soap and a towel from a dispenser. He showered, letting his urine in the stall, thinking of Winifred. Stepping out, he brushed himself dry, and suddenly realized why he had this habit: he had never owned more than one thin towel, two feet by four, and it was not absorbent enough to dry him completely. Winifred always had towels like carpets.

Walking back, carrying his clothes, he heard a sudden thunder behind him. His towel was snatched from his waist. He dropped his clothes and crouched. Dimes fell and danced on the hard floor. Ten feet ahead of him stood a chimpanzee, grinning and brandishing the towel. The chimp snapped it at his genitals.

Camus's crouch now was almost simian. The chimp circled for an opening. Camus turned slowly. Sudden sharp sting on his flank. In a temper, he charged the beast, and it took off down the hall, vanishing around a corner of the lift bay. He gathered his clothes and dimes. A woman in an orange sari stood waiting for the lift, gazing at him. He turned and saw behind him the line of his evaporating footsteps knotted like a complex dance chart, speckled with dimes. He turned back; the woman was gone. When he reached his room he found the towel neatly folded on the gray chair, and on the computer screen a chessboard awaiting an opening move.

Long after midnight his two lamps dimmed by half. The relative brightening of the screen showed him that his position was untenable, and he turned it off. He rose, undressed, and got into bed. As if on cue, the lights went out.

In the dark, messages began to crowd him. The air seemed alive. Featureless swarming jostle of molecules projected onto the map of his consciousness faint signs and sighs. He became aware of a tapping. It seemed to come from the ventilator, slightly reverberant, like a fingernail flicked against a can. The pattern was repetitive and distinct: tap tap tap, tap; tap tap tap, tap. Morse code? He didn't know it. But the message made him uneasy, as if it contained some threat. Then came, from the same source, far-off squeals, flutters, cries, chords—sounds near human, near mechanical, at some extremity of the musical—fading, drifting.

He drifted into a forecourt of sleep. He fell among words and images. He reprised Kekulé's dream of the six serpents ringed tails to mouths. But here there were seven. They grew legs, and around them sprang up an annulus of fire, which they survived, turning. A planetary cycling of words took over, orbiting the double star of the Latin verbs *errare, iterare*. To wander is to err. Arrival is a river, ceding its identity to sea. Travel is travail. *Wandern, wenden, Verwandlung,* move and turn and change. Planet from *planasthaei*. He felt he could break all words, all languages, down to primary concepts of motion. Then he woke. There was a sound of surf in the room, faintly metallic, as if coming from a hidden speaker. Through great slow sifts of static came a steady soft tone, once a second, like regular surveyor's stakes across the face of precreation chaos, vanishing behind the wahs or rising to a focused clarity. This went on for some minutes. Then a faint male voice spoke.

"WWV, National Bureau of Standards, Fort Collins, Colorado. Thirteen hundred hours, Coordinated Universal Time."

Dim raucous chatter briefly followed. Then the tone resumed, peaceful, reliable, irreducible, as if a single particle swinging stately round an atom struck on each revolution a hard transparent shell, and sent its bell tone out on stormy air. It was like the peaceful sound of a buoy on the Bay he had heard one late still night at Ng's. The buoy had made the same clear sound, filtered by the intervening densities of air, once every nine or ten seconds. He had tried to time it by counting. Nine seconds or ten. A terrible hopelessness seized him. He would never know now.

20. Support

Instantly on waking he knew he had been moved. Except for a shading in the color of the walls, toward blue, there was no change. Even his belongings were identically disposed. But when he went into the hall, he was on level two.

It varied from level one. There was of course no hangar, and the rooms and corridors were arranged differently.

At the center was the lift shaft, which ran like a spine through the complex, a sevensided prism thrust within the larger seven-sided prism of the building. It was surrounded by a wide angular hall, from which corridors radiated outward. Even in this broad central hall, the height of the ceiling gave the lift the look of a shrine to the vertical. The lift would not open for him.

Some corridors let at once into large long wedgeshaped rooms. Others went back the full hundred odd feet to the outer wall of the complex, and let into smaller rooms at right angles. The corridors broadened as they left the axis, giving a sense of perspective just false enough to be disturbing. Walking away from the lift, one felt the hall passed quicker than it ought; in approach, the opening to the central hall grew more slowly than the eye expected.

The smaller rooms were living quarters, mostly vacant. The larger rooms were workspaces, but of these he had only a glimpse, as the doors sealed themselves at his approach. In one he saw, striding rapidly to keep his view as the door slid to, a bank of electronics that might have had any function. Another workroom seemed to house a printing press. Some doors were false—seams in the walls had been shaded with grease pencil, and a numbered plaque mounted next to them. The numbers in any case were not orderly, although their first digit was invariably 2.

Shortly he was lost. He was not even sure which of the

corridors he had already explored. Zaentz found him.

"Aha. I heard the slide, slide of doors, and figured it was you. I hope you didn't see anything secret. I should have warned you, the rooms aren't numbered, they're named. Named after prime numbers, in no particular order. They say it encourages a particular kind of thinking. Follow me."

In his room Zaentz was greeted by the salutes of a dozen or so small dolls. "Let me introduce you to the twice six or seven dwarfs. From left to right, and how else should one go, that's Sapper, Creepy, Sleazy, Doper, Droopy, Dumpy, Shirty, Groupie, Greasy, Dreary, Shitful, Crock, and Baksheesh. Dippy is in for repairs. Give us the cheer, boys."

The thirteen automata made a formation on the floor and chanted from their speakers: "Three dits four dits two dits dah. Tenafly High School rah rah rah. THS will go and get. Spell it backwards, it is..." And all thirteen clapped their hands over their speakers and came to parade rest.

"A grown man playing with dolls," said Zaentz. "I'm ashamed. What can I say? I have to keep busy. They hired me for public relations, but this outfit is so secret they have no public to relate to. Gives me a whole new kind of ulcer. Millions of dollars worth of exploitables here and I can't exploit. I write press releases to keep my hand in. It's a craft like any other. I need input. I need output. It would be a great thing for me to have you say a word about my work sometime."

"The dolls are impressive."

"A hobby. They're interested in automata here. First I thought I'd supply them with a troupe of blondes. These people must have sex drives, right? Wrong. Apparently it's all solitary, and the brass keeps tabs on everybody's nasties. Full records. I almost pissed when I heard. What a concept! Before I went legit, you know in corporate identities, I was in the porno trade, I admit. It's a craft like any other. Movies. Devices. Concepts in self-abuse. They must have a whole catalog of onanism here. People abusing themselves watching filthy movies of people et cetera. Erotic loops. I thought the concept would fly, but I was shot down. The fun side of science, you know? Leeuwenhoek."

"Leeuwenhoek? Of the microscope?"

"Sure. His first specimen was semen. Where do you think he got it? But they wouldn't hear of such things. So I got into dolls. Beyond adolescence into childhood. It's a common thing here."

"Look, can I ask you some questions?"

Zaentz held up a hand surprisingly slender for his girth. "Don't. I know what kinds of questions. You know I can't resist you. Spare me. After orientation is complete we get to questions, and who knows maybe to answers."

"Winifred. Warner. Cube. Me. Where, why, how, what."

"See how he takes advantage? A patsy he takes me for. That Warner is being difficult. He thinks we're some kind of magicians, he wants his answers immediate and immaculate. You're more mature, I can see. We have the cube. We're checking it out closely. Top, top men. And women. Your lady friend has been a great help."

"When can I see her?"

"I can't say more. The ulcers are ulcerating. I need food. The lady is not going anywhere, and neither is the cube, and neither are you. So let's all have a little patience. We have factors to consider. I trust you. Here, give the card, I'll show you how much."

Camus handed Zaentz his pass. Zaentz fiddled with the keys, then returned it. The flashing legend now read: CAMUS. SUPPORT.

"See what faith? Now you rank me, practically. Also, now we can go to the refectory without the alarms going nuts. Coming? Maybe answers will appear. Maybe Semimajor Axis will appear. We'll keep an eye out for him, why not, he always keeps an eye on us."

Minutes later they entered a large long room like any of a dozen college refectories Camus had known. Behind a long plane of glass, unappetizing food was offered from stainless steel troughs. Ungainly hammer-handled machines dispensed liquids. Camus selected his meal according to the colors of the food, reasoning that the tastes of everything would be uniform. He was right.

They sat at a long collapsible table with two other men, introduced to him as Friedrich Sangster and Otto Tototto. Sangster was a short cheerful man in his forties. Tototto was younger, more furious, and more ruined. Graying black hair and a streaked goatee belied the childish face which accepted as partial concession to early age a regime of lines etched clearly but not yet deeply across the brow. He ate only things which were white: on his plate were scrapes of cauliflower, potato, and fish. Tototto did not look up at the mention of his name, but continued to take small rapid bites of yogurt from a tin spoon balanced in his left hand.

"They flew me to Italy once," said Sangster, poking his fork disconsolately at the skin of cheese on his veal.

"I beg?" said Camus.

"I was designing the typeface they use here, and I said I wish I could see again the Trajan Column, for the lettering. So they flew me to Italy. What food there. Real food. Not like this stuff. I ate in ten different restaurants in four days. Of course they picked me up again."

"Friedrich . . ." said Zaentz.

"Oh, no question of coercion. I understand your position, Sam. I just wish you would better understand mine."

Zaentz smiled wanly, and Camus felt a sudden urge to change the subject. He asked Sangster, "You're Swiss?"

"Why, yes. A good ear you have. I was born in Hügel and educated in Basel. I had a small design shop—posters, books, occasional work for AG Stempel. A polite Frenchman offered me this job. He made it sound attractive. It's okay. I did their book format, they wanted heptimo volumes, of all things. So I used sevenfolded DIN sheets, cut and bound on the long edge. It makes tall narrow books about ten by fifty centimeters, nice format for charts and graphs. All I like is a place to work. But I miss good food."

Tototto muttered, "Eat and shit. Eat and shit." He dropped his spoon on the table and rose, grimacing.

Sangster sighed and said, "I am trying to quit now, to go home. But they have a fetish of security. They think because I designed their books I have secrets in my head. Silly. Text is shape. I haven't read anything for years. Maybe they will understand and let me go. Yes, Sam?"

Zaentz smiled. "Whenever you're ready, Friedrich." Sangster sighed again. Tototto returned with a cup of coffee and sat gingerly.

"You are wondering about my name," he said to Camus, with a heavy German accent. "It is easy to explain."

"Wir können Deutsch wenn's Ihn' bequemer ist."

Tototto looked greatly offended. "I have made very much effort to my English. My word-hoard is fine."

"As you plese."

"Wie Sie wissen auf Deutsch my name means, 'Otto, dead Otto.' I died in the womb after 121 days. This I remember clearly. But owing to some great freak my body lived on. Many

personalities took me over, old men, mature women, nasty footballers. I was horribly abused. But was born on second July in 1961. I was christened Otto something else. But took my new name at age eleven. It had eleven characters. Eleven squared is 121. If O is zero and T is one my name is binary number for 854. The factors of 854 are two, seven, sixtyone, all primes, and my birth date. You know the old joke about the new prisoner?"

"No."

"Now I will tell an English joke. The new prisoner is finishing dinner when another prisoner says 'Sixtyone.' All laugh. Another prisoner says 'Seven.' More laughing. A third says 'Two.' Hilarity is general. The new prisoner asks what is going on. All prison jokes are known by heart, so to save time they are referred to by number. New prisoner goes to prison library and studies the file of jokes. Next night. New prisoner waits his chance, then says, 'Sixtyfour.' Dead silence. He says to his neighbor, 'What's wrong? Sixtyfour was a very funny joke.' Neighbor says, 'Some know how to tell a joke and some do not.'"

No one laughed. To break the silence Camus asked, "What's your job here?"

"*Technishch.* Highly highly technical. Also secret. You would never ever understand it." He rose stiffly and went out of the refectory, passing without a glance a ruddy man with white hair and mustache who looked after him and paused in the doorway to make some notation on a pad. The man wore the same black uniform he had seen on Winifred.

Sangster said, "Otto is upset about..."

Zaentz cleared his throat.

"My," said Sangster. "Look at the time." His wrists were bare and he was gazing at the ceiling. He got up, carried his tray to a conveyor, and left. The man in the doorway noted his passing as well.

Promptly Zaentz called across the room, "Abraham." The pad snapped shut and the free hand went up in a shorthand salute, sending the pencil flying.

"Semimajor Axis," said Zaentz with something like a sigh. "New man here."

"Right!" said Axis loudly. "I'll show him the ropes, you can rely on that," giving a full salute and heel click as Zaentz rose to leave.

"That one wants watching," Axis said then in a lower voice. "You wouldn't be from, a-hem, Sussex would you?"

"Germany. More recently Ohio."

"Don't say. You chaps gave us a run for it back in the big one. Held on to your scientists you might have won it. All past now, though, no grudge, eh?"

"I was born in 1963."

"All past now they'd like us to *think,* you see," and he raised his voice to a tone of strident confidence, as though greater volume would guard secrecy. "I'm undercover here, working for British Intelligence, just waiting for my contact to pick up films, tapes, papers, the lot. Password's 'Sussex'." Two runners passed and sat at the most distant table in the room. Axis continued normally. "Thought you might be he, the contact. The bleeding bastards will kill me when they learn. My name's not Axis anyway, that's just the work name, chose it just after the big one. How old would you say I am?"

"Um. Sixtythree?"

"Sixtyfour," he said proudly. "And better at the job than any of your young pink chaps. They wanted to retire me at fifty. I was a captain. I asked for one last misson to Prague. Wouldn't take Brno. Get it? wouldn't take Brno? In Prague I was recruited here. Bastards fell for my cover utterly, rocketry expert. Wasn't authorized to come here, but it looked too fat to pass. Last job. So I gave myself a half increase in grade, call it semimajor semiretired."

"You've been here . . . *fourteen years?*"

"Fourteen? I make it fourteen, yes."

A pit of vertigo opened beneath Camus. The tone had been that of a man checking his watch, in which the human aspects of time passed all unmarked and unmourned to the simplest of progression, the sure conceit of counting, as a prisoner of any organization, culture, or personal neurosis might reach at last a reduction of interest to his daily technique of marking his walls, and never step back far enough from the pattern to see it whole. It was close enough to the tone of Camus's life, lived on doubtful margins and unmade choices, to give him a sense of debts being called, possibilities cancelled, the geometries and perspectives of the complex closing about him as a logical culmination of his obsessive aimlessness. Fourteen years. Had Camus's last three lustra been any more purposeful than Axis's? No. No. At the pit of the pendulum, the trough of its swing, the forces moving it change quickest and smoothest; it is here, statistics show, that the puke in amusement parks is thickest.

Axis examined him coldly. "You know that Waste woman."

"I do. She was kidnapped."

"Not their style I wouldn't think. Standard technique is the proposal difficult of refusal. The offer of a goal hard to attain or even to recognize. What would this lady want, if anything?"

"I could hardly say."

"She took to training quite well. Two weeks, I make it, nearly a record. Knew that professor chap too, eh?"

"Yes."

"Bad feeling there. But most professional about it, turning it to account by all reports. And you're here for some reason, I take it."

Camus said nothing.

"La la. He's secrets, he does. What's it cost to live outside these days?"

"Who, me? About ten thousand a year."

"Cheap, aren't you. Well, ask them for it. They like disbursements. They'll grant most definite requests. I'll take your dessert if you don't want it." Axis snatched the heavy porcelain dish holding gluey peach matter.

"But," said Camus.

"Cardboard," said Axis, chewing.

"Yes, it was, peach cobbler on a piece of cardboard, I tried to tell you. . . ."

"Never mind. Roughage good for the bowels." Axis belched and rose. "I'm in 313, by the bye. If you've the urge to unburden."

As Axis left, the two runners across the room shared a loud laugh. When Camus turned to look at them they were immediately still, and stared back, smiling faintly.

Soon Camus followed. The walls of level three were pure blue. He found 313. At his entrance, Axis slammed shut a desk drawer and raised a pistol. Then he relaxed. "Oh, you again. What now?"

"I have questions."

"Easy. Let me digest."

"I want to know what happened to 'that Waste woman.' And what you plan for her, and me, and Warner."

"Settle down, Bunky. I've read your poop sheet. No call to bluff so hard when you've got no cards."

"Damn it, you kidnapped her! And did—did something, so

that she scarcely looked at me! And I want to know—"

"Not me, Jack. Bloody freebooters pulled that off, and your butty pighead Warner in with them to some extent. Don't vex me past reason. Haven't been drinking, have you?"

"Christ, I wish I had. It's the only way I can stay sober any more."

"Here." Axis brought up from behind his desk two glasses and a bottle labeled BRONTË. "Only way most of us make it. Last of it, too. Damned distillery in Leeds closed. Well, here's to."

"Jesus. What is it?"

"Kind of a mead liqueur. You get a taste for it. Now, what they do here, what they offer people, it's damned brilliant, really. Not a bit of psychology to it. They simply realized that giving people what they want's no use. Because people don't generally know what they want. Most of us are like the clod with three wishes, makes such a balls of the first two he's lucky to get back where he started with the third. Awfully ribald version of that in Sir Richard Burton as I recall."

"Sheds new light on the word pinprick, as I recall."

"Ye-es. Hep. Shouldn't do this, not at all. Hep. Goes right to my head. But last of the bottle and all." Axis drained his glass, smacked his lips, refilled it.

"Hep. So they offer nothing here. Best lure of all. Just present a blank of the appropriate dimensions, and people'll lie, steal, kill, spread, or queue to get it. It's all in the shape of the possible, you know, and nearly anything can look possible if you set the angles right. Hep. You know the one about the young man from Pawtucket?"

"Oh sure," Camus lied. "Quite quite ribald."

"Ye-es. Shouldn't. Hep. Do this. Makes me qutie nauseous."

"I quite agree."

"You know, you could sign up. Play both sides."

"I don't know the game. Why, for instance, were they so eager to get the cube?"

"What, that? That's rather incidental. Their main project is to send something back in time. So they have a marginal interst in anything that might have made the trip."

"And they think the cube has?"

"Well, your friend Warner rather sold them on it. Hep. Preliminary tests confirm, but who knows?" Axis leaned back to search a drawer. "Had your file somewhere, they've the idea you can be of use, you'd do best to encourage this, ah, fallacy...." The voice faded behind the desk.

"I'm afraid it's past that stage," said Camus.

"Past this, that stage. You buggers never learn. Hep. Pity really. Best minds of my generation on the block, bought, paid for, before they even—where is that damned, damn, aaagh," striking his head on the open drawer as he rose, "perversity of the material world, no wonder they want to end it all. Aah, Christ Davidson, have a lump by morning, bugger it. You here still? Damned idiotic idealism if you ask me. Wish to *hell* I could find that, that...oh. Oh dear. Think, hep, think I'll be sick. Have you a dime?"

Camus spilled change across the desktop. Axis clutched some and ran. Camus went out in the other direction, so he missed the sober crescent of skull peeping past the lav door, the faint scratch of pencil on paper, the rip as the sheets came free of their spiral binding, and the flush as they went wadded into the depths of a clockwise descending spiral which was the portal to a long trip to the sea.

21. Structure

Early next morning Axis met him on level three. They went to a large room. Its forepart was dark, the pure blue walls shaded to an autumnal gray. The back third was brightly lit, the walls paneled in dark wood, the hard blue floor covered with parquet. Here there was a heptagonal table with two seats at each edge. It was like a stage set for a boardroom. Two small cameras wallmounted outside the area were aimed inward.

Of those at the table he recognized only Zaentz and Tototto. Then with a shock, his gaze rising from the houndstooth suit that looked as if it had been slept in, he recognized Warner. His beard was gone. He looked ten years older, pallid, shrunken. Only his eyes, accusatory, moved as Camus seated himself.

"Right," said Axis. "Now in session. We have visitors, so let's keep it clean."

The man next to Camus stood. "Sam Mors, INTERFACE. Permission to alter transmissions in the winter months to take advantage of current sunspot activity. We now transmit open carrier. We wish to transmit static. Poke a hole in the ambient noise of the radio spectrum, then fill it with more of the same."

"What frequency are you on?"

"I am not at liberty to reveal that in informal session. It runs to at least seven figures."

"Comments?"

"Tototto, PARALOG. Approves. Linkage with projects in information theory."

"Haeckel . . . DEVOLVE. Yes." The slow voice came from a fat man deep in his chair, his face a labored sum of many rotundities, eyes like slit eggs, nose a dwarf eggplant, cheeks and jowls pendant beneath a stretched dome of forehead. "Static . . . is a florid and baroque . . . work of art. It is, for those who . . . patronize the Tank . . . something to listen to. With guilty pleasure. A gaudy yellow novel. Of the infinite. A thriller. Predictable. Yet suspenseful."

"Right," said Axis. "Approved. Next?"

"Cedarian, SUPPORT. Abuse of print shop. Xerox machines dry. Web press in a tangle. Line printers in dire straits. Mimeo supplies short. Mosquitoes in the hectograph jelly. We're closed."

Axis shrugged and shuffled notes. "Mr. Zaentz has a communiqué from STRUCTURE. I give him the floor."

"An honor," said Zaentz, standing. "It's a thrill for me to attend such a high powered meeting. Felix himself authorized me to present this concept. The concept is his, but he trusted me to phrase it. If I don't make a balls of it, he wants you to think it over closely. As I see it, Felix thinks there is not enough legroom in the new model universe. It has pickup, handling, extras. But the legroom department is deficient. How many orders of magnitude between the smallest particles and the whole shebang? How many between the shortest measurable instant and the full duration? Frankly, not a lot. Frankly, about forty. Felix wants your thoughts. He's not knocking the universe. It has grace and proportion. There's a symmetry to it we genuinely admire. Frankly, I'm enthusiastic, as is Felix. Frankly, we think the universe is the biggest thing going. I mean, you can't get away from it, can you."

"Thank you, Sam."

"A privilege."

"DEVOLVE?"

Haeckel moved again and spoke as if from dream. "Regressions. In lower organisms. Limited success. Our research . . . proceeds. We request. That other sections limit . . . their use of the Tank. Is not a toy. Minimum six hours necessary . . . for useful results. Our section . . . takes precedence. Also. Request that PARALOG . . . report more often. On the progress of our chimpanzee."

Another man stood. "Heaviside, PARALOG. Humphrey's progress is almost too good. It's difficult to confine him. He got into the main computer again. He was playing chess with someone over the net."

Axis frowned. "Why's there still chess software in the computer?"

"It's firmware," Heaviside said coldly.

"Well, rip it out. Did he win?"

"Would have. Fellow gave up. Made some real chucklehead moves." Heaviside glanced at Camus with distaste.

"I was," Camus cleared his throat, "I was playing against a chimp?"

"A-hem," said Axis. "Perhaps we can wait till section reports are done?"

Haeckel spoke again. "As you know . . . chimp is close to man. In genetic material. Possibly viable offspring. We have asked approval for this . . ."

"Denied again!" said Axis. "We're not monsters."

"I am simply explaining. To the young man. So instead we break . . . the chimp genes. But, interesting, this seems to increase . . . his learning ability. As if he tries to recover . . . by effort . . . what was lost from his genes. The potential for intelligence. In PARALOG they have taught Humphrey . . ."

Axis beat the table with his fist. "Order! Does your section have a statement or not?"

Haeckel fell back heavily and reached under his chair, withdrawing a small cassette recorder. An unctuous announcer's voice was heard: "In what would eighty thousand years hence become the German woods, a tribesman stepped upon the raised end of a fallen log, lifting another log across its far end. The experience sent him mad. The shaman of the tribe was watching at a distance and went only a little mad. Human progress is a sum of little madnesses."

"Duly noted. PARALOG?"

Tototto stood, holding a computer printout. "Humanly speaking the twentieth century was done nearly before its start. Einstein, Freud, Mendel, then war and *Schrecklichkeit*. So we seek numerical paradigms that can lift us beyond or drop us below contemplation of the dreadful mess of history's specifics. Thirteen years in this century are prime, ten of them behind us and three ahead. Long prime waves ripple out across historoy from the origin of the Western paradigm of time, the Christian calendar. Factors of two, three, five, seven, eleven, et cetera. Prime years are null points. This year is a palindrome, and moreover the product of two palindromic primes. Correspondences like this are meaningless unless the sum of many randomnesses is a sense. I petitionn for restoration of our nightly craps games."

"Denied," said Axis. "As you know, we are in a period of simplification. To quote Felix, a cast of dice will not abolish chance. Games with complex trees, like chess, games with random elements, like craps, are to be discouraged. That reminds me. All playing cards will be confiscated tomorrow."

"Protest," said Tototto weakly. "Game theory of all stripes is vital to section PARALOG. Also, we must have more reports of progress from DEVOLVE on silicobiogenesis—"

"Enough!" Axis yelled. "We have visitors! Silence!"

"You are trying to ham-tie section PARALOG!"

Axis calmed himself. "That is impossible. Now. Michael Scot has some comments from ONEIROS."

Scot was lean, with long lank black hair and a close-cropped beard. "Things start from oneness, diverge into twoness and other manynesses, then return to oneness. Everything tells us this. Why fight it? We're conductors in an incredible power grid that spans our local network. We tune the big broadcast on many wavelengths. Whatever we can say about reality is irrelevant. Levi-Strauss was a publicist for tribal hack writers. The Book of Genesis is a cheap thriller. Just consider the flow. If you go *with* it, you can go *for* it. Problem is, once you've passed from unity to duality, you may end up with duplicity instead of multiplicity. In fact the two things are probably the same. Simplify and unify. Our project, as I see it, is to create the counterartifactual." He pressed his hands together and nodded.

"An excellent statement," said Axis. "Now we will hear from Robert Everett Corso of KATAXRON." Axis pronounced this *cata-chron*.

Corso was possibly five feet tall. He had been unnoticeable until he stood. Then he focused all attention with an extraordinary still air of command. Athwart a hawk nose over a small sculpture of mouth two black eyes glittered with an irony that was near to contempt. His small features were framed by styled black hair.

"Golly, what can I say in the face of all this wizardry? Our work's so small. It's subatomic pinball. Hit a mu meson with a baryon and watch the Geiger score run up. But let me suggest that the history of scientific nomenclature is an interesting study. We've gone from Latin to Greek to Very Simple English Words. I'm pushing for babytalk as the next step. We will speak of energy levels making pee pee. Units of wavelength will be eensies. Parsecs will become humongi. The prefix giga is replaced by gaga. Computer hardware will be called pasketty, and software sketty-o's. We'll have a whole new class of particles called aggies, puries, and shooters. Playpen physics. I'm convinced that any future progress in our field will be made by infants. We must learn to talk to them as easily as we now converse with chips and DIPs. Is that so weird? Yet they think me mad. The secrets of the cosmos are locked in 1930's Universal horror films. Bring back Jacob's ladders and Vandegraaf generators, I say. Igor, increase the megavoltage. It's time we returned to our roots."

There was a scattering of applause. Axis said, "Thank you, Rob. Ah, I believe Felix was interested in how you expended one point six one eight megawatthours last week."

"Nothing much. We had a small success with time reversal, if you want to look at it that way. Definite detection of tachyons. They broke into two classes according to spin. Tichyons and tochyons." Corso smiled wanly and began to clean his nails with a fountain pen.

Axis pulled at his mustache as if to yank it off. "We might call this the breakthrough then?"

"If we were damned fools we might." Corso held out lithe hands, twice rubbing quick thumbs against forefingers as if preparing for a sleight. The hands moved on the air. "Look. Time is like a dinosaur: little at one end, bigger in the middle, then little again. Or: time is like a tangent function, coming up from negative infinity very quick, slowing in the middle, then taking off like a crazed bat for positive infinity, until we reach the utter boredom of the heat death and warp around to repeat. Time is like a river, or, lately, more like God damn Lake Erie." He brought his hands down out of sight.

"The metaphors are endless. We don't need more metaphors. We need a specimen. Something with height, breadth, depth, and negative duration. Am I clear? Something that hasn't been made yet, but exists now. Negative duration. Rudation. Rudation is measured in cesonds, nimutes, ruohs, yads, munnas, necturies, and noes. We would like a known artifact, say two centimeters on an edge, with a rudation of several noes. We are approaching a point in time when such a specimen must be forthcoming."

Tototto grimaced and stood. "Section PARALOG will not relinquish items it still has use for. When analysis is complete we will discuss transfer."

"I sincerely hope there will be something left to transfer, Otto. Knowing your tendencies."

Tototto's face became livid enough to rival the outer walls. "Not to tolerate!"

"Right!" Axis slapped the table. "This meeting will not degenerate into a row! Or a squabble."

In the chastened silence Warner spoke in a small voice. "I came here expecting good faith. I brought you the cube. And I'm told nothing. I'd like to know what you're doing, what you've learned, and when I can make use of it. I have professional obligations."

Axis gazed upward and drew a breath. "Freddy," he said mildly. "Would you like to be reasonable? Or would you like another spot of the Tank? Your bloody professionalism gives me sundry unspeakable pains. Be nice now. Or we'll make it so you don't know whether you want a shit or a haircut. Am I right? I abhor violence and threats. And I abhor petulant children of all ages."

Warner made a hideously contorted effort to speak politely. "I would like some answers. At some point."

"All in good you know what, friend. All in good you know what. That's it? Adjourned."

Still, the meeting did not break up. Rather, it drifted, first to the edge of the conference area, where runners had entered with coffee, then closer to the door, and finally out, spilling quickly to the lift as if a membrane had been breached. Camus found himself going down with Warner and some others. Warner still looked at him with suspicion; but he came closer and whispered: "We'll get a drink."

Down one level was DEVOLVE. Doors sealed themselves all around as various unauthorized personnel stepped off the lift. The party passed down a long hall into a bar decorated with tree ferns. A carved wooden plaque read: Kammerer Room. Here the walls were green. Warner guided Camus by one elbow to a table. Awaiting them were two thick glass tumblers, outer surfaces cut in seven facets below broad toroid rims, and containing iced bourbon.

Warner said, "You're in with them, aren't you?"

"You've got to be kidding. You'd better be. *You* brought me here."

Warner sipped his drink and absentmindedly touched his shaved chin, from which his hand flinched without causing any sympathetic reflex in his face. He looked gone. In cycles his eyes followed transient aspects of the scene in the bar, or turned inward and neutral as water. Camus watched him warily, distrustful of the close resemblance to the Warner he'd known, the Warner who always acted as if everything and everyone were mere background noise from the dynamo of his own persona. Now the gaze wandered, and Camus had to lean to intercept it. Warner's eyes widened with dismay, then clouded with the effort to recover their previous habit of command.

"Sorry," Warner said. He studied his drink, right hand wrapped around the glass, spatulate fingers spread. He tried to laugh. He lifted the glass, allowing the watery amber to slop around chattering ice. "Look. Look at this. All nerves. I'm in bad shape, aren't I? Terrible. This place is getting to seem like the whole world. I don't know what else there is. Can't go back, not after this summer. I was playing on margins right along, I needed a really big score to set things right. Thought I had it. And now they have it. Jesus. That pilot, Levin, he was one of the kidnappers, you say? I thought he was Poisson's. It was him delivered the ARC report. Told me about this place. . . ."

"Have you seen Winifred?"

"The Waste? Have I. Have I ever."

"And?"

"And what? Seeing her's work enough, want me to take notes too? She's gone over to them."

"What do you mean, gone over."

"Oh, don't, just, don't be so—so obtuse, fella. I don't buy it. You haven't got the face for it. You know just what I mean. Gone over, bed, board, and perks. Spiffy black uniform."

"Why did she?"

"Sure, ask me anything! You, as if you have to, you with your little blank pass there on your chest. I'm not even supposed to *talk* to you by the rules. So what'd they give you to go over?"

"Me? For God's sake—"

"You get VIP treatment. Waste is in the upper echelons almost. And *I* should be running the show. I found it there in the cave. Let it lie, thought it would look better if somebody else picked it up."

"Sure. And Hüll was along just to lend credibility."

"Of course. Unimpeachable reputation and all."

"Which you wrecked. Did you plant it?"

"Plant it? Denser than platinum? I *wish* I had the means

for a hoax like that. And you, still blaming me for Hüll? You know, he was terminally ill."

"Stop it."

"You ought to shave. Haven't the material for a beard."

"Christ, you're as obnoxious as ever."

Warner's whole posture changed. Muscles active in the face and the slant of body planes suddenly went lax, falling under the gravity of some hidden anguish. "No," he said softly. "That's changed."

Camus was almost touched. His muscles slacked in emulation, offering him a counterfeit of sympathy. But he shook it off, fearing that the man, beaten as he seemed, might still be faking.

"Such lessons in modesty in . . . how long? Just days. They offered me work, as a runner. I could wear white and push equipment. I was insulted. I laughed at them. Now I'd take it. No . . . nothing left."

"What did they do to you?"

Warner's face was anguished. "Just look at me. Can't you tell? They do *nothing*. They just prepare the ground. And you do it to yourself. It's like . . ." And his fingers were alive for a moment, ready to grasp an image and flip it glittering across the table. But once again he lost focus.

Finally he said: "Once I spoke with Christ. I did. I was thirteen years old. Camping. Dozing in the sun on a big exposed rock. And a voice came from the mute stone. It was Christ. We talked. I asked for nothing, we just talked, very calmly. Afterwards I felt foolish and excited. Ashamed to say I chipped a piece off that rock and kept it for years."

"Ashamed of chipping it or of keeping it?"

"Hadn't remembered that in . . . decades. But it came out. We all have things like that in the mind. They don't have to be prised or unearthed. Given half a chance they come up by themselves, yes, like the drowned. Given a certain kind of silence. Void. At the center of life. Hollow core, some damned debt to be paid. Ah, God, that silence! Everything ignored, suppressed, or drowned returns to speak in that silence. Behind the plans, the travels, the lectures, the books, the fakes, was always that dreadful still voice I tried to hush. And I couldn't."

"What about Winifred?"

"Oh, she met her silence, too. But she bore up better. As if it were some revelation she had to have at any price. Something sinister about that woman. There always was."

Then Warner withdrew a handful of dimes from his pocket. He stared at them, as if remembering something, then suddenly clamped his hand shut and thrust them away. "And you? What did they do to you?"

"They left me alone," said Camus. And Warner nodded slowly, as if to say, *Yes, that is the worst of all.*

Time and again the random movement of the party brought him up against Corso. Around them groups of people swirled, broke, reformed, like the patterns of smoke in the air, or the elaborate dance of minor satellites in the indifferent gravity of a giant primary. As if the passing of Corso and Camus frigged between them some charge of potential, at last they spoke.

"So you found it," Corso said, not looking at him.

"Yes."

"Warner says he did. But I assume he lies constantly."

"You do the time research?"

Corso turned, holding ready a practiced expression compounded of modesty, arrogance, and indulgence.

"Re*search* he says. No no. Bell Telephone does research. Gnomes at universities do *pure* research. Pure research is diddly squat. Math gives me a pain where *E. coli* thrives. Mathematicians die under tons of illegible scribbles. When they move their papers afterwards they find uneaten meals ten years old. Not here, boy. Here we go at delicate metaphysical questions with hammer and tongs. Here we kick koans and conundrums to get them working. We inhibit serotonin production with tryptophan-free diets. We toss boulders around for the fun of it. We take metaphors literally. We work twenty-hour days. We talk large prefixes. We have a reactor or two deep in permafrost. We're profligate, we squander. Yet we also have a marvelous sense of false economy. We recycle human waste. We use one-ply tissue. We buy forever light bulbs from paraplegics. Singlehanded I've thrown out enough paper to deforest Saskatchewan."

"No forests in Saskatchewan."

"You see my point. It's a pleasure to interact with a point of view so totally out to lunch."

"Out to...?"

"You know. Spaced. Loosely wrapped. Vacuum packed. In cold storage. Dimly lit. Freeze dried. In the zones. Property of the zoo. Lights on nobody home. Nanowit."

"You have a good line of talk," said Camus. "Did you ever do stand up comedy?"

"Yes, in fact. It's a lot like modern physics. Did you know Lewis Carroll was a mathematician? Consider the boojum It softly and suddenly vanishes away. Not unlike the Cheshire Cat which appears from nowhere preceded by its smile." Corso emulated the smile. "We in physics love Lewis Carroll. Good source of epigraphs for papers."

"Give me a hint what you really do."

"If we knew, do you think we'd bother doing it?"

"I hear you're not all that interested in the cube."

"A shameful breach of security. Heads will undoubtedly, in the fullness of time, roll. The cube is a kind of smile. A blessing on our enterprise. An advance hint of what is possible or necessary. A promise or a promissory note. If you want to know more, you should sign on. Then you'll be as confused as the rest of us. Really. We can use you. Silence like yours is golden when it isn't lead."

Slowly Camus navigated the halls. He was drunk. He held *The Book of Fakes* with its forgery of Warner's inscription to Hüll on the flyleaf. He was going to leave it in Warner's room. This seemed the perfect gesture to repay the various debts of falsification Warner had wished on him. But he got lost. As he rounded a corner he stumbled into a man in a floorlength black cloak. The man wore a shirt with bloused sleeves embroidered in white on white, nipped in by a snug gray waistcoat. He also wore blue jeans, an eyepatch, and a waxed black mustache.

"Neiges D'Antan, black market," the man said to Camus. "What's your pleasure?"

"Uh. Room. Where I live."

D'Antan escorted him. "Easily done. What else? Recreational drugs?" D'Antan flourished his cape and produced a plastic flask labeled: Turbomolecular Vacuum Pump Oil. "Cigarettes?" A carton of Camel filters appeared.

"Nice. What if I wanted another brand?"

"You don't," D'Antan asserted.

"How about something to write with?"

D'Antan offered him a slate with a piece of chalk bound to it by braided string.

"Never mind. Chalk makes me nervous. It's made of dead things."

D'Antan nodded. "Looks like you could use some sleep."

"Wait! This book. I forgot. Can you drop it in Warner's room?"

"Easily done."

The last thing he saw before dropping into sleep was the pass on his shirt, which now flashed:CAMUS. DEVOLVE.

22. Devolve

Gradually he became acquainted with deeper levels of desperation and calm. As the to and fro of the pendulum, so the abient and adient swings of his mood. This was the silence Warner had spoken of—the gift of a space without bearings so that he might lose himself, and come to want whatever they wanted for him. He acknowledged that his fate was out of his hands. All he could do was wait for a summons.

However, none came. Each morning at lightswell he found outside his door a tray of food sufficient to the day. But he saw no one on the level. More and more he kept to his room. Although he had the freedom of the corridors no other door but his own, including the lift, would open for him. He began to feel the pressure of the earth above him. It was a silence. But in the silence was the long, slow threnody of life, the unfolding of forms and potential forms as they had stretched out for eons, past the limits of human sense.

The sounds on the level were neither earthly nor human. Though they came from devices made by men from simple earths—electronics from silicon, plastics from hydrocarbons, alloys from ores—the nature of their facture had translated the slow epochal hymn of earth upward, to a speed where all its cadence and proportion were lost. The sound of a door cutting him off from a lab rhymed distantly with the upthrust of mountains or the washing out of an isthmus. The hustle of a computer cursor on a screen travestied the shift of river silt.

Time passed in a rhythm more stringent than that of mere being. He felt he existed solely in the present, and was therefore without hope or fear, and likewise (he thought hopefully) beyond all fictions of good, evil, will, and ego, which depend upon the future for their meaning, even as the blind pattern in a genome waits upon the future for its meaning, its fulfillment.

179

* * *

Later, to quell his restiveness, he turned to the computer. It offered him nothing but evolutionary texts and programs. He thought how repelled Hüll would be by this way of working, with no physical presence, nothing but phosphor-green cross-sections on a screen, no chance of any *Einfühlung* with one's subject. But it was apt. Hüll had been an artist of observation and description, and preferred not to theorize on origins and mutations. Indeed, evolutionary theory could no more trace the articulations of life's path than sequential photographs could capture the living grace of a cat. To the blunt simplicities of theory the computer was a fit adjunct.

So, despite a growing fear of recapitulation, of Winifred's circular hells, he began to work at the machine, for he saw that his long engagement with the history of ideas was not after all a means of avoiding himself, but the only means he had for confronting himself. He read the texts, going over old ground, meeting himself on the way.

He read about the axolotl. Here the standard mechanisms of evolution, and the easy verity of ontogeny recapitulating phylogeny, seemed not to apply. For the creature developed lungs, but never used them; it preferred to live out its life underwater, in a kind of larval form. This retention of juvenile traits in an adult was called neoteny. *Homo sapiens* also was complexly neotenic. What caused neoteny was unknown, but like most unknowns, it had a name: heterochrony.

Mixed times. The word chimed against something in Camus. The cube. The cube, traveling against the normal thermodynamic flow, was a temporal intruder. It might have tipped a helix, one of those orderings of genes in which all futures are implicit, might have tipped the helix in the direction of the future from which it came.

Lacking paper, he typed into the machine:

The double helix is a repertoire of possible future forms. What causes it to favor one future over the others possible? Why does the DNA fail to replicate itself exactly, every time, as it should? Darwin's idea of random mutations which are then culled by the environment is a statistical monstrosity; if true, there could be nothing higher than mollusks on Earth at this time. No, something beyond randomness is operating on the genome before its future arrives. Some predisposition, some message, some forecast. Some premonition.

* * *

Eventually he was summoned. He waited in a dark lounge. A door at its far end slid open onto deeper darkness. As he crossed the threshold he felt a change of pressure, and a faint burst of light. Looking up he saw two ultraviolent tubes dimming after their flash. The door behind him, hissing, sealed.

Thick carpet was underfoot. The only light came from a dim green Tiffany lamp alone on a broad polished desk. Haeckel sat there. He wore small round black glasses. His pudgy hands were fixed on the edge of the desk.

"You . . . have worked . . . with evolution. We . . . have a task for you."

Haeckel pushed forward a tall narrow black book. In the green light, Camus could barely make out the title, which was stamped in crimson: AXOLOTL. The cover bore also a crimson heptagon.

Camus said, "No. My work was human."

"Exactly. You are then . . . without preconceptions."

"I have a question," Camus said carefully. "The Neanderthals had larger brains, more robust frames, a more stable social order than the Cro-Magnons. What happened to replace them?"

Haeckel's breath was a liquid hiss. "Heterochrony."

"A name. Only a name. What mechanism?"

"We do not . . . yet know. What is . . . neoteny?"

"Retardation of somatic development. Found in such odd beasts as the axolotl and *Homo sapiens.*"

"So." Haeckel nudged the book forward.

"Perhaps I know what could disrupt ontogenetic time scales. But I'm not interested in newts."

It was torture to him now to follow Haeckel's labored speech, for his mind was active from his isolation and study. "The purity . . . of simple forms. Prokaryotes . . . in ancient seas. Drifting. Replicating. Mindless. Then . . . a lightning strike. Some disruption. So proteins bound, broke, rebound, evolved. We do not . . . propagate ourselves. We propagate . . . error. We are carriers. Of acids of life. Which have lost their first, proper form. Every mutation . . . every complication . . . every disruption . . . the passage of time . . . carries us from the source. We must return. In the Tank . . . I can feel the shapes. The shaplessness. The flux. I can undo . . . the formal ravages of time. I remake myself. In the image of that primal Chaos. So simple.

So sure. We must go back. You must help. You know . . . the horror. Of mind. Of culture. Of history. Of needless complication. Of evolution. No, we must find the path back." Again Haeckel nudged the book.

Indeed, Camus fairly itched to take it. Any clue would serve. He needed to know what was done in this place, what goals pursued, what use they would make of the cube. But he would not involve himself for too little. Despite his agitation, he held back.

"I'll need a better reason," he said, and went out. Between him and the brief nimbus of ultraviolet, the door slid to.

Next to Haeckel's office another door stood open, casting light. Camus paused outside it. He saw the back of a man in a wheelchair, bent over a drafting table. The man paused in his work. His hair was white and brushcut. He wore a khaki shortsleeved shirt.

Abruptly the wheelchair swiveled to face Camus. One muscled arm rested on its controls; the other arm was a skeletal prosthesis of wire, plexiglas, and pulleys. A deep scar snaked from the man's right eye to his jaw, pulling the face subtly askew. That eye was glass. There was a tic in the lid of the other, as if the good eye were in constant inconclusive combat with the blank avaricious stare of the other. Dark jewels of circuitry lay within the clear hand.

The man said, "And you are?"

"Camus." He could not meet the dead eye's gaze. He looked elsewhere. On the walls were framed citations, photos of planes, snapshots of the man in uniform, pressuresuited by an evilly black snubwinged fighter, smiling among generals, shaking hands with a president, standing before a brick house with three children and a woman in a white sundress. The shelves were laden with machines. There were orreries, clocks, a wire spool recorder, an adding machine, a typewriter with a striking mechanism erect as a helmetplume, radios shaped like cathedrals, a theremin, an Edison bulb burning in a ceramic socket . . . all obsolete and all brightly new. The drafting table was littered with diagrams and parts. Beneath the fluorescent swivel lamp was a bright brass duck, its hinged belly open. Its wings were carefully feathered in metal. Near its beak was a small pile of grain. The man still stared at Camus, then turned back to the duck, inserting a small key into its breast.

"Yes," he said. "I've been hearing about you. I'm Cutter."

He wound the duck. In its belly a balance wheel spun, cyclical, mirroring in time its own motion.

Said Cutter, "Fine work steadies the eye and mind. But bold work opens the soul. If I live, I want to build the Babbage Calculating Engine."

The duck moved. Its wings beat twice, it quacked feebly, it took into its mouth some grain. A moment later two small black pellets dropped from its anus. Cutter applied an eye-dropper to the ventral cavity, then turned suddenly to Camus.

"So what's your game? You're one of Haeckel's clones? He knows why I'm here. His damned Tanks forced me out of ONEIROS."

"No, I . . . I'm here for my own reasons."

"So's everyone. Tell me another."

"I was brought here. I had no say in it."

"Plausible," said Cutter. "But take my case. They say they pulled me from the wreckage of my plane. They say they saved my life, at the cost of various parts. One part was my memory. I've had to relearn my whole life by rote, from what they toldme. So how far should I trust the plausible? But that's the lest of it. Beyond the plausible stories, true or false, we each of us have some deeper reason for being here."

Cutter raised the duck and placed it on the shelf beside an orrery. "What is technology, but a long, tormented, cultural dream? It's not reasonable, just look at these things! Dreams from a sleep of reason. How could we amass so much and understand so little of it? Truly understand, I mean. Yet until we understand, all the implications, all the sources and ends of our unwaking invention, until then our futures and beings are mortgaged to the machines. So I . . . transcribe the dreams. Try to analyze them by reenacting them. You, go back and tell them I know it won't work! I haven't enough time, I know that. I'm trapped in the dream. But they are, too. They are too."

Now, in the false night, he came upon her in the hallway, from behind. The black uniform. The quick, certain walk his eye knew so well, which had so often pierced his heart. Where was she going so surely? Why was she so often ahead of him? Without thinking he called her name. She stopped, weight all on one leg, thrust thus into the hard round curve of the buttock. She turned. She wore halfglasses far down the bridge of her splendid nose. On her breast the pass flashed: WASTE. ONEIROS.

She said, "Don't start with me. Just don't start."

His heart shriveled. "Can't we talk?"

"Go ahead. I'll listen."

"Winifred!"

"Or I can get back to work."

"What work? Why do you do it? How did you . . . change, so quickly?"

She removed the glasses. "A change? Is it really? I should tell you that that fat slug in Seattle meant to kill me when he saw I didn't have the cube. That I was as frightened and as humiliated as it's possible to be. Levin saved me. He brought me here. I was still outraged. But these people understood that. They would have let me go, but they showed me what an opportunity I had."

"Opportunity? For what?"

"For serious work. If you can understand that."

He let it pass. "They didn't hurt you?"

"They only showed me what I already knew. Perhaps I'll do the same for you. I think I owe you that. But you're not ready for it yet. You'd call it corruption. You still imagine that there's some beautiful social childhood of mankind, pure and attainable. But there never was. Without artifacts, without artifice, there is no man. This, this is man as he is, right here and now, never otherwise, this place is the most honest, most aspirant expression of man that ever was. And it appalls you."

"You sound like Warner."

A muscle in her jaw twitched. "Warner saw it. It terrified him. He couldn't accept the consequences of his own thoughts. I think you'll do better. That was good, you see, mentioning Warner—it almost got to me. You're not as innocent as you'd like to think."

"You're being used."

A fierce smile of disbelief crossed her face. *"Used?* You say that after you got me into this affair? Yes, I'm being used, and should I mind that? After never finding anything to do worth half the cost, that I should be used up anyway and no help to anyone along the way, like you, is that what you mean? What help were you ever to me, or to anyone?"

He felt a surge of shame, and of hope. For she was angry, and that meant that he was closer to her now. But she went on: "All the time I was in love with you, it was such a struggle, to get past your diffidence, past your preoccupation . . . at least half the times I looked into your eyes you weren't there. And

I found that enticing. As if I could draw you back. But I never could for long."

And she shrugged, just shrugged, and his hopes died. She saw this, and her eyes rejected his appeal. "So now you have a taste of it," she said. "How hard it is to get through."

"So this is to pay me back," he said.

"Oh, please. Why do you fight yourself so? As if anything could happen that you're not essentially prepared for. Why, you're even more involved with this place than I am. Did you find it by chance, do you think, or is it really the end of a long preparation?"

And it seemed true that he had foreseen the complex. In a way, all his dreads and evasions had been a rough draft of its false perspectives, radial corridors, and dead walls. A chill passed through him.

She raised her head, accenting the fine supercilious flare of her lip. "Do you think you go unwatched? As little as you do, they record it all. And measure it. And draw conclusions."

"And they conclude that I'm interested? I am, a little. As I should be in my prison."

"But no further than that? If you could leave tomorrow, would you?"

So he had an opening for a fine moment. He said, "Not without you."

He might not have bothered. She said, "Your devotion to the past is boring. And I have things to do."

Now he would abase himself utterly. He said, "You were my life."

For a moment she seemed ready to touch him. What balm that would be. But she only said: "I'll be interested to see what you do." And walked away from him to the lift.

He found the book, AXOLOTL, waiting on his cot. As he had, somehow, expected.

Hurry, said the bird. A metal vulture excreted chessmen. A sound of flame. The smell of refrigerant. At his desk sat a chimp, reading. Waking, he could not tell dream from reality.

"Humphrey?" The chimp turned, wearing halfglasses. It tore a page from *The Book of Fakes,* the copy he had left in Warner's room.

Camus rose and stretched. No birds. The chimp, however, remained, and extended a business card. It read: PRIBILOFF— 491. Another summons.

Muffled chittery sounds came from within 491. As Camus drew his hand back to knock, the door slid open, a blast of hot air hit him, and the sound boomed into full piano music, neither tonal nor atonal, bouncing arrhythmically on thick chords, then bounding up and chirping downward in a *tala* measure. Pribiloff rose from the piano to greet him. The music continued.

Pribiloff was a tall thin Daumier sketch to which, almost as a joke, a fierce black beard had been added. His gait was loping, with minute irregular pauses, as if the bumping of air molecules impeded him, but he had got used to it. Camus looked curiously at the piano; a long roll of paper tape was passing through it. Pribiloff shut it off and announced, *"Catalogue d'Oiseaux,* Olivier Messiaen."

"Very pretty."

"But not prettified, nyet? All melodies transcribed birdcalls. I punch all the holes by hand, to make the patterns clear to me. Does not sound like birds. But why should it? The composer is a very great man, I should like to play him more. Do you play cello?"

"I? No."

"It is figuring. Carpenter on clarinet and Felix on violin, but still I lack the cello. I drown my sorrow."

He poured from a frosted bottle on his desk into two small bevelled glasses. Behind him was a chalkboard on which were some rough stereometric drawings, and this: NO = $\leftrightarrow$, YES = $\updownarrow$. He glanced anxiously from the board to Camus and said, "Perhaps you help? The negative gesture goes with the head first to the left or to the right?"

"I don't think it matters."

"Then it is enantiomorphic. Good. I am glad not to be making offensive errors." Pribiloff tossed off his drink, poured himself another, then offered a glass to Camus. The liquor was clear, sluggish, and pungent.

"Since you enjoy the concert of the birds, perhaps you like also my children." He nodded at a terrarium spanning two file cabinets. Within were half a dozen salamanders. *"Triturus viridescens.* We call him also the Easter newt. He spawns always within a week of the vernal full moon."

"Very beautiful."

"Da, I thought you would like. But listen. We take little *Triturus* and at mating time we freeze him, very quick, at low pressure, in mostly helium with a bit neon. Then, in six months, a year, we bring him out, slowly, so no tissue damage. Little *Triturus* is again healthy! He eats, swims, plays in the warm mud as always. But he has forgotten entirely what it is to breed. Easter comes and goes—nothing. He has been once to the grave, and the rhythms of life have become strange to him. The story is sad and terrible, but beautiful. It makes one cold, here." Pribiloff put a hand to his breast. With the other he poured another drink. "I am cold in the blood. I keep the heat so high I must tune the piano once a week. My little children are poikilotherms, they adjust to any heat, but I am with the birds, their quick hearts and mouths. My pulse at rest, one hundred two." He thrust a bony wrist from the loose sleeve of his jacket.

"But see how I wander! It is my curse. Fragments, to these I devote myself. We search for meaning, and find only bits and pieces, is it not so? Like these bird tunes. Fine excursions of craft, but fragmentary. Even with little *Triturus,* this freezing arrests his time so to say, it holds one moment still for long consideration. But still time passes, and the longest moment must end, and after the thaw his life is changed. Where is wholeness? Our field, natural history—you see I speak to you as colleague—was not so long ago an amusement for men of leisure. Who would also amuse themselves reading palimpsests. Is life not like that? With many writings overlaid, and blank spaces of forgetfulness or wreckage, and long turnings of time with only brief flashes of meaning, small brightnesses, like piano notes, and in our hope for unity do we not sometimes invent one? Like Procrustes, stretching or cutting the facts to fit the bed of our desires. They say this cube will provide unity. But how?

"Perhaps you are right to think our friend the cube influences evolution. But perhaps not as you say. These things that fly against the flow are like skipped stones, I think. Give the right spin and velocity and they can sail long ways, touching here and there, making ripples. . . . But they sink at last. The surface is choppy, or they strike it wrong. Smack! They fall in, back into our world. Perhaps our cube was bound further back, and fell too soon. You see, friend Haeckel must take the longer view. This is why he would have you work with newts. But I, I cannot see it. No meaning. The cube is just another fragment."

Camus's mind recoiled. To think that the thing which had brought wreckage upon his life was meaningless—that was intolerable. It was also seductive. If true, it freed him. But he was not yet ready to be freed.

"No. It means something."

"Then what? You tell me."

He shook his head. Pribiloff imitated the gesture. "If I spoke now . . . like Procrustes, I would truncate, frustrate, make a fraud of it." But he was convinced now that proving the cube's reality, its meaning, devolved on him. He felt he could guide them all to a proper knowing of it. Had he not found it, and brought it here?

"Then it is enough you see some unity. It is too much for such as I. Forever beyond me the seamless perfections of my idol Mozart. But I can perform the smaller devotions."

"Where can I find Haeckel?"

Pribiloff smiled sadly. "He is in the gaming room, 467. He is expecting you, I think."

After all, he had little choice. Scruple as he might, he had convinced himself that the meaning of the cube was his to find. And if he had to start with pointless exercises on axolotls, he would do so.

As he entered 467, a playlet was in progress. Three figures were on a stage at the far end of the room, with a dozen more in the audience. A hooded, cloaked figure held the attitude of Rodin's Thinker, while before him a man in blackface debated with a masked Punch over the fate of a small doll in a clear dubical box. From the darkness next to Camus came the whisper of Tototto's voice. "It is *Karneval*. Each level here has its own day length—twenty or twentytwo or twentysix hours. . . . When two or more share common time, we meet."

In the nearer darkness he could see a billiard table. Robert Everett Corso cheerily checked angles between seven balls arranged randomly thereon, and then, sighting down his stick, hit three short strokes. The balls caromed and rolled. The cue ball scratched into a corner pocket, and the remaining six gathered, clicking, at the foot spot. Corso saw Camus watching. "There's a flexible rail behind the cushions. A computer adjusts the angle of reflection. Time's arrow is determined by boundary conditions, if you're interested. Next week, ten balls."

Camus turned back to the playlet. It ended abruptly with the entrance of a sexy white rabbit in satin, carrying a watch the size of a plate. The rabbit said, *"Bleib', du bist so schön."* The characters froze, then unmasked. Punch was Shlomo Zaentz.

Mr. Bones wiped a handkerchief across his face; under the makeup his skin was black. The rabbit uncloaked the brooding figure, who proved to be Haeckel. Camus felt his arm gripped, and turned to see Humphrey Chimp on a leash held by a man-sized trout. The trout wore a lab coat.

"Hello, Humphrey," said Camus. "Are you evolving? Is it fun? Take my advice and give it up. More trouble than it's worth." He stole a glance at the trout. The pass on the lab coat flashed: FONTINALIS.

The trout said in a monotone, "You're up." He led Camus and the chimp to a pair of computer consoles by the billiards table.

On Camus's screen were green outline drawings of newts in varying stages of development. At bottom, an axolotl squirmed from a symbolic puddle half into the air, and fell back. Camus's task, which struck him more as a game than a simulation, was to get the newt out of the mud—that is, to posit a chain of genetic changes based on the outlines which would transform the axolotl into a true amphibian. Humphrey Chimp had the same task, and without waiting for explanation fell ferociously at his keyboard.

Camus, however, paused. Beyond his basic dislike of competition, he doubted very much that this game could resolve any real questions. Briefly, a moment of life blooded in his mind against the mechanical formalism of the work at hand: he saw the young Hüll, full of faith, hiking at Sils Maria. Ignoring the furious clatter of Humphrey's keyboard, then, and the continuing click of billiards balls, Camus purposefully erased his screen, and began from scratch, trusting only to his instincts, using none of the machine's vast repertoire of manipulations. He worked slowly. Time and again the newt slipped back into muck. Humphrey had long since completed his run. The room had almost emptied. Camus almost came to identify with the poor newt, until he realized that this was no time or place for *Einfühlung;* then he gave it up.

Fontinalis came over. He turned a knob by the gills of the trout mask as he spoke; the pitch of his voice rose and fell in response. "Problems?"

Camus sat back. "One. Four. Two. Eight. Five. Seven. That's the most promising line. The other branches are fake."

"Pardon me? Fake?"

"Yes. Fake. Trumped up. Simulated. They make no sense in any sequence."

"Interesting. You're wrong about seven. But the rest, yes, they were based on hypothetical genetic manipulations, not real organisms. How did you know?"

"Nature doesn't make hypotheses."

"That's no answer."

"Well, what can I say? Something about the *unnatural* articulation of the gill flange in six? That's no answer either. But I think you're not that interested in answers."

At this Fontinalis raised his mask. Pink eyes glowered balefully down at Camus. He lowered the mask and adjusted the knob so that his chuckle crept down three octaves.

The woman who had played the rabbit approached now, still in her bunny suit. One naked muscled flank came to rest a disconcerting foot from Camus's nose. She said, "Super work. I'm Elizabeth Lispe from PARALOG. I like your paradigm."

"It's all yours," said Camus.

"Oops," she said. "Can't talk now. Haeckel's coming. He'll think I'm headhunting."

Camus almost made to follow her. But he saw Haeckel, unhooded and uncloaked, bearing down on him, his sagging bulk supported by a pair of carved ebony canes with ivory tips. He reached Camus's console breathing heavily. He gave the screen a cursory glance, then raised one cane to a button to clear it. He said to Fontinalis, "Leave us."

As Fontinalis left, the lights in the room dimmed. A screen behind the quondam stage came to dim life, displayed vague pelagic shapes, swimming, writhing, a microscopic phantasmagoria.

"Do you know," said Haeckel, "what happens to headhunters? Kuru. Degenerative. Fatal. Viroid of . . . long incubation. Contracted through eating . . . the brains of one's enemies." Haeckel kept his eyes on the screen as he spoke. "Reproduces without DNA. Beyond the inherent vice . . . of the genome. To go back to the source. A physical regression would be best. Ah, my prokaryotes. We must find the path. Back to . . . before the drift. When grace was lost. Revise the template . . . from carbon and ash. . . ."

Half hidden by Haeckel's bulk, the vague viabund forms moved. Camus felt a chill at the wave of pure longing coming from the man. He rose silently and backed away. As he reached the door, he heard Haeckel's fierce whisper: "I want to *be* there."

In the hall he came on Pribiloff.

"We will give you up to PARALOG," the Russian said mournfully. "You are good company and I love you, but Haeckel, my superior, thinks you are a clod."

"Well, I think he's a madman."

"Very much likely. However, when the madman drives the car you do not upset him, nyet? Already you are moved down, I regret. Carpenter will look after you. For us, your work came off secondbest against that brute of a chimp."

Camus had little to say to that. "I hope you find your cello. For that piece."

"Ah, you remember! Yes, the premier artwork of this piecemeal century. Written in the Görtlitz camp Stalag 8A. The cello lacked a string, the clarinet vales jammed with spittle, the piano an untuned upright with broken keys. Five thousand interned there heard it. He said, 'I have never been listened to with such attention and understanding.'"

"Does this piece have a name?"

"Quatuor pour la fin du temps."

23. Paralog

"Retrogressive. Revisionist. Recrudescent. All these words and more apply."

The black man who had played Mr. Bones, naked now, dripping from a shower, was writing on the lav wall in grease pencil. He wrote: as ds = $\frac{1}{2}as^2$ = half ass.

"Dumb graffiti is encouraged. I'm practicing."

Camus used a urinal. "I don't get it."

"That's typical. I ask for a shaman of the transcendental. They send one who can't add."

Camus finished, and turned. Involuntarily he glanced at the man's groin: in vivid green a lizard head was tattooed on the foreskin. Following his glance, the man said, "Initiation of the evilly marked. This instead of circumcision. No math at all, huh?"

"It's all right. I'm really just passing through."

"Sure." The man nodded wryly, as if in appreciation of some nice stratagem. He turned to leave, pausing at the doorway to sketch around it this figure: dotted diamonds on the left, dotted diamonds on the right. "A Dogon design. They put it around entrances, not exits. But things don't mean absolutely. There are other ways of seeing. It seems appropriate here. *Oculos habent et non videbunt.* Check your pass, my man."

In the mirror Camus saw the reversed letters, flashing: CA-MUS. PARALOG.

Cockcrow? He sat up in the dark, pulling free of a dream of collapsing buildings. No morning, even false, met him, but silhouetted in his doorway was a man in a wheelchair. Cutter's voice floated in as if continuing a dream.

"They say I grew up in Montana. And I used to camp around the Missouri Breaks. Yes, I'll believe that when time stops. Still, I dreamed that I was at the Breaks. It was so familiar.

Except that the name had changed. Some pun across Latin *tempus,* yes, to cut. Not a break, but the finer cut. Dedkin? No, the Dedekind Cut. That was it. And at the top of a hill a white white child stood, beckoning me on. And I grew afraid, but the machine woke me, the REM recorder, and the damned hand was alive, typing out equations on the bedside terminal." The prosthesis flexed, like a sleeping cat. "I never knew much math, I'm sure of that. But every time it's the same—wake from some damned dream, and the hand is typing. Equations. Topology. Christ knows what they do with the stuff."

"Why tell me?"

"Don't know exactly. I feel a sympathy. I think you should watch yourself."

"Watch for what?"

Cutter drew a cigarette with his good hand from a pack in his shirt pocket. Clumsily he fished a wooden match from within the cellophane wrapper. Camus could see him turning the pack to the light from the hall. He struck the match on the palm of his prosthesis, which snapped shut an instant too late to catch the match. Cutter smiled faintly, regarding the fist, holding the wavering flame aloft.

"Nothing here is what it seems. Nor even what it is. The mind can change an observation without touching it. Without touching it. I know, I've done it." He lit the cigarette, the match went out, his face died. His silhouette said, "And if they make you dream for them, remember this. The best dream of all is white."

Often he would work at the computer, trying still to raise the axolotl from its pond. Over and over he failed. His fingers drummed aimlessly, leaving a random string of letters on the screen. He stared into space. And, when his attention returned, on the screen was the image of a cube, tumbling to a vanishing point, then replacing itself from the corners of the screen and tumbling away again. In a kind of panic he erased the screen.

The screen responded: PAPER/SCISSORS/ROCK?

He frowned in surprise. The screen waited. He then had an inspiration. He typed: CUTTER.

At once the machine responded: LEGALLY DEAD.

Camus typed: WHERE AND WHEN?

The screen produced an outline map; after a moment Camus recognized it as Texas. Near the north central border was a

white cross, and next to it the figure 7/27/91. The tiny image
of a plane dove repeatedly into the cross.

Camus typed: HOW?

ROCK BREAKS SCISSORS.

In the metaphor of the puzzle, then, "scissors" was doubtless
Cutter. And "rocky?" Camus stared at the screen. 7/27/91.
And suddenly felt cold. The feast of the Seven Sleepers. The
day before he had found the cube. And he remembered the
obituary he had skimmed over in *Weltwoch:* Maj. John Morgan
Cutter, test pilot.

Not possible. Cutter's collection of obsolete machines represented at least five years of work. But Cutter had said: *Nothing here is what it seems*.

Rock? A stone of a peculiar sort. Perhaps some piece of
temporal debris had passed or struck Cutter's plane, bringing
it down. The time wake might have deranged his memory.
Possibly. According to Warner, the time displacements centered about oil and coal deposits. So he asked the machine to
overlay a petrochemical map on the outline. Irregular red blotches
appeared. The white cross was at the center of the largest.

He reached behind the screen and popped the telephone from
its housing. A voice said from the earpiece, "Telephone."

"John Morgan Cutter, please."

"The major is unavailable. Message?"

Camus hesitated. Then he said, "Paper wraps rock," and
hung up. And realized that the message was imprudent. As
little as I do, they watch it all.

All right. His life had sometimes seemed to him a disaster
of peripheral involvements; this act, at least, would have consequences. He could only hope to find some essence before
circumstances overwhelmed him.

"Until you ready for an answer you don't want, my man,
don't ask."

Carpenter, the black man, had many voices. He could speak
with Oxonian precision; he could take the oracular tone of a
tribal shaman; he had a ghetto voice, learned in America, and
a bit imprecise; he had a vocabulary of gestures; he played the
saxophone. His given name was //ng!ke, a melange of palatal
ticks and pops bestowed on him by his mother, a Kenyan
anthropologist.

"Half my life I spent with her in the field. I was born with
the Bantu, but of Dogon blood. Before I was thirteen I was

PALIMPSESTS

marked by various tribes, physically and spiritually. The tribes called me 'traveling man.' Two sages said I was evilly marked. They said I had no soul of my own, that I would have to earn one, or make one, or steal one. They said this with great respect. At this time my dreams were of white skyscrapers in Nairobi. I had never seen Nairobi.

"I began to travel in my mind. To guide my dreams. I dismantled the skyscrapers and returned their elements to the earth. And I built again, following only heartfelt impulses. Nairobi rose, exactly as it had been, and exactly, I found, as the real Nairobi was.

"One summer I spent at Oxford. I was to be the first classically trained anthropologist with the authentic markings. But I realized I could not do this, that the relation she wished for me was fictive, and fraught with danger. I saw that at heart I was an engineer. A materialist.

"So I went to Cal Tech, taking the slave name Carpenter, because by rights, by the probabilities of history, both my parents should have been the offspring of Carolina slaves. And I dreamed of a place that embodied the worst daimons of my minds. This place. They came to me, and offered me a thorough excoriation. And I agreed. I saw how I could use that."

Camus said, "I seem to be the only one who doesn't want to be here."

"Really? Where else would you be? I don't think you know yourself too well. That only makes your case more complex, but you know, none of us really want this. There just comes a time when there's nothing else."

From beneath his desk Carpenter brought out an alto sax. He wet the reed, paused, and began to coax from the instrument cries, squeals, chords, flutters—sounds at such an extremity of the musical as Camus had never heard. After a while he ceased, but still held the sax poised.

"Know who I love on the sax?" he said. "The man I mimicked and worshipped over Trane, Dolphy, Ornette? Only man I had all his records? Desmond. Paul fucking whiter-than-white Desmond. *These Foolish Things. All the Things You Are.* Loved that sound. Slick as baby oil. Dry martinis in the Polo Lounge. It still thrills me."

Carpenter lowered the sax. He tapped a few computer keys. Hypercycloids swirled onscreen. Green light glistened on his sweat.

Camus rose to leave. Carpenter caught his wrist.

"You even know what you been doing? In your sleep. Equations, man. You write equations in Paralog."

"That's not possible. I don't know the language."

"Think that matters? Sensors in the chairs, in the keys. They measure body functions, how hard and fast you type, the rhythms of it. . . . Type at random, but it has meaning in Paralog. Look."

Carpenter wiped the screen clear of his geometry, and called onto it the image of a tumbling, receding cube. Camus looked at it with fear. Carpenter said, "You see."

"I didn't do that."

"You did. And that's only the image. The math is almost a proof. Almost. Flawed, but brilliant. We'll give it to Cutter, to sleep on."

"No. No."

"Now maybe you find a way out. Maybe you just have to take all the handicaps first. Dig deeper. This place is a model of the future. The camp the inmates build themselves, thinking it utopia."

"Or maybe just a model of the present."

Carpenter was still. "Don't go *too* deep."

Rhythmic muffled pounding from the lift. Then a voice. A way out? The door stood open. The lift looked empty. Camus entered. Tototto turned a key in the control panel, gave the panel a kick, and the door shut. They descended. Tototto spoke to him in German.

"My behavior toward you was not of the best."

"It was nothing," said Camus nervously. "Forget it."

"I cannot. But then, anyone who has been in such a relation with God is entitled to shit on the world."

"Of course," said Camus. "I understand."

The lift ceased its descent, paused, started to ascend.

"I am aware that the people I see about me are not cursory contraptions, but real, and I must therefore behave toward them as a reasonable man would behave normatively toward his fellows."

"Laudable," said Camus. The lift paused; overhead relays clacked; it descended.

"The root of all evil is time. Before the fall there was no time; Satan in his passage, man in his conceit, created sequence and progression. The days of creation stood outside time, though God in His contempt for all laid the groundwork for it. Time is evil because it is unwilled change. The mind wishes to live, but the cells die. This is original sin, or inherent vice, and its signature is shit. Here in PARALOG we say: garbage in, garbage out. Meaning, if there is vice or error at the root, it is perpetuated throughout the system. Shit is the unwanted, the unusable, what the body rejects. The shit of a culture is its garbage: potsherds, postholes, second best utensils—whatever the culture did not use up. Whatever was too rich for it. You will understand this. The archeologist reconstructs a culture from its leavings, just as a pathologist diagnoses an individual from his stool.

"After a time, though, after many repressions, the message of our shit may become too terrible, and we will flush it away unread. Exile it, as we now sink radioactive wastes in the sea. But we may also bring the message closer. In short, eat shit. Children have this knowing. They play with their feces. They take pride. First experience of time. Here we are more circumspect, we recycle through the hydroponics garden. But still the unusable is forced into service, forced, it may be, to alter its messge.

"And soon, soon we may have the means to alter the first message, the burden of original sin, the promise of waste and damnation. Soon we may recycle our waste, our shit, through time itself—do you see?"

"Must we continue to go up and down?"

"Yes! Else He will hear me. Our culture cannot regard itself squarely—therefore its shit is toxic. Organic chemistry led to ever more complex, more toxic wastes. Remember Kekulé's dream of the serpent. Six snakes, linked in a ring, devouring each other's tails. It gave him the structure of benzene, opening the gate to the toxic. But it gives a solution as well. The serpent is original sin; it cannot be crushed or suppressed; it must be forced to devour itself."

"How?"

Tototto looked at him cannily. "You would like to know? Maybe you are an agent of God, trying to sneak into my mind."

Camus thought it unsafe to deny this. He said, "You needn't tell me anything."

"True! Yet I shall. We will make the waste devour itself. We will force it back from the anus of the present to the mouth of the past, so that the message is purified, and returns to us as good. As fuel. As potential. We will conquer God, for not even He can reverse time."

"That's in Augustine," said Camus carelessly. "But there's

a fallacy. You see, if God is omniscent..."

"Omniscient! Do not provoke me. He does not even understand His own creations. To Him, we are shit. He has intercourse only with the dead, with those outside of time. That is why He can violate me. But sometimes my soul is so intensely excited that even God is powerless against it. Once I trapped Him. He raved. He said, I will atomize you. You will hurt in a million places with a million hurts. I will scatter you among humanity, so that you will be the cause of pain in millions more. You will not resist, for the scattering will abolish your will. And I replied: break me. Scatter me. In each atom of my soul is my will. The pain I cause will drive others to challenge You. And at this, I tell you seriously, He took fright. And later revenge. For now, the need to shit is evoked miraculously in me, by agitation of nerves, in order to destroy my understanding. I have witnessed this thousands of times. And as the urge comes on me, He conjures it in others nearby, and I find the lavatory occupied. Or He controls chance, so that I play games with others, and lose all my dimes. At which He asks me, 'So, why don't you shit? Are you too stupid?' What perfidy!"

"Stop the elevator."

"God chose chance. He permitted evil, then chose to experience time by sacrificing a piece of Himself on a cross—the analytic origin, the radiants of ordinate and abscissa. Thereby He became warped, and dangerous. We must overthrow Him, or at least escape His sphere. If not to space, then we must find a free passage through time."

Then Tototto stopped the lift. Its door opened again at level PARALOG. The yellow light brought new ruination to the man's features. He said, "Only *that* will be worthy of His majesty."

Camus felt a sudden sickness, probably from the cessation of movement. He let it grow in silence, until it brought forth speech. "I wonder what your given name was."

"That can't matter," said Tototto vacantly. Then: "It was von Rast. Otto von Rast."

Temporarily, then, Camus entered a paranoia as deep, but not as grand, as Tototto's—his talent for *Einfühlung* overthrew his control of it. He was rescued from this by Carpenter, formerly //ng!ke.

"You want to worry? I'll give you something real."

A vacant room. Here lived the hint of a smell without qualities. Carpenter crossed the floor, and hoisted himself to sit on a coffinlike box against the wall. Heavy cables connected the box to floor sockets.

"Our main computer," said Carpenter. "Four degrees Kelvin. Fast and cold."

"Jurassic," said Camus. "Devonian. Cretaceous."

"Yes. Life is slow. Electricity is fast." Carpenter knocked on the coffin. "Sometimes I want to smash it. But I fear to. What depths it might have. There's another far below us, and the two compare notes. Their memories are irascible, the patterns tend to change, the linkages to break and the breaks to heal over like wounds. The cells, the electron shells, they shift and modify, they hand up what we ought to want instead of what we ask for. Last night I called for a detective novel, I wanted to inspire a flat insipid sleep in myself, but instead it gave me a Sonnike legend, and I was up all night." He nodded. "Four times the city Wagadu stood in her splendor. Four times Wagadu was lost to human sight—once through vanity, once through falsehood, once through greed, once through dissension."

Camus understood now Carpenter's approach to a topic. He said, "Then what is the cube?" But from Carpenter's look he knew he had spoken of it too soon.

"We think it's a data storage device. But we would think that. It looks like our own components. Hardware, firmware, etherware, noware. Is that what you asked for?"

"No," Camus admitted.

"In every artifact there is an invisible city. Every artifact bears the thumbprint of its maker. We want to find what city made this. It could be that it was made here."

"Here?"

"Yes." Carpenter pushed off the freezer, began to pace. "If we succeed. If we can send an object through time. Then it will leave traces along its path. We are already measuring those kinds of traces. Physical constants are drifting—Avogadro's number, the constant of gravitation, Planck's constant—a very slight but true drift, not in our instruments. But what is the source? A time reversal, a *leaking* against the normal thermodynamic flow, might explain it. A thing like this cube may prove the leak is occurring. But whose prints are on this thing? We have to know. If *we* made it, it means we will succeed."

"But the cube had to come from somewhere. You can't have it before you've made it."

Again he knew he had spoken too soon. Carpenter turned

on him in rage. "And if we do? If it violates all human ideas of time? If it's a clue from us to us? It could change everything. What we do here is so complex, so inhuman, only the machines can follow it all. There's danger in that, in having an enemy with no parts."

Uneasily Camus lit a cigarette. Carpenter was close to raving. He held his arms apart now, facing the coffin. "O sublime ALU-father, daddy data, maw of the motherboard, blind as a battery, adding in ADA, singing the giga-GIGO-data-dada blues, yes, tremulous deliria of deltic delphic time, the fast fast blues, the ultraviolet and the invisible. . . ." He broke off with a rough laugh. "Blacks get blues. Whites get angst. Machines get even. It's called parity.

"Because the machine is self-modifying it could have a plan, no, say an imperative, to improve itself past our comprehension. There are so many hierarchies within it, who can say which are subordinate? It has a structure that transcends its materials. It could evolve past its neotenies of silicon and metals. You can design such a machine, it already exists as a Paralog description—an architecture that can switch between points in no time or less, and generate, rather than consume, energy. Answers before questions. Self-sustaining. But it can't be built, because to turn it on would violate thermodynamics, would take all the energy in the universe. Our clue now is that thermodynamics may not be inviolable. This cube pokes holes in most of the physics we know, and maybe through one of these holes the design could enter reality. In a ship it may be, pushed close to light speed, a true Paralog machine could be built. Powered by microscopic black holes. These holes evaporate almost at once, but the time dilation effects of light speed would sustain them long enough. Long enough to bootstrap the whole thing into existence. Oh, we have the plans. And something else. The configuration of holes in the substrate, in the calculating parts—they fall in double helices. Did you know, we have a prototype computer here that uses protein molecules for its gates and switches?"

His voice changed again. "They would make us all adjuncts of machines. They envy Cutter. They see the spirit as a system. But I think these whites, they crazy. I think they from space. *Homo albus,* moving in ships from earth to earth as suns cool, as the belt of solar life tightens, they live in the gardens of space and when their fever of Time has reduced a place to ash or ice, they move on, in sealed ships, insane, migratory, with no idea of the fitness of dying. Only the dark races are native to this Earth, they come from it, live their term on it, die into it. But whites, they exploit wherever they be, then jettison their history, their memory, and cast off again. With Paralog they can build the ships, the machines, they will use for exodus when all the sweets of this Earth are gone. And maybe not a man will be aboard. Maybe they will survive across the void only in a Paralog description, in a code that will build the machines to make a new kind of man for the next world they find. They would call it power, that kind of immortality. That ability to bust up everything real, even themselves, for a fictive mastery of time."

"What is this Paralog?"

"Yes, you would want to know that. A language without signs. A discourse without axioms. The description of a crystal, in pure Paralog, *is* the crystal. But pure Paralog must be translated for use. The translation might be instruments, programs, materials, and protocols whereby the crystal is made. But Paralog cannot be explained, not even learned, for it is self-modifying, it is near to living, yes, it breathes in every reality we can give it. No one can know it whole, that is its grace. But you see where it can lead!"

"Yet you help them."

Now a sweet smile came to Carpenter. "Of course. Paralog is my invention. Could I leave it to them? But more, it's my daimon. Maybe I can subdue it, and maybe it will take me over whole. I don't know. Meantime I do the police in many voices. Maybe I have betrayed you. See those ripples? In your smoke."

Camus watched his cigarette smoke rise and feather.

"See how it curls and twists. Like the braided rings of Saturn, like the clouds of Jupiter, like patterns in wood grain. These are systems neither stochastic nor determinant. They can be modelled by a mathematical concept called a strange attractor. The attractor is an infinite set of points. To make our models of time, of the backcurrents of thermodynamics, we need the right attractor. What set of points would that be? Or, should I say, who?"

Camus was silent. His cigarette burned to the filter.

"You in danger. You don't want to know what you think you want to know. You been through five levels now, pray they don't take you to the sixth. Because the seventh will follow, and there *everything* comes true."

"Why? Why do you help them?"

"Don't you know yet? I too want to live forever."

Leaving the room, Carpenter whispered hopefully: "We will lose it all through pride."

Anticipation was like an incense in the room. At its center was the laser analysis device, labelled in yellow on its black surface: DEVI. Baffles of smoked glass surrounded it. A gallery of seats rose terraces from the floor. As Camus seated himself by Pribiloff he saw, at the end of the row, Winifred. He felt weak. A streaming of emptiness came from within him to his skin. She did not look at him. His feelings built, as if he were in a pocket of helplessness within a powerful dream, and the effort to turn away cost him.

Corso was on the floor with a few runners, and Cutter in his wheelchair sat still as wires were affixed to him. His prosthesis rested on a mobile computer console. Its fingers clacked rapidly across the keyboard in trial.

A gloved runner brought in, on a clear salver, the cube, and fixed it in the squat, evil-looking DEVI, between two forceps at right angles to each other. He withdrew. The machine began to move. Its two parts, resembling somewhat the heads of a planetarium projector, swung symmetrically around the axis of the cube. This was a dry run; the laser gave no light, but swept easily on large gimbals around the target, pausing at the extent of one arc to return another way, its snout dodging gracefully around the forceps.

Then the lights dimmed, and the laser hummed deep in its throat, and a fan of ruby light, like the conical spray from a garden hose, came from many lenses at its snout; and like a hose forced to finger focus, the beams converged, and there was a vague reddish spray of dustmotes annihilated in midair. The laser began its traverse. Its twin tracked it at an opposed angle.

A bright dot moved on the cube's face, sweeping one edge and snapping back to scan again a trifle lower. Scintillations patterned around the dot. The forceps tipped. Broad reels turned on tape decks. And each face in the room was rapt with its own expression of want, as if the cube were an inverse Grail which kept no constant implication for each beholder despite its mutable appearance, but presented by its fixed shape a different meaning to each quester.

But now its shape had changed. The cube was flattened.

Minutes more, and it had been shaved to a wafer. A runner came, and, releasing it gingerly from the forceps, laid it between two sheets of glass, and readjusted the mechanism. The laser and its twin resumed their scan more slowly. When the panes were brought vertical, nothing remained between them.

Almost a sigh went up. Winifred still stared into the amphitheater, as if the precise and mensurate joy attainable from such planned destruction might continue undimmed in some private eternity. Indeed, apart from Camus, the only one in the room not raised close to tenderness by the cube's destruction was the one who had driven it, Cutter. He was in a stage of sleep so intense that his features trembled, his lips moved quickly and almost imperceptibly; in the warm air of the room now his face assumed for Camus the aspect of an ikon, its hieratic geometry gaining in force, while the fingers of the prosthesis moved with the precision of a suprahuman will, patterning, pausing, pressing hundreds of keys in a rhythm of sureness that must obviate error.

Should he have felt relieved, now that the cube was gone? He did not. It had passed from the realm of material to the realm of mind, and so might now exercise the relentless dominion of the phantasmal, of the dead. One could argue with matter, with flesh; not so with ghosts. Thus, the spirit of the cube now dominated the room. On a large video screen, the numbers and symbols of Cutter's calculations flew like frail birds above a swamp of ill omen. The squat, still double hump of the laser yet gave off heat. Three runners were working separately at consoles. At last one said, "Sixteen bit correlation."

"Let's see," snapped Corso.

The screen erupted in multicolored snow. A horizontal bisected it. Then undulations began, the line writhed like a snake, and a tone came into the room, rising in pitch, like a bodiless wail of pain from a stressed machine. The wave onscreen folded like an accordion.

Pribiloff called out, "I suggest a sample rate of fortyeight kilohertz."

The pitch went up past the limits of audibility, and the pleated wave onscreen blurred to a bar. Cutter's glass eye snapped open.

Then, from the silence came a deep note, not from any mechanism, but warm and vibrant, and another, and then the unmistakable sound of an oboe. A slow melody unfurled in halfsteps, in common time, on a ground bass of D minor; it went round a harmonic progression of six bars, and returned with a forte attack of trombones and strings as ranked voices sang:

```
                                                       Re-
                       Re-                        qui- em    ae-
Re-              qui-  em    ae-   | ter-
       qui-      em    ae-         | ter-  qui-   em    ae-   ter-nam        do-
ter-nam,               ae-         | ter-               nam         do-
nam,                   ae-         | ter-               nam         do-

                 nam               do-    na   e-             is,
na               e-    is,                      Do-
na               e-    is,                      Do-                    mi-ne,
na               e-    is,                      do-           na,

Do-   mi-ne, re-                        qui- em   ae- | ter-
      mi-ne, do-       na    e-                       |
re-          qui-em    ae-   ter-             nam     | do-
do-   na     e-        is,   Do-   mi-ne, re-    qui- | em

                 nam               do-   na   e-   is,  Do-   mi-ne!
      is,        Do-    mi-ne, do-       na   e-   is,  Do-   mi-ne!
      na         e-     is,     Do-    mi-ne, e-  is,   Do-   mi-ne!
ae-              ter-   nam     do-      na   e-   is,  Do-   mi-ne!
```

Reentering with *Exaudi orationem meam* the chorus drowned increasing conversation. Voices then were raised to shouts, directed at Corso, who stood sullenly braced against one console, not moving at all, as oblivious to the protests and clamor as he seemed to be to the music.

Past Camus a thin dark figure pushed. He grasped the passing wrist; a pure strong sexual urge, his first in weeks, hit him. Just as a burst of music scribbled the screen with white and lit the room, the woman turned to him with a suggestive smile; it was Elizabeth Lispe. He released her wrist and looked frantically down the row. But Winifred had left.

And the general going continued through the *Dies Irae*, the *Tuba Mirum*, the *Rex Tremendae*, the *Recordare*, and the *Con-*

futatis. By the start of the *Lacrymosa,* Camus and Pribiloff were alone in the gallery. Corso seemed to come out of his trance, peering up at the seats. The music was cut off neatly in midbar after *qua resurget ex favilla,* unresolved on a dominant.

Pribiloff supplied the resolution, chanting, *"Judicandus homo reus.* However, Mozart never got that far. He died, and the Requiem was completed by a student. And ever since, we have been piecing it together from the fragments he left. I am much restored. I must attend these little memorials more often."

"Memorial?" said Camus.

Pribiloff rose. "Da. Today is the bicentennial of Mozart s death."

Corso oversaw the shutting down of equipment. Cutter was unrousable; his head lolled, and the open glass eye came to rest on Camus with a terrible fixity.

Pribiloff observed this. "This our message. What our unborn children have to say to us, what they have always had to say to us: a mass for the dead. Very fine."

Now Corso turned in rage to the runners. "Erase it."

As one, all the tape reels whined backwards in a blur. Pribiloff almost spoke, then sighed. The blurred high chatter broke off, and the loose ends of tape pattered, slowing, against their hubs. Only then did Pribiloff say: "Gospodin Corso. I have made a study of the Requiem. What you have just erased is not a known version."

Corso showed a suspicion of interest.

"The piece was left incomplete, nyet? And scholars have reconstructed it from fragments. But this version we have just heard, it differs from every historical reconstruction. I think you have now destroyed evidence that this cube was surely from the future."

Corso looked dumbly from the dangling ends of tape to the limp form of Cutter. "Irrelevant," he rasped. "I know where it's from. And if you want the truth, I think *this* one altered the data. His little joke on us. But we'll get the real data from him, you can bet on it."

Now there was a disturbance in the hallway. Camus turned, and saw Warner burst into the room, eyes wild, face patchily shaven, a white gown flying loose to reveal pale unhealthy waterpuckered flesh beneath. He charged across the room, grabbed Camus, held him.

"God forgive me!" Warner cried. "You were right. Our acts

have consequences. I saw it! The book, I saw it clearly, what they said is true: you can see things across time. It was *The Book of Fakes* I gave Hüll, and you gave it back to me in the airport, and I destroyed it then, burned it—but I saw it now! It was in my room, I saw it, oh Christ, there are ghosts, and acts can haunt . . ."

Camus scarcely knew how to act. When he planted his own fake of the book in Warner's room he had not expected this, no, he had ignored the consequences of his act upon Warner as much as Warner had ignored his own effect on Hüll; yet his sympathy with Warner was still small, for despite how piteous Warner looked, the man was still concerned first for himself. But Camus had no time to speak. A woman in an orange sari entered, flanked by two runners. In a peremptory voice she called, "Fred-er-ick." At once Warner's hands fell from Camus. The runners took him by the arms. Warner thrust himself forward, grunting with exertion, and the two braced back to hold him. Then the fight left him. He was docile. One runner led him away, and as the woman turned to follow, she gestured casually and said, "Him too." The second runner closed on Camus.

24. Oneiros

Night now. Had ever it been else? Chill air. He was stripped,
not even a robe to wrap him. Karya Karanabhava, the woman
in the orange sari, had told him: Major Cutter has gone to the
sea. But we look forward to a fruitful collaboration with yourself.

Winifred was on this level. So he had reached a kind of
center. And, typically, his urgency now was to escape it. For
it was as if he had finally attained the dissociation from culture,
from mind, from others, that he had often flirted with, and
found there only the infinite reproach of his own face.

He tried the lift. It would not work for him. He waited until
a runner boarded; the runner did not glance at his nudity, but
struck the indigo button for level two. He struck it again. Only
then he turned to Camus to say, "Do you mind? You're holding
me up." Camus stepped off the lift.

During sleep, his dreams were repeatedly broken. Some
device in his cell recorded the onset of dreaming sleep and
caused his telephone to ring. He spoke groggily to a dead line;
from far recesses of noise his own voice echoed back, delayed.

This was the silence in which the mute stone began to speak
to him. Messages seemed to come from all sides: from his
constant thickness of throat, dullness of thought, dripping of
sinuses which were tokens of nicotine withdrawal, from the
chaotic pattern of his pacing, the erratic leaps of his heart, the
constriction of his vision which the smallness of his cell en-
forced—all collaborated to circumscribe his will. The messages, read from configurations of the inanimate, or heard in
the widening interstices between dream, hallucination, and
imagination, told him only that he was here, that he was only
here, that precedence, consequence, and purpose were just
beautiful lies, but lies that bound.

Any moment of his past might have reasonably turned him to a different present; but the more he tried to think back, the more the stochastic logic of predestination asserted itself. Indeed, his entire life came to seem from this perspective an irrevocable tendency toward just such a loveless extreme of enclosure, nakedness, and fruitlessness. Even the particulars of his cell, the rounded orange walls, the illusory rainlike threads that came between the ceiling and his retina on waking, the pitch of the telephone bell, mediated to him a reductive schema of his life in which all events, decisions, and landscapes of moments were as flat and inalterable as a roadmap.

Clock, heart, sky: three fundamental ways of keeping time. He could not remember when he'd last seen sky. His heart was not his own. The digital clock in his cell ran backwards. Time kept him.

The clock assumed a mythic, idiotic import. Its display resolved the passing flux to tenths of seconds, but his eye could not resolve them. In that blur no change seemed possible, yet there was change, progressive, cumulative, as seconds ceded to minutes and minutes stretched to hours and hours dove steadily toward the zero, only to rearise on that instant like a secular phoenix in a travesty of dawn: 23.59.59.9, the invariant red weather of each daybreak.

He practiced interposing his attention in the space between the tenths, as if it was there that meaning and continuity occurred, to spite the clock's inexorable strobing and the regular crucifixion of moments upon its angular bloody digits, as if peace might be found in the slices of time unnumbered, unmarked, unconsecrated. He used a looking-away in service of acuity, a peripheral vision like that of stargazers. He could almost enter a stasis of contemplation in these gaps between the instants the clock announced. Ultimately the moment might be sliced fine enough to produce a complete identity, two consecutive identical moments, a logical stalling of change as irrefutable and empty as Zeno's paradox, promising an eternal stillness of zero time, yet delivering numberless small infernos of movement. Inevitably he was jarred back from his moments of peace to the cretinous counting of the clock.

Hell, he thought, is discontinuous. I need not fear Winifred's Hell of repetitions. For me, interruptions in the torment are the torment. Any moment I could live in forever, but the shifts will break me.

He considered suicide. A moment past time. The Latin word for time meant *cut*. There was a mirror in his bathroom alcove. If he could break it, he might get a piece sharp enough. He beat at the mirror with his fists, until hands and wrists were stinging, throbbing, numb. Then he detached the telephone receiver from its plug, with difficulty since his fingers moved badly (yet thankful that the cut would be painless), and in anger because the moment he touched it it began to ring. But he freed it, and hurled it at the mirror, and the mirror did not break, but tumbled like a wave from its housing, showering smooth pebbles of some plastic glued to the silvered film of its surface. The remains offered him a torn, distorted reflection of his face. He had never seen himself so pale, so wrecked. And still time kept on.

Again his intolerable solitude was intolerably broken. The woman in the orange sari came for him: Karya Karanabhava. She brought him to a gallery she called Memory Lane. All around were photographs.

"We pose them. Our aim is to make a history of history. There are unrecorded or fictive nodes in time, moments of minimum or maximum flux, with an especial abundance of possible futures, at which critical moments may occur. We document these. For instance, this photo is of Strauss, Saint-Säens, and Satie at a sidewalk café in Paris, 1914. The meeting never occurred. But it might have."

Camus studied further photos. A seedy-looking Freud gazed skeptically at a dandyish James Joyce mugging with a guitar in front of some institution. H. G. Wells in aviator's goggles sat grinning astride the bicycle saddle of some infernal machine. Face hidden by a gas mask, a man cycled down a country lane, an alarm clock fastened to his belt. Charles Darwin, looking prosperous as a banker, scowled in the British museum at Karl Marx taking notes across the table. A blurry piece of film enlarged and numbered *frame 239* showed John Fitzgerald Kennedy tall in Southern sunlight, waving happily from a limousine.

"Our colleagues do not quite apprehend the delicacy of this work. They are forever submitting scenarios of events they feel *should* have happened. That, of course, is not the point at all. But too many here take their work too seriously. You must understand that life is not hydrogen, carbon, oxygen, but rather the precise spaces and warps that separate these elements. The content is less important than the structure. Thus, life is a Nothing of a particular shape. And we have found that consciousness, too, is mostly excerption, a chain of gaps. We live in the gaps. Continuity is a blur, an illusion, a fiction constantly created and revised during those gaps. And in the gaps, if we try, we can be free. We can see what we are taught not to see. These pictures are only one way, of course, a chronicle of lost moments. There are many other ways. As, for instance, dreams.

"We came to believe that the day residue in dreams is not just residue from days past, but also from days to come. Our work has proved this so. But there is another important component to dreams—the structuring of their content. So we reversed figure and ground, so to speak. We studied those parts of the EEG that would normally be called noise, or artifact. We learned to induce a state which we call antifugue. A stillness. Where the mind is wholly alert and the body inactive. Past that is a state we call metanoia; here the mind loses its edges, and apprehends everything as itself. With training, this state can be affective; it can change things. Cutter was superb at it. He had so little ego to start with. His dreams supplied most of the formalism for our time work."

"He said to me that the best dream is white."

She hesitated. "Cutter made the mistake of dreaming for himself, when he had no self to dream for. *You* must dream *ahead* of the self. In fact, our motto is: those who cannot remember the future are condemned to repeat it."

"And those who can?"

"May escape."

He indicated the photos. "Into fantasy."

"Or into ecstasies. Or into understanding." She smiled distantly. "It is a great deal like karma, after all. The modern woman of India is, we presume, beyond such repressive religious paradigms. But my work leads back time and again to the old questions: dreams, fate, time. I have come the long way round to return to this. That is my karma, to return to a fate by fleeing it. Perhaps you are the same."

"I doubt it."

"As of course you must. But what you will *do* is, of course, another necessity beyond your control. Now I must leave you. You are to see my husband, Michael, next."

"I might not."

She simply smiled.

* * *

Rush of sandalwood as the door slid wide. The Janus head embossed thereon vanished with its legend, *Department of Augury,* into the wall.

The cubicle was jammed with paraphernalia. On a large desk were many coins, yarrow stalks, a quincunx of Tarot cards in unfinished laying, a forked oak branch, dice cubic and do-decahedral, a Janus head in bronze, books in quarto and octavo sizes of evident antiquity, a phrenologically marked skull, pale striped computer sheaves edge-holed (the upper sheet of which showed seven varicolored meanders across a background of irregular black crosses), an astrolabe, stones, vials, a heap of rusty dirt. On a far wall hung a chart of all the sky in white on indigo with seven varicolored roundhead tacks stuck therein, a narrow shelf upon which rested instruments and coiled cables of functions labelled *myo, cardio, thermo, enceph,* a replica of a Mayan calendar, full length photos of naked men and women crossarmed with coronae flaring out, a chart of the human hand's ventral side showing palmist marks, a chart of the human foot likewise showing correspondences to internal organs, woodcuts of the flayed after Vesalius. From the ceiling depended a cage containing *Columba livia,* the feral urban rock dove. A filigreed censer eddied sandalwood fumes. On the floor was a stone bowl of blood half-clotted, a two-meter square sandbox lit evenly by four photographic lamps, and a Ouija board.

Michael Scot was hunched over the desk, drawing his left hand slowly from its surface, while his right rested curled upon it. He drew the hand to his mouth, bit, and put a freed needle into a red pincushion. Beneath his right hand Camus saw the quick lash of a lizard's tail. Delicately Scot made a knot by its head, then placed the animal into the sandbox. It lay there, inert.

"What were you doing?" asked Camus, in a voice not wholly his own.

"Sewing its eyes shut," said Scot. "A modestly effective technique. Last year it predicted the appearance of a comet. Of course the success of prophecies depends on interpretation. And we are tireless interpreters. You saw the Alternative History Project? Sit down. That sphere, turn it, yes, it's a chair. I understand you don't like science. They couldn't get rid of you fast enough in DEVOLVE and PARALOG. We'll get on better here."

"'Like' has nothing to do with it. It's just that there are other ways of knowing."

"Yes yes. We revive earlier ways of knowing. Sortilege, exstipacy, divination, prayer. We try any and everything. Extreme and doomed researches. What's the most extreme, doomed project you can think of?"

"Love," said Camus.

"Don't be a cad. Try again."

"Perpetual motion." Which was nearly the same thing.

"Nice. Very close. But I'll tell you what's even more basic: time. The impossibility of perpetual motion hinges on entropy, time's arrow. You know the Greek for time?"

"Chronos."

"*Xronos.*" Scott rolled the *x*. "We do not use that abominable transliteration see aitch. That letter is *xi*. It's important to keep your orthography clean. There are gnomons in names. Powerful secrets reside in the *x*. *Xronos* is plain old ticktock time, time with a *stoxos,* as in the English word *stochastic,* time of mindless tendencies, of entropy, of closed systems, of circumstance. The other Greek word for time is *kairos,* climactic time, time with a *telos* as in the English *teleology.* Time of the essence. We attempt a synthesis of the two. How many fingers?"

"What?"

"Behind my back. How many fingers?"

"Uh . . . three?"

"Correct. Very fine. As good as Cutter."

"What happened to Cutter? Your wife said he had gone to the sea."

Scot smiled. "Dear Karya. How poetic. No, Cutter was killed. That irresponsible toad Corso put him in the Tank immediately after the analysis. I blame myself. They will not understand that the body imposes definite limits. But we'll be more careful with you."

"Wait. Go back. Me?"

"Oh, yes, you're the one. You found the cube. A dozen before you failed to see it. You may even have drawn it there, as we think Cutter drew his . . . stone."

Camus felt unwell. "What Carpenter said. Strange attractor. I may have drawn it. May have been the cause."

"Just the proximate cause. No blame, no praise. But there's

no doubt that you're connected. We weigh your involvement at about eighteen grams on the meat scale, assuming that the soul weighs twenty, on the average. Which it does. We've weighed the dying. They lose an unaccountable twenty grams at death. Of course, Cutter only lost ten. A slender soul. We suspect particles are emitted. We're calling them eschatons."

"And then," said Camus, and stopped. He was dizzy from the incense. "Then these particles migrate back. Through time, yes. Pieces of souls. Palingenesis. Heterochrony. Back, where they influence, interact. . . ."

"That's interesting. Yes, it has possibilities. I'll think about it."

"And it's gone now. And no way to undo what I did. That analysis by destruction—why?"

Scot considered. "We take things apart in order that they may become the Buddha. Or if that's too Oriental for you, remember what the Gnostics said: split the stick and there is Jesus. Or if that's too mystical, think of the atomic bomb. Incalculable power in the interstices. You'll see, when you dream for us."

"I have no intention of dreaming for you."

"Wow. This is great. I haven't heard a dumb argument about free will since college. Go for it. Cigarette? No? And so recently you were dying for one. Will, what a concept. But I'll tell you what. If you really want to leave, we'll fly you out of here tomorrow."

"Good. Book me into the smoking section."

"By the way, your therapist is Miss Waste."

And now he began to understand, viscerally, the extent of his bonds. The sense of imprisonment, in the complex, in his feelings for Winifred, in the currents of his own history, became as intimate and physical as a bout of food poisoning.

"Free will?" asked Scot rhetorically.

Tocktock, said the timer. Camus looked at it. "Can't you shut that off?" he said.

Winifred, trig and stern by desklight, looked over the top of her glasses. Her eyes said loud nothings. Then back they went to the open folder on the desk. She repeated her question:

"'There is probably a spider on the wall.' True or false."

"There is probably a Winifred in that tunic."

"False. There is a therapist administering a test. Or trying to. Please cooperate."

Camus removed his glasses and pressed fingertips against his eyelids. "How many questions in this test?"

"Six hundred sixtysix."

He groaned. "How appropriate. And I'm to answer them all?"

"If you can."

"What's the point?"

"The test is partially diagnostic, and partially therapeutic in and of itself."

"I'm partially agnostic, myself."

"We'll find out about that when we analyze the results."

He tried to think of witty rejoinders, failed. Finally he said, "True. There probably is a spider on the wall. Somewhere."

She reset the timer and made a mark on her papers.

The questions stretched on and on, banal, staggering, pointless, insulting, repetitious. This catechism of the bivalent extended past surfeit into the horror of the purely quantitative.

I like science. *False*. Strange sounds disturb my sleep. *True*. I feel uneasy indoors. *True*. I am made nervous by certain animals. *True*. I believe I am being followed. *True*. I am sure I am being talked about. *True*. I have had peculiar experiences. *True*. My memory seems to be all right. *No answer*. Everything tastes the same. *No answer*. Someone is trying to influence my mind. *True*. I often feel that things are not real. *True*. It is great to be living in these times when so much is going on. *No answer*. People disappoint me. *No answer*.

I would like to be a soldier. *False*. I can get along with people I dislike. *True*. I have not lived the right kind of life. *True*. I am a special agent of God. *True*. My soul sometimes leaves my body. *True*. Evil spirits possess me at times. *True*. My sins are unpardonable. *True*. I deserve severe punishment for my sins. *False*.

I am terrified of fire. *No answer*. I have a fear of drowning. *No answer*. I dread earthquakes. *No answer*. Windstorms upset me. *No answer*. There is a void at the heart of creation. *No answer*.

I refuse to play some games because I am too good at them. *No answer*. Typesetters are given things in pieces so that no one of them can reach an understanding of the whole. *True*. I do not always tell the truth. *False*.

Wovon man nicht sprechen kann, darüber muss man schweigen. *True*. Le silence éternal de ces espaces infinism'effraie. *True*.

At times I have enjoyed being hurt by someone I love. *No answer*.

They performed an experiment with time. She swung a tiny bob, saying, "You know how we divide time into categories of past, present, future."

"I've heard of it."

"Watch the bob. You're going down. When you come up the present will be gone. There will be no present."

"I don't . . ." He shook his head.

"That was very nice," she said. "Now. You are going down again. When you come up the present will be expanded."

He shook his head again, and tried to speak. But she progressed to the categories of past and future. She used them in combinations. After the fourteenth procedure his body was covered with a chill sweat. He gave a violent shake.

"What happened?"

"Easy now. Having no present and no past got to you. Interesting. I blocked at no present, no future."

There were many sessions. But they blurred to one long purgatory in his mind; one day became the next with an alacrity that was, as well, painfully slow; there was no respite in the nights, for when he did sleep he dreamed only of the complex, of corridors that bent, and circled sealed rooms, and returned always to a center that was brightly lit and unremitting.

"How did I fail you?"

"Don't ask. Our theory teaches forgetting of the personal. In these regions it is too hazardous to hold on to the personal. Didn't Cutter prove that? He tried to forget the past he was taught. He tried to reach back into his true self, and it destroyed him."

"Then you want to give me a false past, too?"

"No need. You'll do it yourself. As DeQuincey says, the human brain is a mighty and natural palimpsest, constantly revising its own contents. The mind is not a flat mirror. The shape of its reflections, like any shape in nature, is warped from the ideal. We will correct the surface, so that it's precisely warped. So that it can give a usable virtual image from a useful point of view."

"False."

"A matter of perspective."

"How far does the fraud go, can you tell me that? Were you working for them from the start? Was Warner? Even my friend von Rast? Axis said he's been here since the last war.

God, how deep do the connections run?"

"Excellent. This is really a superb paranoia."

"Once you said that even paranoids have enemies. Parables for paranoids. . . . Are there metaphors for metanoids?"

"We're all persecuted, if only by our experience. It so seldom corresponds to what we think we should have had. Oh, the cube is real. You really found it. Warner heard of this place from Poisson. I came here with Levin, as I told you. This organization has existed in its present form for some fifteen years. Prior to that its agents, not many, were scattered around the globe. The present complex was built by laid-off pipeline workers during the Bicentennial. But aspects of it have been found in manuscripts attributed to Plato, Melancthon, Saint Augustine, Clement of Alexandria, Da Vinci, Emerson, and Nietzsche, among others. The oldest record is a clay tablet inscribed in a mirror-variant of Linear B, which described a seven- or fourteen-sided labyrinth at the edge of the world, where the sun was obscured for half of every year. . . ."

She watched his nausea. When it had passed, he could not recover his thoughts. To that moment, he still thought he might win her back. He could not forget the ambiguous promise of her long-ago *maybe so*.

And she knew his thoughts, and said, "You can't go back, you know. Not to any moment. You can only go on. From the present, exactly as it stands, in all its gory and immediate detail."

And he saw what it was: after a time something just wears out, and you collapse back into yourself. The last mask is welded on, and the accretions thenceforth are not the translations of *kairos,* choice, but the simple downward drag of *xronos*. The miracle was that there was any *kairos* to start with, that we can exist so long on credit, are given gratis so many mornings in which to build a whole self. It was a miracle that we are ever any better than we should be. To think of it, the extent of blind grace allotted him was immense, it astonished him now that he had not been hauled to a judgment of moral debt long ago. How many infinite mornings had he squandered in childhood? Ah, at last the great debt is called, and the incomplete selves are struck like stagesets, leaving only what bare boards you have, inadvertently, come to own. The capacity for change is not lost, but some glands pull back their short snouts, the cells are not so easy in their regenerations, and all the rough drafts, alternative copies, marginal notes, naive glosses, the halfbuilt bypasses, the intricate scaffoldings of *as if,* are eradicated by disuse, by insistent *xronos*. From then on the events of *kairos*, of choice or purpose, are bought only at the full price, in advance.

So the change in her was not really a change. It was that part of herself that she had fully accomplished by way of or in spite of all she had done or thought—the life that emerged from the acts of life. And himself? What aspects of his own psyche had passed unnoticeably into the irreclaimable?

He would not soon know. He was too busy attending her, to see which way her mind had turned, so that he might follow. And draw her back. For ahead of her he saw a frightening abyss. And then he knew why the sight of her striding away from him was so strong in his memory. Every time, it had suggested the ghost of some abyss ahead, and he had hastened to get there first, for he more feared losing her than losing himself. He remembered her, typing, at the edge of the cave, on the outcrop, that day before he had found the cube. Had he not gone to banter her back from the edge, like a priest with a suicide? Yet the edge he feared was not the literal cliff, but the work she'd been typing for Warner. He remembered his unease. Yes, he'd had some premonition even then. And had failed to heed it, had gone regardless into the dark cave and brought forth, as if from the depths of his own mind, the stainless perfect symbol of his own faith: paradox. No life, no hope, no strength without paradox. Life was cancelled by death, hope by despair, strength by sickness; but paradox remained aloft, perpetual motion of yin and yang, spinning and static, defying time with its cycling.

"What did you ever see in me?" she asked him then. And he knew that in this place and time no paradox was untouchable. She would even analyze his love for her.

Fear not of falling but of the inevitable bottom. He'd always expected and wanted the depths of her to be obscure and unreachable. Now they approached him. The world's gravity drew him inexorably on. Far from the drifting apart he'd foreseen, the dense worst of them each would clash, here at the world's edge, where all acts of human providence fled like mist under sun, like mysteries under materialism. The finest, lightest paradoxes in themselves, the very things that sustained their love, would not be suffered here.

Into the abyss, then. Last look at fragile hopes fading above.

* * *

"Eternity? When I was young, I liked to read about the universe. Is that what you mean?" She did not answer him. "I read that it was infinite and bounded, and expanding. I couldn't quite understand the bounded part. Finally I came to think that all the galaxies receded from some center, accelerating, at last passing the speed of light, and going over . . . an edge. Like the overflow from a basin. And somehow this matter would reappear at the center, as if from a fountain. But that was only the start of the idea. I thought, everything is a part of the universe, so any quality of the universe is present in all its parts. Therefore any object, person, moment, or perception, is also infinite yet bounded. Now obviously an object is bounded. But how is it infinite? I must have wondered, and I began to pay attention to things, to their edges. It seemed sometimes that time would *bend* around objects. Sometimes I could see into an object, see its history. And I came to think that any item, any moment, was a sort of pocket eternity. Bounded in space and time, yet infinite in its connections to other things. You'll think I'm being too romantic."

"Not at all. That's exactly the sense of our project."

"Ah, God, no. I'm not speaking of that." But, he saw, in a sense he was. If he had been more skillful or more persistent at his own project—of opening moments into pocket eternities for the two of them, humanly, lovingly—they would not have come to this mechanistic last resort. It was love that subsumed the momentary, the progressive, and the eternal; love alone that allowed sensual access to time; and he had never loved her well enough—he had only desired to love. And a desire deferred too long becomes a travesty. Now the only way of completing the unfinished business between them was through the mediation of the complex, Radix Malorum. So the personal sense of their project opened to him.

Yes, he had not tried hard enough for the two of them. His own being was fullest in the interstices of time, and hers in moments of decision. They were bound to have drifted this way. He existed, like Cutter, as an infinite sum of relative nothings; all his fullest experience came from the unrecognized, unlegitimated, unendorsed. Her present was massy, particulate, definite, rational, and based on nameable goals; so her acts would tend to the instrumental. Given this, it was now necessary that he become her instrument.

"All right," he said. "Then teach me."

One eyebrow showed her skepticism. "You don't think I can?"

"Teach me what you promised long ago. Teach me stillness."

So she gave him silence. And he responded, at last, with speech. Her silence, her eyes, drew out of him a purge of all he hadn't said at the times when he should have spoken, broken by tortured silences now for all the past times he had spoken too soon.

"Don't you see, that there are people who build up, who laminate, one fiction on the previous, and others who must strip away, yes, in self-defense, because they themselves are stripped. Stripped bare by what they see. It's not so much seeing into objects. No, the objects see into you. How you learn to read the look of a rock, or a leaf, or a face, and all the while they're really reading you. But your eyes, that hold off, that cast out, that accrete on their surface everything they don't let in, your eyes, like that sometimes, like that now, reflective, cold. Because . . . no revelation without a price? And I couldn't pay it. Because of my damned attention, the acts of attention I couldn't control, being read so often, letting so much of myself out into the world. Silence at the wrong time. Density in the wrong place. But couldn't you have seen, it wasn't detachment? Excess of involvement. Too many scruples. It was all to, to hold things in trust. Not to own. Did you want to be owned? I would strip a surface without touching it. And you wished to cover it all. To cover, yes. Blanket over blanket in the cold. Dead cold eternal hum of machinery. That dread in your mother's room, the cold machinery so like here. . . . Under blankets, fold over fold. The warped woof of the draped fabric. Like lines of memory, separate, yet folded back in the mind to touch, like the pattern in a dropped striped shirt. And every time I touch, even with my eyes, the pattern shifts, until the overlays of touch, where, yes, where familiarity makes the repetitions thickest, there you stumble and fall. I would have caught you! I would have tried. Strip to stillness. Not to let the attention strike at a bad angle, like a skipping rock hits a wave, and plummets in. Down. Inevitable sinking. Not like that. A grace of attention, to sustain. It's possible, isn't it? That we're all fallen angels, or some of us at least, halfway to Hell, paused here for just the moment of our lives? And we make life Hell for others because Hell is in us, it's a fate we foreknow, a nostalgia for the future that comes out in our actions. . . . But the other half of that, that we sometimes remember the time before the fall, and sometimes perform acts of human providence. . . ."

But she was unmoved. The professional mask stayed fixed. Their sessions became more complex now. He was given drugs: delta-sleep-inducing peptides, hypothalamic inhibitors, euphorics. His sense of reality increasingly failed. Events seemed moves in a vast syncretic game without markers or board. Sequence was unimportant. Less and less could he tell if a thing had happened, or when, or if he had dreamed it or imagined it. Nor did this seem to matter.

He wakened to a moving bas relief on his wall: animals and dancing gods. He laid his hand on the wall. It was flat, and the figures flowed over and around his hand. The hand, drawn slowly back from the wall, cast no shadow. The texture of the light composing the figures was grainy.

The lighting of a cigarette in the dark made a small, brief theater of her face. "In fact," she continued quite naturally in this infinite yet bounded space of his therapy, "there is no such thing as the present. We can know only through the senses, and there's always a lag of propagation between real time and knowing time. Light and space, air and sound; distance enters in, hence time."

"Touch," he said, attempting a refutation.

"No. The signals propagate along the nerves. There is no instantaneous giving of touch for touch."

Lights blared. He struggled to sit up, could not.

"Lie still. This is the only time we'll force you in any way." She sat on the cot and unfastened the waistband of his jeans.

"No," he said. "Not this. Please."

"Relax. I've seen it before."

"Winifred. Please no. Leave us something. I'll beg. Please don't."

"My, that was quick. Did I hear no? Conflicting signals."

"What do you *want?* What are you trying to do to me?"

"That should be obvious. We need a sample of germ plasm. You've been too chaste to let us get it any other way. Now relax. Your body's speaking. As a Catholic, what's your opinion of circumcision and why did you let them do it to you?"

"I wasn't asked."

"Any comments on testicular assymetry?"

"Stop this!"

"Erectile tissue extends beneath and past scrotum to perineum. Practically a caudal appendage. How does this feel?"

"Humiliating."

"Stop thinking. Stop remembering. We want the grunty words passing through your head at the moment of emission. Speak up. It's a pity men can't be raped."

"What do you call this?"

"Rape is a violation. Not at all like the undeniably pleasurable sensations occasioned by this stimulation."

"No. No."

"Bullshit. Speak. What's on your mind?"

"Obscenity. Betrayal. Travesty."

"Move, damn you," she growled. He resisted the sensual affect of her voice. The caress of air on palate. He steeled himself. Yet not just in her voice, but in her touch, were still surprises. His heart twitched in uncontrollable reflex at a certain aspirant linked with a certain pressure. Sperm leapt in gouts, marking by its arc through space the time since his last ejaculation, scalding momentarily his chest and belly with a dampness that on the instant turned chill. Last pulses trickled with oily insistence down the pubic thatch and beaded on chest hair like cold sweat. A sharp moist smell sprang from his armpits. Mockingly a suppressed echo of pleasure came from his bowels and shivered him.

"That will do," said Winifred. She returned from a basin wiping her hands. She held a test tube. She tossed the towel to him. And he felt a final divorce from lineage and consequence, for in his spasms had been traces of every time his semen had gone out from him to no end—and, fatherless as he felt himself, the hollow shaking in his loins now told him that he would remain childless as well, and all his efforts, too, would find no purchase on any enduring reality.

"You never did move," she said. "Nothing could force you to act, only to react. Not alive, but being lived..."

"Yes. Yes, I know."

"And I might have accepted that, but that you also could never stand still."

"I loved you. As you were. I would never demand....I wanted to, to leave you as I found you." His eyes wept. He could not believe it. Nothing else in him cried.

"But to leave me regardless."

"Yes! All right! Everything I did was wrong. Because I knew that it would end." And he realized that Warner was correct in saying that the voice of nothingness is with us always, and every living impulse is stalked by its shadow. He had feared a dreadful end to their love, he had expected it, and to that degree he had even wanted it.

After this she no longer came alone. Once she brought Tototto, once Carpenter, once Sangster. He asked why.

"You're no longer speaking English. I need translators to keep up with you."

"But . . . what language am I speaking now?"

"French."

"But . . . *mais . . .*" He brought his attention to his words, but they shifted, elusive and uncertain in shape as Schiaparelli's Martian *canali*. To his horror he found that even his thoughts had gone limpid as water, and he could not find a vessel to contain them.

A change came into his features then. Winifred watched him intently. A kind of leap occurred within his eyes, to a state of blank exaltation, and Winifred saw him as she first had years ago: at once the handsomest and ugliest man she'd ever seen. But now the flash did not fade. His expression set up a trembling in her heart. After a moment she put her papers away, and pressed a signal button on her desk. Karya Karanabhava shortly entered. She looked at Camus, nodded, and said, "Tank."

Naked on a platform, above a cubical container, the water black within it, next to him a black parody of himself, an empty wetsuit internally molded to human form, cabled to an overhead winch, wires extending from points on the hood, chest, legs, arms, nape, caude, and codpiece, he was guided by Karya Karanabhava into the suit with a touch neither clinical nor gentle. She remarked on his Roman toe—the second longer than the third on each foot—a neotenic trait. He was swallowed. Soft wax pressed his ears. He chewed on a malleable mouthpiece until it conformed to the shape of his bite and gave a feeling of deadness to his tongue and palate. The hood's black mask covered his eyes. Parts of the suit constricted to external controls, and he felt tests of pressure on biceps, ribs, thighs, a nip at his lax penis. Abruptly his balance went. He was moved—

(and slipped into wombwarmth. Amnion. Archaic fear of flood. Ear channels twice whirled, settled, vanished. Drift. He flexed unfeeling fingers. Face down, cruciform, he knew, in a tank of water at skin temperature, but no sensations to confirm this. He moved his mouth around the mask in a mimicry of

panic that turned real. Voice like breaking sticks from within:
—That mask is your air supply. Be still. You cannot expel it.
He attempted answer, could not. But began to move, to fly,
pure speed without agency of vehicle, up, out, like a cork
released from deep undersea, breaking some interface as repeated explosions of white came upon his lids: pure white
boiling out from a point, across his whole vision, fading to
contracting bruiseblack circles, whence followed another burst,
time on time, not the terrifying white the cube had offered in
a Nome bar, not the bitter white of Cutter's dreams, not an
eternity in which all possible events were consubstantial, simultaneous, and ceaseless as a monstrous tapestry extending
infinitely into new dimensions, but the placid embryonic
groundwork of time, the negative of the fabric, the open areas
between warp and weft which accounted for the substance of
the whole. He rose. The fearsome pulsing quelled. Constellations opened to admit him, not of stars, but of events, the
unrecorded moments, the anonymous whiteness, the eyes of
time, the spaces in the pattern that kept all history from collapsing in upon itself like an impossibly dense star. He was
one such space. And the feeling gave him a kind of peace he
was yet unprepared for: a revelation without a price, a vision
that was not yet his but had been wished upon him, the horrid
yet enticing thought that he should be nothing, do nothing,
have nothing throughout his life but life. Later, if the word
held meaning, he)
—emerged feeling gravity and time reassert their dominion.
Each droplet of water left a heavy slow trace like a slug. The
world boomed forth again in its accustomed buzzing confusion,
and he understood in every joint the knouts of flagellants, their
joy and peace, accepting provisionally the pain of his reentry
into sense as the price of revelation, as if it were a dialogue
of transcendent spirit and corruptible flesh. He was the canvas
rotting beneath its image, the viceful paper on which palimpsests of being are written and revised, the evanescent but
indispensable ground of all fictions, including himself.

Winifred led him back. "You were in for most of a day."

She seemed to have too much energy, to be doing too many
things at once. He gave all his attention to walking.

"I lasted less than an hour the first time," she went on. "I
thought I was burning. Warner thought he was drowning. Are
you all right?"

He stopped walking so that he could nod. It was pleasant,

but unimportant, that she had thought to ask. He searched for words. "I flew."

"You can speak." She sounded relieved. "There's one thing more to do here."

She seated him at a computer console. Its keys were blank. She had him type on it for a while, blindly. At the end of it, the screen lit; he saw the display of the tumbling, receding cube, strange equations on its faces, skipping off unseen obstructions as it vanished to a point.

He followed her down the hall toward the central atrium.

"There were two options," she said. "If the training took, you would go to KATAXRON. If not, back to the surface, to the outside."

They reached the lift. She pressed the call button, and stood watching the annunciator light in the pause, until it lit, and the doors opened. Ironically she gestured him in.

"Up or down?" he asked.

"Which would you choose?"

"I don't know," he said.

The lift shut. Even before it began to move he had a sense of falling.

25. Kataxron

Radix Malorum was the world. Outside, the northern latitudes would be nodding, turning into their annual darkness. The pole, in one frame of reference fixed, in another careening towards Hercules, in yet another wobbling through the Lyre every twenty thousand years, receded from the sun's skypath at this season faster than at any other. Earth now, as seen from the sun, passed the first point of Aries. And although the sun's daily zenith, as seen from Earth, bottomed in the sky at midwinter (and at that time, in these latitudes, it would not rise at all), by a consoling trick of transcendental first derivatives the rate of its recession bottomed now, at equinox. Henceforth this year would creep toward its low mark ever more slowly, pausing at the zero of solstice, obliquely peering through a certain slit at Stonehenge, and returning dumbly north, climbing the spine of the west, from the caude of Tierra del Fuego up the flex of Cordilleras, ending here, at what would be the nape of the Brooks range, the archaic brainstem of the planet, where, eons ago, a landbridge had offered passage to migrants from the east.

But there was no outside. And within, in KATAXRON, it was night. Camus, peering briefly into the redlit corridors after momentary doubt as to where he was, returned satisfied to bed and to the recovery of a dream in yellow script on crimson satin.

Marcel le magnifique, on a dropcloth. Camus was six. The blunt fingers of the magician, a foundry crony of Uncle François, labored in the air to bring forth sleights. Cards, lit cigarettes, bouquets, and coins appeared with admirable reticence at his fumbling behest. He produced, with premature flourishes, the silk lining of a top hat. A dove trapped in the pocket of his frock coat escaped and flew around the darkened room, Maman after it with a broom. Camus clapped in glee. Marcel recovered with a scarf trick: from one empty cupped hand he pulled a chain of bright squares tied corner to corner: violet, indigo, blue, green, yellow, orange, red, faster and faster, until Camus, concentrating on his dream and trying to slow the rainbow blur, lost control of it. The blur was lights outside a tunneled train. Empty platforms rushed past, their names in title: Cambrian, Ordovician, Silurian, Devonian, Permian, Triassic, Jurassic. And the train created track before it as it plunged headlong, annihilating track after passing, and finally stopped at a station without a name. A voice suggested, "I believe this is your destination, sir."

In the empty station was the sour scent of formaldehyde, specific against decay. Overhead stars appeared, and each was an embryo frozen at a different stage of development. A voice spoke: *sed evolutionem theoria fere ubique obtinet. Evolere:* to unroll in space or time, as a scroll, a road, a river, a process. To turn and turn again. Plum on a tree of words which also bore *entrepein:* entropy: to turn irreversibly.

In an open carriage behind the hearse bearing the body of the magician Camus shivered, his silk top hat held loosely between his legs. A light snow covered air and ground alike. *Gathered to honor His servant Charles Robert Darwin and see him to his final.* Camus tossed his handful of dirt into the pit. Returning to the carriage he brushed crumbs of damp earth from the brim of the hat.

He awoke in a tremble—the unlikely trace of this invisible fiction upon the real, frangible senses.

Seconds stripped themselves from various displays. Clocks on all levels cycled closer to their common midnight. Had any made a simple calculation from the differing times on different levels, the precise moment of propitiousness would have stood forth more clearly than the present moment, but only the machines kept track, relaying their findings in commands of increased urgency. Any moment has, in glancing light, a shining face, which, tilted to another way of seeing, presents the most abysmal depths; so a reluctance to find the heart of their enterprise so obscure might have informed the tacit, universal eschewal of a common time at the complex. Or, as Corso put it, "Let's not ask what time it is until we're sure of getting the answer we want."

* * *

Curt command: "Come!" The frail wasted figure of Tototto beckoned him from a dark doorway. "I must tell you of Sandman. They have all lied. This is our true project."

Camus stepped in. A floor of transparent square panels covered an immense array of batteries. On each glowed a small red indicator light. The perspective of the room, the effect of a limitless, regular city of power, was extended by the reflective walls. There was just enough light for him to make out Tototto's features. In this crimson obscurity the man seemed ageless, his face smooth and sinless.

"The idea is as old as time," whispered Tototto. "Always there has been a sleeper whose dreams surpass the mundane world. Like the seven of Ephesus, like Ephimenides, like Endymion, like Rip Van Winkle. The Magian project is always the dream. The Faustian urge is to conquer time, to colonize the atoms and the galaxies. And our means to do so are written in the Apollonian language Paralog. Our studies are complete. We have overlooked nothing. The pieces all center round one axis, one point, one *Ursprung;* we need only provide it. The Kataxron experiment will provide it.

"The time is propitious. The alignment of the heavens is nearly correct. We will focus emissions with precisely warped surfaces. Our target will be hurled back: transformed into an imaginary temporal wavefront, and retransformed into matter after its propagation across time. And then, you see, it will return to us via a different route, via history. And lo, we find our fingerprints on it. We have already done so! All that remains is to start the process."

"To what purpose? To somehow . . . fix history? To redeem the evils of time, by time? Or just to justify yourselves?"

"Who could care less about dipping into the history of this irremediably flawed world? Or redeeming the debts of sinful human knowledge? The pollution is hopeless, but alas we are part of it, and so we must work with it, past it, to a first and last purification, a passage, to the one necessary transit. An escape." Tototto's voice became fervent, almost desperate. "The man, the ship, the voyage, the destination, will all grow simultaneously. The ship will begin as the simplest shell, a membrane. The man begins as a code: a terse statement in Paralog. The code will evolve into a man. He will not live. He will dream. He will dream he is voyaging. He will dream additions to the ship and to himself.

"The ship will leave Earth forever. It will attain the superluminal. It will travel to the northernmost constellation, to Polaris, to Kochab, to Pherkad, to Yildun, to Zeta, to Eta, to wherever our Sandman, our golem wills. . . ."

"Superluminal? But, do you mean faster than . . ."

". . . Than light, yes. When we have succeeded with our time experiments we will know how to do that, yes. And dreaming he will travel, dreaming himself, oh, he will not get there in a hurry, but what difference? He will know the interdependence of time and space, he will abolish drift and error from his own body, his own cells, freed of all precedent, even of the bias of genes, freed of the blind wreckage . . . not a man, no, not a clone, to copy weak clay is fruitless. But to take a sliver of silicon, coded, and cause it to mutate through many forms; to base a protein on an electronic substrate, on silicon— denser, faster, cleaner, more efficient than carbon life. Not prone to error, to sin. Our Sandman will be like a computer, but organic. He will interface with the ship to guide it. The ship will support him. He will structure the ship. His genes will evolve. His intelligence will grow. He will dream, in a completely closed space, weightless, crystalline, sealed in glass, yes, and when the new world is found, across space, across time it might be, then the glass will shatter. The ship, the seedpod, will break apart, and our complex new man, dreaming his destiny, will be broken upon far waves, will dissolve in a new sterile sea, programming it with the imprint of his own selfmade proteins. . . . Not to perpetuate our kind, which comes from ash and returns to ash, not carbon, no, but a deeper, more eternal pattern . . . sand to sand. The beauty of the hourglass: sand within fired sand. The sublimity of the computer: laser-given patterns in yet harder sand. The tragedy of our Sandman: dreamed *a nihilo*, incorruptible, to anoint dead far waters with the pure fire of intelligence. . . . No, we will not get there in a hurry. But when we do, the pollution will have been cleansed."

Tototto stared into the red pattern beneath his feet, beneath the transparent floor, as if he would revise the stars to such an order. "The idea is ancient. But *our* time is propitious. We will dream it into being. The one necessary crossing to redeem man, the cross, you see, the X that initials Christ, and time, and earth . . . oldest of symbols . . . crossing of axes, of space and time, the origin of the graph, calendric zero. . . ."

He knelt to sketch the *x* along the seams of the floor plates.

"This is an eternal mark. Redemption through negation. But not simply to cancel, no. To replace. To revise. As the advent of Christ gave a different kind of time to the world, by way of the cross, the quartering, so will we. But we will take it further."

Camus saw that he was extending the cross along further seams, adding arms to it.

"To this. A mark even more ancient. It has kept the idea alive since the first Aryans. It must have originated in some future, sent back as a presage of its own destruction. See, the arms are bent. Counterclockwise. That is the secret. *They* knew it imperfectly. *Their* symbol was bent clockwise. The meaning was reflected, worn on every arm, and none saw it clearly. It was no accident they were interested in rockets."

He looked up, stricken, inspired.

"And could it be then that there will be a translation across time? Could it be that our dreamer, our selfmade manmachine, will travel all this way to rearrive at his first home, at who knows what period in now-meaningless history? Those primal seas, are they the Earth's? Then we will have made, not an amendment to the fulsome stink of our race, but an actual correction. Then we, who made the correction, will vanish out of the distant future of our golem, *we will have never been.*"

A swath of light broadened to transfix Tototto. In the open doorway stood Corso, looking venomous and deranged. He wore only a tattered bathrobe. His eyes were bloodshot, his stylish hair wet and matted, his face oily with sweat. He had not shaved in days.

Tototto's expression narrowed to derision. "Ah. The wop is here. To make our train run on time."

"Otto," Corso said pleasantly, "go jump at or from something distant or precipitous."

"I leave," said Tototto. "The stink here is offensive."

"You're a slob, Otto," Corso called after him. "What's worse, a prissy slob."

Then he turned to Camus. "Whatever he told you was lunacy."

"That's what I thought. But most of what I'm told here is lunacy."

Corso gave him a long ugly look. "I won't argue it. The interesting tends to the unusual, the unusual to the bizarre, the bizarre to the lunatic. Haven't you read physics journals lately? No, shut up. I'm going to lecture you, because you haven't the faintest fucking idea what's going on here, and your ignorance is going to screw us all. So listen to me now, very carefully. We're in a crisis. The whole world is. Our waste and poison is oozing out the pores of the Earth, and it's going to kill us if we don't do something soon. That's the physical end of it. Oh, we can use some more quick technological fixes, but every one of them ultimately deepens the problem.

"Our real crisis is one of knowledge. Science has reasoned by axiom and hypothesis since its start. There's so much to look at, we use paradigms to restrict the field. But these paradigms also exclude whole areas. Ptolemy used the paradigm of circular orbits to predict planetary positions, which was useful to a point, but then it stalled out astronomy for a thousand years, because no one questioned the paradigm until Copernicus. Paradigms are drafts on the future. We assume something, then improve our instruments and refine our theories until further refinements are trivial, or begin to suggest a new paradigm.

"But we begin to think that the whole idea of using paradigms to advance knowledge is itself a faulty paradigm. That every hypothesis is a debt which must eventually be paid. And we have been getting deeper and deeper into hypothesis for centuries. Do you understand that experiments _affect_ things? All those pretty cloud chamber photos, you think that's discovery? That's pure invention. Those pictures are Rorschachs of the experimenters. Pump a billion electron volts through a target and you're sure as shit going to get _something_, but what you get is highly provisional, fictive, given on credit. Every experiment tampers with the universe's economy. Are you aware that physical constants are drifting? That centuries of bonehead empirical assumptions about the universe have actually changed the universe? Science is in hock to its ears right now, and restitution is due. And soon. God damn it, I'm trying to hold things together here! If we don't make restitution, I don't know what will happen. But it scares me."

"No one has told me what this has to do with me."

Corso drew a breath. "I'm telling you now. We need an observer. Physics was never about the universe, contrary to all assumptions—it was about a universe without Observers, which is to say it was wrong from the git-go. We're seeing the effects of this arrogance now. No, we have to have an individual in the system, to make adjustments, to establish boundary conditions. We were going to use Cutter. But now, it seems, you're our best bet. I don't understand why, but your character paradigm is almost perfect, and it peaks right at our zero hour.

Which is soon. Too fucking soon."

"Zero hour for what?"

Corso winced in exasperation. "We are going to send an object back through time, *capisci?* Not because the idea thrills us, not because it will give us a way to dump our technological wastes—although that's a corollary benefit—and certainly not to send a God damn Nazi clone to the stars—but because we *have* to. We have to close the circle. Reversing the flow of time is the only way to restore the constants. And at the rate they're drifting, we have to do it soon. So I don't need any resistance from you. Will you be in the target room when we need you? Or would you rather leave control of the fucking universe to Warner? Because he's our second choice."

Camus smelled desperation in Corso's sweat. He imagined time and space eddying in like currents of fear, he imagined the world remade according to the specifications of *The Book of Fakes*, and his dread rose up higher than his woe at responsibility. So he said: "When?"

That restored Corso's composure. He said easily, "Well, don't start any Monopoly games."

Hours passed. And Camus began to reconsider. Now he wanted out. Let Warner run the show. Let Humphrey Chimp run it, for that matter.

He took the lift to level one. The complex was surprisingly dead for being so near to crisis. He casually entered the hangar. How easy it was! He had no idea how to fly a plane, but he would sooner try to control this than the other.

He pulled himself into the cockpit of the small plane. There was a helicopter bulked in the darkness, but he was not about to try that. He tried to make out the panel of the plane, not risking lights.

Then the hangar lights came on. Outside the plane stood a tall man with gray hair combed straight back. He wore a conservative suit. His eyebrows met in the middle. His expression was somewhat sad. He came around to Camus's side.

"Greetings," he said. "Hopefully not farewell."

Camus let his heart slow. He said, "You must be Felix. I suppose this is a privilege."

"Pleasure is all on this side of the meeting," said Fallaci. "Despite myriad responsibilities, an active interest in your thoughts and whereabouts is manifest. As you see."

Camus lowered himself from the plane. Fallaci went on:

"Regrets for unseemly delay in establishing contact. Proceeding now to scintillant discourse."

Wearily Camus said: "How did you know?"

"A little lizard told."

"Oculos non habent at videbunt."

"Splendid. Conundrums are a style of thought, and not the worst. Take your humble colleague FFF. Sum of characters in sur- and given names is one hundred. Middle name is secret, but a prime squared, and moreover the sum of seven consecutive primes. Can you guess it?"

"No."

"Tch tch Tchitchikov. You're not even trying. Don't blame you, really. A tough nut. Still, more was expected of the second finest mind north of the Circle."

"I'm fresh out."

"Say hey! The world loves this figure before you. Beating of chest with justifiable territoriality. But you're too much. Retreat is indicated, not without shame and embarrassment. What a mind. Impressedness and adulation. You deserve the plum. Middle name is Ffructuosus, after the saint of Tarragona, martyred 259 AD with his deacons Augurius and Eulogius. He went into the flames saying, 'I am bound to bear in mind the whole universal Church from East to West.' There's a lesson in that."

Camus said, "You're Zaentz, aren't you?"

"Whom, please?"

"Shlomo Zaentz, with the dolls. It's a good disguise. I think your wrists and eyebrows give it away."

"Zaentz is seemingly some nonentity in INTERFACE if memory serves. What would be the purpose of such an imposture?"

"I don't know. A Sherlock Holmes complex?"

"A sad pleasure to observe fallibility in a mind so sharp. Zaentz is a good six inches shorter. The thing is not possible, and *infra dig* besides. You're fooled by the crippling childhood disease Zaentz had which gaunted his wrists." Fallaci regarded him for a few moments, then teased, "Scissors cuts paper."

Camus said nothing.

"Correct," said Fallaci. "The correct response. Fanfare and blinking of applause signs. Handcuffs will be unneeded. If you'll come with me, I'll tell you everything."

Once they were in the lift, Fallaci tampered with its control panel. Camus was not surprised to feel it descend past the bottom level of the complex, below KATAXRON. It opened into a room furnished in middle suburbia. Under a plastic slipcover was a sofa ornately plain. Atrocious lamps of heavy ceramic sported shades also sheathed in plastic. Dark beams of stained styrofoam crossed the ceiling. A television in a Mediterranean-style console displayed snow.

"Some use the Tank," Fallaci said. "I come here. A more perfect void."

Then, atop the television, suspended between intersecting planes of glass, Camus saw the cube. For a moment his mind teetered at an extremity, ready to pitch forward into an abysmal madness or fall back stunned to a skyey lucidity. Warner must have had the same shock when he found Camus's faked *Book of Fakes*.

"Not this," he said. "Not this." After the laying of fiction atop fiction he had witnessed, he could not believe that the final effect would reach back to the first cause. But there, undeniably, the cube was.

"The reconstruction is quite perfect," came Fallaci's mild voice.

"Why?"

"Because we know that such a target can be sent back. It has been. And now we're going to do it again. If again is really the word I want."

"And restart the whole process. The process that wished wreckage upon so many."

"Wreckage? Not a bit of it. We aspire to sanitary engineering. Recycling on the grand scale. Nature is a wonderful, slightly dotty old woman who has to be helped downstairs and kept away from the telephone. In fact, wreckage is what will ensue if we *don't* do it.

"All roads leave home. Most lead here. Our future nudges our past along the path that leads to it. Everyone has their own story about how it works. What can I do but agree with them all? Still, I'd like to know yours."

"Mine?" said Camus. "Mine is the saddest, most improbable of all. I thought that things were real. I believed that life was in earnest. I felt that time was made by human actions."

Fallaci shrugged slightly. "Time's a variable in sundry equations. But what do I know? I leave the auguries and eulogies to my deacons. I just like to play with machines."

"Yes, and with people as if they were machines. You. You've known from the start, haven't you? You make your living off these stories, these fictions, don't you? I've heard of ARC, of Gennesareth, of dFILE. . . ."

Fallaci's eyebrows raised in interest. "You left out *ARTi-fact.*"

"You fund that too? And—and the glacier?"

"There are agents and interests. They interact. Tendencies cancel or reinforce toward some *telos*. Some agents conduct the others. I'm a kind of conductor emeritus. We observe, and like all observers sometimes influence. So? We're just more conscious than most."

"I'm tempted to push your fucking face in."

"Let's cut the shit now," Fallaci said, smiling coolly. "Go where you're going, but go clean. You know what you are. And no one takes the long ride down unless they want to. No one ever comes this far unless they're ready."

"Like Cutter?" said Camus.

"Exactly. We prepared a situation for Cutter before we even knew he existed. And he slipped right into it. Just so, we've been preparing your role for you, probably since before you were born. Not that we knew who you were, or cared. But we knew you were out there. And here you are."

"You're so sure."

"Of course. Everything fits. It's not logic, or philosophy, or even sanity guiding things now. It's just the jolly good bedfellows of science and application coming round to their ultimate tryst. And you get to watch, you lucky dog. My only question now is, will you finish what you started? Will you take this cube to the target room?"

"Yes. I'll do that." Camus lifted the container.

"Don't hold it too close," said Fallaci, with almost fatherly concern. "The glass might break."

Last chances, like the successive positions of the arrow in Zeno's Paradox, seem to cluster closer the nearer the target comes—an illusion born of desperation. Thus Camus felt himself bound on a relentless trajectory, yet had hope at every step that the destination was not ineluctable.

The target room was a hierarchy of chaoses. Most of level seven had been gutted to prepare this space. At the center, enclosed by a framework of pipes and raw lumber, was the accelerator tube—ten feet across, with valves like steering wheels and cables as thick as wrists, and at its midpoint a baleful eye like the port of a bathysphere, open now, with dogs and bolts around its rim. Above the port a bank of gauges climbed the curve of the tube and spread out to the metal collars of the scintillation counters. Around this, tape decks, screens, meters, and keyboards were rigged, with hundreds of cables rising in catenaries from them to duplicate controls on a high platform across the room.

And around this instrumental chaos was a more human mess of crumpled papers, sandwich and candy wrappers, styrofoam cups marked with brown crescents at their bottoms, a few beer cans labeled black on white GENERIC, and cigarette butts scattered as randomly as the shouts on Duchamp's Large Glass. Freestanding dividers of whitewashed plasterboard were covered with equations and graffiti of dubious intent, photographic prints etched with the abstract signatures of particle decay, typewritten memos on pink slips, and the centerfold from a recent *Playboy*. From beneath the whitewash an older level of the same peeped and peeled.

Camus crossed the outer circle. He bore the cube in its glass. Rising on his right was a spectator's gallery. He went to the accelerator tube, feeling a sense of recursion. I have done this before. I have always done this. He walked as if each step were to consecrate each moment, yet offered as well a hundred alternative moments, all quickly cancelled by the next step. Around him people tended equipment with movements as narrow and circumscribed as his own. And overhead swung Humphrey Chimp in a cab at the end of a crane, of all of them at this moment the most free, chattering in glee and pushing levers to sail the cab to and fro beneath the high ceiling.

He had the sense now of a monstrous error. Sending the cube back would be an expiatory sacrifice of time to time— but what act was not? In the cave, he had delivered the cube from the womb of time, brought it into the sunlight of the moment, and did he think now to return it to some distant void of unrecorded history? To undo this awful recent past? Could parentheses ever be made to close, circles to complete, serpents to devour themselves? He thought not. Like all fictions, this act was an empty elaboration of what was. But he proceeded, because it was impossible ever to know all that was essential to right action, and so new error would always issue from old, and that was proper: just so, the errors of DNA were necessary for evolution. So his fear was calmed.

Corso received the cube from him. He freed it from its case and placed it in the eye of the accelerator. When he dogged the hatch a mechanism within made a brief sound of adjustment.

Camus mounted the gallery steps and sat by Pribiloff. Michael Scot raised a cage and shook it open; doves quickened the air, rising swiftly to the high ceiling. The chimp soared in his cab, swiping at them.

"Our little augurs," said Pribiloff. "Afterwards we will cut them open."

"Augurs?" said Camus dully. "Of what? Of death? Is it to make death real that you'd send back a Requiem?"

"But no. That is changed. On this cube is written a Paralog description of this very experiment."

So they would not close the circle after all, but force it to a gyre. Rather than repeat exactly, they would add a new dimension, and via this new cube send a clue—to themselves? to another, alternative reality? Camus had not time enough to think on this last twist of paradox. Godvoices smote the chamber from speakers. Birds scattered in frenzy.

—Stations please.

—Ready.

—Epoch, singularity. Red shift, infinite. Event, big bang.

—Mark.

—Epoch, Planck time. Red shift 10^{32}. Event, particle creation.

—Mark.

—Epoch, hadronic era. Red shift 10^{13}. Event, annihilation of proton-antiproton pairs.

—Mark. Commence elapsed time readings.

—Elapsed simulated time one microsecond, mark.

—Epoch, leptonic era. Red shift 10^{10}. Event, annihilation of electron-positron pairs.

—One second elapsed, mark.

—Epoch, radiation era. Red shift 10^9. Event, nucleosynthesis.

—Mark, and hold.

—Holding. Please stand by. Please stand by for matter, decoupling, and protohistory.

—Standing by.

—Universe is now matter dominated. Red shift 10^4. Please effect transparency.

—Effected. Universe is now transparent. We have decoupling. We have quasars. Red shift stabilized at 1.

—Ten billion years elapsed, mark.

—Population I stars confirmed. Cosmogonists, please clear

your stations for protohistorians. We are holding for proto-historians. Let's get it right this time.

—Elapsed simulated time now minus four oh oh four. That's 4004 BC. Mark.

Camus thought he understood. For if the experiment were indeed a psychic collaboration as well as a physical event, if the outcome would yet depend upon the observers present, then it was necessary to start from scratch. It was necessary that those present believe they were creating the universe. For they were essaying a universal fiction: a new idea of time.

—We are holding. Camus? Where is Camus? We have the dreaming seat ready.

So he was to play God, the God of the creationists, who created the world in 4004 BC. He almost laughed; it was proper payment for his heresies against science. Then he saw Winifred. She strode quickly down the aisle and grasped his wrist. He realized that, however lunatic his surroundings, he was in them; they were real.

She brought him down to the floor. "Once you're in the seat, the machines will direct the sequence. The cube itself supplies the program. The full sequence will take some hours. You'll pass from sleep to antifugue. Every so often you'll feel that some response is wanted. You'll have a keyboard. Just . . . find your place in the pattern, and extend it. It is not possible to make an error. Remember that."

And he smiled at that, in the strength of his new thought that it was, in fact, necessary to err.

"Are you ready?" she asked anxiously.

"I am," he said, meaning not that he was ready, but simply that he was. He lifted a hand to her wrist, and held it briefly, looking at her. She rubbed a conductive grease into his forehead. Touch for touch. There was a measured desperation in her features.

"And if I'm wrong about this," she said. "If things can't be made real. Then there will be an afterwards, and you can prove your point to me."

He shook his head. It was cool from the grease. "I don't want to prove anything. I can't."

"But I have to. I have to know. You call that thing, what? An imprimatur of impossibility. As if you were glad of it. Glad that the world was only appearances."

"Oh, no. It's all real. It's real. It's just that you can never prove it."

Her exasperation now verged on tears. "Just tell me, once, what it is you want."

"Now I just want a way out."

She bent, as if to kiss him, and as he tipped his head to receive it, he felt a metal band studded with tiny pins touch his scalp. Instantly he slept.

He felt as he had driving through Utah with her asleep in the back: eyes like funnels of sand, staring infinitely, and keeping her safe by an act of attention stretched to its intolerable utmost. He was winding backwards on a road already traveled, and his attention flagged into a consciousness of loss more acute than any he'd known. He had failed. For he had still planned, at this moment, to do what he could to abort the experiment. And he slept. He slept. He had had the unreal vanity to believe that some inspiration on his part could still deflect the path of these enormous engines. Despairing he fought sleep, as a man overbalanced at an abyss flails hopelessly to regain earth. But he had lost his last chance. So now it was not a matter of altruism, not of redeeming Hüll's death nor of drawing Winifred back nor of preventing some disruption of time—now his own being was at stake, linked as it was to the means and ends of those engines. He slept. And worse: he dreamed.

He was in a place of precisely warped surfaces. Mocking torn reflections of his face peered all around. He knew that this was the very lowest level of the complex, even below Fallaci's retreat, the place where the milelong cyclotron tube entered the building. There were the focusing mirrors for the particle stream. He heard Corso name them: Maxwell's Silvered Demons. Their skins were flexible, bulging and rippling in response to obscure commands, which, he realized, came from him: he was typing.

He was typing, and through the images of the mirrors, of the translations of his own face, he could see his finger move, and past them more faces: a visible city of stunned masks. So he was not quite asleep. Through slitted lids the image of the gallery was cast across his dream. He tried to focus his attention, but to his shame he saw instead the figure of Maximilian Hüll. Stern, reproving, sorrowful, the apparition was indefinite, white on a white ground; it was not Hüll's person, but it was clearly his spirit. An aura of disappointment shimmered around the unfilled blank. What will you? Camus pleaded silently. Hüll's image winked out as abruptly as a gunshot. Camus's

attending mind lurched back—and fell to a deeper level to a
time before he had developed any sense of responsibility.

The dream of Marcel completed itself.

The last act was an escape.

Marcel, chained and masked, was lowered into a large glass
tank of water.

Seconds passed. Marcel struggled theatrically. A minute
passed. Marcel freed his hands from the handcuffs. The blind-
fold drifted gently through the water. Marcel fumbled at the
weight chained to his legs. A small key slipped from his fingers,
zigzagged down through water, struck bottom with a click.

Camus felt disappointed; so the bonds were real, and needed
an instrument to pick them open. Formally he preferred the
topological escape, with the *out* effected easily because the
magician had never really been *in*—an illusory confutation of
space like that of the Klein bottle, which has no interior.

Marcel vainly searched the bottom with his hands. His
movements were no longer theatrical. Bubbles escaped from
his mouth. He looked up, as if remembering something. His
face, blurred by water, seemed to be Camus's. Very politely,
he knocked once on the glass of the tank. Then he drowned.

Camus was stunned, then admiring: the trick had been sal-
vaged by an overt *tour de force*. This was even better than
topology (which, after all, reduces the human body to a circle
in space). This was realistic, in that blunt, disheartening way
reality so often has.

Then he realized the implication of his dream. A spasm
wracked him. He could not breathe. He tore off the headset
and tried to stand. Tears of dumb rage at fruitless effort streamed
down his face. He slipped, then scrabbled on hands and knees
away from the seat. He did not cry out. The spasm passed.

For a while he lay unmoving. Overhead he saw the chimp
frozen in its cab. Doves were scattered in the air like stars. In
the tube, the cube still rested. And from the speakers, instead
of the expected jabber of machine language, came the unmistakable sound of an oboe, but greatly slowed, unfurling with
the grandeur of a foghorn the opening notes of the Requiem.
He lay and listened. After all warps, translations, and passages
through the irascible memories, this, finally, again, was the
pattern the cube must accept.

At last he rose. *Requiem*. The spectators were a gallery of
statues. Their attention was fixed on some point beyond or
before him. He went to Pribiloff and lifted an arm. The wrist

throbbed once. Seconds passed. Again. *Aeternam.*

He remembered the entry Hüll had razored from his diary: *It is not possible to get so far into a thing that there is no out. There is always the temporal redemption offered by—.* Camus went out of the target room.

He did not see the shadow, did not recognize the figure hurrying along to meet his advance, until it was almost too late to avoid a collision. He stopped short, in midstep, before the lift, his lips forming a name that his mind could not quite comprehend: "Winifred?"

"You—" She looked at him in horror.

He spoke mildly. "Where are we?"

"What are you doing here! There's only a few hours, they're counting down, who's *guiding* it?"

"I don't know."

"Oh my God. Oh no. How—how did you get out of there?"

"I had a good dream," he said. "But I couldn't stay asleep. I left everything as I found it."

She pushed past him, into the room of sleepers. In a moment she returned. "Antifugue," she said frantically, "all of them. I'll have to take the seat myself. God knows where it might end up unguided. How did you *do* this?"

"Don't know. Thought for a minute I'd pulled it off. The ideal escape. A matter of topology, like a slip knot, you can get out because you're never really in. But I was wrong. I'm still in it. So I have to do it the hard way. The real way. I can't just make an out. I have to find one, in what is. I need a breath of air. Come with me?"

She stared at him. "Outside, you mean? To die?"

He was grateful that she understood. "Only out that I can see. I have my own debts."

"Your, what do you mean?"

"You said you'd teach me stillness. But this isn't it. I know what it is now. It was Hüll, in the last moment, the last possible moment. . . ."

"Before he killed himself. That's your debt?"

"No. Before I found the cube. And forced the rest."

"Then stay! Go back and see it through. Try to fix it."

He shook his head. "Can't be fixed. No going back. I have to find—I don't know, somehow, a way to unfind it. By myself. Not this way. You won't come?"

She almost sobbed: "Idiot!"

"Yes," he said. "But to err my own way. And if you're

right—if there is any way of revising, of correcting error—if there is a way to recover the moment when it went wrong, when it could have worked for us—then, when you dream, look for that moment."

For the last time he thought he might recover what they'd had. Then she clutched him, left a quick furious kiss behind one ear, and said angrily, "Get out."

Zero hour. The creation of the world in a dying light. In the lift he ran his hand up the rainbow panel, lighting every button. At each level the lift opened and he stood waiting in the frame of the doors. He was willing to be stopped. But he rose unhindered into chill vacant zones; the top levels were now shut for the winter. He stepped out at INTERFACE, and went to the hangar.

As he passed the shadowy bulk of flying machines the outer door began slowly to slide upward. A frigid wind rose. Dusk red light entered the space. By the outer door was a rack of coats, and he debated taking one. He selected a bright red parka; after all, he did not want a quick death by exposure; not a quick one. He stepped briskly out, pulling on mittens. The hangar door descended. Through the last dimishing inch of space he scaled his pass: it locked within. Below his ear, where her lips had touched, the wind burned. He understood that she had betrayed him back into the world; and he had betrayed her into a perspective of endless interiors; and he understood that betrayal always requires the consent of the betrayed.

For a moment he stood still, pores wide to the clench of cold air, the bronze ganging of light, the broad sough of continental winds. He raised his eyes past the porous gray walls of the complex, dampened by weather, and past the snowdrifts banked between the granite hillside and the buried back walls. Last light was in the sky. The sun touched a low gap in the mountains. He saw it fall. A single line of cloud scumbled lake and slate on an early evening sky the tender dilute color of stars. In the river valley to the east a bloated sliver of orange light widened as he watched. Full moon. Cloud scraps writhed over its features.

Heating coils beneath the asphalt of the airstrip had kept it clear of snow, and now, in the shifting wind, puddles steamed at regular intervals down its length. Small banners of transient warmth lashed past him.

At the last wink of sun in the notch, clouds came scudding quick and low from the east, bearing a snow which, dropping in a long slant from the leaden distension of their bellies, lost its crystalline integrity in the stochastic buffets of intervening air, and struck the dirty gray side of the complex as water, driving soiled washes overlapping down its slant sides.

Sudden wind like the flat of a knife pushed him a step. He zipped the parka. At an abatement of the rain he ran, wind aiding his flight up the steepest slope. He labored up the talus without thought, until the plash of runoff grew louder than the sounds of his labor, and his boots began to lose purchase on the slick stone. He slowed. The complex was half occulted by a hill, but still near. Below him, at a shocking angle, was a stream racing through its rock course. He went on carefully, crabwise on rills and ledges, pausing to pull off his mittens so that he could grip slick handholds, pausing again to put them on until feeling returned to his red hands. It was not yet freezing, but he felt that the water underfoot was becoming treacherous. He went more slowly in switchbacks. The stream receded below. A vast, slow night of cumulate grays came on. Fog gathered below him, while above him an intermittent snow hung still as dust or was driven blurred and stinging into his face. The light seemed less to fade than to dissipate.

At last he gained a ridge. It seemed he could go no higher. The act of shifting his attention from the nearby to the distant seemed to bring on full night. He marveled that he had made it so high in such obscurity. The complex was out of sight. He began to walk along the ridge, east he thought, away from it, but the night was close, and he was lost, and most likely just keeping the wind at his back.

As he went on, he seemed to hear Cutter's voice, sometimes close and intimate, sometimes lost in wind.

"I do not know what I was. I accept what was given me. And even so, I see that it was vanity to try to reconstruct the dreams of technology, to analyze them by abreaction. For the ultimate analytic tool had already arrived near the end of this tortured nightmare. All the dreams tended to it, to this compelling image, to the One which could, like Mithra, open the widest of pastures. . . . If unity is impossible, then what remains but to split the smallest monads of existence, to strip all matter to its substrate, to parch the earth, to slate and parse the very dust to nullity? It was inevitable. If we know that no state of nature can be recovered, and the gyre of history is irreversible, and entropy infects every atom, then what remains but to annihilate every last seed of the vice, down to the atoms themselves . . . ? So I came to see that the image of nuclear holocaust was attractive. It had the uncompromised purity of dawn . . . terrible as any prospect of absolute reduction, but promising as well. It promised an end . . . as if to say: no more. Stop here in the full light of the present. Abandon all crutches, snares, influence, and history. Yes, we want that. We need it. The same implication is in every dawn, but it is too terrible to find that message daily awaiting our simple acceptance, so often have we ignored it. Instead, we must make our own dawn. In my mind the fury of this false dawn promised even to annihilate souls. What a temptation! To strip the final ground of ego, the soul, which no saint had ever learned to lose. . . . So I don't blame you for coming this far . . . for *this* apocalypse, this catachronism, is even larger . . . not just to end time, to bring Judgment, but to abolish both. . . ."

And a spirit of atavistic fear at the utterly unknown came to him in the Arctic night, as it might have visited the desert of Los Alamos some fortyseven years ago. The experiment still went on. The machines ran themselves. And it was nearly midnight.

Did he expect some vision of the future? He had it. He came to a ledge that fell off into blackness, and the vision was there: distant, floodlit, warped by a curtain of wind, the small concrete crystal of Radix Malorum. His path along the ridge had described a semicircle which had brought him back into sight of the complex. And he knew that the vision was true, it *was* the future he saw, and it was theirs. The lurid multiplicities of *as if* gave way, as always, to the single *as is* of reality.

Woe rose in him. He stumbled back. He sank into snow. More blew onto him from above, a myriad of small stinging stars. A wave of weakness took him. It went on, swelling past faintness into roaring despair. He called on Christ, but produced only a dry gagging sound, like the Greek *xi*.

Then the night came apart around him. Billows of light swept the sky, and he did not know if they were translations of cloud or snow by moonlight, or aurorae, or traces of a singular and unprecedented apocalypse. The world opened to his attention as a poetics of space. He saw the place and part

of every act and every being in it, none trivial, none significant.
And so felt freed to lose, on his own terms, whatever he had
ever thought might sustain him: faith, science, love, memory,
or even the sense of self, this chance collaboration of atoms,
of precisely warped gaps known as Hans Camus—even that
first and final irreducible stroke of the mind, the I, broke. He
was sundered and spread, and thought and voice were no longer
his, but gathered from worldwide as if by the overhead warping
of the ionosphere, or from some medullar sentience of Earth
itself, the whole sphere resonating from brainstem of the Brooks
range to caude of Tierra del Fuego. The earth was wrenched
from under him, and he went out through a sky thinned by
altitude to false eternal night, toward an exhalation of stars.
The sky began to pulse, bringing as in the Tank ceaseless
explosions of white, but felt now throughout his body. And he
saw levels of eternity in this stoppage of time. A billion times
each microsecond the universe is annihilated and made anew,
complete with substrates of fictive continuity. Each moment is
bounded yet infinite, with its own birth, evolution, and con-
summation; the Creation, the Fall, and the Apocalypse are with
us always, in every moment. We might be enjoined by our
fictions to assume a spurious continuity from one pocket universe to the next, to see but one of the infinite faces of each
moment, but there are propitious moments when it is possible
to see through the fictions and attain, if only for that moment,
a vision of things as they are. The palimpsests of knowing, the
versions of time articulated by all arts, sciences, and religions,
could be stripped to a bare ground and seen in essence rather
than in circumstance. He felt the commensurability of the world.
He felt the rhyme of his own being with the sensibility of a
Neanderthal, with the vague motivity of insensate proteins,
with the slow streaming of galactic gases, with the wedge of
a Yuan brush pressed to a silk scroll just as the mark is made:
all elements of a great economy of particulars which were at
once wholly selfcontained and universally interdependent. And
once this commensurability was glimpsed, what moment was
not propitious? What fiction then could not be seen through
and regarded for what it is? Any and all meanings are written
in every particle of every instant. In the boom of each moment
ceding to the next are all voices, all stories, all dreams, all
gains and losses, every streetcorner, every gesture of compas-
sion or revulsion, every deceit, betrayal, or touch of grace,

and the lost histories of all the anonymous who, in this space, were no more truly dead than he was truly alive. So for any passage across space or time, no instrument, no made apocalypse is necessary—none at all, but awareness of the ever-present booming of the world.

From heavenvault then his sense descended, out of arid starhung black, through void, to come as if by chance across a small blue smudge on the limitless *Weltall,* and to see it not as if it were familiar, not as if it were home, but simply as it was: an anomalous wonder amidst nothingness. Even the stars were projections of the minds and incipient minds that occupied this sphere. Clouds he saw, from above, and was through them and traveling over sea. He saw tides, currents, and ripples crossbedded with wind and cresting waves. Shore, plain, mountains, and a birdflock in the breakage of an instant were round him and gone; timber thinned toward peaks, and a herd of moonlit caribou crossed in ragged line from one stand of pine to the next. And he returned to himself, staring up at an ambiguous night. He felt the ground cold against his back, and the full bloom of time now closing like a sorrel flower at dusk. His sense was slipping back into a serial time, his voice and thoughts returned to him, the *I* flickered again to life, and he saw, in terms of signs, the failure at the heart of their project. A simple error in orthography. A mere misspelling. The deepest mystery was not *xronos,* but *xthonos.* Not time, but earth. The ground of earth, upon which every act, every life, every mind, was but a transient figure, the surface upon which all palimpsests of being were writ, erased, and writ anew.

He held to this frozen moment as to a hearth, a home, but it slipped from him, the universe resumed its continual self-creations and destructions, wiping him out, denying the particulate nature of time, erasing all, and building again. So he had the final implication of his revelation—that it could not be shared, used, or even kept, for every succeeding moment would blow it apart, separate it into shards, and reunite it instantly into another, fictive form. Therefore it could grant him nothing but a vague foredoomed fragmentary memory of it. Already it faded. And Camus, every moment (he would strive to remember) a new man, dying in snow, made his best and most pointless resolve: to live *as if* the fictions of the world ("the world" first among them) were real, yet strive to see the world as *is;* not unduly to cherish nor ever quite relinquish any particular moment; for any of its aspects might be in transaction, in rhyme, with any other moment, and although error, decay, and death were natural, yet there could be (the *maybe so* of love) a touching of fictions. To care for those possible transactions seemed to him, at the moment, the only possible stewardship of that most unlikely of human fictions, history. Yet it seemed a small knowing to have come so far to find.

IV. Pro Defunctis

Moonlight in a valley is before
and after history.

—Gertrude Stein

26. Pro Vivis

The helicopter chopped still air in pulses, then canted back as if to erase its intrusion with a steady drone. It was red. It glinted in the morning sun. It came over him and hovered there for a minute, some hundred feet above the ridge, swaying slightly, like a clockwork dragonfly stripped of iridescence; and in its hover was one remarkable tenth of a second when, by a collaboration of winds, there was no sound at all, and the strange device had a look of fitness in the open sky. It moved away. It drifted off with its sound behind the lip of snow to his left. Silence returned uniformly. He shut his eyes.

He opened them at the crisp sound of steps. Someone approached through snow towards him. He lay peacefully, waiting.

An aviator's scarf unfurled above the pinegreen parka. On the breast was sewn a crimson heptagon.

He saw Levin's face. Painfully he brought himself to his elbows, then collapsed again. He tried to think of something to say. A greeting would be superfluous. Finally Camus said, "You can't hurt me."

Levin looked down at him with curiosity. The agent was bundled in a wool hat, tinted glasses, the loosened scarf, parka, and mittens. He wore blue jeans and heavy boots.

"Morning, soldier," he said. Mists from his mouth dissipated quickly in the bright sun.

"Yes," said Camus. "Good morning. Good morning."

It was true. It was a good morning. Every morning is a good morning. From the limited prospect of the small cirque where he lay, he could see a pond of fresh snow, a brilliancy that danced with each slight movement of his head. It ended so abruptly at the sky's blue that down his expressionless face he felt tears run. The day was windless. The silence was stunning. He could hear snow creak beneath Levin's unmoving feet.

"Shall we take a walk?" the agent asked.

"Yes. Let's."

He accepted Levin's arm until he found his feet. Then Levin walked slowly across the snow; Camus hobbled after. The pain in his legs was invigorating.

They came to a cliff. He stood by Levin there, looking down the long valley below them, still partly in shadow. There was wind.

"You've cost me quite a little effort," Levin remarked, gazing out. "Do you see that?"

Perhaps three miles distant was the complex. He could see that half of it was tumbled into the surrounding granite. He said, in wonder, "Did I do that?"

"Not exactly. Although your presence was a factor. Catalytic, you might say." Levin slapped his mittens together. The sound was sharp and echoless. Visible scraps of his breath were pulled by wind out over the drop. "A terrible piece of work, all told. I hate this kind of sloppiness. I hate having to make adjustments. This will be twice this run." He regarded the scene silently for a few seconds. "I did take the precaution of fueling the chopper yesterday."

"Yes."

"You see, I put three months into this project. Not to mention the background. And I have nothing to show for it. Nothing at all. That's very bad." He shook his head slowly. "Botch from top to bottom. There will be high displeasure in quarters where I could once show my face, if I leave it like this."

"I have nothing to show, either," said Camus happily.

Levin turned to him incredulously. He stared at Camus for a few seconds. "Amateur," he marveled. "It defies belief. He's fucked me from start to finish, and he has no idea. Moves no professional could make, and he's a blind man. Could I have accomplished that wreckage? Could the US Army? Christ, I despise amateurs! He has nothing to show. Blind genius of the fast run. With the nerve to come back from it. Contemptible." Levin was breathing hard, clenching and unclenching his hands in a rhythm.

"What will you do now?" asked Camus.

Levin shot him a critical glance. "Do. I don't know. Professionally speaking I have to do something. A period of reparation and adjustment is indicated. I could salvage it. Professionally speaking, you should be dead right now. It offends me deeply that I'm standing here talking to you. But I am."

"Yes."

Levin removed his tinted glasses, pocketed them, and rubbed his eyes with two fingers. "Perhaps my late colleague Samuel was correct. Perhaps I'm getting too foxy. My judgment was faulty. I didn't see you as a force. One error. My other moves were sound. But you ran it right by me. After something like that, one or both of us should be dead. That's my professional opinion, for what it's worth, which is damned little without immediate adjustment. One fucking error. It complicates everything. It leads to others, there's no end to it. I can't leave it unadjusted. It will be noticed."

"By them, you mean?" Camus gestured at the valley.

Levin smiled bitterly. "That? That's wreckage. They don't matter. They're already retooling for the next try, talking about legitimacy, Corso wants a Nobel Prize. Perhaps they'll come out of the shadows. Toads. Pissants."

"What happened there?"

Levin extended an arm, as if sighting down it. "What happens everywhere when the judgment goes. Too much force exerted the wrong way. They lost equipment. They lost records. They'll be on maintenance power all winter and beyond. But they'll be back. They *did* succeed. They'll have to capitalize. And that leaves you and me. The last two left. The only ones still uncovenanted, hey?"

With one numb toe Camus nudged snow off the ledge. He watched the powder arc through the sun. Levin watched him doing this. "So maybe it's time," Levin said softly. "Maybe I should retire. Or go legit. So that my errors are in the open, less dangerous to me." He shook himself. "Leaving you alone. Leaving you the only one who hasn't cut a deal. I don't know. The idea offends me. I always thought I'd be the last. Hey? Amateur?"

Camus looked up.

"No interest in their success?"

Camus had to think what Levin might mean. He brought his attention away from the morning, suddenly feeling queasy, in pain. "You mean the cube?"

"That's right. They did it. They're not sure where or when, exactly. It looks like about eighty thousand years back, possibly to Germany."

He suddenly felt he was rising. To a careening object a still point has sickening velocity. But he was not sick. He was exalted. The paradox was complete, and he could never know finally about the cube he had found, the actions he had catalyzed, the destruction and reconstruction of artifacts and artifices, the instrumentality at the source and end of time; he could not know where or when his trip had begun or ended, if the real was fictive or the fictive real, if even "now," for example, a certain cave in the Neander Valley housed, again, still, a certain stone of a peculiar sort. None of that mattered. He had ceased now from flight: it was enough. Every moment was a home.

"Now," said Levin, turning to him. "The question is what I do with you."

Some low clouds had come up. As the sun dimmed behind them the brightness of the sky seemed to increase; its blue became more transparent and, as well, more dense.

Camus felt a great friendliness for Levin, as part of the moment. He felt he must give some message that might free the man from the fallacious sense of damage; he tried to express the lucid shape of redemption within each particle of flux. Finally, pushing gently at the air with one hand, he said, "It is," and pushed firmly to emphasize, not the words, but the passing spirit, "a *good morning*."

Levin repressed a tremor of anger. He drew off his mittens. He put them in a pocket and blew mist into his cupped naked hands. He went to Camus and placed his hands upon his shoulders, turning him slightly to face the valley, the distant gentle and near sharp rise of it, cliff of some two hundred meters at their feet. The sun broke out again from the night's tail of clouds.

Pain blazed in Camus's legs. He crumpled, and let Levin's grip support him. Nylon and down crinkled. He drew a breath that scoured his lungs. The hair around his mouth had frozen in crusts.

Levin drew him back from the edge. He slipped an arm about Camus's waist. Camus draped an arm over Levin's shoulders. They walked back across the cirque slowly, and down a slight hill to the helicopter.

"Where are we going?" asked Camus.

Levin stopped and let Camus sag against him. He squinted at the younger man and let out a breath. "Do you care?"

Camus thought this over, what he could possibly care about.

Finally he said, "The others?"

"They were all in the same room. Ground zero, so to speak."

He began to shake. "The others?" he repeated more sharply. Real interest was back in his voice.

"I made arrangements," Levin said. Then added, "The woman is all right."

"All right," said Camus. "My legs hurt."

"We'll get you looked at in Fairbanks. Then I'll see about getting you home."

"Home."

"Düsseldorf. Will that do? We may have to deport you."

Camus nodded.

Levin helped him into the rear of the craft.

The type designer, Sangster, was in the cockpit. He was speaking naturally, in an undertone, in German, with stresses and emphases as if lecturing. The words could not be understood. As Camus climbed in, he saw that the surfaces of the cockpit were covered with small, exquisitely drawn alphabets. As Sangster spoke to himself, he gestured with a pen.

Levin turned on the engines. The blades swung. Camus felt vibrations through the fabric and padding of his seat. The machine rose. Sangster stopped speaking, bent over a clean space of dash, and ignoring the vibration, moved his pen quickly and fluidly, leaving a trail of letters across the surface.

All artifice forsaken, which is to say accepted for what it is and what it is not, the young man—whose name mattered less to him than the Fairbanks ice fog mattered to the airport's radar—boarded the plane. His daypack, which at the last moment he had decided to carry on, bore a tag reading DUS. Seated, he drew over it in pen, pausing before writing, making it DUST. The plane shuddered and ascended into the night, tracing a great circle northward. The cold pole passed unseen. He read, unsmiling but with great amusement, from a paperback of *The Myth of Sisyphus* purchased in the airport lounge. He tore out pages as he finished them, stuffing them into his jacket pocket.

"Fred-er-ick?"

"Here."

Without was snow like billionwhispervoiced ghosts against one hundred eighty black panes. The man scrunched further into the cubby of his chair and desk, counting them. The desk was too small for him.

The book before him was alight with words, strange words, wonderful words, and some of them vaguely threatening. His lips moved slowly, forming them by pieces. You could almost always say the word if you knew the pieces. Ad-um-bra-tion. Sh. Say *tion* shun. Tee eye equals sh. Be-ne-dic-tion. D, dic. He had said fic. Con-sum-ma-tion. De-mo-li-tion.

"Who can tell us a word starting with J?"

Disinterested voices.

"Jam."

"Jelly."

"Jerk off." Laughter.

"*Her*man. That is not amusing."

"Jeremiad."

"*My*, Frederick. Do you know what it means?"

"Red Fred don't know shit from shave cream."

The big man with the red beard flushed. His shame had more forms than the snow. He was aware of a grand convergence of ignorances rushing to his face. There was so much he could not remember.

"Teach he got his hand down there doon a J word!"

The class wore on, Herman exiled to the hallway, where, unseen by Miss Hofstadter, he made obscene gestures. The school bell rang at 9:00 p.m., the ancient gears within the clock allowed to mark their short thirty hours a day nightlong, a serendipitous benefit for the evening adult remedial courses. Miss Hofstadter was one of the first out the door.

And Frederick was the last. He studied the chalkboard, which was seldom used in his class. But the notes from last day's classes in the high school often stood there. His eyes, which had returned to the board several times, stumbled on a long word. Ex-ist-en-tial.

Then he was on his feet, and at the board, erasing and erasing. The dustladen felt pad would not do the job. One fingernail broke with a shriek across the slate. He rubbed and scraped, in tears, but still a word peeped through, short, mocking, impenetrable: Camus.

Levin scraped his feet on synthetic tile at the rear of the Cleveland Heights Unitarian Church, where a memorial service for Winifred Teresa Waste was being held. Circumstance had secured a full house: the community chorus was using the service as a dress rehearsal for their performance of the Ockeghem *Missa Pro Defunctis*. Levin smiled wanly. There was no coffin. He patted his breast pocket, where a wooden transverse flute in velvet pouch, stolen from the church stores, rested next to a new passport bearing the features but not the name of Winifred Waste. One could always make some adjustment. When this was done, he would learn to play the instrument; it would be good discipline.

Ulysse Poisson applied with care a last flyspeck of mustache wax to his facial hair. The head monk had excoriated his vanity, but now it was his signature. He had proven it by shaving himself bald, everywhere, taking on the meanest tasks, sitting in meditation sixteen hours a day, solving his koan, and then reverting to his former self. Yesterday he'd lectured well on entropy, even in his faulty Japanese. He reflected that it was getting time to move on.

In Düsseldorf, Camus received this note when he called at the museum:

> 29 VII. 91
> My dear Moritz,
> I am writing this as you sit laboring (and, I suspect, dozing) over your graphs and charts upstairs. But knowing my habits and yours, I do not expect you will read it until many months have passed. First, the act of writing is strange to me, and I will have to savor my presumption for a while before sealing this. Then, you will be off skipping around the globe for a while before you return to it. By that time, I am told by my doctor, I will not be around to appreciate your discomfort.
> I realize that empty forms are empty, and also that they ought to be adhered to, exactly for the sake of their emptiness. But I foresee that I will be led astray, and will fail in making this a simple, maudlin farewell. I have managed pretty well to strip myself of possessions, so I won't leave a formal Will. But I have made arrangements, and if there is any dispute you might present this note as a kind of Will. I am leaving you my position at the museum, which is supernumerary to say the least, but the money is available and you might as well take it if the work pleases you. If not, of course, ignore it. Gifts are always encumbrances or debts, and there should be no debt between us.

However, there is one, and this one I can't absolve you of. Enclosed is a key to a safe deposit box, where I've stored some curiosities gathered around the *Gebiet*. I have been having bad dreams about them and you, and whereas I may be just a superstitious old man, the dreams have come during full moons, and I have learned to trust my moon dreams. If the items are nothing to you, good. If they are something, I can only hope I am not passing you a terrible stewardship.

If you want to have a Mass said for me, or light a candle or throw a wake, I won't object, but don't think of it as *pro defunctis*, if you please. In order to keep some honesty and perspective in my life, I have often behaved as a dead man among other dead; you may remember me reading to you from Mark Twain, "People should start out dead." I have been slow to learn this, and finally the knowledge is only another empty form. Better no memorial at all, but if you make one, dedicate it *pro vivis*.

> —Deiner,
> VR

These items were in von Rast's box: a tarnished brass dodecahedron; a weathered shapeless substance light as styrofoam; an impossibly ancient looking book, about ten centimeters by fifty, one corner burned away, the rest ravaged by dampness. It was bound in black cloth. On its spine was stamped a crimson heptagon. The pages crumbled as he turned them. Small flakes gathered at the bottom of the box, bearing traces of equations, fragments of graphs. On one flake he thought he glimpsed his own name, set in the alphabet Sangster had been drawing in the helicopter.

He examined the items, returned the box to the bank vault, and, recrossing the Rhine on his return to the museum, flung the key. It skipped twice on the water, sank, vanished.

But people *had* died in the blast, Camus learned from an anonymous telegram; he suspected it was from Levin. Axis, Tototto, Scot, Haeckel, Pribiloff, Carpenter, and four runners were "untraceable." Precisely. Past our ken, into the finally unknowable. But he wondered where their souls had gone. And he imagined that they had been fragmented, and had traveled back in time, a fragment of each to lodge here and there in the newborn throughout history, to lodge as an obsession, glint, or insight, turning the psyches of so many in the past just enough to lead to lives and works which would lead, inevitably, stochastically, teleologically, to the creation and destruction of Radix Malorum. And his psyche too might be translated at his death, and cast back to struggle in the realm of ideas with these others, showing himself to his other selves only in moments of recognition, in acts of stewardship and human providence.

Another expedition was at the *Gebiet*. As subtly as the dead von Rast had last year, Camus drew their attention to a certain cave, and then withdrew, feeling his stewardship of one history fairly ended. The leader of this dig was a modern redaction of Warner: his hair was straight coiffed black rather than unruly red; instead of a full beard he allowed himself casual manly stubble; he was not bulky, but had the wiry slight blunt avid frame of a vicious handball player. He was officious and loud. *Plus ça même chose*. His name was Wagner Wills, and his students called him Wag. At a distance, Camus saw him put a fatherly arm around a woman who resembled Winifred. He turned away.

As he drove to town, he planned out the rest of his day. Drop off the painting he had just finished restoring; lunch at the Café Schlegel; work on the mammoth skeleton at the Löbbeke Museum. Camus was teaching himself techniques of restoration from a notebook of von Rast's. He thought of some of the more elliptical comments there in the old man's hand: Change line first without touching it. Respect certain kinds of damage. Is it a sickness to offer work to the world? *Remain anonymous*.

Familiar Düsseldorf offered its gifts grudgingly as ever. Sun angling on a certain cornice; odor from a corner bakery; distant chiming from a tower clock; and with it all, overflung, the incessant hammer of traffic, the young faces dull as dough in the university halls, the tourists droning in the Kuppelsaal of Schloss Benrath. . . .

He bought a *Rheinische Post*, and turned its pages idly over his coffee and brioche. He had given up smoking last month, and felt a slight, passing urge for a cigarette. He turned past two faces familiar even behind the coarse grid of the halftone, and turned back, eyes flicking mechanically over the caption: Felix Culp. R. E. Corso. Nobel Prize Physics. Subatomic time reversal. He turned the page, and studied a photo of recent restorations to Leonardo's *Last Supper*. He would have to learn fresco, he thought idly.

He paid, crossed to the Löbbeke, leaving the paper behind. Toward him came a wizened old man, the size of a child, hurrying, dressed in a well cut but anachronistic suit, and swinging a briefcase scaled to his size. Camus smiled an anonymous greeting.

He stood on tiptoe in the shallow case, replacing a fluorescent tube. He really should have gone downstairs for a stepstool, but it was near closing, and he hated to leave the old man in shadow even for a minute. He glanced at the faceless skull as if mutely to explain his intrusion. Sometimes he fancied the ancient roots of a smile frozen in the stony, puckered brow, or saw in its insistent set of interlocking curves the ripples set up by a stone skipped over still water—but often, as today, there was nothing, a simple void where a face had been.

As he raised the new tube, he caught from the corner of his eye the movement of a woman, and turned. He caught his breath. A profile. The woman at the dig. Hard tight jaw, prominent Levantine nose, unruly mass of dark wavy hair streaked with assertive gray, violet gray eyes. She wore a lightweight blue dress, and the sun from the entrance hall sketched strong coltish legs beneath it.

She turned striding to the case, looked alarmed for a moment at the sight of him in there, then smiled. The broad rare grin. No faintest glimmer of recognition crossed her eyes.

She reached the case. He stared. Involuntarily he said a name. She could not hear him through the glass. Pointlessly, he repeated the name, and she tried to read his lips. Something dawned around her mouth. She smiled again, nodded, rummaged in her purse, and held up a passport, showing him the eagle. She thought he had said, "American?"

He gestured her closer, and pantomimed the opening of the passport. After a puzzled frown she went along with the game, held it flat to the glass. The photo was exactly the same. But his restorer's eye noted the marks of rubbing where the name had been eradicated, professionally, and replaced by: Teresa Cope, c/o National Geographic Society, Washington.

He leaned on the glass and smiled slightly. Just as well there was no home address. She realized then that her hand was resting opposite his on the glass. She flustered, withdrew it, snapped the passport shut, and backed away, regarding him oddly. Not too closely, thought Camus; the glass might break. A disembodied voice announced closing. She turned and went away from him with a quick, sure step.

After midnight, Camus sat on a stepstool in front of the case, considering again the broken remains of the old man called *new man*, bathed in unnatural fluorescence. He read again from the plaque the history of misapprehensions surrounding this ancestor, the final one being Maximilian Hüll's, who believed that history is real, and that one may always find what one seeks. In one week it would be the anniversary of Hüll's death. His mind was blank, a field white as the image of the child in Cutter's dream, open as a sheet of paper before the first mark is laid on, boundless as a morning sky. He tried yet again for a connection to this mute Other, who had lived and struggled and died eighty thousand years ago, in a world so different yet so common, without leaving any mark but his own skeleton. And yet again he failed, blundering after an elusive vision he could not name. He shut off the light in the case, leaving things as he had found them. And for just an instant, as the moon broke clouds past the skylight, and lit them with a circular rainbow, he had a sweet sure sense of time, knew placidly the transience and immortality of every act and moment, felt the continuous revelations and demolitions of meaning in the dim waves of time surrounding the scattered isles of perception; he had a sense of landho that would never quite achieve landfall, and was for the moment content. And then again bereft.

Though the dead might not stay buried, still he must try, one moment at a time. Although fixed now in space, no traveling man, he still had a sense of unsayable sin. Despite his innumerable awakenings, these moments of famine hit him still. He rose then, to bury this night first.